Praise for Meredith Schorr

"Schorr mixes and matches couples with charming aplomb in this sweet-natured romcom...The author manages to easily reel readers in from the start...Pieces of the puzzle are thoroughly and appealingly mixed up in this well-paced tale."

– Publisher's Weekly

"With a premise that rivals the best film rom-coms, *The Boyfriend Swap* is filled with romance, humor and heart—a delight from beginning to end. Meredith Schorr delivers chick lit gold!"

– Jamie Brenner, USA Today Bestselling Author

"Fast-paced and fun. I loved this charming story."

– Michele Gorman, USA Today Bestselling Author

"What a fun book. The characters were incredibly well-written. I felt like I understood everyone's personalities and quirks, almost as if I knew them personally myself. Meredith Schorr is a talented author and I'm glad she has other books out for me to read!"

– Becky Monson, Bestselling Author of the Spinster Series

"Friends swap shoes, purses and gossip. Why not boyfriends? Warm, witty and winning, *The Boyfriend Swap* is wonderful entertainment you'll want to share with your best friend."

– Karin Gillespie, Author of Divinely Yours

"Sassy, sexy, endlessly entertaining, and full of laughs (as well as some heart-wrenching moments), *Blogger Girl* is one of those books that keeps you up at night because you can't wait to see what happens next."

– Tracie Banister, Author of Mixing It Up

"America finally has its own version of Britain's Bridget Jones!"

– Books in the Burbs

"Meredith Schorr is an author to watch."
— Tracy Kaler, Founder and Editor of *Tracy's New York Life*

"A strong and confident heroine, a sexy boyfriend you can crush on, supportive friends, and plenty of conflict leading to comical results, culminating in a very satisfying ending...Once you start this book, you won't be able to put it down."
— Erin Brady, Bestselling Author of *The Shopping Swap*

"A perfect mix of romance, conflict, and humor, *Novelista Girl* solidifies Schorr's place among best-sellers Sophie Kinsella and Emily Giffin."
— Carolyn Ridder Aspenson, Bestselling Author of *Unbinding Love*

"Absolutely brilliant chick lit, I couldn't put it down, and I highly, highly recommend."
— *Chick Lit Plus*

"Meredith writes with wit, candor, humor and vulnerability that illuminates the struggles of dating and relationships."
— Nancy Slotnick, Author of *Turn Your Cablight On*

"The perfect vacation read. The dialogue flows like beer at a beach party."
— K.C. Wilder, Author of *Fifty Ways to Leave Your Husband*

"I laughed my way through this novel. A must-read."
— *Chick Lit Plus*

"I am a huge fan of chick lit, but this book was so much more. It has become one of my favorite reads!"
— *The Little Black Book Blog*

"You won't forget this delightful cast of characters or Schorr's sharp, candid insights about the plight of the modern woman."
— Diana Spechler, Author of *Who by Fire* and *Skinny*

Bridal Girl

Books by Meredith Schorr

JUST FRIENDS WITH BENEFITS
A STATE OF JANE
HOW DO YOU KNOW?
THE BOYFRIEND SWAP

The Blogger Girl Series

BLOGGER GIRL (#1)
NOVELISTA GIRL (#2)
BRIDAL GIRL (#3)

Bridal Girl

Meredith Schorr

HENERY PRESS

Copyright

BRIDAL GIRL
The Blogger Girl Series
Part of the Henery Press Chick Lit Collection

First Edition | April 2018

Henery Press, LLC
www.henerypress.com

Trade Paperback ISBN-13: 978-1-63511-330-3
Digital epub ISBN-13: 978-1-63511-331-0
Kindle ISBN-13: 978-1-63511-332-7
Hardcover Paperback ISBN-13: 978-1-63511-333-4

Printed in the United States of America

To fabulous and dedicated book bloggers everywhere.
Kim's story would not exist without you.

ACKNOWLEDGMENTS

Thank you to everyone at Henery Press—Art Molinares, Kendel Lynn, Christina Rogers, and especially my fabulous editors, Maria Edwards and Rachel Jackson.

A world of gratitude to Samantha Stroh Bailey and Natalie Aaron, the best beta readers a girl could ask for.

Thank you to my friend since the third grade, Amy Ehrnsperger, for all your insight into event planning (and for always making me laugh).

I am so thankful for the support and enthusiasm of so many bloggers, authors, and members of my small but loyal street team who connected so well with the characters of this series. Without your encouragement, the series would likely have stopped at one book. Special shout-outs to Melissa Amster, Ashley Williams, Kelly Perotti, Bethany Clarke, Amanda Lerryn, Isabella Anderson, Gina Reba, Kaley Stewart, Samantha Janning, Mary Smith, Susan Schleicher, Charlotte-Lynn, Linda Levack Zagon, Lindsay Lorimore, Rebecca Moore, Aimee Brown, and Stacey Wiedower.

Finally, I am grateful for being blessed with people in my life who inspire so much of the strong, loyal relationships found in this series: my family, the Beach Babes (Sam, Francine, Eileen, Jen, Julie, and Josie), Ronni, Jenny, Hilary, Elke, Deborah, Megan, Lily, Shanna, and my guardian angel, Alan.

Chapter 1

SEVEN MONTHS UNTIL "I DO"

Two stars: Fluffier than a bag of marshmallows

Dentists all over the world rejoice: A Blogger's Life *might make your teeth fall out. Popular book blogger Kim Long's debut novel has about as much depth as a Kardashian sister.*

Published one hour ago by Thirsty Reader

"Something wrong, Kimmie?"

Nicholas's breath tickled the back of my neck, and I quickly minimized the screen on my computer. "It's nothing," I muttered as a lump settled in my belly. I didn't want Nicholas, my fiancé, to know I'd been stalking my book reviews—again. He knew how upset I got by negative ratings and implored me to accept it was impossible to please everyone. He was right, as he almost always was, but I couldn't help myself. Hoping his question was merely rhetorical and not in response to the groan I'd accidentally emitted, I swiveled my kitchen stool to face him. From the way the inner edges of his dark eyebrows curved toward each other in concern, I knew he'd heard my sounds of distress.

"You're looking at your reviews again, aren't you?" The silent "tsk, tsk" attached to his question was deafening.

"Why do you ask?" I waved my hand. "Never mind. Yes, I was. Too bad none of your siblings are dentists instead of physicians."

Nicholas regarded me with amusement before rubbing a strand of my long light brown hair between his fingers. "What do Neil, Nathan, and Natalie's careers have to do with reviews of *A Blogger's Life?*"

I chuckled at the names of Nicholas's siblings, but soon enough, the text of the two-star review flashed before my eyes and threatened to turn my laugh into a sob. "Apparently my book is sweet enough to cause tooth decay." If my readers were going to cry while reading my romantic comedy novel, I'd hoped it would be happy tears, not because of a toothache. My lips quivered.

Nicholas let go of my hair and opened his mouth to say something I assumed was positive in nature, but I cut him off. "It wasn't meant as a compliment." I gave him a pleading look, silently begging him to lift my spirits with his next words—like the reviewer had the intelligence quotient of a gnat, no taste, and was probably a fifty-five-year-old woman who lived in her aging parents' basement with a dozen cats.

Nicholas appeared to contemplate, as if letting Thirsty Reader's opinion set in before responding. "What advice do you think Blogger Kim would give to Author Kim right now?"

As the creator of the popular chick lit book blog, *Pastel Is the New Black*, I was very familiar with mixed opinions on novels. But being on the receiving end of mixed reviews took some getting used to, and Nicholas knew it. "I think Blogger Kim should cut Author Kim some slack. Sure, she's experienced at the art of writing two and three pink-champagne-flutes reviews, but she's a newbie at receiving them." I rotated my stool so I was again facing my computer, where it sat in the kitchen nook in the one-bedroom apartment I shared with Nicholas in Manhattan's West Village.

Nicholas squeezed my shoulders gently. "I'm sorry, Kimmie, but bad reviews come with the gig. Especially if you expect anyone besides your friends and family to read your books. Besides, most of the reviews have been fantastic."

With my eyes closed, I took in his truthful words while his skilled hands attempted to loosen the tight knots in my joints. Since my debut chick lit novel had been published a month earlier, sales were more than decent. Numerous reviews from bloggers, readers, and at least one of the major trades cited me as the "next big thing in romantic comedy" and "an author to watch." But along with the shining accolades came hurtful comments that I should stick to reading and leave the writing to the professionals. I wished I could focus on the positive, like I'd always urged my author friends and those who did review tours with *Pastel Is the New Black* to do. As a book blogger, I was a hypocrite to the nth degree, but I couldn't make my skin grow thicker overnight. Making the transition from Blogger Kim to Author Kim was a dream come true, but if I'd learned anything in the last thirty or so days, it was that even the best dreams were peppered with nightmare sequences. The recurring one where my agent, Felicia, rejected all of my pitches for new novels and then dumped me as her client was especially disturbing.

"By the way, can you please tell Natalie you're not dressing up as a mermaid for the wedding? I'm betting you'll be the sexiest bride no matter what you wear, but a *Splash* or *The Little Mermaid* theme does nothing for me."

Nicholas's voice buzzed in my ear, snapping me out of my own head. I turned around to face him again at the mention of his younger sister, Natalie, who was twenty-nine and a year younger than me. "What's this about a mermaid? Sounds kinky." I'd never thought about role playing Tom Hanks and Darryl Hannah from the classic eighties movie, but Nicholas could make anything sexy if he put his mind...and other parts...to it.

"I'm sure it would be, but I'd like to keep our wedding a kink-free reception. The honeymoon is an entirely different story." He waggled his eyebrows.

I imagined Nicholas playing with my mermaid tail and blushed. "Count me in. As long as it's pink."

Nicholas scrunched up his face. "You want to wear a pink wedding dress? You're far from virginal—thank God—but I was thinking white or off-white."

"Oh. You mean mermaid-style wedding dresses." I withheld a giggle at my overactive imagination, although Nicholas *did* like to keep things interesting in the bedroom, and sometimes bathroom and living room. Nicholas would have me on the kitchen table if I let him, but I preferred to keep activities in the kitchen PG-13 for sanitary reasons. "It doesn't actually have a tail, silly. It's just form-fitting at the bodice and the skirt flares to the floor." I gave him a playful punch in the arm.

Nicholas's cheeks turned pink. "When Natalie said mermaid dresses were sexy, I argued that Ariel had nothing on you. Now I know why she rolled her eyes. I thought she was just being Natalie. It all makes sense now." He chuckled. "Don't forget, your appointment at Kleinfeld Bridal is next weekend. My mom and Natalie won't shut up about it."

"Of course I remember." An appointment at the world-famous bridal shop was unlikely to slip my mind. Thankfully, I'd done my research and made the appointment shortly after Nicholas proposed. When it came to shopping for clothes, I didn't play around, but I couldn't fault Nicholas for double checking. We'd been engaged for nine months, but aside from the date, venue, and entertainment—Nicholas, whose passion for music ran deep, had already booked the house band of a popular club—our wedding to-do list had very little check marks.

"Hopefully, you'll have so much fun trying on dresses and drinking champagne, you'll manage to go the entire afternoon without checking your reviews," Nicholas said, his voice dripping with hope.

"I think I can manage it," I said with only a hint of doubt. I wondered if my shopping session at Kleinfeld would be aired on the reality television show *Say Yes To The Dress*. It was doubtful, since I wasn't a bridezilla, no one in my entourage was a bully, and despite a rocky path from casual colleagues to future husband and wife, Nicholas and I didn't have a tragic story to win over the hearts of viewers, like a battle with cancer or an imminent deployment back to Afghanistan. Not that I was complaining.

"Atta girl," Nicholas said with a wink, causing my knees to wobble. He could still incite the butterflies to dance in my tummy with a mere facial expression—like a wink or the trademark rubbing of his hand along the ever-present dark scruff on his jaw—as effortlessly as he could when we first fell in love more than two years earlier. Our love story might not make exciting television worthy of a reality show, but the hills and valleys kept me on my toes.

"I need to get back to the hotel with the number of rooms we want to set aside. How many people do you think will stay over?" We were holding the reception at the Soho Grand. It was where the magic of our coupling first began the night Nicholas met me for a drink after my ten-year high school reunion, and it was also where he had popped the question. We planned to reserve a section of rooms at a special rate for our guests.

I counted on my fingers. "Your parents and siblings, my parents, Erin and Gerry, out-of-town relatives." I ran out of fingers. "Maybe we should look at the guest list."

"What is this list you speak of?" Nicholas asked with an eyebrow raised.

I bit my lip. We hadn't yet vocalized how pathetically unorganized we were, but it was the white elephant in the room. We'd picked a date more than a year away so the wedding planning wouldn't need to compete with the release of *A Blogger's Life* for my attention. But now the big day—a Saturday night in early November—was only seven months away. "I suppose we should figure out who we're inviting, huh?" My stomach curdled at how much we needed to do before we could finally say our "I dos" and live happily ever after, but as the bride, I felt it was my responsibility to take on the bulk of the preparation. Nicholas had nearly short-circuited our relationship the year before, when his obsession with getting ahead in his high-profile legal career trumped our time together. I didn't want to add more to his plate and tip the balance we'd worked so hard to achieve. Even though I was now juggling my role as a published author with my full-time gig as a legal secretary and managing *Pastel Is the New Black*, I had it under control. My dreams—both professional and romantic—had all come true and I'd be damned if I'd complain about "having it all."

Nicholas was only five foot seven, but at a mere four foot eleven, he towered over me and I had to stand on my tippy toes to give him a reassuring butterfly kiss on the nose. I squeezed both of his sides and presented a confident smile. "We'll get there, sweets. One thing at a time."

Chapter 2

The following Saturday, my entire body shook with nerves as I sat down on a brown-upholstered couch and took in the crème-colored walls and white columns inside Kleinfeld Bridal. I wasn't a stranger to luxurious department stores, but this was the first time I'd been in one entirely devoted to dressing a bride-to-be. I pinched myself to confirm this was really happening—I, Kimberly Michelle Long, was going to marry the love of my life, and my friends and family were at a world-famous bridal shop to support my search for the perfect gown. Nicholas's mom had come in from Vermont, mine from Florida, and my younger sister, Erin, from Boston. The local crew included Nicholas's little sister Natalie, who was now a surgical intern at New York-Presbyterian/Weill Cornell, having graduated from the University Of Vermont College of Medicine, and my closest friends, Bridget and Caroline. Erin was my matron my honor, Bridget, my BFF since the seventh grade, was my maid of honor, and Caroline and Natalie were my bridesmaids. My relationship with Natalie was still a fetus, but I asked her to be in my wedding party as a way to grow our bond. I hoped we'd eventually be as close as real sisters.

From next to me, my mom said, "Hopefully, Jeanine and Natalie will arrive soon so we can get started." She accepted a glass of champagne from one of the bridal consultants with a gleeful twinkle in her brown eyes and whispered, "This is so exciting."

"But not more exciting than when we shopped for my dress, right?" Erin asked, a hint of a frown on her full and flawlessly painted purplish brown lips. She twirled a finger through a coffee-colored spiral of her long hair.

I met Bridget's green eyes from where she sat on a neighboring couch and we shared a knowing look. My younger sister by three years got hitched before me and already owned a four-bedroom house in the suburbs with her husband, Gerry, but she would forever be my baby sister. "I'm sure saying yes to your dress was equally scintillating," I responded. "Of course, I can't know for certain since you insisted on it being a mother/daughter only event—no sisters allowed." Yes, I had some petty in me too, but I was gutted when Erin left me out of her big shopping day all those years ago. Despite being single and my sex life consisting of an occasional casual shag with Jonathan, my friend with benefits at the time and Bridget's current live-in boyfriend, Erin was the only sibling I had. My love for her trumped any jealousy or bitterness, and I wanted to share in her dress-shopping experience. Since Caroline had eloped the year before with a sexy Brit she'd met on a plane and Bridget and Jonathan didn't believe in marriage, the next opportunity I'd have to shop for someone else's wedding dress might be for my own daughter.

"Nicholas's family is almost ten minutes late," Erin said, pouting into her watch. "I hope they don't give away your appointment."

I heard someone shout, "There they are!" and looked over to where my future sister-in-law, Natalie, dressed in a red and white polka dot hoop skirt and a white short-sleeved turtleneck sweater, was scurrying toward us as if on a mission. Between the outfit, her chin-length ebony curls, and her huge brown eyes, she resembled Minnie Mouse. I'd have to remember to send a picture of her to Nicholas. I didn't know her well enough yet to tease, but he'd been her brother for twenty-nine years and nothing was off limits.

Natalie, who was dragging Nicholas's mother and another girl behind her, stopped in front of us, put her hand to her chest, and took a deep breath. "Sorry we're late. Tiffany had low blood sugar and we stopped for a bite." She skimmed the room. "Where's the booze? I'm not on call again for thirty-six hours. First I drink. Then I sleep." She waved at my mom, Bridget, and Caroline. Then she bent down, kissed me on the cheek, and sat down next to Erin without acknowledging her. Erin, who was examining her unchipped maroon-painted nails, smirked in faked nonchalance. My stomach churned at the thought of Erin and Natalie vying for an equal voice in any wedding-planning decisions. If my sister was Martha Stewart, tailored and color-coordinated, Natalie was Katy Perry, quirky and mismatched down to her personalized tie-dyed scrubs. I prayed the two could get along for the next two to three hours at least.

I scooched over and patted the couch next to me. "Sit here, Jeanine." When my soon-to-be mother-in-law sat down, I hugged her thin frame fiercely. We'd hit it off right away, unlike Nicholas's father, who I'd warmed up to only after he stopped making my sweetie feel less than just because he chose a career in law instead of medicine like the rest of the Strong clan. And then it hit me. "Who the hell is Tiffany?" I clapped a hand against my mouth, hoping the query didn't sound as rude to the others as it felt floating off my tongue.

The pretty blonde who'd accompanied Natalie and Mrs. Strong into the store cleared her throat. "I'm Tiffany. Close friend of Natalie's since our school days."

"Tiffany just moved from Queens to my apartment complex in Murray Hill, so we get to hang way more often. When I'm not working eighteen-hour shifts, that is." Natalie beamed at Tiffany.

"And you must be Kimmie." Tiffany's aquamarine eyes took me in from under long eyelashes and she flipped her wavy golden blonde hair across her lanky shoulder.

"Yes, I'm Kim." The nickname "Kimmie" was reserved for Nicholas, but unauthorized users sometimes slipped through the cracks. "Nice to meet you." I wondered what she was doing at my exclusive and very intimate appointment-only shopping excursion.

As if reading my mind, Natalie said, "I hope you don't mind I let Tiffany tag along on your special day. We have plans later."

She didn't clarify, as if having plans later explained all. It didn't. I had plans with Nicholas later and I didn't invite him because the groom wasn't supposed to see the wedding dress until his bride walked down the aisle. It would have been weird. Almost as strange as having this random chick weigh in on whether the bling on my dress added just the right amount of pizzazz or made me look like I'd been shot by a BeDazzler gun. But I wasn't going to cause a scene by asking her to leave. How much harm could a friend of Nicholas's sister cause?

"I've known Nicholas forever. I know what he likes," Tiffany said, smoothing down her form-fitting black jeans.

This got my attention. "How do you know Nicholas?"

Natalie responded for her, "She grew up in Burlington too." Then she looked at Tiffany and made a slashing motion across her throat.

"Don't be so dramatic, Nat. Kim won't care that I dated Nicholas. It was ages ago." Tiffany laughed, while I felt Caroline, Erin, and Bridget's eyes on me. My mom was having an in-depth conversation with Jeanine, something about the pros and cons of wearing a veil.

I jutted my head back. "You dated Nicholas?" Nicholas had never mentioned her name. He didn't talk much of past relationships, except I knew his girlfriend before me, Amanda, cheated on him.

"Back in high school," she said.

My friends' shoulders dropped an inch in relief in unison as if it had been choreographed, probably since high school was a long time ago for all of us.

Tiffany continued, "I was a freshman, he was a senior, and we fell in love."

"Ah, teenage romance. Don't we all think our first relationships will last forever?" Bridget gave me a knowing look since she was currently crazy in love and living with my high-school boyfriend.

Tiffany faced me. "Like I said, it was ages ago. You have nothing to worry about." She sat down in the small space between Natalie and Erin, practically on Natalie's lap.

"Yes, it was so long ago, it wasn't worth mentioning." Natalie stood up.

I smiled sweetly. "Good to know."

"Which one of you is Kim?"

I beamed up at the stunning bridal consultant standing before me, happy for a subject change. She had smooth brown skin, her long raven hair was pulled back into a braid, and she was dressed in head-to-toe black like all the other specialists. "I'm Kim," I said, rising from the couch and straightening my posture. I had a feeling she had close to a foot of height on me.

She told us her name was India and she'd be my bridal specialist for the day. I introduced her to my companions, informed her of my budget, and a few minutes later, I followed her to the back room to get started. The collection of turquoise bangles on India's right wrist made a clanging sound as she led the way, asking me questions about Nicholas and our wedding plans.

I told her about the Youtube video Nicholas posted for me in a grand gesture the previous summer to express his devotion and apologize for neglecting me in favor of work.

India's amber eyes twinkled. "He sounds like a prince, and you definitely have the glow of someone in love. I enjoy nothing more than styling a blissful bride. Do you have a particular dress type in mind?"

I bit my lip. "I know I don't want a ball gown or anything with a huge skirt. And I don't want anything with ruffles or tons of layers. I was thinking a sheath style might be best, given my shape. Maybe lace. Or not." I told her I had an open mind to any style except ones in which I'd be mistaken for Glinda the Good Witch or one of her loyal munchkins.

India tapped her finger to her chin and began going through the racks. I took calming breaths in and out while I watched her put a few dresses to the side and pass others by.

A few minutes later, I was in a dressing room stepping into the first gown—a beaded lace sheath with an empire waist—when I heard a ruckus from down the hall.

"Kim? Where are you? You can call off the search. I found your dress." It sounded like Natalie.

Erin countered, "Not possible, since I'm holding the perfect gown in my arms."

My mom said, "Girls, keep your voices down. This is Kleinfeld, not H&M."

"They belong to you?" India asked.

I nodded guiltily as she zipped me up.

As soon as India opened the door a crack, my entire entourage came barreling inside.

Natalie looked me up and down. "So not the dress."

I hadn't even had the chance to view my own reflection but took her word for it when everyone else nodded in agreement. "Okay then. Next."

Natalie shoved a dress in my face. "This is it."

"Not so fast." Erin stepped in front of Natalie. "I think you'd look gorgeous in this one."

"How about we view one gown at a time?" Even with her voice raised, India managed to sound completely poised and in control. Her no-nonsense attitude shut everyone up while I tried on the two new dresses.

Thankfully, I wasn't the modest type or it would have been super awkward getting naked in front of seven other women. I couldn't remember a single episode of *Say Yes to the Dress* where the bride-to-be's family joined her in the dressing room.

Natalie jumped up and down like she'd just saved a life when I tried on her pick—an offbeat mini high-low gown—while Erin didn't hold back her aversion. She said it was the perfect gown, if I was getting married in "the best little whorehouse in Texas." Everyone else was quiet, but I could tell they agreed with me—it was not The Dress.

Erin's "perfect" dress consisted of a princess ball gown with several layers of tulle on the skirt. My first instinct was "hell no," but I tried it on to prove how unflattering it was. Erin's eyes danced as if resembling a pinhead was the desired effect while Natalie made gagging motions behind her back. "I don't love either of these dresses, but I adore you both for trying." I hoped I sounded grateful for their enthusiasm despite hating both their choices. "I was thinking something more like—"

"You'd look lovely in a strapless gown with a sweetheart neck," Jeanine said.

"She's too chesty for strapless," my mom argued.

I cleared my throat. "Guys, India already selected a few—"

"A miniskirt? What were you thinking?" Erin rolled her eyes in Natalie's direction.

"Better than a ball gown—the one style your sister ruled out," Natalie scoffed.

"I know you both meant well," I said, but my words fell on deaf ears. I glanced helplessly at India, who was watching the spectacle with her mouth agape. She was probably thinking this would have made a great episode of *Say Yes To The Dress* after all.

"How about mermaid, K? Nicholas would love you in it," Bridget said while Caroline nodded in agreement.

"I agree with Birdie. Or fit and flare. I wore one to Nicholas's senior prom. He couldn't take his eyes off me all night." Tiffany looked dreamily at the ceiling until Natalie nudged her in the elbow.

Birdie?

"My name is Bridget." Bridget crossed her arms over her chest and glared at Tiffany.

My tummy dropped in disappointment. The day was supposed to be about me, but not a single member of my entourage, invitees and crashers alike, had even asked what kind of dress I wanted. Not even my mother, and I expected more from her. She was still explaining to Jeanine, who was probably an A-cup, how difficult it was for busty women to wear strapless dresses. Jeanine thought the style would emphasize my lovely décolletage. My first choice was sleeveless, but no one cared about my preference. I blinked back tears of frustration and embarrassment as India, no longer poised and in control, shouted, "Enough."

Enough was right. While everyone ignored India and continued to talk over each other about what style would be most flattering on me, I removed my phone from my purse and shimmied out of the dressing room, careful not to trip on the full skirt. I assumed if I ripped it, I'd have to buy it. I'd give the bill to Erin since it was her stupid fault I was wearing it in the first place.

With tears stinging my eyes, I hid behind a rack of dresses and called Nicholas. He picked up on the first ring.

"You found the dress already?"

"Not exactly." I sniffled.

"What's wrong, Kimmie?"

"I can't do this." I desperately needed to wipe my nose and forgot to bring a tissue from my bag. I assumed I'd also be charged if I got snot stains on the dress.

I heard Nicholas gasp. "You can't do what?"

My pulse quickened knowing he must be thinking I meant getting married and I wanted to ease his mind immediately. "The dress shopping. It's horrible. No one's listening to me. Natalie's too offbeat. Erin's too traditional. Your mom wants me to show off my tits, but my mom says no. Tiffany said you'd like fit and flare—"

"My mom wants you to show off your tits? Lady after my own heart." Nicholas chuckled. "Wait. Tiffany? Tiffany who?"

I snorted. "Apparently, the original love of your life. But we'll talk about it later. Help?"

"Do you need me to rescue you?" He sounded disappointed for me.

I swallowed hard. I couldn't leave. "I just need a pep talk." Even though the wedding planning had taken a backseat to the release of *A Blogger's Life* in general, I'd been totally juiced up for the dress-shopping part. The appointment was booked ages ago and we were already seriously behind. "There was a long waiting list for this appointment. I should try again." This was *my* day and I'd take back control.

After a pause, Nicholas said, "If you're sure. I know how excited you were, but it's supposed to be fun and you sound miserable."

I sighed. "My family, your family, I suppose eventually *our* family sucked all the enjoyment out of it. But I should cowgirl up." I'd find a quiet place and practice mindful breathing for a few minutes before I attempted take two.

"Kim? Yoo-hoo. Where are you, Kim? We have more dresses for you to try," Erin said.

I squatted as best as I could while wearing a dress two times the length of my body. If Erin spotted me, she might insist I try on another dress that made me look like a puffy marshmallow.

"I think a pink or blush shade would scream Kim," I heard Bridget say.

Someone—Tiffany?—snorted. "A pink wedding dress?"

"I found another gown you will *love*," Natalie said.

I wouldn't be surprised if it had multi-colored ruffles on the bottom.

"As much as she loved the other one?" Erin said in a snotty tone.

I whispered into the phone, "Can you hear this?"

"Last chance. I can get you out of this."

I begrudgingly accepted defeat. "Okay, but how?"

"Trust me."

Two hours later, I was snuggling with Nicholas in the queen-sized bed we shared.

He brought a spoonful of mint chocolate chip ice cream to my mouth. "All better?"

I swallowed the creamy goodness with my eyes closed and nodded. "You're my hero." A few minutes after we'd hung up, Jeanine rushed out of the dressing room to tell me Nicholas had called her. He'd told his mom the founder of his company was in town from Denver and had asked if Nicholas and his fiancée were available for a last-minute dinner to discuss his future. Nicholas told Jeanine he felt guilty asking me to cut my big day short, but this could be huge for his career. Did Jeanine think it was okay to ask to reschedule the dress shopping or would I throw my engagement ring into the Hudson River at the mere suggestion? Since everyone was aware it was Nicholas's obsession with work that threatened our relationship the year before, my selfless fiancé basically threw himself under the bus with his escape plan. I wasn't sure I'd ever loved him more.

I told the group I needed to be there for Nicholas and apologized profusely to India for wasting her time. Even though there was only kindness in her eyes when she hugged me and wished me luck, I wouldn't be surprised if she initiated my permanent ban from Kleinfeld the second I left. As mortified as I was at the prospect, I was thrilled to get out of there and away from my overbearing bridal party. And since the founder of Nicholas's company had been dead almost twenty years, the two of us were enjoying a quiet evening at home for two.

"I still need to find a dress." I shuddered at the thought of repeating the day's events.

"You have plenty of time," Nicholas said.

I nodded despite the heaviness in my center reminding me seven months was the opposite of plenty of time. According to the article I'd read in *The Knot*, you should begin dress shopping twelve months in advance of the wedding. I'd technically "started," even though my first attempt was a disaster. At least I was now certain I didn't want a princess ball gown or a mini high-low. I recalled what Tiffany said about Nicholas's reaction to her fit-and-flare style prom dress. With a playful nudge at his side, I said, "Tell me about *Tiffany*."

Nicholas flipped onto his side facing me. "We dated a very long time ago and she remained friends with Natalie. They've become closer since Natalie moved to New York and my mom said they're practically conjoined now that Tiffany moved into the same building." He tickled my arm. "What else do you want to know? I have no secrets from my sexy bride."

"Did you guys have sex?" Obviously, I wasn't Nicholas's first lover.

With any luck, our marriage would survive "till death do us part" and I'd be his last, but my heart didn't share my nonchalance at the question. It galloped furiously the moment the words escaped my lips and my mouth went dry as my mind recalled all the young adult novels I'd read about intense first loves. Mine and Jonathan's relationship didn't qualify and I hoped Nicholas and Tiffany's didn't either. I selfishly wanted to be the only novel-worthy love story in Nicholas's life.

"We did. Does it bother you?" His brown eyes were pools of concern as he studied my face for a reaction.

I considered the question for a moment before responding, "Not really." Nicholas's previous partners had been irrelevant to me until one showed up at my bridal appointment. "It's kind of pervy though." When he furrowed his brow at me, I clarified, "Your age difference."

"You guys are the same age. Does that make what we did thirty minutes ago pervy?" His hand traveled the length of my bare leg under the covers.

I scooted closer to him. "Our three-year age difference means nothing now, but fourteen and seventeen?" I crinkled my nose. "Pervy."

Nicholas chuckled. "She was the freshman 'it' girl. If it wasn't me, another senior would have deflowered her."

Any hope I had that Tiffany was the ugly-duckling-turned-swan type who'd only come into her own in her twenties was expunged. "Was she your first too?" I hoped he'd say no even though my logical side knew it didn't matter.

"Yes."

I frowned.

"What's with the pouty lips?" Nicholas said, mirroring my expression.

"I could have lived without meeting the first girl you ever made love to."

"I survived knowing about your first boyfriend. And I haven't seen Tiffany in years, unlike you and Jonathan." He raised an eyebrow.

Nicholas and his legal mind made a great point. I was hypocrite *ultime*. "You're right," I muttered before bringing my knees to my chest to make myself even smaller.

Nicholas snickered before spooning his body around mine and squeezing me gently. "Tiffany means nothing to me now, except as part of my history. You, on the other hand, mean everything to my present and my future." He kissed the top of my head. "Nap time."

I nodded, suddenly too tired for words. I wasn't seriously intimidated by Nicholas's past with Tiffany, but I'd have been happier if Nicholas's past wasn't such a head turner. I also found the timing of her reappearance suspicious given he was engaged to someone else. Even his sister seemed annoyed by Tiffany's reminiscing, but Natalie was the one who invited her in the first place. Who would think inviting a guy's ex-girlfriend to watch his current fiancée try on wedding dresses was a good idea? The smarts she possessed to pass the medical boards were a sharp contrast to her lack of common sense. I let out a deep exhale. It wasn't worth worrying about. Hopefully, it was a one-off and I'd never see Tiffany again.

As I closed my eyes, I realized I hadn't even checked my reviews all day.

My eyes flew open and immediately fixated on the nightstand where I'd left my phone. I slid my arm out from underneath Nicholas's and carefully reached for the device. I could tell Nicholas was already asleep and I didn't want to wake him. He'd only urge me to wait until later. *As if.*

My pulse raced like it did every time I pulled up the page for my book on Amazon. *A Blogger's Life* had fifty-three reviews, one more than the day before. All consideration for my darling fiancé forgotten, I bolted out of bed and scrolled to the most recent customer review— four stars! I released a quiet exhale knowing a scathing review was unlikely to accompany a four-star rating.

Four stars: Nice if unrealistic portrayal of life.

I really enjoyed this novel. It was the perfect book to snuggle up with on a rainy spring day. The author has an engaging and humorous voice, the pacing was perfect, and the romance enjoyable. My one criticism is that all the conflict was superficial and could easily be resolved in the real world. It would have been refreshing if at least one of the characters, main or supporting, experienced something dire, like a death in the family or a terminal illness. In real life, people die! I'll read this author again, but I do hope she learns to sprinkle some depth and darkness into her otherwise-idyllic fictional world.

Published seven hours ago by Bernadette Lapone

I lay back in my bed with the phone resting on my chest and contemplated Bernadette's feedback. As an author of romantic comedy, the biggest calamity I made my characters endure was a vicious breakup, a lost promotion at work, or some other equally reversible conflict. I'd never considered killing anyone. In my opinion, adding such darkness to a novel in the genre defeated the purpose of a story meant for escape from real life. But if I wanted to grow as an author, I couldn't toss aside constructive criticism without careful consideration. Ms. Lapone wasn't the first reader to complain my writing lacked depth. Maybe she was right.

With romantic comedy, it was all about the blissful conclusion. I needed to figure out a way to put my characters through more weighty conflict without depriving them—and my readers—of their happy ending. I'd already sent the first fifty pages of my second novel to my editor, Sadie, and was waiting to get her thoughts, but I had a good ways to go before completing the draft. I had my work cut out for me, but I wouldn't quit until I got it right. I'd start tomorrow. I had almost eight months until my December deadline to deliver the completed manuscript to my publisher—plenty of time. With my decision made, I closed my eyes and joined Nicholas in his repose while a bevy of catastrophic subplots danced in my head.

Chapter 3

The following Monday, I was on the phone with my mom. Her flight back to Florida was the day before, and I hadn't seen her since I ran out of Kleinfeld to "rescue" Nicholas. She didn't know I was the damsel in distress who required rescuing.

"It was very selfless of you to give up your big day for Nicholas. I hope he appreciates it," she said.

"Of course he does, Mom, but there's more to it." My mom adored Nicholas, but she hadn't forgotten the previous year, when I showed up in tears on my parents' doorstep in Boca Raton after a failed attempt to reignite the spark between Nicholas and me during his business trip in Florida. I knew she was concerned Nicholas was back to his old habits of putting career advancement before our relationship. I couldn't bring myself to confess the lie Nicholas had concocted to get me out of the bridal shop, but I needed to take some of the blame off him. I also thought she should know I wasn't as torn up about cutting the appointment short as she thought. "The truth is I wasn't having as much fun as I imagined. I think eight was a crowd." I explained how overwhelmed I felt with everyone tossing out their opinions and never once asking what I wanted. I laid most of the blame on Natalie and Erin. I swallowed down my guilt as I waited for my mom's response.

"Oh, sweetheart, I'm sorry. I suppose we all got carried away and were living vicariously. You know what? There are many bridal shops in Boca Raton and neighboring towns, and believe it or not, they don't only cater to the over-seventy crowd. Why don't you pick a weekend and come down? It will be just the two of us. Your dad and I will pay for your flights."

My limbs tingled with warmth at her words. "It's a date." I looked up from my phone into the dark blue eyes of my boss, Rob. "I need to get back to work. I'll call you later." We said our goodbyes and I hung up. "What can I do for you?" I asked Rob.

"How about your job?"

Typically, a question like this from your boss would be accompanied by beads of sweat forming on your forehead while your chin trembled in fear. But I knew better, and the quiver of Rob's lips was confirmation he was teasing me. "Whatever you say, *Daneen*," I said, referring to a former attorney in our department who didn't think a lowly secretary like myself deserved Rob's loyalty, Nicholas's affection, or even to breathe the same air as her. By some miracle, condescending Daneen had found another law firm to bless with her skills and probably another poor assistant to torment, but Rob liked to imitate her to get a rise out of me. There was no denying I lacked passion for my day job, but Rob knew my devotion to *Pastel Is the New Black* and my writing career never got in the way of my work assignments. He fully supported my publishing dreams, and I suspected he'd prefer to work with a less-than-enthusiastic me than a more motivated anyone else.

"Can you do a mail merge for me? I sent you the documents." The jesting portion of the conversation was clearly over.

I nodded. "You got it, Boss Man."

By the time I completed Rob's task, it was time for lunch. With my e-reader tucked into my purse and my laptop in tow, I headed to the firm's cafeteria, ready to dive into my latest novel for the blog. The book was the second in a series about a wedding planner. When I got to the scene where a bride was trampled by her overzealous bridesmaids, I put the e-reader aside—way too close to home—and checked my personal email instead. There was a new one from Felicia. My idealistic side imagined my literary agent was writing to tell me a film company was interested in optioning the movie rights to *A Blogger's Life*. The realist in me wasn't holding my breath, and knew it was more likely she was asking the status of my standalone sophomore novel, *Love on Stone Street*. My two-book deal was based on a proposal of the second book, and I was well aware of the clause in my contract stating the manuscript had to meet with the publisher's approval in order to move forward.

Hi Kim,

I hope you're well and adapting to your new role as a published author. I thought you'd like to see the attached. I spied someone reading A Blogger's Life *on the subway today!*

I have some news from the publisher. It seems Sadie has resigned from the company and you've been assigned a new editor for Love on Stone Street. *Her name is Melina Rhodes. She's an ace editor who's been in the business for almost two decades. Don't be alarmed, but she's more old school than Sadie and doesn't have much experience with chick lit. I'm not worried and you shouldn't be either. You got a starred review from* Publishers Weekly *with* A Blogger's Life *and I'm confident you'll wow Melina the same way. You should be hearing from her soon, if you haven't already.*

Felicia

Choosing to focus on the positive news first, I downloaded the attachment and squealed when I saw the picture of a young woman reading a paperback of *A Blogger's Life*. I couldn't tell which line of the subway it was since the advertisement above her seat, for the School of Practical Philosophy, was popular on all of them. I sent the photo to Nicholas, my parents, Bridget, and Caroline with only the phrase, "A dream come true."

I bounced a curled knuckle against my mouth as the news of Sadie's resignation sunk in. We'd worked so well together on *A Blogger's Life*. Like Felicia, Sadie had loved my writing style, and her edits served to make the book stronger, tighter, and funnier without threatening my voice. I was crushed to lose her on my team and more anxious than ever about my second book.

I rolled my shoulders and watched my fellow employees enter and exit the cafeteria. I considered my day job a necessary evil to pay my bills. It was a pit stop on the way to what I hoped would be a full-time writing career. Having an editor who "got" me was a big part of making the dream a reality. Felicia's warning that Melina didn't have much experience with chick lit didn't inspire confidence and, instead, made me even more determined to add a more serious or sad plot line to *Love on Stone Street*. I'd devoted my life's work to squashing the claim that chick lit was dead, and I'd jump into the murky waters of the East River naked before I went Benedict Arnold on the genre. No book heroine of my creation would be dealt a tragic blow like cancer, but I could probably wreak some havoc on some secondary characters without being tried for treason.

According to the time on my watch, I had fifteen minutes left of my lunch hour, and every sixty seconds counted when writing a book. I clasped my hands together, intertwined my fingers, and stretched my arms out in front of me. It was time to go deep.

Chapter 4

Speaking on a writers' panel was way outside my comfort zone, but Caroline and Bridget talked me into participating in one at the Brooklyn Book Festival. The festival was a free week-long celebration with programs highlighting New York City's diverse literary scene. I'd attended before as an avid reader and blogger, but this was my first gig as an author. I was a last-minute replacement for Hannah Marshak, who Bridget and I had known in junior high and high school as the resident "mean girl." We'd reconnected two years earlier when Hannah's debut chick lit novel, *Cut on the Bias*, was published and she asked me to review the book on *Pastel Is the New Black*. After initially refusing to do *anything* to help advance the career of my high-school nemesis, I eventually pulled up my big-girl panties and gave it an honest four-pink-champagne-flutes review. Later, when I was having difficulty securing an agent, Hannah shocked me by making an introduction to her own agent, Felicia Harrison. Felicia loved *A Blogger's Life* and offered to represent me too.

I flashed back to the email I'd received from Hannah a few weeks earlier during a girls' night with Bridget and Caroline.

> *Bonjour, my little agent sister,*
> *I'm at JFK Airport, in the first-class lounge for Air France. I'm off to Paris to celebrate my birthday. I agreed to be on a panel of female New York-based authors at the Brooklyn Book Festival a week from Saturday, but the tickets were a surprise and we won't be back in time. I hate to disappoint my fans, but how could I resist another trip to the City of Lights, especially whilst in the midst of penning my third Paris-based masterpiece,* A-Line in the Sand? *I thought you might want to*

take my place—on the panel, not in Paris, obviously. I have other authors who are interested, but thought you could use the promotion and you'd make the perfect substitute given we write in the same genre and share an agent. Of course, I'm better known, but you have the famous blog going for you as well. You can thank me later with drinks. Or with a five-pink-champagne-flutes review of A-Line in the Sand. *Jk.*

I'll expect to hear from you soon.

Au Revoir

It was typical Hannah—never without a backhanded compliment even when she was trying to be nice. Despite the dubious execution of the invitation, I conceded it was a great opportunity to advance my writing career.

Between the nightly pep talks over the last week—Nicholas—and the no-nonsense lecture on the subway ride into Brooklyn on the value of this type of event for exposure—Caroline—I was as composed as I was going to be. I was comforted knowing Nicholas, Bridget, Jonathan, Caroline, and her husband, Felix, would be in the audience to support me. The six of us had plans to celebrate Jonathan's birthday after. Bridget reminded me no matter what happened, there would be a tall glass of something alcoholic at the restaurant later. I was counting on it.

My event was taking place at the Brooklyn Public Library at three thirty and I'd arrived forty-five minutes early as instructed. Even though I wanted to cling to my posse like a drowning woman to a life raft, I told them to check out the outdoor booths and come back when the event started. I had to fake some semblance of cool in front of the other authors.

When I spotted Christine Bannah, another one of Felicia's clients and one of my favorite romantic comedy authors, on the other side of the room, I restrained my inner fangirl. Today, I was acting as her equal even though I felt like an imposter. Then I remembered I wasn't a fraud. I was a published author whose debut novel was available online and at brick-and-mortar bookstores country wide and was being read by commuters (or at least one of them) on the New York subway system. I might not be as accomplished as Christine Bannah, or even

Hannah Marshak, but every success had to start somewhere. With the confidence of a much taller person, I approached the other authors and made introductions.

It turned out Christine was a fan of *Pastel Is the New Black* and even offered to read *Love on Stone Street* and write an endorsement. She'd also seen Felicia's tweets about *A Blogger's Life* and had a copy on her e-reader. The other panelists, a combination of psychological suspense, mystery, and upmarket women's fiction writers, were equally kind and I almost forgot to be nervous. And then I was seated at my spot on the podium looking out into an ocean of at least two hundred people, and my nerves woke up as if someone threw a bucket of freezing water on them. I searched the crowd for my honey for a reassuring wink but couldn't spot him.

I listened to the moderator introduce the panelists, most of them award-winning and best-selling novelists, and felt every muscle in my body tense as she introduced me, a debut author represented by Felicia Harrison of Harrison and Gold Literary, and founder of the well-known book blog, *Pastel Is the New Black*. I'd been tasked with providing my own bio, and acknowledged it was a bit lame compared to my literary comrades on the panel. Maybe my lack of experience would work in my favor, making me more relatable to the audience. Like Caroline had said while urging me to accept the gig, there were probably many aspiring authors in the crowd who'd be interested in how I'd made the transition from blogger to author. It would be fun to share my story in a live medium as opposed to a blog post. My excitement mounted as the moderator opened the floor to the audience. I only hoped my voice wouldn't shake when I answered my first question.

The first query was directed to Christine Bannah. The audience member wanted to know if her *Orange Orchards* series was based on a real location. The next few questions were aimed at a suspense author whose recent release was described as "Alfred Hitchcock meets Gillian Flynn." Several members of the crowd were curious how the author dreamed up such sinister scenarios and was she as dark in her real life? The author was actually very lighthearted and jovial despite the gruesome nature of her storylines. I listened carefully to how she found her dark place, since I'd had to go to mine when making my most recent additions to *Love on Stone Street*.

Twenty-five minutes later, I wished I could crawl into the wall and hide until the event was over. I'd learned everything I ever wanted to know about writing suspense, heard the story of how the demise of Christine Bannah's first marriage inspired the character arc of her latest heroine, and took note of master world-building author Ally Wiship's advice for creating a fantastic yet believable universe. What I hadn't done was share my own success story, insist *A Blogger's Life* was not a fictionalized account of my own life as a blogger, or even open my mouth, except to drain the contents of my water bottle. Not a single question was directed to me, which made me feel a bit like a seat filler at the *Oscar Awards*. I wondered if the crowd was waiting for the real author, perhaps Hannah Marshak, to come back from the bathroom and take my place.

I ran my hand against my sweaty neck and tried to maintain a poised expression even though tears were perched at the back of my throat, dying to make a dramatic entrance. I wondered if the other authors noticed and felt sorry for me. Were they avoiding eye contact on purpose? I slickly checked my watch and hoped the time was almost up. I needed a drink bad. I also craved the strong arms of my fiancé to hug the embarrassment and devastation out of me.

The moderator said, "You, in the Lenny Kravitz t-shirt. What's your question?"

I was staring down at the red soles of my favorite designer shoes— the ones I could have left in my closet since I might as well have been barefoot for all anyone in the room cared—but my head jerked back at the phrase, "Lenny Kravitz t-shirt."

"My question is for Kimmie…" Nicholas cleared his throat. "Kim Long."

I gasped in surprise and choked up, my belly heavy with love. Nicholas had heard my silent prayer and come to my rescue. I could kiss that man.

Nicholas grinned at me. "First, I'm a huge fan. I loved *A Blogger's Life*. Since you're a blogger too, I wondered how much of Laurel's story was based on your own. Did you have similar issues with your fiancé as she did with Henry?"

My heart melting, I lifted myself to a standing position. "Thanks for your question. I'm so glad you enjoyed *A Blogger's Life*." I tried to look at him without making it obvious he wasn't a stranger or give away how badly I wanted to do much more than kiss him the first chance I got. "I initially wrote Laurel to be the opposite of me in both appearance and personality because I figured readers would assume the book was based on my life. I'm way more stubborn for one, and she's about six inches taller than me, but when I completed the first draft, I realized her romantic conflicts somewhat mirrored what I was experiencing at the time with my then-boyfriend, now fiancé." I gave Nicholas a meaningful look. "We worked them out and are stronger than ever. I can't tell you if Laurel and Henry were as lucky without spoiling the book for the others." I grinned at the crowd and sat down.

"Thank you, Kim," the moderator said with a nod in my direction. "Next question. The woman with the long red hair."

"This is also a question for Kim Long," Bridget said. "I loved *A Blogger's Life* as well and wondered if you were planning to write a sequel."

A wave of gratitude rushed through me as I stood up again. I wouldn't trade my best friend for all the fans in the world. "I'm thrilled you enjoyed *A Blogger's Life*. I hadn't planned to make it a series. I'm currently working on another standalone novel right now, but I'd never say never." I beamed at Bridget, who waved at me before flushing red and sitting down.

Even though I wished someone in the crowd—one who wasn't betrothed to me or been my best friend since the seventh grade—had been genuinely excited to meet me, at least now I could leave the event with some semblance of dignity. I'd been drowning in anonymity and my fiancé and bestie pulled me out of the abyss. No one needed to know they already knew the answer to their questions.

I listened with half concentration as the attention of the room went back to the more popular authors on the panel until the moderator announced the next question would be the final one of the evening. She pointed to a thirty-something woman with shoulder-length blond hair in the second row.

The blonde stood up. "This question is for Kim Long."

My heart jumped into my throat, and the empty water bottle I'd been squeezing slipped out of my hands and under the table. I tried to reach it with my foot, but I couldn't so I slid down farther in my chair as the woman asked her question. I still couldn't make contact with the bottle.

Focus, Kim. The water bottle could wait. I got up from my chair and squinted at the woman, trying to place how I knew her. "Hi there. Would you mind repeating your question? I had a...water-bottle issue." I cleared my throat. Obviously, the girl was taking pity on me, like Nicholas and Bridget, but the harder I looked, the more convinced I was she was a complete stranger. Could it be? Was there someone in attendance I didn't know who was genuinely interested in me as an author? Maybe she'd ask what my next book was about. Or how long I'd wanted to be a writer. I was giddy with anticipation.

"I read on Hannah Marshak's blog that you took her place today. Are you planning to review *A-line in The Sand* on *Pastel Is the New Black*?"

My heart sank. So much for a stranger's sincere interest in me as an author. Even though it took my iron will not to crawl under the table with my empty water bottle, I planted on a smile. "Yes, of course. I'm looking forward to the read."

Ninety minutes later, I raised my blueberry mojito in a toast to the birthday boy. "Happy birthday, Jonathan." We'd arrived at The Saint Austere, a dimly lit tapas restaurant in Williamsburg, too early for dinner, but took over a nice space at the bar for pre-dinner drinks and one-dollar oysters.

Caroline's husband, Felix, grinned at me. "And to the famous author, Kim Long. Brilliant job today."

I smiled shyly at Felix and tried not to make eye contact with Bridget. We were madly in love with our respective mates, but Felix's sexy British accent made our knees wobble every time. "Thank you, but Nicholas and Bridget were the real stars of the afternoon." I placed my drink on the mahogany wood bar and squeezed Nicholas's hand. "I felt like the biggest loser before you saved me with your questions."

Nicholas patted my back. "Who cares who did the asking? You responded like a rock star."

"Agreed," Bridget said with gusto. "It will be even better next time."

"Once was enough for me," I mumbled before taking ownership of my cocktail again. I was hoping to drink the memory of the event out of me, but given my size and lack of alcohol tolerance, I'd pass out before dinner if I didn't pace myself. I forced a smile at Jonathan. "What else do you have planned for your birthday?" The portion of the day dedicated to me was over. It was time to make it all about Jonathan.

Caroline wasn't having it. "Cut yourself some slack, Kim," she said with a frown. "You were a late addition to a panel of seriously famous authors. There wasn't much time for your own fanbase to get word of the event and be there to support you. But the exposure you got today was priceless. I bet droves of readers will buy *A Blogger's Life* now."

"Caroline's right," Jonathan said. "According to the rule of seven, a potential customer needs to see your ad seven times before they consider buying the product. It's possible many people in the audience hadn't heard of you before this event, but next time they see your book on Amazon or in Barnes and Noble, they'll remember you spoke today and might buy it." He shrugged. "Focus on the positive, Long."

My mouth dropped open, although it wasn't the first time Jonathan's famous rules resonated with me. "You're right." I met the eyes of all my friends. "All of you." For the first time since we'd left the book fair, I honored my peeps with a genuine smile. "But, seriously, it's time to make the night about the birthday boy." This time I meant it. "What's your wish this year?" I asked as a baby howled from somewhere to my right.

Jonathan groaned. "At the top of the list is for all the babies to go home where they belong." He scowled in the infant's direction. "If you can't find a babysitter, stay in for dinner."

Nicholas snickered. "Drink faster and you won't even hear the kid." He emptied an oyster into his mouth.

Looking from Nicholas to me, Jonathan said, "Please promise me you won't insist on bringing your kid every time we go out." He ran a hand through his unruly head of medium brown hair. Bridget had trained him to shave his head when they first got together, but it appeared the honeymoon was over. He was now back to his lazy hair-maintenance habits and in desperate need of grooming.

"I wasn't aware we were pregnant." Nicholas bumped me on the shoulder. "Something you want to tell me?"

Unlike Bridget and Jonathan, Nicholas and I wanted to have a baby—babies—but we looked forward to a year or two of being on our own first. Rolling my eyes, I said, "Let's get married before we discuss procreation, please?" I guzzled the rest of my drink at the unwanted reminder I was less than seven months from my wedding day and had no idea what I was wearing. And we hadn't picked out invitations either. When did *The Knot* suggest doing that?

While Bridget got up to use the restroom, Jonathan continued to gripe to Nicholas about babies in bars and Caroline and Felix got lost in a two-person conversation, I slipped my hand into my purse and pulled out my phone. I hadn't checked my reviews—

"Don't even think about it," Nicholas said, removing the device from my hand and raising it above his head.

I hopped on my toes to get the phone out of his hand. "But—"

Nicholas shook his head. "No buts." He dropped the phone back in my bag and stroked my cheek. "At least wait until later. If there's a bad review and we're home, I can make you forget about it with my many talents. There isn't much I can do about it here unless you've changed your mind about getting busy in public restrooms." His dark eyes dilated as if imagining me dragging him into the bathroom for a quickie.

But I had a one-track mind. "You think there will be a bad one?"

Nicholas sighed as Bridget returned from the bathroom.

"I waited for you. Let's go out for a smoke," Jonathan said to Bridget.

I watched their retreating backs. She and Jonathan always smoked in tandem. I wished they'd quit in tandem too.

Felix and Caroline separated from a lip lock and joined our conversation. "Caroline told me you got a brilliant review in *Publishers Weekly*. Way to go, Kim." Felix's eyes crinkled at the corners.

"See?" Nicholas rubbed my shoulders. "Who cares about negative reviews from anonymous readers when a major trade calls your book 'a real winner'?"

The answer to his question was me—I cared. But Nicholas's face shined brightly as he looked at me with pride, and it lit me up from the inside out. I'd be damned if I wiped the glow from his cheeks.

Hours later, as I lay next to Nicholas in bed, I thought about the book fair and whether I could deem it a successful event. I knew Hannah would ask how it went, and while I didn't want to stoop to her level and exaggerate how *splendide* it was, I wasn't about to confess I was a non-entity until my groom-to-be and best friend, or as Hannah described her, "my slightly taller Siamese twin," put me out of my misery. I would thank her again for the opportunity and call it a decent first experience on a panel. It was the truth to say I was asked three questions—she didn't need to know one was about her—and I met several fellow authors, including one who agreed to blurb my next book. I wouldn't volunteer it was Christine Bannah in case Hannah swooped in and stole her from me. Who was I kidding? She would definitely ask. Or she would tap my nose like I was a puppy and say, "Good doggie." With Hannah, one never knew.

I was too wired to fall asleep, unlike Nicholas, who was sleeping soundly beside me, but since tomorrow was Sunday and not Monday, I didn't care. I could do some writing.

I pulled my laptop onto my lap and checked my email. I sucked in my breath at the sight of an email from Melina Rhodes.

> *Dear Kim,*
> *It's nice to e-meet you.*
> *As you probably know, Sadie Campos has left Fifth Avenue Press and I've been assigned as your editor* for Love on Stone Street. *I'm looking forward to working with you. I've read the first fifty pages and am curious where you're going with it. What is the central conflict and how will you resolve it? Please send me the synopsis and any additional pages you've written as soon as possible.*
> *Thanks so much,*
> *Melina*

I rubbed my fingers against my temple. It had become obvious to me while querying *A Blogger's Life* that condensing a book into a one-to-ten-page summary (depending on an agent's preference) was harder than writing a three-hundred-page novel. Sadie knew I wasn't a plotter and had trusted me to proceed without a synopsis. Clearly, Melina didn't share her confidence. My chest tightened with anxiety and I resisted the temptation to cry myself to sleep. I couldn't afford to rest. I had a synopsis to write.

Nicholas entered the kitchen the following day and pointed at his watch. "It's time for the family video chat."

I blanched. "Already?" I'd been so focused on writing my synopsis since early in the morning, I hadn't even noticed the sun setting through the window.

Nicholas sat next to me at our kitchen nook and we joined the chat already in progress. With any luck, we'd finish early enough to make a nice dinner for two and relax a bit before bedtime. I'd worked so hard all day, I'd earned a break and maybe some sexy time.

"Since everyone is here, let's get started," he said in a loud enough voice to be heard over our moms, who were using the chat to have their own two-person conversation.

Before he could say another word, Natalie's face popped onto the screen. Her raven curls were pulled back into a multi-colored paisley-printed chiffon headband. This time, she looked less like Minnie Mouse and more like a Bohemian Snow White. "Hi, everyone," she said, waving frantically.

Trying to maintain a poker face, I glanced at Nicholas and whispered out of the side of my face, "Who invited your sister?"

He widened his eyes and, still facing the computer monitor, responded, "No idea."

Jeanine pursed her lips. "I told Natalie about the call, but I didn't expect her to join." She ran a hand through her shoulder-length dark hair. "I'm sorry."

Natalie pouted at the screen. "I have no idea why you're apologizing, Mom. I'm sure not including me in the first place was an oversight and I forgive you. We're here now so let's get to it."

Before I could contemplate who she meant by "we," another face popped into view—Tiffany's.

I sat up straighter in my chair. Why was she here?

"Hi, Kim!" Tiffany brought her head closer to the screen and looked at Nicholas. "Hey…your eyes have a little green in them." She laughed.

Nicholas's mouth twitched. "You gonna puke on me now?"

I glanced from the computer to Nicholas and back to Tiffany. "Um, what?"

Tiffany's eyes opened wide. "Oh, sorry. Inside joke from back in the day. We used to quote *10 Things I Hate About You* all the time."

"All the time being fifteen years ago," Natalie mumbled.

"I guess you had to be there," I said with a sigh. This meeting was being held to go over financials with the people helping to fund the wedding and the honeymoon. As far as I knew, the funds in Natalie's bank accounts weren't on offer. I was willing to humor her because she was about to become my family, but the same didn't apply to Tiffany. His mom wasn't kidding when she told Nicholas the two were conjoined. And Hannah Marshak called Bridget and me Siamese twins. We had nothing on those two.

I kicked Nicholas under the table. He grabbed my foot and wouldn't let go. I knew he was trying to distract me. It worked. My number-one priority became getting my foot back before his tickling made me pee in my pants.

Warren, Nicholas's dad, cleared his throat. "My wife tells me the happy couple needs a swift kick in the butt regarding the wedding planning and she asked me to deliver it. What's going on?" He directed his green-eyed gaze at Nicholas. "Is it because work is keeping you too busy?" It was obvious he hoped the answer was yes.

Nicholas released my foot. "We're completely on track," he lied. The tone of his voice was confident, but his hunched posture didn't escape me. Nicholas had come a long way from desperately seeking his father's approval, but Rome wasn't built in a day. I squeezed his knee.

"Not true, big brother. If Kim doesn't get a dress soon, she's screwed. Alterations take months," Natalie said.

"Nat's right. Kim's proportions don't match any of the sample sizes. Trust me, I work in fashion. I know." Tiffany frowned at me. "I'm sorry."

I feared she was right and willed my legs to stop bouncing.

"Kim's shape is perfect," Nicholas said.

Natalie snickered. "Kim's body type might be ideal if she could wear a Victoria's Secret Dream Angels bra and panty set to the wedding, but her measurements don't match off-the-rack wedding gowns. She's too short and her chest is too big."

Tiffany laughed before clamping her hand against her mouth. "For a doctor, you have a crappy bedside matter, Nat."

The air in the room felt thick and my hair felt hot against my neck. Although her delivery could have benefited from sensitivity training, Natalie spoke the truth: I was never going to find a dress in time. Rather than leave Kleinfeld early, I should have kicked everyone else out and let India work her magic.

"Call me old fashioned, but it seems wrong to discuss my daughter and bra and panty sets in the same sentence," my dad said. "Maybe we should—"

Cutting him off, Natalie said, "We've done research into the style of dresses worn by actresses of similar shapes—Jennifer Love Hewitt, Kristen Bell, Amanda Seyfried—at their own weddings and when they played brides in movies and television shows. They almost always wore sleeveless fitted sheath or fit-and-flare dresses to show off their ample booty."

"Booty," Tiffany repeated with a giggle. "Remember when I became obsessed with Pirate's Booty, Nicky? It was practically all I ate for an entire month."

"I...um." Nicholas glanced at me and raised his palms in an "I give up" gesture when I mouthed "Nicky?" Nicholas didn't do nicknames— not even Nick.

"We're getting off topic," Natalie mumbled.

"I missed rounds for this?" Warren barked.

Raising my voice, I said, "Maybe we should table the wedding-dress talk for another time, but please email me what you found, Natalie." Even though my future sister-in-law and her unwanted sidekick crashed the video chat, I had to admit researching the dresses of similarly shaped women was kind of brilliant.

Natalie beamed at me. "I sure will."

I scratched my head. "What else was on the agenda for today?"

"I need to get back to the hospital," Warren said.

"You'll have dinner first," Jeanine said. "Which reminds me, I have a roasted chicken in the oven. Can we continue this next weekend?"

"Peter, we're late for the weekly tenants' association meeting," my mom said before frowning at me. "Sorry, sweetheart."

I blew her a kiss goodbye. The sooner this chat ended, the quicker I could pour myself a generous glass of wine.

"We have to bail too. Date night." Tiffany pouted her bubblegum pink lips at Nicholas. "Sorry."

It was unclear whether she was apologizing for having to leave the conversation or because she was going out on a date, but I couldn't care less. "Okay then. Bye, Tiffany. See you later, everyone." I closed out the chat and let my head fall back.

"What exactly did we accomplish with that call?" Nicholas asked.

I let out a deep exhalation. "Absolutely nothing, *Nicky*."

Nicholas rolled his eyes. "Please tell me you're not threatened by Tiffany."

Early on in our relationship, my insecurity had almost come between us when I accused Nicholas of not taking me seriously because I didn't have an advanced degree, but it was all in my head. Nicholas hadn't cared whether I was a secretary, a lawyer, or the President of the United States, as long as I was happy. And none of the many women who'd tried to turn his head, including Hannah and Daneen, had succeeded. If Tiffany was looking to recreate history, I knew she'd fail too. I shook my head. "Not at all."

"Glad to hear it." He rested his head on the kitchen nook. "What a waste of time."

He was right. I'd had more productive conversations in the ladies' room at work. The knots in my belly twisted and turned. "Honey?"

"Hmm?" he mumbled.

"How do you feel about me wearing a Victoria's Secret bra and panty set down the aisle?"

Nicholas sat up straight. He placed a hand on both of my cheeks and peered into my eyes until his lips slowly curled into a grin. "Best. Wedding. Ever."

Chapter 5

SIX MONTHS UNTIL "I DO"

"You sure you don't mind?" It was later that week, and I'd just asked Pia, my assistant reviewer for *Pastel Is the New Black*, to take on more books. I stretched out my arm and extended my phone away from my face. Communicating via Facetime was more personal than texting or simply talking on the phone, but I didn't need to see up her nose (or vice versa). We'd never met in person, but she was a stellar book reviewer—almost as good as me.

"Not at all. I'm ahead of schedule for the thesis and my workload is otherwise light right now. Send me what you've got." Pia's almond-shaped brown eyes twinkled and her hips moved as she danced in place.

Pia was twenty-four and studying for her MFA at the University of Michigan. She was tiny in stature, but I'd bet her energy could charge all the computers on her campus. I'd taken her on the year before to alleviate some of my review backlog, but over the last six months, I'd handed off more than half of the requests I'd received. Felicia had warned me it would be impossible to maintain the blog without help once I became a full-fledged author and she was right.

"How's the writing going?" Pia asked. Her boogying must have worn her out because she was now sitting on the edge of her bed. I spotted a black and white throw pillow behind her. I couldn't make out the words, but knew it said, "A room without books is like a body without a soul" because I owned the same pillow.

"I sent the synopsis and fifty more pages to my editor earlier today. I hope she doesn't hate it." What if she thought it was garbage?

Pia smirked. "She won't hate it. She loved *A Blogger's Life.* She loves you!" She vaulted off the bed and paced her room.

My heart fluttered with nerves. "You're thinking of Sadie. This is my new editor, Melina. According to Felicia, she's more 'old school.' Whatever that means. I'm taking this book in a different direction in an attempt to attract a broader audience." I chewed on my lip, debating whether to get Pia's opinion.

"Like what?" Her eyes opened wide and she added, "No spoilers." She sat back down on her bed.

Her constant movement was making me dizzy and I hoped she'd sit still for the rest of the conversation. "One of the subplots is a bit...um, dark." I felt my face flush.

Pia furrowed her brow. "In what way? No cancer, please." We both hated one of Olivia Geffen's more recent offerings because one of the main characters was diagnosed with a very rare form of Leukemia.

I chuckled. "No cancer. Just murder." I tapped my foot against the ceramic tile floor of my kitchen.

Pia's head jutted back. "You didn't tell me you were writing a mystery."

"I'm not."

Her eyes bugged out. "Thriller? Really?"

Twirling a strand of hair around my finger, I said, "No. It's chick lit, but the sister of one of the secondary characters is a victim of a serial killer. Not a main character, obviously. In real life people get murdered. I'm trying to bring more realism to my writing."

Pia blinked. "Did your editor ask you to do this?"

I shook my head. "It's something I thought of on my own in response to some reader comments. What do you think?" Pia didn't respond and she was surprisingly still. "Pia?"

She winced. "My honest opinion?"

"Yes." I braced myself.

"A romcom is supposed to be romantic and comedic, not deadly."

I released the breath I was holding. "I always felt the same way, but now I'm not so sure. Even readers of chick lit want depth these days."

"Depth doesn't have to mean murder, Kim." She snickered.

My stomach clenched and I fought back tears. "I'm so out of my element, Pia."

Pia's face softened. "Look, it seems odd to me, but I haven't read the book. I'm sure you nailed it. And, who knows, maybe you'll be a trailblazer for the next genre crossover: romantic comedy meets murder in the first degree. Sophie Kinsella meets Stephen King." She grinned.

I returned her expression even though I was already second-guessing my decision.

Chapter 6

I swallowed down my nerves as I entered New Genesis Bridal, where it was located on the second floor of a building in midtown Manhattan. The family video chat had been an epic failure. We still had no idea how many guests both sets of parents wanted to invite, we didn't have a room count to give the hotel, and we hadn't discussed where to hold the rehearsal dinner. The one thing the call did accomplish was to convince me that unless I wanted to wear lingerie to my wedding, I needed to buy a dress the day before yesterday. Since relying on a future trip to Florida to shop with my mom was too risky, I decided to make another attempt at searching locally. There were no available appointments with any of my second-choice boutiques—Kleinfeld had been my first—for a few weeks, so I asked Bridget if she'd accompany me to the one place I could find that accepted walk-ins.

I glanced around the tiny store and lowered my expectations of finding The Dress there. The selection was probably as limited as the square footage. But at least I wasn't alone. Or with my entire bridal party. I wasn't sure which would be worse. "Thanks for coming with me, Bridge."

Bridget placed her hand on my arm. "Are you kidding me? This is the most fun I've had in months. We're living out our teenage fantasy, right here, right now. And, besides, I could use the distraction."

I cocked my head to the side. "From what?"

Bridget waved me away as a saleswoman approached. "Not now," she whispered out of the side of her mouth.

"Welcome to New Genesis Bridal. How can I help you?" asked an attractive woman who appeared to be in her late forties.

Bridget pointed at me. "She's getting married and needs a dress. Can you help her?"

The woman smiled. "You're in the right place for a wedding gown. It's a good thing she's not searching for swimwear or pajamas." She winked at Bridget and turned to me. "Do you have a dress style in mind?"

I repeated what I'd told India at Kleinfeld, and ten minutes later I was in the storage room (the store was too small to house a formal fitting room) trying on a beautiful La Sposa mermaid-style dress in crepe with chantilly and lace work on the bodice. I gaped at my reflection in the mirror in awe—I looked like a bride! "I'm digging this V-neckline. And check out my ass. Bootylicious!" I twirled in front of the mirror. "What do you think, Bridge?" I couldn't tear my eyes away from my mirror image. When Bridget didn't respond, I stopped staring at myself and faced her. She was crying. The gown was stunning, but the tears were unexpected. "Really? You think this is the one?" I desperately needed to find a dress today, but I also didn't want to miss out on the fun of trying on a variety of them.

Bridget buried her head in her hands and dropped to the floor. "I'm kind of pregnant."

My mouth opened and shut in rapid succession while I let her words sink in. Finally, I said, "You're kind of pregnant? How can you be *kind of* pregnant?"

"I'm not. I'm one hundred percent preggers." She stood up and wiped her eyes, leaving a mascara stain. "I'm with child. I've got a bun in the oven. I'm harboring a fugitive. You get the picture? I'm full-on knocked up, K. Four weeks along."

I swallowed hard as my own eyes welled up. Bridget was having a baby and I loved her already. (I just knew it was a girl the way you *knew* things about your very best friend in the entire world.) "Oh my God, Bridget. That's..." I walked toward her with my arms outstretched. Then I remembered Bridget and Jonathan didn't want children and froze in place.

"Jonathan's going to kill me."

My eyes opened wide and I clenched my fists. "Oh no, he won't. If he so much as pulls on a luxurious strand of your hair outside of the heat of passion, I will rip off all his limbs with my bare hands. And then I'll go to prison and break Nicholas's heart." I glanced down at myself in the wedding gown. If I was in prison, I'd probably have to wear an orange jumpsuit and shackles to my wedding, which would make this shopping session moot.

"He's made it very clear he doesn't want marriage and kids."

"What about you? I thought you guys were on the same page." I bit my lip, uncertain how she would respond to the question. When I'd expressed doubt she and Jonathan wanted the same things the summer before, we had our first real fight, and our eighteen-year friendship almost went up in flames. Since then, I'd learned to keep my opinions to myself.

"I thought we were too, until..." Her voice dropped off and she sighed. "Until there were two pink lines on my pregnancy test." Her chin trembled and she hurled herself into my arms and sobbed.

I gently extracted myself from her embrace. The last thing I wanted to do was push away my best friend in her time of need, but if she stained my dress with her makeup, she'd have to pay for it. Patting down her hair, I said, "It's going to be fine. You're going to be fine. Just let me get out of this dress and we'll go someplace quiet and talk over a glass of prosec..." *Crap.* Booze would not be appropriate in this scenario. I forced a smile. "Let me buy you a cupcake."

Bridget helped me out of my dress while blubbering her apologies for ruining my special day. I assured her it wasn't a big deal, which was a big fat lie, but an "oops" pregnancy took priority over shopping every day of the week and I still had six months.

I explained to the boutique owner there was an emergency and we had to leave, but I'd be back. I was getting quite practiced at rushing out of bridal salons under the guise of an emergency, and wouldn't be surprised if there was a clandestine list of blacklisted wannabe brides making its way through the underground bridal circuit with my name now at the top.

A half hour later, we were comfy on the top floor of 2Beans, a gourmet coffee and chocolate shop near Grand Central Station. We'd both catch the train home from there later, only I'd head downtown and she'd make her way uptown. Bridget didn't say a word during the ride in the Uber over from the dress shop and now she was hunched down in her seat. But at least she'd stopped crying. I ordered a latte for me, a hot chocolate for Bridget, and a chocolate sampler for us to share.

"You all right, Bridge?" I asked. We'd talked each other off the ledge countless times over the years, but we were in foreign territory now. For the first time in my life, I didn't have the words to make my best friend feel better. If only I knew what she wanted to hear, I'd say it.

"I don't know." With her head bent toward the brown wood surface of our table, she looked so lost. She lifted her head and met my gaze, her green eyes pleading. "Promise me you won't say anything—to anyone. Even Nicholas."

I grimaced. "You have my word." This was the only right answer, but I didn't think she understood how hard the task would be. "It's only a matter of time before Jonathan will notice something is up. You won't show for a while, but you can only feign a sore throat for so long before he questions your lack of smoking, and how long do you really think you can get away without drinking? Lent is over. Unless you tell him you're on an antibiotic for a 'cold.'" I used air quotes around the word cold. When Bridget beamed at me, I did a double take. Maybe she'd come to her senses and realized being pregnant was a great thing and not something to weep about, unless it was tears of joy. Cautiously, I asked, "Why are you smiling?"

"You're a genius. I'll tell Jonathan I went to the doctor and he put me on an antibiotic. It will buy me about two weeks and give me time to come up with a plan."

I slid down my seat. "What kind of plan? You need to tell him the truth. The sooner the better." I had no idea how I was going to keep this from Nicholas. He was going to ask how the shopping went and I'd have to lie. My first attempt to find a dress earned me a heaping bowl of ice cream. This one found me shoving assorted truffles in my piehole. By the time I did buy a dress, I'd be a size bigger, at least.

As if reading my mind, Bridget said, "I'm so sorry I messed up your day." Her lips trembled dangerously.

Since I didn't want to add to her worries, I shrugged it off. "No biggie." My heart stopped. "You'll be seventh months pregnant at the wedding. You're going to need a new dress. A maternity one." I told the girls they could wear whatever they wanted as long as it was a shade of dark purple. Even if I wanted them to wear the same dress, it was more likely Erin and Natalie would kill each other than ever agree on a style. All the dresses had been purchased since, unlike me, my bridal party was on the ball. Bridget would look stunning in a burlap bag, but she'd gushed over the one-shoulder pleated dress she'd picked out. I thought she might even make out with the whimsical bow across the left shoulder.

Bridget's eyes opened wide. "My fat belly is going to ruin all your wedding photos. I'll opt out of the party if you want. You can make Caroline your maid of honor." She chewed on her lip and averted eye contact.

I groaned. "For the love of God, Bridget, I don't care what you wear. If George has to drag you down the aisle by your chinny chin chin, you'll stand at my side as my maid of honor. End of story." George was Nicholas's closest friend and his best man. His girlfriend, Sarah, was our caterer. Even though the Soho Grand had an in-house caterer, we wanted to support Sarah's new business so we had it written into our contract. "And, besides, your belly won't be fat; it will be pregnant. I need you."

Bridget's eyes welled up. "You're my BFFAEUDDUP." This was the acronym we'd devised as tweens. It translated to "Best Friends Forever and Ever Until Death Do Us Part."

"And you're mine. Now stop blubbering and eat your chocolate." I brought up the notes app on my phone and added "tissues for Bridget" to my shopping list. If her hormones were already raging now, I'd be handing her a lot of Kleenex over the next nine months.

Chapter 7

"I'll send positive vibes your way," I said to Nicholas over the phone. His boss had asked him to stay late and Nicholas assumed it was related to his future with the company. "I love you more." I ended the call and stretched the length of the love seat in our bedroom. Nicholas designated it my "lady couch" because it was pink and too small to fit both of us unless I sat on his lap.

I flipped to the first page of the brochure of wedding invitations we'd obtained from a well-regarded printer on the Upper East Side. I was excited about being ahead of the game on at least one aspect of wedding planning—or at least on time.

I knew from previous research I was partial to white and gold invitations and figured it would be easy to narrow it down. As I continued to scroll through the binder, I saw more and more variations of the same theme and my pulse raced in the beginning signs of panic. Which font should we choose? Should we limit the gold to the lettering or did we want something more ornate? Were we modern or traditional? I bit back a sob of frustration and shut my eyes. Couldn't anything be easy? Behind closed lids, I decided it was time for a break. A check of my email would do nicely. I opened my eyes and pulled up my Gmail account. There was an unread note from Melina. I chewed on a nail and opened the email.

> *Hi Kim,*
> *I read your synopsis and additional pages of* Love on Stone Street. *Parts of it are very promising. I like your idea for the competing restaurants and the* Romeo and Juliet *inspired love story. Unfortunately, the serial killer subplot doesn't work for me. I'm sure you can come up with something more*

enticing. I'd be happy to look at your next attempt.
Melina

My mouth went dry. Pia was right—I'd gone too far and now I'd blown my first chance to impress Melina. She probably hated me. But what now? Did I come up with something slightly less dark than murder but still grim enough to placate those desiring more than "mindless reading" or was it better to stick to what I did best—warm and fuzzy sprinkled with comical conflict? When I was a teenager, scribbling stories in my looseleaf binders during class, I'd assumed my favorite authors, like Sarah Dessen and Meg Cabot, held all the power. The truth was, unless you were a huge name, authors were at the mercy of agents and editors to tell them when their words were worthy of being read by the public. My editor had given me a flashing red light.

I was in no condition to do any writing tonight—not with my thoughts all jumbled like items in a kitchen junk drawer. My deadline was almost seven months away, but it was looming out of my comfort zone. I had a full-time job. I had a wedding to plan! And now I had to re-plot my book almost from scratch. I had no idea how I got myself into this mess or how to get out.

I curled in the fetal position, tempted to put my thumb in my mouth and rock like a baby. Then an idea came to me. Maybe Melina would give me an extension on my deadline. Publishers granted extensions to authors all the time. There was no reason why I'd be an exception.

I sat up and emailed Melina back, expressing thanks for her comments and promising to work on my draft. Then I asked if I could get a brief extension—even just a month or two—in light of my competing personal issues.

Feeling better, I closed out of my email and shut the lid of my computer. On the plus side, I was now eager to return my attention to shopping. Picking out invitations had to be less stressful than choosing a direction for my novel. I resumed my comfy position on the couch and placed the binder of sample invitations on my chest. It was time to focus on my wedding.

"Kimmie."

"No," I said, brushing away the hand stroking my face. I wasn't ready to come out of my comfy place.

"Kimmie."

I continued to ignore the sound of my name until I felt myself being lifted off the couch. My eyes fluttered open. "Nicholas," I said against his neck. I inhaled the delicious scent of him. My mind slowly waking up, I said, "Your boss. What did he say?" It took effort to get the words out.

"Shh." He placed me on our bed and kissed my forehead. "It's all good, but we'll talk tomorrow. Go back to sleep."

I wanted to press him for details, but it could wait. Vowing to obey your husband was way sexist, but I'd concede just this once. I closed my eyes and let myself fall.

As I walked to where Nicholas stood with the rest of the bridal party, my eyes welled up. He sure knew how to wear a tuxedo. He was the most beautiful man, inside and out, and he'd chosen me to be his bride. Butterflies danced from the tips of my Badgley Mischka ankle strap shoes to the top of my—I looked down and froze in place. Oh my God, where was my dress? I snatched my elbow out from under my dad's grip and used my right hand to cover the exposed area between my thighs. Thankfully, my bouquet of peonies was large and lush enough to cover my ample and equally uncovered breasts. I was grateful the bridal party was ahead of me in the precession and not staring at my bare ass, but I couldn't say the same for our guests. I whipped my head from side to side. The breeze from the movement tickled the back of my neck and I fought the urge to touch it with one of my otherwise-occupied hands. I hadn't planned on wearing my hair up. I braced myself for the gaping mouths and expressions of horror on the faces of my friends and family, but the seats were all empty. Where was everyone? I kept walking toward Nicholas, my skin flushed with shame at my nudity on such a momentous occasion.

When I stood before him, he laughed. "It's all right, Kimmie. No one's here. We never sent out the invitations. Remember?"

My eyes flew open and I sat up in bed. My breathing was ragged and my kelly-green tank top was drenched in sweat. It was a nightmare of the highest caliber, but at least flower shopping should be easier now. I opened the notes on my iPhone and, before I forgot, jotted down a description of the bouquet I'd used to cover my boobs in my dream.

The shoes were fabulous and comfortable too. I hoped a pair just like them existed in real life.

After I showered and got dressed, I joined Nicholas in the kitchen. "Morning." I poured myself a cup of coffee and sat down at the table.

Nicholas was facing the sink with his back to me but turned around with a grin. "Sleep well, Kimmie?"

A vision of him carrying me to bed flashed before my eyes. "I did. Sorry you had to physically remove me from the lady couch."

"Yeah, my arms are killing me today," he said with a smirk.

I ignored this. "What did your boss want to talk about?"

Nicholas leaned against the refrigerator. "Remember when my dad pushed me to become general counsel of the company?"

Nicholas's father's relentless pressure on Nicholas to devote his life to work left a caustic taste in my mouth even almost a year later. "How could I forget?" I snarled and quickly brought my hand to my mouth. I'd never fully forgiven Warren, but I didn't want Nicholas to know I was holding a grudge. "Is the general counsel leaving?" I refilled my coffee.

"No, but they're creating a position for executive general counsel. It's a step above assistant general counsel and comes with a significant increase in pay and stock options. My boss wants me to apply."

"Do you want it?" I held my breath. I fully supported Nicholas's ambition, but we'd worked so hard to get to a place where our devotion to our careers didn't come at the expense of our relationship and I was terrified of losing him to his job again.

He nodded. "According to Gideon, the promotion won't necessarily result in more work; just different. I'll also have more ability to delegate. Best of all, if we combine my raise with your salary and book royalties, we should be able to afford a two-bedroom apartment without needing to move out of the city."

My eyebrows lifted. "You want to move?"

"Not tomorrow, but someday. We can't raise a kid in this place," he said, making a sweeping motion across our small apartment.

His words made me think of Bridget and her secret. I wondered if she and Jonathan would stay in their one-bedroom apartment or if they'd move after they had the baby.

I feared the kid would be five before Jonathan even knew he was a father.

"What do you think?"

I returned my attention to Nicholas before I accidentally mentioned Bridget's condition. "It sounds great. What happens next?"

Nicholas explained the position would be posted internally and anyone eligible could apply. There would be several rounds of interviews and presentations before the position was filled.

He said his boss, Gideon, would throw all his support Nicholas's way, but there was no guarantee.

"They'd be crazy not to pick you."

He walked over to me and rubbed my arm. "You're slightly biased, but thank you all the same. Anyway, enough about me. How was your night?"

I sighed. "My editor hated my synopsis and pages. I have to start over." My insides quivered with anxiety.

Nicholas sighed deeply. "Oh, no. What did she say?"

Collapsing onto a chair, I said, "My attempt at plotting a 'mindful' read was a failure."

Nicholas frowned. "What are you going to do?"

"The only thing I can do—keep writing. But I asked for an extension."

"You've got this," Nicholas said, sounding way more confident than he should based on the facts.

I downed my coffee and glanced at my watch. "Crap. I need to get to work."

"Me too. By the way, after I carried you to bed last night like the prince I am, I went through the binder of invitations and marked the ones I liked the best. I remembered your preference for white and gold. I'll let you choose your favorite, but at least it's narrowed down now."

"You did that for me?" As a wave of relief washed over me, I stood from the table and beamed at him.

Nicholas scrunched his forehead. "I did it for us. No reason you have to plan this wedding all by yourself. You have a book to write."

I lowered my gaze and mumbled, "Thanks for reminding me."

He lifted my chin with his finger and kissed me gently on the lips. "You did it once. There's no reason you can't do it again."

I nodded agreeably even as the names of famous one-hit-wonder authors, like Sylvia Plath, Margaret Mitchell, and J.D. Salinger, flashed before my eyes. At least if I only had one book in me, I'd be in good company.

Chapter 8

Thanks to Nicholas narrowing down the choices, we picked out invitations and ordered them from the vendor later that week. We chose a simple but elegant print with a white background and gold lettering. On the side was a gold satin ribbon with two die-cut hearts in the middle. The owner of the store said if we hurried, we'd still have time to send "save the date" postcards, so we ordered those as well. Since we were on a roll, we reserved the Saturday afternoon of the following weekend to make more progress. We looked forward to creating a list of wedding-related tasks so we could enjoy the satisfaction of checking them off one at a time. Earlier that day, I'd booked a flight to my mom's for later in the month to go dress shopping. I could shop locally in the meantime, but quite liked the idea of sharing the experience with my mother. For now, it was time to discuss where to go on our honeymoon.

"Someplace warm, but not a cruise," Nicholas said from next to me on the gray leather couch in our living room. "Too many kids."

"You sound like Jonathan," I said with a chuckle before my shoulders tensed. Jonathan's overt aversion to children entertaining until he sowed his seed in my best friend. Changing the subject, I said, "If we plan the honeymoon for right after the wedding, we can probably avoid families and kids. There's still school in November aside from Thanksgiving weekend."

Nicholas nodded. "True. You're so smart, Kimmie." He leaned in for a light peck on the lips, which somehow rendered me topless within a matter of seconds. I was panting for more and eagerly positioned myself to give him access to the front of my jeans when there was a knock on our front door.

From the hallway, a voice called out, "Anyone home?"

I pushed Nicholas off me and grabbed my t-shirt. "Were you expecting anyone?" I asked, my breath ragged.

Nicholas called out, "One second," and turned to me. "It sounds like Natalie. This is an unexpected visit." He waited for me to put on my shirt and opened the door. Natalie and Tiffany walked inside. Natalie wore her scrubs, but Tiffany looked ready for a night out in painted-on black jeans and a floral-printed off-the-shoulder tunic.

"I just came off a sixteen-hour shift and need to stay awake until a reasonable hour—intern jet lag," Natalie said.

Tiffany piped in, "We were going to do some consignment shopping in the neighborhood and it started raining."

"We figured we'd pop in and get some shelter from the storm." Natalie joined me on the couch. "Whatcha doing?"

It was on the tip of my tongue to tell them I was about to get laid before they so rudely interrupted, but I had an inkling Tiffany would bring up some memory of when she and Nicholas experienced their own coitus interruptus back in the day. I had no desire to envision fourteen-year-old cheerleader Tiffany climbing on pre-lawyer Nicholas. "We were discussing the honeymoon."

Tiffany clapped her hands together. "Fun. Where are we going?" She squeezed in between Natalie and me.

We? I glanced helplessly at Nicholas, who had dragged the piano bench from the far corner of the living room and placed it next to the couch before sitting down.

"*We* hadn't gotten that far yet," he said.

"Why don't you go to the Bahamas like the Beatles did in that movie you made me watch a hundred times..." Tiffany scrunched up her face. "*A Hard Day's Night*?"

"You mean *Help!*" Nicholas said, darting a guilty look in my direction. "I've made Kim watch it too."

"Too cliché. What about Vietnam?" Natalie pressed her lips together and looked up at the ceiling. "Or Chile."

"Aruba is a popular honeymoon destination," Tiffany said.

Smirking, Natalie said, "Precisely why they shouldn't go there. How about Tanzania?"

Nicholas jerked his head back. "How are you coming up with these? It sounds like a list of strangest places to go on a romantic vacation."

Natalie pouted. "Precisely. I read it on *The Knot*."

"Are you getting married anytime soon?" Nicholas asked.

I was glad he said it and not me. As far as I knew, Natalie wasn't even dating anyone, although if there was any truth to *Grey's Anatomy*, she was probably getting her rocks off with a hot surgeon in the on-call rooms daily.

"I was trying to lend a hand to my busy big brother and almost-famous future sister-in-law. But if you don't want my help, I'll stop." She folded her arms across her chest.

It was true, flattery got you everywhere. I found myself wanting to hug Natalie in response to her "almost famous" comment. "Thank you, Nat," I said with a pat of her leg. "We're not ready to make a decision, but you'll be among the first to know." I stood up, hoping they would follow my lead and conclude their unexpected pop-in, when there was another knock on the door. "I heard rumors they were relocating Penn Station, but I had no idea it was moving to our apartment," I said with a chuckle before greeting our new guest.

It was Bridget. Wearing a shiny red raincoat and yellow Hunter boots and carrying a purple umbrella, she looked like a cartoon character, albeit an adorable one. I pulled her into a hug and whispered, "Help. Tiffany and Natalie are here" into her honey-scented hair. I wondered if she'd heard me suffering from across town and had come to rescue me, but when we separated, her complexion matched her rain slicker and her green eyes were wet with tears. My heart dropped. "Oh, no. What's wrong?"

She sniffled. "It's Jonathan." She hung her soaked coat on an empty hook in the foyer and slipped off her boots.

"You told him?" Based on Bridget's appearance, I assumed his reaction wasn't to scoop her up in his arms and tell her he loved her and their unborn baby, and I clenched my fists in anger. Whether or not having a family was part of the plan, Jonathan had no right to make his pregnant girlfriend cry. She didn't become with child by herself. It was too bad Melina had axed the serial-killer storyline in *Love on Stone Street* or I would write Jonathan into my book so I could kill him off.

From behind me, Nicholas said, "Told who what?"

I blinked at Bridget as a silent question. She shook her head in response and followed me into the apartment. "Nothing," we said at the same time.

Bridget walked into the living room and stopped short when she saw Natalie and Tiffany.   I guessed she'd been too distracted by her misery to hear me say they were here. She greeted them with a limp wave.

Tiffany took Bridget in, from the toes of her multi-colored rainbow socks to the hood of her pale-pink sweatshirt. "I like your outfit, Birdie. The colors remind me of something Natalie would wear." She looked fondly at Natalie.

If this girl insisted on showing up at my apartment uninvited, she could at least have the courtesy to get my best friend's name right. "Her name is Bridget," I said sternly before giving Bridget a sidelong glance for her reaction to Tiffany demolishing her name again. Her face held no emotion. This was bad. I took her hand. "Come with me."

Nicholas mouthed, "What's wrong?"

I shook my head and led Bridget into the bedroom as Tiffany said, "While Kim talks to Bird...I mean, Bridget, let's get back to the subject of honeymoon destinations. If you want non-traditional, what about a dude ranch? Remember when we went after homecoming, Nicholas? I was an expert rider by the time the weekend was over. Even though I didn't even get on a horse." She snorted.

I stopped walking and turned around in time to catch Tiffany swipe her hand up my fiancé's arm. I took a step forward, ready to rumble.

"Oh my God." Natalie groaned. "Give it a rest."

Nicholas backed away from her and dryly responded, "I can't say I recall it." Then he winked at me. I gave him a desperate look but completed the journey into the bedroom and closed the door behind us.

"What happened?" I asked Bridget, who was already stretched across the lady couch with my black and white afghan draped across her legs.

"I tried to tell Jonathan about..." She placed a palm against her belly. "My situation." She pushed out her lips. "We were watching television—a marathon of *The Middle*. Jonathan was laughing out loud, which I took as a good sign since it's a family show." She stopped talking and sat up.

I sat on the edge of my bed, facing her. "Then what?"

She scratched her head. "I decided you were right. I needed to tell him. He'd be shocked, but eventually he'd get on board. I mean, we love each other. What's a more beautiful tribute to our mutual devotion than making a baby? Right?"

I opened my mouth to respond, but it must have been a rhetorical question because Bridget didn't wait for my answer.

"Before I had a chance to make my true confession, Jonathan muted the television, turned to me, and said..." Her chin quivered. "Do you know what he said to me, K?"

I bit my lip and whispered, "What did he say?" I curled my fingers along the edge of the bed to brace myself.

Bridget stood up and paced the length of the room. "He said, 'Thank God this will never be us. Middle America, middle class, and middle aged with three useless kids? Thanks, but no thanks.' Then he raised the volume and continued to crack up at the pathetic married couple and their loser children and didn't even notice me frozen next to him."

I gulped. "Then what happened?"

"When I was able to move, I grabbed my coat and said I needed to run an errand. I had no idea I was coming to you until I found myself heading downtown on the subway."

"Oh, Bridget," I said. I stood up to give her a hug as the door squeaked open.

Nicholas popped his head in. "All right to enter?"

I couldn't very well keep Nicholas out of his own bedroom, so I waved him inside. I was desperate to tell him about Bridget, but it wasn't my place.

He gave me a pleading look. "Please don't leave me alone with them. Natalie is trying to convince me we should go to Siberia on our honeymoon. And Tiffany suggested having a destination wedding wherever we decide on a honeymoon and inviting all our guests to join us for one big extended party. She said it would be sublime." Nicholas did jazz hands and said, "Woo hoo" in a high-pitched voice. "I'm sure your parents would love to lose the deposit for the Soho Grand so we can plan a destination wedding."

"And I'm sure Tiffany would love the chance to rekindle your flame on our honeymoon," I said sarcastically. "Wait. Tiffany's invited to the wedding?" Nicholas said she was Natalie's friend, not his.

"She seems to think so," Nicholas said, sitting next to me on the bed.

I glared at him.

"She's in for a rude awakening," he said before nuzzling my neck.

Closing my eyes at the sensation, I said, "Good." He was forgiven.

Bridget cleared her throat.

A wave of guilt washed over me and I slid away from Nicholas as I remembered why Bridget and I had escaped to the bedroom in the first place.

"Are you all right, Bridget?" Nicholas asked, as if finally realizing we weren't alone.

"I'm swell. And I'll be swollen soon enough too."

Nicholas furrowed his brow and gave me a questioning glance.

I shrugged. *Not my place.*

"I'm pregnant." She stood up and pointed at Nicholas. "If you tell Jonathan, you won't need to worry about a honeymoon because I'll hunt you down and kill you before you make it down the aisle."

I yelped, "Bridget!" as Nicholas slowly backed his way out of the room.

Bridget sunk back on the bed. "Sorry. I didn't mean that. But please don't tell him," she said with her back to Nicholas.

"I won't." Nicholas widened his eyes at me and gestured toward the living room. "See you out there?"

He was such a good sport, I had to smile. "We'll be out soon, sweets." After he closed the door behind him, I turned to Bridget and blew a stream of air out of my mouth. "This can't go on."

"I'm sorry I yelled at your fiancé and future father of your children. Nicholas would probably make a Youtube video if you were pregnant. Why can't Jonathan be more like him?" she whined.

"If history repeats itself, you'll be dating Nicholas in about fifteen years." I giggled until I remembered if Nicholas dated Bridget after me, we'd need to split up first and so would Bridget and Jonathan—so not funny.

She stood up again. "I know I need to tell him soon, but I can't do it right now and I have no desire to go back out in the rain. Can I hang here for a while?"

"You can stay as long as you want." During Nicholas's "workaholic stage" the summer before, I'd moved out of our apartment to take time to figure things out. Bridget and Jonathan let me bunk with them for weeks. As far as I was concerned, she had an open invitation. But I hoped it wouldn't go on too long, mostly because she'd left Jonathan completely in the dark without giving him an opportunity to prove her wrong. The romantic in me was certain Jonathan would be thrilled to find out he was going to be a dad despite it not being on his life plan.

A few minutes later, we were back in the living room. Natalie was perched over Nicholas's laptop doing unsolicited honeymoon research while Tiffany braided her hair from behind. Every few seconds, they would giggle like teenagers, and I grimaced at what bizarre locales they'd suggest next. Nicholas had returned the piano bench to its rightful position and was practicing scales, and Bridget was curled on one end of the couch spooning peanut butter out of the jar. Across from her, I brainstormed alternate subplots for *Love on Stone Street*. I was determined to add complexity to the novel with a storyline aimed at one of the secondary characters. I hadn't heard back from Melina regarding my extension request, but I was forever hopeful.

I studied Bridget as she ate from the Skippy container like it was ice cream and inspiration hit—an unwanted pregnancy. "You're a genius, Bridget."

She looked up at me, a glob of peanut butter on her upper lip. "I prefer creamy."

"Yes, I can tell how much you despise the crunchy kind." I was still laughing when my phone rang. "Hi, Erin."

"Clearly you didn't lose my number."

I frowned. "Um, what?"

"I heard you had a family video chat and left me out."

I groaned. The fun portion of Saturday was officially over. "It was with both sets of parents. Are you my mom now? Or Nicholas's? What about my dad? Is there something you need to tell me?" I chuckled.

She harrumphed. "No, but neither is Natalie, and Mom told me she was included too."

I was surprised my mom mentioned it since she was aware of Natalie and Erin's stupid rivalry. I wondered if she secretly enjoyed the drama.

From the other end of the phone, Erin said, "Kim?"

I glanced over to where Natalie had now turned away from Nicholas's laptop to observe Tiffany sitting next to Nicholas on the piano bench. "I'm going to kill her," I mumbled, clenching my fists.

"Who? Why was Natalie in on the call? I heard she's trying to help you buy a dress. Don't even deny it."

"Erin." I'd have rolled my eyes if I wasn't too busy making sure Tiffany didn't touch Nicholas inappropriately.

"I'm your sister and I have much better taste."

"Erin." This time I did roll my eyes.

"Do you really want to wear—"

"Erin!" When I heard her gasp, I lowered my voice to a whisper so they couldn't hear me on the other side of the room. "In the name of all that glitters, I didn't invite Natalie to the chat. She crashed. Just like she did today when she showed up at our apartment with her Stepford friend under the guise of wanting to help us choose a honeymoon destination." I snuck another glance at Nicholas and Tiffany. Tiffany had scooched her way to the center of the bench and Nicholas's butt was practically hanging off the edge. It was obvious he wasn't comfortable with the invasion of his personal space, so why didn't he just get up?

"First she thinks she's Kate Young and now she's Jason Couvillion too?"

"I know Kate Young is a celebrity stylist, but who the heck is Jason whatshisface?"

"Couvillion." Erin enunciated each syllable. "He's a travel agent to the stars."

This was getting ridiculous. "Trust me when I tell you we have no interest in Natalie's travel-agent services. She suggested Siberia."

Erin giggled and I was back in our childhood home more than a decade earlier. When I wasn't kicking my little sister out of my room or teasing her metal mouth and clumsy tendencies, we managed to enjoy each other's company like only sisters can. A rush of loyalty swept through me. "If you can swing a trip to Boca the weekend after next,

Mom and I are going dress shopping. You're welcome to come." I'd wait until later to insist she give up on the idea of me in a princess-style dress.

Erin clucked her tongue. "I can't exactly up and leave my husband with two weeks' notice, Kim."

And, just like that, the sentimental urge for sibling bonding was gone.

Nicholas finally excused himself from the piano. He shook his head at me, his brown eyes sending me a private message—he loved me and only me, and wished everyone else would leave so we could finish what we started on the couch.

I mouthed, "Me too." To Erin, I said, "Was there anything else you wanted to talk about?"

"Have you seen Hannah lately?"

And we're done here. "Can I call you later? I've got a full house. Bye." I ended the call and let out a long, deep breath.

Four hours and twelve containers of Chinese delivery later, we finally had the apartment to ourselves again. Only, we were too stuffed to do anything but cuddle on the couch like sloths and binge-watch *Empire.* It was Nicholas's newest addiction. "The day wasn't a complete bust. At least I booked a flight to visit my mom for dress shopping."

Nicholas grinned. "And, thanks to my sister, we know all the most romantic destinations in Siberia."

My chest constricted. "Speaking of Natalie, why is Tiffany always tagging along with her?" It was obvious Natalie was bothered by Tiffany's antics, so why did she keep bringing her around? They lived in the same building, but surely they each had their own lives and semblance of personal space.

Getting up to bring our leftovers to the refrigerator, Nicholas said, "Maybe she's her Bridget?"

I followed him to the kitchen. "Well, my Bridget doesn't inappropriately grope other women's property."

Nicholas leaned against the fridge with his arms crossed. "I'm your property now?"

I narrowed my eyes. "You know what I mean."

He grinned. "She's always been touchy-feely, but I'll talk to her about boundaries."

"Thank you." We resumed our positions on the couch. "Back to the honeymoon. What about St. Lucia? I did some research for David when he was deciding where to go with Amy on their honeymoon last year."

"Rob's paralegal, David?"

I nodded.

"You liked what you saw?"

Nodding, I said, "I did. I'll look again tomorrow."

"We're making progress, Kimmie."

I snuggled closer to him. "We are." I remembered my new idea for *Love on Stone Street*, as inspired by Bridget, and smiled to myself. "In more ways than one."

Chapter 9

FIVE MONTHS UNTIL "I DO"

The dream (nightmare) I had a couple of weeks earlier where I walked down the aisle wearing nothing but designer shoes and a lovely bouquet of peonies served one purpose—I was super stoked to pick out the flowers for the wedding. Since the flower market on Twenty-eighth Street in the Chelsea neighborhood of Manhattan wasn't too far from where both Caroline and I worked, I asked her to join me during our lunch hour to see what kind of options were available. I'd take pictures of the ones I liked, and Nicholas would either give me the thumbs up or down to help narrow down the choices. The idea was if we went to the flower shop already knowing what we wanted, we'd save time and avoid stress.

As we walked up the block, I told Caroline about the impromptu gathering we had in my apartment the past weekend, including Tiffany's irritating habit of hitting on Nicholas as if I weren't there. "It's bizarre. One minute, she's touting Hawaii as a perfect honeymoon destination for us and the next, she's waxing nostalgic about their puppy love and trying to mount him on the piano bench." I wrinkled my nose. Even though I didn't see Tiffany as a threat, my body tensed in her presence and my jaw ached whenever I spoke her name.

Caroline scrunched her face. "She's got serious gall." She stopped in front of a batch of orange roses outside one store. "These are so pretty, and orange is fitting for an autumn wedding."

I leaned forward and inhaled the sweet scent. "I'm not sure how I feel about roses or how orange will look against your purple dresses." I doubted the flowers would end up in my bouquets but took a picture on my phone just in case. "These are pretty," I said, pointing to a batch of blue hydrangeas at the next storefront.

Caroline smiled. "Very. Remember, whatever you choose will need to be in season in November."

Having not thought of that, I frowned. Leave it to Caroline to be logical. We didn't have much time, so rather than ask someone who worked there about the best options for a November wedding, I would check online. I reached for my phone as it rang—Nicholas. "Any chance you know what flowers will be in bloom in November?" It was unlikely, but he never failed to surprise me with the depth of his knowledge—one of the many reasons I loved him.

"Not a clue. Listen, I need your help."

The edge in his voice concerned me. "What's wrong?" I stepped to the side and mouthed, "Nicholas" to Caroline. She nodded and removed her e-reader from her purse. Her habit of reading anytime and anywhere she had a free moment was almost as bad as mine. I would have chuckled if I wasn't troubled by Nicholas's call.

"I'm supposed to give a presentation at work this afternoon. In an hour and a half to be exact."

I remembered. As part of the vetting process for the executive general counsel position, all the candidates were required to present their thoughts on the direction they thought the company should take over the next five years. Nicholas had spent all of Sunday working on it and had stayed late at work the last two nights.

Nicholas continued, "I uploaded the presentation onto a flash drive, and the halfwit I am, left it at home." He mumbled something unintelligible, but I was fairly certain he was cursing his stupidity.

"Can you go home and get it?"

"I could, but it will look really bad if I miss one of the other applicant's presentations. Can you do it? Please?"

I glanced at my watch. I was supposed to be back at work in twenty minutes. "You just need me to email it to you, right?"

I heard Nicholas sigh. "Unfortunately, it's not that easy. The presentation includes at least twelve different large exhibits and color files, which is why I put them all onto a flash drive for easy upload. I'm afraid our home computer doesn't have the juice to email them all in one message and it would probably take you longer to split the files into multiple messages than to just bring me the flash drive." More to himself, he muttered, "Unless you could convert everything into a zip file, but it would still be risky."

I had no idea what a zip file was, and asking him to explain would use more precious time. "I'll leave right now." I grabbed a confused Caroline by the hand and dragged her down the street.

"Hurry. I'm not going to be able to stall, and if I'm not prepared, we can kiss this promotion and our two-bedroom apartment goodbye."

"I'll move as fast as my short legs will take me," I said, already out of breath.

"Thank you, Kim. I love you."

"I love you more," I said before ending the call and giving Caroline the Cliff Notes version of what was going down. A minute later, I was in a cab heading downtown. I called Rob, told him Nicholas had an emergency and I'd have to take a long lunch. My phone rang—the Soho Grand. I let it go to voicemail. First, I'd save Nicholas's presentation. Then I'd plan our wedding. The red light we were at was unusually long. It took another moment to register we were stuck in gridlock. I couldn't tell how far we'd gone while I was on the phone with Rob, but I doubted we'd moved even ten blocks. I muttered, "Crap," and leaned over the front seat. "Any idea what's going on?"

"Mid-afternoon traffic," the driver said with about as much emotion as a robot.

"Can we switch routes?" I pleaded. I glanced at my watch. Once I grabbed the flash drive, I could take the subway directly to Nicholas's company in the Chrysler Building, but first I needed to get home—and fast.

The driver pointed to the cars in front of us lined up like lemmings and laughed. "Nowhere to go."

"I'll get out here then." I'd jog to the nearest subway station. My eyes traveled to my three-inch tobacco leather mules and my stomach churned nervously. At least they had a block heel.

"I can't let you out until I can pull over. After next light."

While the taxi remained in its motionless state, I rocked in place and willed myself not to scream. I repeatedly checked my watch and prayed the minutes would go by slowly. My phone pinged a text message from Nicholas querying about my progress and I responded,

"On my way!" because I couldn't bear to tell him the truth. Finally, when I had chewed off all my nails as well as the remnants of my lip gloss, the driver pulled over to the curb. I gave him a twenty. "Keep the change." Shutting the door behind me, I ran to the Union Square subway station. It was warm for early June and I was sweating by the time I arrived.

I assumed it wouldn't be crowded at this time of day—the tail end of lunch hour and way before rush hour—but I was wrong. My heels tapped impatiently on the dirty floor beneath me as I waited in line to swipe my MetroCard through the turnstile. When I reached the front, I had to battle with people going through it in the other direction. I practiced good manners until I couldn't take it anymore. A thirty-something guy in a suit approached with his MetroCard out and an entitled look on his not-as-cute-as-Nicholas's face. *Not gonna happen, dude.* I leaned over and gave him a peek of my cleavage, which he eyed appreciatively. Sometimes a woman had to use her feminine wiles to get the job done. And it worked. He stepped to the side and motioned for me to go first. I presented a coquettish smile and swiped my card— insufficient funds. My shoulders drooped and a tear of frustration fell down my cheek as I rotated my heel and left the line to refill my card at the kiosk.

A few minutes later, although it felt like a decade, I finally stepped into a subway car. It was as crowded as a Walmart on Black Friday, but thanks to my small stature, I managed to shimmy my way in. Trying not to breathe in the combined scent of too much cologne, not enough deodorant, and tuna fish, I held tightly to the rail, and closed my eyes. Then I waited for the conductor to quit announcing, "Stand clear of the closing doors" and close the damn doors. At last, my prayers were answered.

When the train arrived at my stop, I pushed my way out. I was on a mission. I was Super Fiancée. All I needed was a cape, preferably a pink one. I'd deliver Nicholas's flash drive and save the day. My adrenaline rushed as I got closer and closer to my apartment and the spring breeze in the air tickled my teeth as I grinned to disguise the pain in the back of my throat from breathing through my mouth. Yoga hadn't prepared me for this type of endurance. And, there it was—my building. Just a few more steps. So close and…oh no. Where did that rock come from? I was already nearer to the ground than most but as my feet lifted off the ground without my permission, it was too close for comfort. A stinging sensation zipped through me as my bare knees made contact with the pavement.

I was sprawled on the sidewalk with my arms extended in front of me. The fingers of one hand gripped the strap of my purse for dear life. My keys were inside and I'd sooner make a deal with the devil to read one-star books for the rest of my life than get mugged right now. Wincing in pain, I pulled myself up to a standing position and looked both ways. No one had witnessed my fall. I straightened out my skirt, took a deep breath, and entered the building. I didn't have time to dwell on the burning sensation in both my knees from falling.

I proceeded to the elevator and stopped short at the appearance of three maintenance men wearing matching blue uniforms.

One said, "The elevator is down."

My breath caught in my throat. "I need to get upstairs to my apartment."

"Sorry. Can you take the stairs?"

I released a nervous laugh. "I ran all the way here from the subway. What's a few flights of stairs?"

Clearly mistaking my trembling lips as a smile, they greeted me with fat grins. "That's the spirit."

My knees throbbed with each step, but I finally made it into my apartment. I located the flash drive exactly where Nicholas said it would be and placed it securely in the zippered compartment of my purse. Then I locked the door behind me, walked back down the stairs, and jogged back to the subway station. By then, I was almost used to the pain. I was too afraid to check the time, nor did I want to waste more of it by doing so. There was no turning back now.

Blessedly, the Spring Street subway station wasn't crowded and the local uptown six train arrived less than a minute after me. My stop, Grand Central Station, was the seventh. I sat down and counted the stops with my fingers. Once we made it past Bleecker Street and Astor Place, I relaxed marginally. Rookie mistake. The fast-moving train turned into the little engine that couldn't, and my pulse raced. The teenager next to me looked up from his iPhone and raised an eyebrow before gesturing at my feet, which were tapping the dirty floor like a poor man's Shirley Temple. I muttered, "Sorry" and willed the train to speed up—without crashing, of course. Then I closed my eyes, practiced mindful breathing, and tried to trick the train to think I had all day to reach my destination. Reverse psychology worked and, at last, we arrived at Grand Central. I wobbled my way to the exit, sucking in my breath at the soreness in my knees from sitting too long.

I hurried through the underground tunnels to the lobby of the Chrysler Building and to the elevator bank leading to Nicholas's office on the twenty-seventh floor. "Almost there, Nicholas," I whispered to myself as I attempted to push my way through the turnstile. It wouldn't budge. I let my head hang back and choked back a sob. Then it hit me, Duh. I needed identification to get into *my* office building. Why wouldn't Nicholas's firm—in a landmark building no less—take the same level of care in protecting against unauthorized and possibly dangerous individuals? But I wasn't a threat to anyone. Quite the opposite. I was here to help. A groan escaped my throat at the same time a security guard approached me.

"Can I help you, miss?"

"I'm trying—" My phone rang before I had a chance to complete my sentence—Nicholas. "One second," I said to the guard in the most polite tone I could muster. "I'm downstairs, but I need to get through security." I removed the phone from my ear and to the guard said, "My fiancé, Nicholas Strong, works at Gracefully Made Soap and Cosmetics. I need to bring him a flash drive for a very important presentation."

The guard gestured for me to follow him to the security desk. When we arrived at the end of a three-person line, he said "Tell her where you're going and who you're here to see. She'll give you a temporary pass up to the twenty-seventh floor."

Nicholas was still on the line and I heard him say, "Kimmie? Are you almost here? I'm set to go on in five minutes and still need to upload the flash drive." I looked pleadingly at the guard—a bear of a man with full ruddy cheeks and thick gray hair. He looked kind and accommodating. "Can he authorize you to let me in directly?" I crossed my fingers, resisting the temptation to flash my cleavage again.

The guard shook his head. "We need to follow procedure, but it's the second to last elevator bank when you're ready."

The air in my tires deflated. *So much for being accommodating.*

Into the phone, I said, "I'm third in line to get a pass. Hold them off. Sing a ditty. Just not 'Kimmie Long was in my pants.'" I forced a giggle, clearing my throat when Nicholas didn't join in. Only one person was manning the two-person desk at security. Where was the other person? "One down, one to go," I said excitedly as I moved closer to the front of the line.

Nicholas didn't answer me, but I heard him say, "I'll be right there" to someone else. "The promotion isn't worth this stress," he muttered.

I stared at the back of the one person ahead of me and discovered a watched line didn't move any quicker than a watched pot boiled. "Of course it is, sweetie. This is merely a bump in the road. My turn! Hi, I'm here to see Nicholas Strong at Gracefully Made."

"Show her your ID," Nicholas said.

I rummaged through my purse for my wallet. My license fit into the allotted space like a fat guy in a little coat and I struggled to set it free. I cursed under my breath until I finally pulled it out and handed it to the woman.

She mumbled something into her phone and looked up at me. "He's not answering his phone."

My eyes bugged out. "I'm on the phone with him now. This is him." I handed her my device.

She shook her head. "Tell him to hang up so I can call his extension."

Hearing her, Nicholas said, "I'm not at my desk. Tell her to phone reception on twenty-seven and they'll authorize you. Three minutes."

"You must be freakin' kidding me," I muttered. I passed on the message to the woman. To Nicholas I said, "Are you sure the receptionist won't need to hunt you down to make sure the four-foot-eleven woman with bloody knees isn't a danger to the cosmetics industry?"

This time, Nicholas chuckled. "I'm standing at reception now. What is this about your knees?"

"You can go," she said, handing me a temporary paper pass. "It's the second—"

"Second to last elevator bank. I'm on it. Thanks," I said, grabbing the pass. I raced to the elevator bank and waved my temporary pass over the glass. Nothing. I waved it again. Still nothing. I turned to the security guard from before in a panic.

"Let me." With the guard's magical touch, the turnstile door opened. An elevator arrived. I stepped in and quickly pressed the button for the twenty-seventh floor followed by the "close door" one. If I was lucky, it would be an express ride.

The door shut halfway before a hairy arm waved it open. The arm was attached to a forty-something man who acknowledged me with a nod. I nodded back. Maybe we were headed to the same floor. He pressed twenty-six. I sighed and hit the "close door" button again as three giggling twenty-something girls holding iced coffees from Dunkin' Donuts walked in. Before I could hope their destination was the same as mine or hairy-arm guy, they pressed the button for twenty-five. If after all this, Nicholas didn't get the promotion, someone was definitely getting killed in my next novel or at least being cursed with a super long sexual dry spell. I needed an outlet to release some rage. The door closed without further interruption and I fished the flash drive from where it was safely ensconced in my purse. I was confident my chances of misplacing it during the elevator ride, however long it might be, were slim.

I watched the numbers light up as we ascended higher and higher until we reached the twenty-fifth floor. The girls took their time exiting and my leg twitched with the need to kick them out myself. I pressed "close door" and avoided eye contact with hairy-arm guy. If he knew what I'd been through in the name of love, he wouldn't think I was rude, but I didn't have time to tell him. We were probably down to thirty seconds at this point. The door opened on the twenty-sixth floor. For a dose of good karma, I said, "Have a good day," and pressed "close door" before he could say it back. In the seconds before we finally arrived on the twenty-seventh floor, I choked up as if I'd finished a first draft of a novel, ran the New York Marathon, and given birth on the same day.

Nicholas was waiting for me when the doors opened and with tears in my eyes and a lump in my throat, I handed him the flash drive. "Go."

"Thank you. Thank you. Thank you," he said before dropping his gaze down the length of my body. He paused at my knees before looking back up at me. His eyes were wide with concern. "What happened?"

My legs were shaking from pent-up nerves. "Later. You have a presentation to make. I'd say 'break a leg,' but all things considered, I'm afraid to risk it. Good luck."

He leaned down and kissed me ever so softly. "I already hit the jackpot when I met you, Kimmie. But I do have to run. I will make this up to you."

"My imagination is running wild. And dirty. Go!"

I watched his back until he was no longer in sight before pressing the down button on the elevator. It came right away. It was empty. I was back in the lobby in less than thirty seconds. Using the underground tunnel, I headed back to the subway and jumped on a waiting and uncrowded six train to the Twenty-eighth Street stop. It was time to go back to work.

My body was exhausted, but my heart was filled with happiness that I was able to assist Nicholas in his time of need. Despite a few bumps and literal bruises, everything had worked out. It was a beautiful day and I had so much to be thankful for. With a smile on my face, I stepped onto the street. A moment later, I felt a drop of moisture hit me on the cheek and I swiped my finger along my skin to wipe it off. Startled by a loud boom, I looked up at the gray sky as pellets of rain crashed down on me. It took a beat to register it was raining, I didn't have an umbrella, and I was getting more drenched with each passing second. When I finally awoke from my stupor, I headed back down the stairs of the subway station and onto another waiting train. To hell with work, I had a book to write. I was going home.

Chapter 10

The following day, I came home straight from the office. It was yoga night, but my knees were too raw to do most of the poses, so I iced them and stretched across my lady couch while I worked on a revised synopsis for *Love on Stone Street.*

Nicholas, who had been watching television in the living room, entered our bedroom and stood over me. "Mind if I watch the news in here? It's getting late." After acing his presentation the day before, Nicholas had rewarded himself by leaving the office at five. We'd contemplated going out for dinner, but I needed to write and he was in the mood to binge-watch on Netflix. Besides, it had been raining nonstop since the day before and neither of us had any desire to leave the confines of our cozy apartment.

I glanced at the bottom of my computer screen. It was almost eleven, but I wasn't surprised since time always flew when I got lost in the fictional world of my creation. I extended my arms in a stretch and yawned. I was exhausted and it was time to get ready for bed. "Go for it. I'm finished writing for now anyway." Mere minutes ago, I had emailed the amended synopsis to Felicia. I asked if she'd mind reading it and sharing her thoughts before I sent it to Melina. At this point, I would rather hear whether the new subplot was genius or utter crap from Felicia than Melina.

A few minutes later, against a backdrop of the news, I slid under the covers, kissed Nicholas goodnight, and closed my eyes. I thought about the upcoming weekend. I was flying to Florida the day after tomorrow to shop for a dress with my mom. Besides quality time with my parents and crossing a vital item off my wedding to-do list, the trip would be a welcome distraction from worrying about *Love on Stone Street.*

As I drifted off to sleep, I heard Janice Huff, NBC's chief meteorologist, deliver the weather report. She mentioned something about monitoring a tropical storm making its way from the Caribbean up the eastern seaboard and the danger of it developing into a hurricane. I sat up. "What did she say about a tropical storm?"

Nicholas turned to face me. "This little rain we're having is actually the onset of Hurricane Daneen."

"Excuse me?"

The faint lines around Nicholas's eyes crinkled. "Just a coincidence."

I smirked. "I'm not sure which version of Daneen is more dangerous." I shuddered in remembrance of when Daneen tried to sabotage my first meeting with Felicia by assigning me an "urgent" project and then lying about what time it was. I showed up late, but by the grace of God, met Felicia in the ladies' room and explained what happened.

"Human Daneen's got nothing on you. This weather system is another story. We'll have to plan all indoor activities this weekend." He waggled his eyebrows.

"I'm going to Florida on Friday." When I'd told my mom that come hell or high water, I was buying a dress during my visit with her, I hadn't meant it literally.

Nicholas turned to me. "I forgot about your trip." He shrugged. "I wouldn't count on it, Kimmie."

I felt an ache in the back of my throat. "The reports could be wrong though. Right?" When Nicholas didn't respond, I repeated, "Right?"

"Maybe." He didn't sound convincing.

My body shook with nervous energy. "I need to get a dress this weekend, Nicholas. We're down to the wire."

He pecked my nose. "Try not to worry about it."

I curled in the fetal position with my legs up to my belly and tried to wipe away the image of Daneen—the person, not the hurricane—from my mind's eye. I should have known she wouldn't go quietly.

The next day at work, talk of the weather was all the rage—the squad hovered over me. Since my desk was right outside of Rob's office, it was a popular hangout for folks either finished meeting with him or waiting to be called inside.

Lucy, an attorney in the group, pulled a pencil out of her blonde bun and scribbled something on a legal pad. "I stocked up on water, cereal, and instant coffee. What else do I need?"

"Toilet paper?" David, the paralegal, suggested with a chuckle. "It figures, the hurricane reaches us just in time for the weekend. God forbid we miss a day of work."

Rob stepped out of his office. "What's this about missing work? Only wimps stay home when it's raining."

Normally, I would roll my eyes at Rob's statement. It was so, well, "Rob." But this time, I agreed. "Rob's right. You can't let a little precipitation prevent you from living your life. I'm going to Florida tomorrow. Drizzle be damned." I refused to refer to this weather thing we were having as a hurricane. Mind over matter and all that.

Rob, Lucy, and David looked at me like I'd grown antlers.

"Drizzle?" Lucy said.

I averted eye contact by staring down at the pink gloss Hunter Boots I'd placed under my desk when I'd arrived at work that morning. They were too hot and bulky to wear all day, so I'd changed into navy blue ballet flats with a pink bow.

"While I admire your statement in principle, your airline might have something else to say about it," Rob said. "Have you checked with them?"

If the flight was cancelled, surely I'd have received a notification on my phone from Jet Blue. I removed the device from the top drawer of my desk, clicked on the app, and saw my flight still listed as "on time." My confidence soared and I beamed at my colleagues. "My airline agrees with me. It's just a silly rain shower."

The likelihood of Nicholas leaving work early two days in a row was slim, and since I'd missed yoga the night before, I went straight to the gym for the six fifteen class. After forty-five minutes of deep breathing, meditation, and stretching, the coils in my stomach settled down. I was positive Hurricane Daneen was on its way to being downgraded to a regular old thunderstorm and I would fly to Boca Raton the next morning as scheduled. I wondered if they purposely exaggerated the severity of the weather to induce panic in the minds of the public. Maybe they even partnered up with the grocery-store chains to boost the economy by scaring everyone into stocking their pantries with non-perishable food items.

I exited the gym and stood under the awning while I checked the app one more time—my flight was still on time. I opened my umbrella and walked home with visions of Vera Wang gowns dancing in my head. I was finally going to experience the thrill of trying on wedding dresses without interruption from opinionated members of my bridal party or confessions of unplanned pregnancies. It was going to be all about me and I couldn't wait. The wind was gusting and I struggled to keep my clear bubble umbrella from turning upside down. But even as pellets of rain slammed me from all sides, I sang the words to "Singin' in the Rain" and skipped all the way home.

When my red-brick apartment building greeted me a few minutes later, I quickened my pace until I was through the front door and inside the elevator. I still had to pack, but first, I'd take a shower. I'd put on my comfiest of pajamas—strike that—one of Nicholas's button-down shirts. I was going away for the weekend which meant there would be no falling asleep to the news tonight. Hot sex was in order, and Nicholas loved how I looked wearing his shirts almost as much as he liked me wearing nothing at all.

The elevator doors opened on my floor. I placed the closed umbrella against the wall next to my front door while I searched for my keys in my purse. When I was conscientious, I kept them in the zippered compartment for easy access, but lately my brain was too scattered to do anything besides toss them haphazardly in the bag. I removed my hair brush, my monogrammed pink makeup case, and my phone and threw them next to me on the hallway carpet. I had a text. I hoped it was Nicholas saying he was on his way home. Maybe he'd pick up food. I was craving pad thai. I reached for my device with a smile and swiped the message. Only it wasn't from Nicholas.

It was an alert—from Jet Blue.

My flight was cancelled.

Chapter 11

Once I accepted that short of taking up magic and learning a weather-altering spell, there was nothing I could do to make Jet Blue change their minds about canceling my flight, we made the most of Hurricane Daneen and our forced staycation in Casa Strong and Long for the weekend.

From next to Nicholas on the piano bench, I watched his long fingers tap the keys in a performance of "Piano Man." We hoped to be inspired to choose our wedding song. So far, it wasn't working. I'd suggested "Don't It Make My Brown Eyes Blue" or "Baby Come Back" since they were the songs we'd sang to each other in our respective grand gestures, but we agreed those lyrics weren't declarations of love as much as expressions of apology and pleas for forgiveness—not exactly wedding appropriate. But if anyone could come up with the perfect song, it was Nicholas. I'd already done a stellar job at screwing up enough aspects of the wedding. Let Nicholas give this task his own tender loving care. I told him so after he played the final notes of the famous Billy Joel tune.

"Cut yourself some slack, Kimmie. It's not like you did a rain dance or anything. You have no control over the weather."

I leaned against him. "If I'd been more on the ball, the trip to Florida would have been unnecessary because I'd already have a dress. I should have stuck it out at Kleinfeld. I'm positive India would have found me a dress even Erin and Natalie would agree was 'the one.'"

"It will all work out."

"Yeah, yeah, yeah," I mumbled as another boom of thunder sounded from outside. I pictured myself in a boring white suit like the one Carrie wore when she married Big in the Sex and the City movie. She looked elegant, but I didn't want to wear a suit to my wedding. I was about to say this to Nicholas when my phone rang. It was Jonathan. Since he rarely called me directly, my heart raced in fear something had happened to Bridget. I answered in a shaky voice. "Hello?"

"Kim. It's Jonathan."

Twirling a strand of hair around my finger, I stood up and paced the living-room floor. Out of the corner of my eye, I saw Nicholas, who had relocated to the couch, give me a curious look, but I was too nervous to focus on him. "What's up?" What if something happened to the baby or Bridget?

"This might sound weird, but I'm worried about Bridget."

"What do you mean?"

I heard him take a drag from a cigarette. "She's so withdrawn lately. She claims her work is busy, but it's always been that way. Part of the fun of sharing a home office is taking breaks at the same time to vent, but she keeps begging off. She says she doesn't have time and we'll talk later, but then she goes to bed really early. Has she said anything to you?"

I sat down next to Nicholas and covered my face with my hands, debating how to respond. If I said, "You need to ask her," he'd know something was up. Something was up, but I promised Bridget I'd let her tell Jonathan in her own time. Too bad she was taking forever. At almost three months along, a baby bump would take the place of her normally flat stomach soon. I doubted Jonathan cared if he could bounce a quarter off Bridget's abdominals, but he'd definitely notice the difference. "No. But I've been swamped with the wedding planning and stuff." I glanced over at Nicholas who mouthed, "Tell him." I shook my head. A best friend didn't renege on her promises.

"Is she cheating on me?" he asked, his voice almost a whisper.

"No!" I yelped before I could stop myself. Bridget might keep unplanned pregnancies from Jonathan, but she'd never be unfaithful to him. In a softer tone, I said, "There's definitely no one else."

He sighed. "What if she's sick? She was on an antibiotic a couple weeks ago. She said it was for strep, but what if it's more serious?"

My eyes welled up at Jonathan's concern for Bridget. He loved her and I was positive he'd embrace the pregnancy. He just had to get used to the idea, which meant she had to tell him. But she wasn't going to spill before we got off the phone and I couldn't take being on the receiving end of his apprehension a minute longer. I could tell it was killing him and the guilt of enabling it wasn't doing me any good either.

Nicholas had lost interest in the conversation and was now reading the latest issue of *The Wire*, an indie music magazine. I squeezed his knee until he jerked from my touch. When he caught my eye, I mouthed, "Get me off," hoping he'd know I was referring to the phone call and not something sexual.

His eyes twinkled and I knew he was thinking the same thing. But he stood up, walked into the kitchen, and yelled, "Kim!"

Into the phone, I said, "Hold on a sec? Nicholas is calling me." I paused for a beat. "What? I'm on the phone with Jonathan."

"I think your roast is burning," Nicholas said.

To Jonathan I said, "My roast is..." I blinked. My roast? I'd never cooked a roast in my life. I didn't even know if he meant roast chicken or pot roast. My fiancé had some imagination. A giggle threatened to bubble out of me even though it was no laughing matter. Regaining my bearings, I said, "Since we were stuck inside all weekend, I decided to practice my cooking skills. Nicholas has informed me I've failed miserably and we can't exactly risk our apartment going up in flames in the middle of a hurricane. Can I call you back? Where is Bridget now?"

"She's napping—again. I'm freaking out a little. Do you promise to call me back?"

"I promise." I was getting tired of making promises I wasn't sure I could keep. I ended the call and faced Nicholas. "My roast is burning?"

He shrugged. "You caught me off guard. It was the best I could do."

"It was good for a chuckle, which is more than I can say for the rest of the conversation. Bridget needs to come clean with Jonathan."

"I agree," Nicholas said, leaning against the kitchen counter. "What are you going to do?"

"I'd call her, but Jonathan said she was napping. She might just be avoiding him, but if she's really asleep, I don't want to wake her. I'll send her a text." I retreated to the living room where my phone was resting on the coffee table. I was afraid to say anything incriminating in case Jonathan intercepted the message, but how could I say what I wanted to say without really saying it? And then it came to me. I'd use

Pig Latin. I wanted to text, "Jonathan is freaking out. You need to tell him. You won't be able to hide it for much longer. Bridget, it's time. Love you." Instead, I typed, "Onathanjay isyay reakingoutfay. Ouyay eednay ootay elltay imhay. Ouyay on'tway ebay ableyay ootay idehay orfay uchmay ongerlay. Ridgetbay, it's-yay imetay. ovelay ouyay."

A few minutes later, Bridget wrote back. "You're right. I know you're right. Love you too." Only, it said, "Ou'reyay ightray. Ovelay ouyay ootay."

Chapter 12

When the rain made its exit, it left sunshine and seasonal warm June temperatures in its wake to start the work week. Nicholas said it was the perfect weather for cake tasting, but I countered there was no such thing as bad weather for sampling delicious cake. Nicholas's brothers, Neil and Nathan, and their wives, Clarissa and Pam, had generously chipped in to buy us a designer cake from Sylvia Weinstock as our wedding gift. The two of us were like ten-year-olds as we sat at the aluminum table in her showroom waiting for our tasting to begin.

"I don't want anything trendy like cupcakes instead of a cake," Nicholas said.

I smirked. "I guess a cake modeled after a Christian Louboutin shoe is out of the question?" We had seen one in the catalog, along with cakes in the shape of a reindeer and a corned beef sandwich. "First you don't want me to dress up as a mermaid and now you want a traditional cake. Next you'll tell me we can't sleep together until after the wedding."

Nicholas's eyes widened in horror. "Bite your tongue, Kimmie."

We laughed, but a moment later, our mouths watered as eighty-something-year-old Sylvia, wearing a white chef's jacket over a green and white floral-printed blouse and black pants, placed a tray with an assortment of cake slices in front of us.

Sylvia adjusted her tortoise-shell oversize round black glasses and smiled at us. "You ready for this?"

"Bring it on," Nicholas said while I nodded eagerly but remained silent. I was too star-struck for words. In my most extravagant wedding fantasies, I wore a fancy Vivienne Westwood or Carolina Herrera gown, but I never dared to dream about a Sylvia Weinstock cake. She was a legend. Remembering I might need to buy my wedding dress at the local mall if I waited much longer, my muscles twitched with anxiety. I brushed the thought out of my mind in favor of tastier subjects, like cake.

"First we need to choose the flavor and then we'll talk design. We have German chocolate, coconut and lime, pink champagne, and carrot here," Sylvia said, pointing to each cake in turn. "And here we have lemon, white chocolate with raspberry, red velvet, and vanilla."

I slickly pushed a fork in front of Nicholas when it looked like he might dive head-first into the red velvet. My eyes went straight to the pink champagne since it combined my signature color with my favorite adult beverage. Faking sophistication, I waited to get the official go-ahead from Sylvia to start.

As if reading my mind, she squeezed my shoulder. "Dig in, dear. I'll step away for a few minutes so my feelings won't be hurt if you hate some of them. I have more in the back."

"There's no way we'll hate any of them," I said as a closed-eyed Nicholas moaned from next to me. I glanced at him in amusement. "If anything, we might end up hating each other if we can't agree on our favorite."

"Couples break up over much less," Sylvia said with a chuckle before leaving us alone.

We spent the next twenty minutes trying each of the different flavors, ruling out some and adding others to our list of favorites. As we took turns feeding each other, I made Nicholas vow not to shove cake in my face at the wedding. "I promise to be nice if you are. But if you embarrass me first, all bets are off."

"What if you go first?" Nicholas teased.

"I won't," I said, dipping my fork into what was left of the white chocolate raspberry cake.

"Western European etiquette suggests that ladies always go first."

"We don't live in Europe," I said before biting into the cake and closing my eyes to savor the sweet creamy goodness.

"Should we ask Sarah which cake goes best with our menu?"

I opened my eyes. "I don't think it matters. Cripes." I told Nicholas about the message April from the Soho Grand had left me the day of his presentation. "She said she had some questions about the outside caterer. In all the madness, I forgot to call her back."

"You can do it tonight when we're done here," Nicholas said.

We hadn't picked the menu for the wedding yet. While some people were happy to skip the main course and go directly to the dessert, I was most excited to choose our options for cocktail hour. Hello, pigs in a blanket! Nicholas hadn't mentioned when we were scheduled to meet with Sarah to discuss. "Speaking of Sarah—"

His shoulders drooped and he groaned. "Maybe there is such thing as too much cake after all."

"My poor baby," I said, rubbing his tummy.

Nicholas sat up straight in his chair. "I forgot to tell you what Gideon said."

"No time like the present." I assumed it was positive considering how suddenly Nicholas forgot his stomach pain.

"They've narrowed it down to three candidates, including your sexy fiancé."

"Henry Cavill, really?" I giggled in response to Nicholas's fake wounded expression. "Kidding. I'm so excited for you. Any idea when they'll decide?" Nicholas was a shoo-in if they had any taste.

He shook his head. "It's going to be a while. These decisions always take a long time."

All too familiar with the waiting game from my time querying agents and then waiting for Felicia to hear back from editors at publishing houses, I smiled sympathetically. "Trust me, I understand slow." Sylvia returned to the table before I could go into further detail. Having lived through it with me, Nicholas didn't need additional clarification anyway.

We told Sylvia we'd narrowed it down to the white chocolate raspberry—surprising since neither of us liked white chocolate—vanilla, and pink champagne, but needed a little time to decide. She said we could think on it while she showed us her gallery of custom cakes, and as we oohed and aahed over fountain, royal, waterfall designs and more, all other thoughts were pushed to the side.

At home later, I was still stuffed but comfy in a pair of my baggiest sweatpants. I was about to crawl into bed with my e-reader when I remembered April's voicemail again. I doubted she was still at work, but calling her back would at least return the ball to her court. And if I ignored her for much longer, she might think I was a difficult bride. I wasn't difficult, just a smidge overwhelmed. But today had been huge—we'd picked out a cake—pink champagne in a five-layer rosette and pearl design. Why not keep the momentum going?

When I removed my phone from the nightstand my heart stopped. There was a missed call and voicemail from Felicia. I clicked on the message and squirmed at the rolling in my stomach. It felt like bats were flying around in there. I swallowed hard at the impatient edge to her voice.

"Kim, it's Felicia. I read your synopsis. We should talk."

Chapter 13

Inhale confidence. Exhale doubt.

Maybe meditative breathing would help shake me out of my writer's block. Nothing else had so far. I stared at the empty screen. *C'mon, muse. Where are you?* I'd come to Ground Support, my favorite coffee shop and go-to writing haunt, straight from the office, determined to write some words. I ordered my usual vanilla latte, shook out my wrists in preparation for a long stretch of typing, and waited. My butt had been seated in the chair for twenty minutes, yet I hadn't typed a single letter on the page. My idea well was bone dry. In fact, I hadn't written a word since I'd had my call with Felicia the week before. She wasn't on board with my synopsis. A romantic comedy wasn't the appropriate platform to comment on abortion rights or women's reproductive health rights in general. I'd confessed I was trying to appease those readers craving a pinch of salt with their sweet, but once again, my attempt to add depth was an epic fail.

Felicia voiced concern I lacked a solid understanding of my brand, which even though I'd only published one novel so far, I'd been building since my first review on *Pastel Is the New Black*. She urged me to get back to my roots, trust my gut, and stop reading my reviews. I'd get back to my lost roots if I could only relocate them. For the first time in my life, I was too paralyzed to write.

I took a sip of my latte and minimized the document on my screen. Sometimes inspiration struck when you weren't searching for it. What better way to fool my muse into action by distracting myself with emails?

When the page opened on my screen, I sucked in my breath. There was only one new message in my inbox—from Melina. In all the time I'd been waiting for her to get back to me about the extension, I lived by the mantra, *no news is good news.* For better or worse, the scoop had been dropped on my virtual doorstep.

> *Dear Kim,*
>
> *I apologize for the delay in getting back to you. I reached out to production regarding your request to push back your deadline and just heard back now. Unfortunately, the way the release schedule is set up, there is no leeway with respect to delivery dates.*
>
> *I'm sorry, Kim. I wish there was something I could do. Hopefully, you've made significant progress on the updated synopsis since we last spoke and the point is moot. I look forward to reading it soon.*
>
> *Take care,*
> *Melina*

I lay my head on my keyboard, not caring if I'd get pastry crumbs in my hair or if any of the other patrons thought I'd passed out. That was that—the December deadline to deliver the manuscript—now five months away and a month after my wedding—was non-negotiable.

I was in desperate need of inspiration. It was time to call in reinforcements. I closed down my computer and walked to Three Lives and Company, an independent bookstore in the neighborhood. The moment I stepped through the bright red door and into the tiny space overloaded with shelves and tables piled high with books, my tense muscles relaxed. As a sense of calm and safety washed over me, I knew I'd come to the right place.

When I visited bookstores before I was published, I'd often search for books I'd helped promote with *Pastel Is the New Black.* I delighted in seeing my name in the acknowledgements. When I was hunting for an agent, I also liked to see who represented my favorite authors in the chick lit genre. But mostly, I'd sit in a corner and get lost inside a black hole while I read for hours. I was incapable of leaving a store without purchasing a new novel, even though my e-reader was full of unread books and there hadn't been space on my physical bookshelf since I was a teenager. I'd never thrown a book out. The few times I donated a bag of used novels to Goodwill, I choked up. Even though it was for charity, it made my heart hurt to give them away.

Since I'd been published, I hadn't walked past a bookstore without checking to see if *A Blogger's Life* was in stock. It was a longshot, since Three Lives & Co. was a well-curated shop not known for carrying much commercial fiction, but I couldn't resist. Restraining my natural urge to shop, I ignored the covers taunting me with their intriguing titles in the fiction section and focused on finding the L's. My fingers touched the spine of a book written by A.L. Long, Heather Long, and then...there it was...*A Blogger's Life* by Kim Long. My publisher had skipped the hardcover stage and published directly to trade paperback. Sadie had explained it was because I was a debut author with a young target audience. This was the same reason my first print run was only 7,500 copies. My publisher was trying to minimize their risk. As long as my book was in a bookstore—a dream come true— the format didn't matter to me. Especially since Hannah's books also went straight to paperback. I knew it shouldn't matter, but I couldn't help but make the comparison. I was also positive if one of Hannah's books came out in hardcover, I'd never hear the end of it.

I removed the book from the shelf, marveled at the pretty illustrated cover atop a pale blue background, and hugged it to my chest. Then I opened to a random page and breathed in the contents. There was nothing like the smell of a real book—a special mix of chemicals with a hint of vanilla—and I swore mine smelled better than any other book I'd ever sniffed. And I'd sniffed plenty.

Ever since I could hold a pencil, I'd been scribbling stories. I started my first novel at fifteen years old and many more followed from there. I had a nice little collection of chapters one through five for various books living a quiet existence in a storage facility in Brooklyn. I always burnt out, or more accurately, gave up before I finished. I feared my stories were garbage—unworthy of being read by anyone besides me—and a pointless use of my time. But I thought those days were behind me. I'd overcome my inferiority complex and I had a published novel under my belt to prove it. So why was I having such a hard time with *Love on Stone Street*? Was the root of the problem the book or me? Was I a one-book author? All I had to do was finish the second book. If I didn't, not only would I be in breach of my two-book contract, but my publishing career might be over. I'd let down Felicia and all the others who'd thrown so much support my way, like Nicholas. I didn't want to disappoint him or myself. I could do it. I knew I could.

But what if I couldn't?

Chapter 14

"Would it be terrible if we grabbed a slice first?" Nicholas asked, gazing longingly at Ray's Pizza through the window of our Uber.

We were on our way to meet Natalie for dinner. She'd been enlisted by Nicholas's parents to choose the venue for our rehearsal dinner. They were paying, but she was local and they weren't. She'd called us earlier in the week and said she'd found the perfect restaurant. Given Natalie's penchant for the eclectic, Nicholas and I were understandably concerned and made a reservation to see it for ourselves. Natalie invited herself to join us.

"Can you imagine if it's all raw food like the episode in *Sex and the City* when Samantha meets Smith Jerrod for the first time?" I preferred my food cooked, but could make an exception if our waiter resembled Jason Lewis.

Nicholas turned away from the window and faced me, his eyes round pools of liquid brown. "She wouldn't dare." He never watched *SATC*, so I assumed it was the word "raw" that freaked him out.

I nodded. "She would absolutely dare." My lips curled up. "But she didn't. According to the website, they offer global eclectic fusion cuisine. It got good reviews on Yelp too."

The car dropped us off and we entered At Vermillion. I took in the space—sleek and modern with multiple levels. Natalie and her guest were already seated and the hostess led us to their table. As we followed her through a room with bright red walls and filled with tables where patrons sat in sparkling white chairs, I inhaled the distinct scent of Indian spices. So far, so good. I wondered who Natalie's guest was and hoped it wasn't—

"You're here," Tiffany squealed.

"And so are you," I mumbled, digging my fingernails into

Nicholas's palm. He told me he was going to tell Natalie it was inappropriate to involve Tiffany in the wedding planning given the circumstances. The circumstances being his bride-to-be asked him very nicely to make Tiffany appear much less often. Either Tiffany ignored the request or Nicholas forgot to give Natalie the memo. I'd ask him about it later, but for now, I planted on a smile. "I like your pants." This was true. I coveted the hot pink stretch pants Tiffany was wearing.

Fifteen minutes later, we'd ordered food and had a round of drinks in front of us.

"What do you think?" Natalie asked, her dark eyes sweeping the vast space.

I took a sip of my cocktail. It was called India Meets Pakistan and it was delicious. "I like the space. It's centrally located, which is good. But I think we should reserve judgment until after we eat." I looked at Nicholas. "Right, honey?"

Before he could answer, Natalie continued, "They have several semi-private spaces and a range of price-fixed menus as well. I think it's perfect."

"Thank you for finding it," I said with sincerity. It was one less task for my to-do list. I'd take the help where I could get it.

"Thank Tiffany. It was her suggestion." Natalie's eyes sparkled in Tiffany's direction.

Tiffany waved her hand in dismissal. "We had a fashion week cocktail party here a few weeks ago and I thought of you guys."

Not only was Tiffany stunning, she had a glamorous job at a fashion magazine. She was practically a character out of my favorite old-school chick lit novels. Thank Gawd I'd killed my jealous streak, because two years ago, her past with Nicholas would have freaked me out. Now she was merely annoying. Besides, my legal day job might be less than seductive, but I was a published novelist. Then I remembered my so-far insurmountable bout of writer's block. I swallowed down my writing-related anxiety with a gulp of my drink.

"How's the planning going otherwise?" Tiffany asked.

"Making progress," Nicholas said with confidence. He told her about the cake we'd ordered two weeks earlier.

"What about a photographer?" Natalie asked.

"Done," Nicholas said.

"Invitations?" Tiffany asked.

I responded this time. "Ordered. Just waiting for them to come in from the printer." The lump in the back of my throat settled down as we continued to answer the questions in the affirmative. Maybe we weren't as behind as I feared.

"Have you registered? Where? Please don't say Crate & Barrel, Target, and Williams- Sonoma." Natalie made a sour face.

Her lips pursed, Tiffany said, "What do you have against those stores?"

I wondered the same thing. We hadn't registered at any of those places, but we hadn't registered period. I took a sip of my drink to wash down the rebounding lump.

"Dullsville," Natalie said before yawning for emphasis. "Why not do something different like ask for charitable donations in lieu of gifts? Or sign up for a gift card registry. Or ask your favorite mom and pop store if they have a registry so you can support local small business."

Nicholas smirked. "These unconventional ideas courtesy of *The Knot* too?"

Sticking her tongue out at him, Natalie said, "Buzzfeed, if you must know."

"We haven't registered yet," I said, happy for the well-timed appearance of the waitress with our appetizers. I took in the feast of sharable plates, including coconut shrimp, tamarind pork buns, and an assortment of naan. I rubbed my hands together in anticipation. "Moment of truth time. Dig in."

For the next few minutes, we were silent aside from the sounds of chewing and other noises of approval. I hoped Natalie would stop with all the wedding questions. We did need to register soon, but it wasn't going to happen in the middle of dinner.

"I think you guys should create a wedding website," Tiffany said.

I let out a deep exhalation, tempted to lower my head to the table. "I don't think—"

"Great idea," Natalie said. "It will help your guests keep track of your progress. You can even make it interactive—let them choose your wedding song."

"If I know Nicholas, the song for the first dance was chosen before he even bought the ring," Tiffany said, beaming in his direction.

Nicholas glanced at me. "We actually haven't decided—"

"Remember ours, Nicky? 'The Space Between' by Dave Matthews Band." Tiffany closed her eyes and hummed a few chords.

"Lame," Natalie muttered.

I agreed. Tiffany had singlehandedly ruined the song, and the musical group at large, for me with her sentimental musings.

"My song with Dean was 'Live Like You Were Dying.'" Natalie smiled at me. "Dean was the love of my high-school life. We went through a country music phase." Tilting her head toward Tiffany, she said, "Speaking of Dean, he friended me on Facebook."

Tiffany pursed her lips. "He did?"

Nicholas cleared his throat. "It's a bit late for a website at this point. I think we missed the boat." He squeezed my knee under the table. "Right, Kimmie?"

"It's too late for a lot of things," I muttered before shoving a piece of naan in my mouth. We'd come up with a few options for wedding songs during Hurricane Daneen, but hadn't found "the one."

"What kind of dress did you end up getting?" Natalie asked.

Tiffany nodded eagerly. "Please tell us you have pics on your phone. Nicholas can look the other way so he won't see."

Dress shopping could have been a helpful distraction from my frozen writing mojo, but I hadn't been motivated to make another attempt. I couldn't bear to tell them I had yet to make it through a successful shopping session and was still sans gown. The resulting vocalizations of horror followed by panic and pity might do me in. I swallowed the bread and stood up. "I have to use the ladies' room. Be right back." Ignoring the look of concern that crossed Nicholas's face, I excused myself and walked in the direction I assumed most likely to take me to the bathroom. But when I saw the sign for the restrooms, I kept going toward the exit of the restaurant. The back of my neck was slick with sweat and I struggled to breathe. I'd take a moment for fresh air and then return to the table ready for the second course.

I stepped outside and leaned against the building's exterior. With my eyes closed, I inhaled deeply through my nose and blew the breath out my lips. I instinctively reached into my purse and removed my phone. If I'd thought checking my email would serve to lower my stress level, it was a good thing I wasn't a betting woman. There was a message from Melina.

> *Hi Kim,*
>
> *I wanted to follow up with you regarding* Love On Stone Street. *As I mentioned in my recent email, the publisher is unable to grant an extension. Remember, the longer it takes to get it to me, the less time you'll have before the final deadline, so I hope you're working diligently.*
>
> *In the meantime, the marketing department has made the decision to reduce the second print run for* A Blogger's Life *by half. Unfortunately, this means that based on past sales and the rate of returns, they lack the confidence in future sales to print another 7500 copies. It's not horrible news, and if this run goes well, it's more than possible they'll up the number for a third, but I thought you should know.*
>
> *Please check in with any questions.*
>
> *Melina*

And there it was in fine print. *A Blogger's Life* hadn't sold enough paperbacks to warrant a complete second print run. I'd been told to keep my expectations down with respect to paperback versus e-book sales, but I thought if I wished on enough errant eyelashes, penny fountains, and whenever the clock read 11:11, I'd prove them wrong and the disappointing fates suffered by other authors would skip me.

I sat on the curb and took a deep breath. It was times like this I wished I smoked. I'd have to make do with Latin/Indian fusion food and exotic drinks. Too bad I had to do it with my busybody but well-meaning soon-to-be sister-in-law and my fiancé's ever-present first girlfriend. Alone time with Nicholas would have been better. Although he'd probably find some way to downplay this latest letdown—"Better half a print run than none, right? It means your book is selling, Kimmie!"

I rose to a standing position. I couldn't focus on both my writing and the wedding planning at the same time. First and foremost, I needed to rectify the no-dress situation. Once I did, the words would flow again. So, the next day, I would go back to Genesis Bridal by myself and make it happen. If no one was with me, there would be no distractions—no unsolicited opinions or tear-soaked confessions. And Accuweather predicted a zero chance of precipitation. It would all come together once I had the dress. This was just the black moment before the resolution.

Chapter 15

During dinner, all four of us continued to shovel food into our mouths long after the desire to unbutton our pants kicked in. This suggested the fare was up to our discerning New York City foodie standards. The service was of high quality as well. After combining these factors with the central location of the restaurant and the sleek and modern interior of the venue, Nicholas and I gave Natalie the go-ahead to reserve the space for the rehearsal dinner. We also put her in charge of the food menu, but insisted she confirm it with her mom. Otherwise, we were afraid she'd base her choices on a list of the most unconventional Indian/Latin fusion dishes she found on social media.

We were mentally and physically exhausted when we got home. A full day of work followed by hours in the company of Nicholas's sister was enough to drain the Energizer Bunny, but I was glad Natalie reminded us about registering. I'd fantasized about choosing items for my wedding registry long before I knew who I was going to marry. My stress level was at an all-time high, but there was no excuse for forgetting to register, especially since people had been inquiring about it since the save-the-date cards were sent out a month ago. Shopping was the antidote to anxiety, especially when someone else was paying. It would do me good. So, before bed, Nicholas and I settled on Williams-Sonoma, Bed Bath & Beyond, and Macy's. We were both dying to get our hands on the scanning gun, so we'd go to at least one store in-person the following weekend and if we burnt out, finish the rest online.

I felt much more in control after firming the location for the rehearsal dinner and making inroads toward registering for gifts. This, coupled with the date I planned with myself to go dress shopping after work the next day, left me feeling less anxious than I'd been over the last couple of weeks. I fell into a peaceful sleep and woke up in bright and amorous spirits. And since morning sex served to burn off those extra calories I'd consumed at dinner, I was sure to feel less bloated when I tried on dresses later.

At exactly five thirty, I left work and, with an extra bounce in my step, headed straight to Genesis Bridal. When I was a block away, my heart pounded in anticipation. I'd never imagined being alone when I bought my wedding dress. I'd always assumed, at the very least, my mom would be with me. With a hand on her heart and tears in her eyes, she'd say, "That's the dress." We'd hug, our torsos rocking from side to side, before separating. Then we'd jump up and down in glee. Later, we'd have a ladies' lunch at Serendipity or Alice's Tea Cup and toast to my upcoming nuptials with a glass of champagne. I brushed aside the wave of loneliness that rushed through my core at the image. I'd save that scenario for my own daughter. Today, my entourage would consist of me, myself, and I. With less than four months until "I do," I had no other choice.

I arrived at my destination and was halfway through the front door of the boutique when my phone rang. I let the door close, stepped back outside, and removed the device from my purse. It was Bridget. I stepped to the side. "What's up?"

"Where are you?"

"Shopping. Where are you?" She sounded far away.

"Lenox Hill. The hospital."

My heart dropped to my knees. "Oh, no. The baby. Are you all right?"

"I'm fine now, but I fainted. I've been through triage and now I'm just waiting to be seen. Can you come? I'm in the ER."

"I'm on my way." Without a second thought, I walked to the corner and hailed down a taxi. Not an easy task during rush hour, but I managed. "Where's Jonathan?" I stepped into the car and said, "Lenox Hill Hospital Emergency Room, please." I had the urge to add, "Step on it" but stopped myself. I prayed it wouldn't be a repeat of my cab experience the day of Nicholas's presentation.

"At home. I was at Lemonade when it happened. You know, that new urban-inspired baby clothing store on Lexington? If I called Jonathan, he'd wonder what I was doing there."

I peered over the front seat and out the window. Traffic was moving. *Thank God.* "You have to tell him!" I knew I shouldn't raise my voice to a hospital patient, but it was Bridget and she was infuriating.

"I know," she mumbled. "One of the shopkeepers brought me to the hospital when I came to. She paid for the cab and everything. I'm totally spending a fortune at the store later to show my gratitude."

"Is she still there?"

"No. She left after I was checked in." She paused. "Kim, the receptionist is calling me. I'll see you soon. Thanks for coming."

"Of course. You're my BFFAEUDDUP." I hung up and immediately called Jonathan. Enough was enough.

He answered after one ring. "I'm not speaking to you."

"I can tell. Listen—"

"Seriously. You promised to call me back weeks ago and never did."

"Bridget's in the—"

"She's still acting strange."

I raised my voice, hoping it would prevent him for interrupting me...again. "If you'd let me speak, you'd know I was calling to tell you Bridget's in the hospital."

Jonathan gasped. "She's what?"

"She's okay. I'm on my way to the ER at Lenox Hill. Meet me there."

There was no verbal response. Just the sound of silence on the other end of the phone.

Ten minutes later, I scanned the reception area of the emergency room for Bridget and Jonathan. I didn't see them, which hopefully meant it was a slow night and she was saved from the ridiculously long waits. I sat down on one of the uncomfortable looking chairs, removed my e-reader from my purse, and waited with my heart in my throat. Bridget insisted she was okay on the phone, but what if she wasn't? Maybe there were internal injuries that hadn't manifested into symptoms yet.

To avoid imagining the worst-case scenario, I got lost in a romantic comedy about a man and woman, complete opposites, who were forced to share the same vacation house for a week. A few minutes later, or it could have been an hour, I saw a shadow hovering over me. I closed my e-reader and stood up with wobbly knees. "How is she?"

"Bridget is fine," Jonathan said.

I opened my mouth to respond.

"And so is the baby." The venom in his voice was unmistakable. "The baby she's been carrying for more than three months."

I swallowed hard.

"I can't believe you didn't tell me. I can't believe she didn't tell me." He ran a hand through his thick locks.

"She made me promise, Jonathan. She..." When I saw Bridget approach us, I stopped talking and ran to her. "You're okay? What happened?"

Bridget offered a meek smile. "I had a hypoglycemic episode," she said before glancing at Jonathan. "He knows."

"I'm the father. I should have known months ago. But, of course, you told Kim before me. Why should I expect any different?"

Several patients looked our way. "Keep your voice down," I whispered.

Jonathan glared at me. "Don't tell me what to do," he said. With a lower voice, he turned to Bridget. "Why didn't you tell me?" The hurt reflected in his hazel eyes was gut wrenching.

Bridget shrugged, her lower lip trembling dangerously.

Facing me again, Jonathan said, "Does Nicholas know too?" He raised a hand. "Never mind. Of course he does."

"That's not the point," I said. No one said anything until the sounds of sobbing broke the silence.

"I was afraid to tell you. You don't want children. You're not just impartial or undecided on the issue. You're very absolute about it." Bridget wiped her eyes. "We agreed we weren't going to be parents and now we are."

My heart ached as I watched Bridget's eyes flit around the room nervously, never once meeting Jonathan's gaze. What did she think was going to happen? What was going to happen?

Jonathan turned to me. "Thank you for coming, Kim. But we can take it from here."

I opened my eyes wide and jutted my chin at Bridget. "Are you okay with this?"

She nodded solemnly. "Thank you so much for coming. The doctor said I need to adjust my eating habits now that I'm nurturing for two, but we're fine. He referred me to a nutritionist in my network. I need to talk to Jonathan now."

I drew her into a hug and whispered, "I had to call him, Bridge. Please don't hate me."

"Never," she whispered back. "I'll call you later."

I made my way outside and back to my apartment downtown. It wasn't until I was halfway home I remembered I still hadn't bought a wedding dress.

Chapter 16

"Start at the beginning. When did you first find out?" Caroline asked, before reaching into a bowl of assorted raw nuts on Bridget's coffee table.

Now that Jonathan was in the know, Bridget was more open about her pregnancy. She had me and Caroline over for snacks a few nights later. In keeping with her nutritionist's orders, the menu consisted of the raw nuts, a fruit and cheese platter, peanut butter and whole-wheat crackers, and caffeine-free sparkling fruit juice.

While we nibbled, Bridget caught Caroline up on everything I already knew. She was now at the part where Jonathan kicked me out of the emergency room. "I was positive he was going to yell at me," she said, covering her face with her long red hair as if embarrassed. "I'd never seen him so angry."

"It was obvious to me he was more hurt than anything else, Bridge. Although, I'm afraid there's a picture of me with dart holes piercing my face somewhere in this apartment. It's me he's mad at, not you." I took a sip of juice. I wasn't sure how I was going to make it through at least six more months of strictly non-alcoholic get-togethers with Bridget. Of course, I would never encourage her to drink during her pregnancy. I just assumed it would be years before we'd be in that position, if ever, considering their previous negative stance on children.

Bridget frowned. "He'll get over it, but I'm sorry I put you in a position to keep my secrets."

"I'd bet money he didn't yell at you. Jonathan?" Caroline scrunched her face. "No way."

I tended to agree with Caroline, but with her higher salary as Vice President of a Fortune 500 company, she could better afford to place a wager on it. I also knew much of Jonathan's calm demeanor was marijuana induced. I was pretty sure even if he'd toked up during the afternoon, being summoned to the ER followed by news of his expectant girlfriend sobered him up pretty darn quick.

"We were eerily silent on the walk back to our apartment. A million thoughts ran through my head, but I took it as a good sign when he held my hand the entire way," Bridget said.

Caroline and I nodded our agreement.

"When we arrived home, he got me settled on the couch, poured us both a cup of green tea, and said we had a lot to discuss." She closed her eyes for a beat. When she opened them, she pushed her lips together and raised her shoulders in a shrug. "In a nutshell, he said he's okay with having a baby, but he needs time to adjust to the idea because it wasn't the life he thought he'd live. He took some responsibility for me keeping it from him, given his blatant disgust for other people's babies, but ours would be different. Then he made me promise never to keep anything so important from him again."

Caroline and I locked eyes for a moment and I wondered if she was thinking the same thing as me: Jonathan was "okay" with having a baby?

As if reading my mind, Bridget said, "It wasn't the worst-case scenario I feared, but being 'okay' with having a baby is not the same as wanting it." She looked from me to Caroline with haunted green eyes. "What if he doesn't love our baby? What if he doesn't love me anymore, but is only sticking around because it's the right thing to do?" Her face contorted and she burst into tears.

I moved closer to her on the couch and pulled her close to me. Stroking her hair, I said, "Don't be silly. He loves you. He'll love both of you." I hoped I sounded more convinced than I felt.

As if on autopilot, Bridget stopped crying, removed herself from my embrace, and stood up. She wiped the corners of her eyes and clapped her hands together. "Enough about me. What's going on with you guys?"

Caroline and I exchanged curious glances we hoped were subtle enough to go unnoticed by Bridget. "Nothing new with me, but The Society of Features Journalism nominated Felix for an award." Caroline's face radiated pride at her husband's achievements.

"Awesome!" I said.

"We'll have to celebrate when he wins," Bridget said.

Caroline grinned. "Absolutely." She motioned toward me. "What's new on your end? How's the wedding planning going? Making progress on book two?"

If someone asked me the two topics of conversation I'd least like to discuss, it would be wedding planning and writing, but circling back to Bridget's problems to avoid my own would be mean. "The cake we ordered is superb. It's pink."

Bridget looked at me fondly. "Of course it is."

"What about the dress?" Caroline asked.

After everything she'd been through, I was hesitant to tell Bridget she was responsible for cutting short yet another one of my attempts to suit up for my wedding. "It's magnificent," I lied. "I don't have pictures of it with me, but I'll take some at my next fitting." I swallowed down the unease of being dishonest. Bridget had been so hurt when I lied about having dinner with Hannah the year before and I promised never to do it again. I'd tell her once she felt better about the baby. Swiftly, changing the subject, I said, "Natalie reserved a restaurant for the rehearsal dinner and shockingly, it's normal. And Nicholas and I are going to register this weekend." I instantly felt a pick-me-up from focusing on the positive. I decided to stay on the "glass is half full" course for the remainder of the evening.

"I'm so jealous," Caroline and Bridget said in unison.

"I'm not sorry I didn't have a wedding, but the whole registering process seems like fun," Caroline went on.

I smiled wryly. "I'll let you know." I spread some peanut butter on a cracker.

"And the writing is going well?"

In the instant the words slipped off Caroline's tongue, my face fell, and along with it went my intentions to focus on the positive. I let the cracker slip through my fingers and on to the plate in front of me.

Caroline's blue eyes widened. "What's wrong, Kim?"

I hesitated. I hadn't confessed to anyone, not even Nicholas, how blocked I was. They were my friends. Wasn't it in their job description to offer advice?

"Kim?" Caroline repeated.

I chewed my lip. "The truth is I'm having a bit of trouble with the writing." I went on to describe my attempts to learn from the negative reviews for *A Blogger's Life* by adding a less whimsical secondary plot to *Love on Stone Street*. "My editor and agent hated both ideas and now I'm completely stuck. It's like I lost my voice." It was the first time I'd vocalized my fear. My chest hitched and I brought a shaky hand to my forehead.

"For the non-writers in the house, what do you mean by 'lost your voice'?" Bridget asked.

I picked up my abandoned cracker and popped it in my mouth. I gathered my thoughts while I chewed and swallowed. "It's hard to describe, but until recently, my characters would speak to me almost constantly—while making copies for Rob, during sprints in spin class, sometimes even during sex."

The girls giggled.

Joining in their mirth, I said, "Don't tell Nicholas" before becoming serious again. "I could see my scenes play out in my head before I even sat down to write. Sometimes, my characters would have extended conversations on my commute to the office. If it didn't work on the page, I always came up with a better alternative. Now it's like my characters went on strike. They're ignoring me."

"Have you told Felicia?" Bridget asked.

I shook my head. "It's not her problem. She's my agent, not my shrink. I'm the writer. I need to write."

"You have to talk to someone about it," Caroline urged.

"I thought that's what I was doing." I dropped my gaze to the floor.

Caroline placed her hand over mine. "Of course, and we're happy to listen, but maybe other authors would be able to give you advice. What author hasn't experienced writer's block?"

Hannah Marshak. I thought it, but didn't say it out loud.

"Aren't there writers' groups on Facebook you can join?" she asked.

"I'm on some of them." I was a member of several Facebook groups for authors and bloggers devoted to the chick lit, women's fiction, and romantic comedy genres.

"You should post about your blockage on one of them," Caroline said. "They're all authors too. I'm sure they've been where you are and gotten through it."

"You make it sound like Kim's constipated." Bridget giggled. "But I agree with Caroline, K. I bet your fellow writers could help you."

"You're right. I will." This was another lie, but I knew the surest way to move on to a less tumultuous topic of conversation was to agree with my besties. I'd be too ashamed to tell other authors I had writer's block. What if it got back to the publisher and Felicia? Or worse, Hannah? But I'd do some lurking. Maybe another author, one clearly less worried about what others thought of her, already did the work for me.

Chapter 17

Since Caroline's past history with providing advice had a pretty decent success rate, I spent the next day at lunch scouring the chick lit author Facebook groups. If somebody requested ways to get over writer's block, I'd find it.

First I had to scroll through this week's promo posts, of which there were many, including one I'd done for *A Blogger's Life*. At least twenty people had "liked" the post and quite a few folks had commented, "I loved this book." It should have made me happy, and it mostly did. But sometimes I couldn't help but wonder if these authors truly enjoyed *A Blogger's Life* or if they were hoping to get on my good side for a future review on *Pastel Is the New Black*. Angry at myself for all the doubts I'd been letting creep into my brain and mess with my head (and writing mojo), I took an aggressive bite of my turkey and Swiss cheese sandwich. The quality of *A Blogger's Life* was not the issue, despite the handful of critical reviews. It was time to focus on the fate of *Love on Stone Street*. Moving on.

I skipped over the posts regarding free promotions and advice regarding self-publishing. Even though I was traditionally published, I usually found all these posts very interesting, but I didn't have time to waste. I kept scrolling until my eyes focused on two magical words on the screen—writer's block.

Tuesday Tips: Hi, all! What do you guys do when you're struggling with writer's block? Over the last couple of weeks, I can't get words on the page. I sit at my laptop for hours and…nothing. Any tips on this rainy (in Baltimore) Tuesday?

My heart racing, I read the comments:

Sorry you're struggling, Tanya! I find removing the pressure by taking a break really helps me. Cut yourself some slack for a few days. Watch some movies. Go shopping. Read more books (mine is on sale for 99 cents).

I'd already been on a "break" for weeks now and it didn't do shit. I couldn't afford to take this chick's advice.

I've been there. How about putting your work in progress to the side and writing something else for your eyes only? A short story, a journal entry? Anything to get you back in the groove without the pressure.

I wrinkled my nose. The handful of reviews I'd written for *Pastel Is the New Black* had done nothing to open me up creatively, but maybe it was because they weren't fiction. I hadn't tried to write anything else, like a short story or even a piece of flash fiction. I supposed it could work, although I was hesitant to use my precious free time on something I had no intention of publishing. Still, it was worth considering.

Exercise! Go for a run, take a spin class, even a brisk walk around the block. I find working up a good sweat gets my creative juices flowing.

Now we were talking. Without hesitation, I logged on to my gym's website, scrolled the classes for that night, and signed up for back-to-back spin sessions. Two cycling classes followed by, hopefully, vigorous sex with my fiancé, and my writing-related constipation would be a thing of the past. I leaned against my chair with my arms clasped behind my head and I let out a satisfied sigh. A second later, I remembered where I was, closed out of my computer, and hoofed it back to my desk. Lunch was over.

Thirty minutes into the first spin class and I was dripping in perspiration. I had my back to the one clock in the room, but I knew we were at the thirty-minute mark because a moment earlier, one guy had gotten off his bike, stretched, and walked out. In every class we'd taken together, he always left with fifteen minutes remaining. I bit back my instinct to judge his lazy exercise habits. For all I knew, he was suffering from a health ailment that precluded him from doing more than thirty minutes of cardio in one sitting. Either way, it was none of my business.

I had my butt in the seat, but at the instructor's command, I stood up to a standing flat at second position, returned to the saddle in first position, lifted myself up to second again, and transitioned back to the seat over and over again for eight counts each. I hated jumps. How was I supposed to open my mind to new plot lines if I was too busy leaping from my seat and back down again? The song ended and the instructor told us to get some water "if we needed it." Only a kangaroo rat wouldn't need water after this class. It bothered me when spin teachers shamed you for taking water. Hydrating was healthy and good for your skin.

I didn't have a single idea yet and contemplated skipping the second class, but I wanted to put my brain in the best possible position to write later. Maybe I was more tolerant to sweating than most people. If so, I couldn't quit yet. And so, I persevered. While I waited for the second class to begin, I peddled the bike with low resistance while staring at the Notes app on my phone. When inspiration didn't strike, I resolved to turn off my thoughts the entirety of the second class in case the trick was to get so lost in the workout, your brain worked undercover.

At the end of the second class, I limped home, my legs wobbling like a Weeble. I probably smelled like an open sewer on a humid summer day, but I was ready to rock and roll. I even hesitated to take a shower in case getting clean stripped away the sweat-induced creativity, but for Nicholas's sake, I took the risk.

Twenty minutes later, I sat at our kitchen nook in my pajamas with my writerly accessories—laptop opened to my document, coffee to keep me focused, and a bowl of grapes for mindless low-calorie snacking. Nicholas said he'd watch television in the bedroom so I could write with zero distractions. I hadn't told him about my paralysis, but he knew I had a deadline.

I stretched my arms out in front of me and over my head before wiggling my shoulders. It was time to get down to business. Melina didn't like the serial-killer twist I threw in to my original draft and Felicia nixed the unwanted pregnancy subplot, which begged the question, what would they like and more importantly, what would make for the best story? My mind hummed, but it wasn't with new ideas; it was to the tune of "Bad Romance" by Lady Gaga, the last song played during spin class.

I let out a frustrated sigh. I'd been quite prolific until I'd allowed Bernadette Lupone and her stupid review to stifle me. She urged me to do something awful to my characters, like what happens in "real" life. Why did I even listen to her? Had she ever written a book? I doubted it. Maybe it was best to simply give up on adding a layer of so-called realism. Felicia told me to go back to my roots. It was chick lit, after all, not *War and Peace*, and not *Gone Girl* either. I nodded to seal the decision and closed out of the latest version of the document and back to the original.

I'd modeled the style of *Love on Stone Street* on one of my favorite authors, Milly Jansell, whose books centered on an ensemble cast of characters rather than just one. *Love on Stone Street* was meant to be a take on *Romeo and Juliet*. The offspring of rival bars on Stone Street fall in love and must keep it from their parents. My main heroine, a small-town girl new to the big city, moves into an apartment over one of the competing taverns and uncovers their secret. An unflagging believer in happily-ever-after, she tries to bring the families to peace while struggling with her own romantic foibles—feelings for two different men, also members of the fighting families. Even if I removed the serial killer/unwanted pregnancy subplots, I still needed a catalyst for the main crisis. With constant reminders of the anchored December deadline, I needed to wake up my muse and fast.

I toyed with having the matriarch of one family witness the patriarch of the other family have a heart attack while smoking outside the restaurant and debate whether to leave him there or call for help. But what if Melina hated it? I couldn't risk sending her anything short of perfection at this point. Even so, I scribbled the idea in my journal. A lousy idea was better than none at all.

I closed my eyes, tapped my finger along my laptop, and visualized the setting of the novel. In my mind's eye, I pictured the narrow street and the two rival bars located across from each other on either side. As the smell of smoke tickled my nostrils, I cursed our neighbors for their nasty habit along with the architects of my apartment for building such thin walls.

My eyes flew open. Maybe a fire could break out in one of the restaurants and the owners could blame the other family for starting it as a way to put them out of business. If I went that route, I could later have the families work together to get the bar up and running again.

As I wrote down the idea, another one popped into my head—when an old cookbook goes missing, one family blames the other of breaking into their restaurant to steal their century-old recipes. I hurriedly jotted it underneath the others while another theory danced in my head. One restaurant could be burglarized with the owners pointing the finger at their rivals. Or, what if a gunman held up one restaurant and the other family called the police? The ideas came fast and furious and I quickly added them to my list before they slipped my mind.

"Kimmie?"

At the sound of my name, I looked up to find Nicholas standing above me, naked aside from his boxer shorts.

He scraped a hand through his hair and yawned. "Why are you still up?"

I shook out my aching hand. It was stained with pen ink. "Working on my book." Rubbing my tired eyes, I glanced down at my journal. My vision was blurry, but I could make out bits and pieces of words covering both sides of multiple pages.

"It's almost three in the morning. Come to bed." Without awaiting an answer, he pulled out my chair and lifted me to a standing position. "Did you make good progress?" he asked while leading me to the bedroom.

I opened my mouth to respond in the affirmative, but I clamped my lips shut before the words came out. The night felt like an out-of-body experience—storylines had poured out of me like beer at a keg party—but all I had to show for it was three pages of half-assed ideas. Now I had way too many choices and not a clue which, if any, was right for *Love on Stone Street*.

Chapter 18

Thanks to the two cycling classes the night before, I was now bleeding ideas for *Love on Stone Street*. I was anxious to settle on a scenario, but it would have to wait another day. Today, I was a participating author at an event at Stony Brook University.

An arm wrapped itself around my waist, causing my toes to lift off the ground. I glanced up from the stack of autographed copies of *A Blogger's Life* on the wood table in front of me and into the smiling green eyes of Bridget's mother.

"I didn't mean to startle you, Kim. Can I get you anything? A cup of coffee? A cookie? A stash of textbooks to take home? Educational books aren't your usual genre, but you know what they say about beggars choosing." Mrs. Donahue's wavy red hair, the same color as Bridget's, only tinged with white at the hairline, bounced as she laughed at her own joke.

I chuckled. "You've already done so much, Linda." I did a sweep of the room. "I can't thank you enough for getting me a spot at this event." A tenured professor at the university, Linda used her connections to get me a booth at the book fair sponsored by the school's MFA program. I'd give out swag, like bookmarks and keychains, and hopefully sell some books.

Linda waved me away. "As far as I'm concerned, the school should be thanking me for getting a top-tier author like you. And I have bragging rights, considering you lived in my house fifty percent of the time growing up." The apples of her fair cheeks glowed with pride.

I fought the blush creeping up my neck. "You're not biased or anything."

"Maybe this much," Linda said, indicating a small amount with her thumb and index finger. "Doors open in five. You ready?"

When I nodded my answer, Linda excused herself to work the room. Almost every booth besides mine displayed some sort of Stony Brook memorabilia, whether a red and blue banner or flag, and some of the other exhibitors wore college sweatshirts. I wondered if I was the only one who didn't attend the school.

I felt the breath from Bridget's sigh behind me and turned away from the library entrance, where people were now entering.

She rubbed her belly. "Could the bathroom be any farther away from your table? I think I have to pee again already." Frowning, she said, "I always thought pregnant women exaggerated this particular side effect." As if remembering why we were in a college library eight years after obtaining our own degrees, her eyes lit up. "It's time!" She bumped her shoulder against mine. "You excited?"

My heartbeat drummed in my chest as adrenaline soared through my bloodstream. I didn't think I'd ever get used to being on the author side of a writerly event. I hoped not. My excitement battled nerves at the reminder of my last event at the Brooklyn Book Festival, which didn't quite live up to my expectations. I brushed the negative thoughts to the side. I'd promised myself this would be a stress-free day, which meant no thinking about *Love on Stone Street* and no daytime nightmares of wearing jeans and a t-shirt to my wedding. Although the clock was ticking, I had zero desire to make yet another unsuccessful attempt to find a dress. Anyhow, this event had been planned months ago and I intended to be fully present both in body and spirit. I'd taken the day off from work and, with Bridget along for moral support, rode the Long Island Railroad to Port Jefferson, where the campus was only a short cab ride away.

I whispered, "What do you think?" out of the side of my mouth before grinning at two young college-age girls who approached my table. I held my breath as one picked up a copy of *A Blogger's Life* and read the back cover. Was I supposed to say something? I didn't want to be pushy.

The girl returned the book to the pile, smiled politely, and the two continued on their way.

"Maybe they were underwhelmed by my author photo."

"You can't win 'em all," Bridget said.

Another attendee made her approach, and determined to engage this one, I said, "Do you like romantic comedy?"

"If it's a book, I like it." She swept her long raven bangs off her face to reveal dark blue eyes the color of blueberries.

I grinned at the kindred spirit before me. Leaning forward, I said, "A girl after my own heart."

She laughed. "Did you get your MFA at Stony Brook?"

"Actually, no. My choice of dress color was totally coincidental." I gestured at the short A-line red dress I wore over black tights with a pair of black suede booties.

She gave me a closed-lip smile. "Where did you study?"

"I went to Syracuse, but I didn't pursue a writing career until much later." I blanched at my own words, hoping I didn't come across as ancient to the younger girl.

She raised a bushy eyebrow. "Isn't Syracuse more known for short story and nonfiction writers?"

I bit my lip. "To be honest, I wouldn't know. I went there for my undergrad in communications."

The girl's forehead wrinkled. "Where did you get your MFA?"

I shrugged. "I didn't."

She scrutinized me. "You're not a trained writer?"

"Her schooling is real-world experience. She's a published author with an agent and a two-book deal."

I flinched at Bridget's assertive loyalty which, as usual, bordered on aggressive. "My friend is right. I don't have an MFA, but I do have a publishing deal." I smiled, hoping to restore the light mood.

The girl cackled. "I wonder what genius chose to invite an untrained author to sign at an MFA-sponsored event."

Bridget raised her chin and thrust out her chest. "That would be my mother."

The girl gave Bridget the once-over before turning to me. "Good luck with your book," she said before walking away.

Bridget stared open mouthed at the girl's retreating back. "Jeez. Should we call Doctor Natalie to extract the girl's head from up her ass?"

"It's a tough crowd." I laughed to disguise my feelings of disenchantment with the event so far.

"Don't let her get to you." She pulled me into a hug, squeezed, and released me with a sigh. "I have to pee again." She glanced at her vintage watch. "I think my apartment might be closer to the bathroom in this place, but I'll be back before sundown. I'm positive you'll be flanked by gushing fans in no time and not even notice I'm gone."

Chances were Bridget would be as popular at a psychic convention as I was at this open house. She could predict the future about as well as I could sell a book at this place. So far, no one had done more than glance at my table before passing it by in favor of one of the neighboring booths. My discreet spying disclosed the hosts of both were Stony Brook alumni and writers of poetry and mystery respectively.

My hopes lifted when one woman stopped at my table long enough to toss a decent number of bookmarks in the red and blue tote bag gifted to all registered attendees.

"These are so cute," she said, her eyes twinkling as she attached a key chain to her own set of keys.

I bounced lightly in place. "Thank you so much. My friend Bridget designed all my swag. She's in the bathroom, but I'll pass along your compliments." I pointed at my books. "Do you, um, like chick lit by any chance?"

"Not at all!" Her freckled face turned ashen and she fiddled with her shirt sleeves. "I didn't mean for it to come out so harsh. I respect anyone who can write a novel. It's certainly more than I've accomplished as of yet. But chick lit is a little too frivolous for my tastes." She ran a hand through her long straight ash-brown hair.

My shoulders hunched. "I understand. It's not for everyone." I faked a smile.

The girl frowned, clearly seeing right through me. "I'm sorry." She removed a book from the stack. "Scratch that. The world is full of sadness. I think a happy book is exactly what I need right now." She removed her wallet from her purse. "How much is it?"

I opened my mouth to respond and clamped it shut. It was obvious the girl had no desire to read *A Blogger's Life*. I couldn't in good conscience accept a pity purchase. But I had to. I took a deep breath and let it out. "It's fifteen dollars," I said while my shaking hand autographed the inside. She handed me the cash and tucked the book into her bag before walking away. "I hope you like it!" I called after her.

"Atta girl, Kim!"

My cheeks tingled in shame as I turned around to face Bridget.

She shook her head at me in amusement. "A sale is a sale is a sale."

Later, over an early dinner at a local diner, Linda tried to take full responsibility for my crash and burn. "I should have realized an MFA event would be populated by a bunch of book snobs."

"Like you, Mom?" Bridget asked with a smirk.

Linda pointed a sweet potato fry at Bridget. "I can appreciate the merits of genre fiction. I have the entire Jason Bourne collection." She turned to me. "And I thoroughly enjoyed *A Blogger's Life*. You don't need formal training when you have innate talent like you." She took a bite of her veggie burger, swallowed, and wiped her mouth with a napkin. "You would have killed it at the general student fair. I'll see if I can get you a table at the next one. If my grandchild is born by then, I might stay home and babysit while you support Kim." She looked at Bridget hopefully. "Yes?"

Bridget grinned. "You can babysit your grandchild whenever you want, Mom."

I smiled at the two of them. Bridget's reluctance to tell Jonathan she was pregnant did not spill over to her parents. They were, as expected, thrilled with the news.

Linda turned to me. "It's settled then. I'll check the event calendar and get back to you."

"Thank you, Linda." I stabbed my fork into a pancake and dipped it into syrup. As I swallowed it down like a lump of coal, I sort of hoped Linda wouldn't pull more favors for me. So far, I was zero for two for successful writing events. I didn't like my odds for a third.

Chapter 19

THREE MONTHS UNTIL "I DO"

It was the following Saturday and I was itching to finish *Love on Stone Street* and knock down the wall between being a one-hit wonder and a tried and true author. But if Nicholas and I didn't complete our bridal registry soon, we might end up with ugly or mismatched china patterns or things we'd use once and toss in the closet, like a panini press or ice-cream maker.

A day of shopping would also do wonders for my psyche and I couldn't wait to share the day with Nicholas, picking out goodies for our kitchen, bed, bath, and beyond. I'd tossed most of my college leftovers, mostly cheap items from IKEA or Walmart, when I moved in with him, but his style was a bit too contemporary for my liking. I preferred a more modern country style. This was our opportunity to choose kitchen appliances, glassware, cookware and more to fit our combined preferences. Maybe successful shopping for housewares would inspire me to make another attempt to buy a dress.

Both Natalie and Erin had emailed me The Ultimate Registry Checklist from *The Knot*. Erin urged me to choose the basics, like a food processor, toaster, and hand mixer, while Natalie oohed and aahed over the waffle iron and juicer. They both agreed a slow cooker could change my life. I didn't plan on turning into Martha Stewart, Giada de Laurentiis, or Rachael Ray the minute Nicholas slipped the wedding ring on my finger, but I was curious what even my limited skills could do with a slow cooker. Maybe it could also help Nicholas channel his inner Gordon Ramsay. Nicholas concurred and so, when we arrived at Williams-Sonoma for our appointment, it was the first item we selected. After that, we moved on to the basics.

I was poised to scan a Calphalon Elite nonstick ten-piece cookware set to our list when Nicholas removed the scanner gun from my hand. Frowning at him, I said, "It's my turn. You scanned the ceramic storage containers." In the interest of fairness, we decided to take turns controlling the device.

"I know. I was thinking maybe we should splurge for the fifteen-piece set." His brown eyes dilated with appliance lust as he scrutinized the larger set.

"We only have a handful of guests rich enough to buy us the big-ticket items, like your Aunt Wendy and Uncle Bill. I'd rather save those selections for things we'll really use. We're already pushing it with ten pieces. Seriously, we're not exactly grooming for our own show on The Food Network." I resumed power of the scanner and zapped the ten-piece set. "I like these," I said, pointing at a five-piece place-setting set with tortoise shell-inspired handles.

Nicholas patted the pair of sunglasses tucked into his Jim Morrison t-shirt. "Is matching flatware to eyewear a new trend?"

"I read it in *The Knot*," I deadpanned.

He rolled his eyes before taking a closer examination of the utensils. "You like?"

"Yes." I pushed out my lips and batted my eyelashes.

"Fine by me." He removed the scanner from my hand and entered the selection.

I went to grab the device for my next turn, but Nicholas was too busy staring at something over my shoulder. "What?" I turned around to see what had him in a trance.

He pulled me to where an assortment of wine refrigerators were housed a few feet away. He checked the price tag on a sixteen-bottle wine refrigerator. "Too much?"

I glanced at the cost and back at him. "Remember when I said we had to save the more expensive items for things we'll really use?"

His brown eyes sad with longing, Nicholas mumbled, "Yes" in a grudging tone.

I bumped my shoulder against his as my lips slowly curled up. "This is what I was talking about. We'll definitely use this wine fridge." Motioning toward the device in my hand, I said, "Shall we do this one together?"

Nicholas grinned. "I chose very wisely."

"The wine fridge?"

He bent down and kissed my nose. "My future wife."

We were already in a lip lock when we re-entered our apartment six hours later. The promise of new bed and bath accessories and kitchen appliances was the ultimate aphrodisiac because, even after a lovely lunch at The Smith, we had a tremendous appetite for each other's bodies. Leaving a trail of our clothes in our wake, we fell into bed and came together in the perfect climax to a successful day of shopping.

Afterward, Nicholas snuggled into me. "I love you, Kimmie."

I sighed against him. "I love you more."

We lay there for a few minutes in contented silence. If I knew Nicholas, he was thinking about the Audio Techna Turntable and showerhead speaker he chose for his personal "all about him" selections at Beth, Bath & Beyond after we left Williams-Sonoma. We'd allowed each other up to two items in the "all about me" category. I was imagining how my pick, an invisible bookshelf, would look in the corner of the living room next to the piano versus the bathroom, and how I could even convince Nicholas to allow a bookshelf in the loo. Picturing other authors' books in my bathroom woke up my temporarily dormant worries about my own unfinished book and I sat up.

"Where are you going?" Nicholas pulled me back down.

Nuzzling his neck, I said, "I'd love to cuddle all day, but I have so much to do. Words to write. Drafts to finish." So far, it had been an idyllic morning and afternoon. I was confident my good vibrations would continue into my evening writing session and wanted to get started even if it meant abandoning Nicholas in bed. I sat back up, pushed the covers off my body, and swung my legs over the edge of the bed.

Nicholas followed my lead. "I have a few errands to run anyway." He stood up and scratched his head. "Is it just me or are you craving Mexican food?"

"It's just you." I chuckled.

"You'll be singing a different tune when you get a whiff of my queso dip and homemade guacamole later. I'll go find my clothes in the living room and head out. I'll be back in an hour or so. Happy writing."

"Thanks, sweets." When I heard the front door close a moment later, I threw on a pair of yoga pants and a t-shirt and fired up my laptop in the living room.

The first order of business was choosing a direction for the main conflict. I worried the heart-attack angle was too easy. Who besides an evil person would witness a heart attack and walk away without calling for help? But if she saved his life, it might be too convenient.

If I went with the fire, I'd probably want to interview some of New York's bravest to make sure I got my facts straight. As appealing as it sounded, it wouldn't be cool to pop into a firehouse and request an interview on the spot. What if the firemen were busy putting out fires? I didn't really have time to set up a formal appointment.

The break-in idea could be fun, but it felt familiar. It was possible it came from a Hallmark Movie or even another book I'd read. I'd make it my own, but it was easy ammunition for readers to slam me in reviews as being "unoriginal."

I let my head swing back and whimpered. Time was ticking away, and on a scale of one to ten, my progress was a negative fourteen.

My phone rang—Erin. A distraction, even an annoying one like my sister, was welcome. "Hi."

"How did things go with the bridal registry? Did you pick a slow cooker?"

My lips curled up. "I did."

"I hope you chose the Cuisinart MSC-600 and not the PSC-350."

"I don't remember, but I can check later."

"Are you going to text me a picture of your dress?"

I had no idea who informed Erin a dress had been bought—it certainly wasn't me—but I wasn't going to set her straight right now. "I...um..." Our landline rang. "I need to call you back." I hurried to the kitchen and picked up the old-fashioned rotary phone on the counter. "Hello?"

"Is Nicholas around?"

The voice sounded familiar and my body temperature rose. "Tiffany? What do you want with Nicholas?"

"I, uh, I can't find Natalie and thought Nicholas might know where she was."

"Have you called the hospital? Maybe she's on call."

"Great idea! Thanks, Kim." The sound of a dial tone told me she'd hung up.

I rubbed my temples and shook out my shoulders to release some stress. The Tiffany issue was edging beyond annoying to completely out of control. I didn't buy the reason for her call. She'd use any excuse to talk to my honey. If Nicholas didn't tell Natalie to insist Tiffany lay off my man soon, I would do it myself.

If I was a nice sister, I'd call Erin back, but I had no idea what I'd tell her when she asked about my gown. I buried my head in my hands. How was it possible I was getting married in three months and didn't have a dress yet? I was the girl who bought three dresses for my senior prom because I couldn't choose between black, hot pink, or multi-colored sequins. (I went with the sequins.) If only I could do the last six months over again, complete with a successful appointment at Kleinfeld and a finished manuscript that I loved. Instead, I was in danger of wearing off the rack from Burlington and all I had to show for my writing efforts was an uncompleted and crappy first draft and an editor who probably hated my guts. My phone rang again—my mom.

"Hi, Mom," I said, sinking my back into the couch cushion.

"How are you, sweetheart?"

"I'm good." My lips trembled at my lie and I made an instant decision to tell my mother I was on the verge of a nervous breakdown. Even a shopping spree followed by multiple orgasms courtesy of my loving fiancé didn't undo the fact that I didn't have a wedding dress or a semblance of a completed manuscript. Ever since middle school, my mom had the ability to talk me off the ledge like no one else. "Actually, I'm not—"

"I'm sorry I've been so out of touch. Things have been a little hectic here and I didn't want to worry you."

She paused for a beat and I automatically worried.

"We had to take your dad to the neurologist," she continued.

I sat up straight. "What's wrong with Dad?"

"He's been having some short-term memory issues and they

wanted to run some tests. It could be anything, vitamin deficiency, sleep apnea, stress..."

My heart slammed against my chest in alarm. "Mom? What aren't you telling me?"

She sighed. "There's a slight possibility it could be early onset dementia, but the doctor thinks it's unlikely based on his symptoms and the lack of a family history for the disease, so please don't worry, Kim. I'm only telling you because I know I haven't been as involved in your wedding planning as I should be and it's breaking my heart. You're my baby and I hate that I'm not here for you."

I heard her choke out a sob and a piece of my own heart broke off. "You're always here for me. Right now, Dad is more important. Is he there?" My dad would never win an award for most demonstrative father, but I knew he adored me and I had an overwhelming urge to tell him I loved him.

"He's actually at a Marlins game—community road trip. See? He's fine. He didn't want me to tell you, but I needed you to know why I've been the worst mother of the bride in history." She sniffled.

"Nonsense." I hadn't even noticed her lack of involvement, probably because I was the worst bride-to-be in history.

"I was so relieved when Erin told me you got a dress. Did Bridget and Caroline take you shopping? I'm sure it's stunning."

I gulped. "It is." After what my mother had told me about my dad, I couldn't add to her stress by telling the truth.

"I'm so glad. We'll fly up there the second we get the green light from the doctor that your dad is okay. I know he will be."

"Me too." I closed my eyes and said a silent prayer for my dad.

"I'll call you soon."

After we hung up, I gazed at my computer screen, but all I saw was my dad. He used to read to me when I was a little girl. My favorite books were the *Winnie the Pooh* series. He'd use distinct voices for Christopher Robin, Pooh, Tigger, and Piglet and I'd sit on his lap on the rocking chair in my room and listen in awe. I'd get so lost in the story, I'd forget where I was.

I took a deep breath. Whatever was going on with my father wouldn't be solved this afternoon, and *Love on Stone Street* wouldn't write itself. It was time to get back to business and my list of potential plot twists. I twisted a strand of hair around my finger and pondered my choices. If Melina nixed the serial killer idea, she might also be opposed to the gunman angle. Maybe she had a thing against weapons.

I tapped my fingers absently along the keyboard until I found myself staring at the Amazon page for *A Blogger's Life*. Holding my breath, I read the latest review.

Two stars: Vapid and Boring

They live happily ever after. Now you don't have to waste your time the way I did.

By Gail Bridges on August 2nd

My shoulders dropped and I let out a moan. I put my soul into writing and revising *A Blogger's Life* within an inch of its life and yet readers still hated on it. Was I wasting my time? I covered my head with a pillow as a waterfall of tears perched dangerously at the back of my throat. When my phone rang again, I tossed the pillow aside and glanced at the caller ID. It was the Soho Grand. I couldn't speak to them in this condition and ignored the call. The device pinged and I assumed it was a notification of a voicemail, but it was a text from Erin: If you're too busy to call me back, at least text me a picture of your dress. Who's the designer? Has Natalie seen it yet?

"Leave me alone," I whined. The front door opened and Nicholas walked in. When he saw me, he stopped whistling to the tune of "Penny Lane" and smiled. "Lucy, I'm home."

Desperate to bury myself in his arms and stay there in perpetuity, I hurled myself off the couch and ran to him until I noticed the large box he was holding. "What do you have there?" The heaviness in my chest told me I didn't want to know the answer.

"Our invitations. The doorman stopped me on the way in." He grinned. "Once these go out, there's no turning back. Unless you leave me at the altar, but you wouldn't do that to me, would you?" He pushed out his lower lip playfully.

"Never." My voice broke on the word, and my vision blurred with tears. I wiped them away, but new ones took their place. It was all too much.

"What's wrong, Kimmie?" He placed the box of invitations on the kitchen nook and took a step closer to me.

Even through my tears, I could see my morose reflection in his big brown eyes and could only imagine what he was thinking. He was obviously not expecting this reaction to the arrival of our wedding invitations. I opened my mouth to wash away his concern, but the words wouldn't come. The air got stuck in my throat and I couldn't catch my breath. "I can't...breathe..."

Nicholas placed his hand on the small of my back and steered me to the couch. "There, there. Take it easy. It will be fine. Breathe slowly through your nose." Patting my back in small circles, he said, "It's gonna be okay."

While I attempted to regain my bearings, I studied Nicholas's gorgeous face, wanting more than anything to believe him. But I didn't. "It's not. I've made a mess of everything."

He crinkled his brow. "What do you mean?"

My lips trembled. "We can't have a wedding in three months!" I shook my head vigorously to emphasize my point. "Unless you want me walking down the aisle while I'm wearing my birthday suit and carrying a bouquet of weeds I pulled from a public green space." I wiped my running nose. "With my luck it would be poison ivy." Even with the perfect dress and beautiful flowers, it wouldn't be right if my dad wasn't well. I resumed shaking my head and muttered to myself, "I can't do it. I can't plan a wedding right now. And I don't want to write anymore either. I'm done." Without a reception to organize or a book to write, I could be free of all the stress wearing me down. I could be me again. If the underwhelming response to my book at Stony Brook was any indication, Author Kim wouldn't be missed.

I looked up at Nicholas, whose eyes had welled up. My heart shattered at the sight. "I'm sorry, Nicholas. I absolutely want to be your wife, but we can't send out those invitations." Before he could respond, I jumped off the couch and ran into the bedroom, slamming the door behind me.

I crawled into bed and buried myself under the covers even though it was about eighty degrees outside. I just wanted to sleep, but I was kept awake by the sound of someone weeping. It was only when

Nicholas curled his body around mine and chanted, "It's going to be okay" in a soothing voice over and over again I realized the sobs were coming from my own mouth.

Chapter 20

Nicholas let me sleep through Saturday night and most of Sunday. He probably figured my decision to call off the wedding and quit writing was a result of exhaustion and I'd change my mind once I had a good nap. The truth was, even though I only left the bed to go to the bathroom and occasionally nibble on the snacks Nicholas left for me on the nightstand, I was wide awake as often as I was asleep. I let Nicholas think I was out of it because I couldn't look at him without wanting to do bodily harm to myself for the pain I was putting him through. It wasn't his fault I was weak. And despite his last name, he didn't have the strength to lift me out of the mess I'd created. Eventually, we'd need to inform the bridal party of our decision and cancel the vendors we'd reserved, but I needed more time. Since we'd just registered, we wouldn't have many (if any) gifts to return, and hopefully, my parents could get the deposit back from the Soho Grand. Even at this late date, I was certain such a sought-after venue would be able to book another event for the night of our wedding. Maybe they'd let us use it to reserve a date in the future, when we were in a better place to throw a celebration.

My limbs were sore from lack of movement, but I was afraid Nicholas would pounce on me with questions if I joined him in the living room. Instead, I got out of bed and walked up and down the length of the bedroom to allow for blood flow. When I heard the front door close, I assumed Nicholas had gone out for a run or to pick something up at the store and took the opportunity to dash to the kitchen. I was parched. I stuck my head in the refrigerator, trying to decide if I wanted water, iced tea, or a glass of vodka on the rocks.

"You're up."

My muscles went rigid and I froze in place. Why was he back so soon?

"You know how I enjoy stating the obvious."

The tone of his voice was light, but I knew it was a cover. I closed my eyes and blew a stream of air out of my mouth before facing him. "Hi." I swallowed hard. I couldn't remember the last time I was tongue tied around Nicholas. It was probably after the first time we broke up, when I accused him of not taking me seriously and couldn't find the words to apologize for my misjudgment.

"Are you ready to talk now?" He motioned toward the couch in the living room and I reluctantly followed him and sat down.

"What do you want to talk about?" I stared down at the pink nail polish on my toes. Sure, I was playing dumb, but it was possible he didn't want to discuss the breakdown I had the night before. Maybe he'd tell me the location of George's next marathon. George had run close to twenty already, including ones in Paris and Israel. Or perhaps there'd been a development with respect to his promotion.

Nicholas chuckled. "I don't know. Maybe the weather or what you want to eat for dinner. Or, how's this for scintillating conversation, why don't you tell me why you've changed your mind about marrying me?"

I gasped and looked up at him. "I haven't!" I was desperate to be Kimberly Michelle Strong. Mrs. Nicholas Strong.

Nicholas raised his palms up and gaped at me. "So what's this about canceling the wedding?"

"We don't have to call it off, but maybe we can postpone?" I looked at him pleadingly.

Nicholas placed a hand on my leg. "Talk to me, Kimmie."

The most pressing issue was my dad. I told Nicholas about his memory loss. "What if he's not all right, Nicholas?" A chill ran through my body and I hugged myself to keep from shaking.

Nicholas blew out a breath and assumed a thoughtful expression. Rubbing my back, he said, "I'm so sorry you have to deal with this, but please don't jump to conclusions. I know it's easier said than done, but I agree with your mom. You shouldn't let your imagination run wild. It's probably why your parents didn't tell you until now. If they knew you were postponing the wedding before you had all the facts, they'd feel awful." He scooted closer to me.

I bit my lip. It was true my parents would hate for me to postpone the wedding, but it didn't mean it wasn't the right thing to do. "What about a dress?" The cards were stacked against us in more ways than one. Nicholas had to agree the odds weren't in our favor with respect to a November wedding.

"Go shopping."

My eyes bugged out. "Are you for real? 'Go shopping?' You don't think I've tried?" I held up a finger. "The first time, my overzealous entourage forgot I was in the room. If you recall, you're the one who encouraged me to escape the madness." I held up a second finger. "Then my maid of honor had a breakdown over her unplanned pregnancy." I raised three fingers. "Then Hurricane Daneen came flying in on her broomstick." I stopped to let out a breath. "And then Bridget wound up in the hospital. I'm afraid the fashion police has issued a restraining order between me and anything resembling a white dress."

Nicholas's eyes twinkled and I could see his lips start to curl up, but he caught himself before doing something stupid like grinning at my misfortune. Or maybe my clenched fists scared him away. "Let's go shopping right now. Screw the whole 'it's bad luck to see the bride in her dress' bullshit. If the bad-karma police make an appearance, I'll let them arrest me instead."

Conflicting emotions surged like a storm in my heart. I so loved the man sitting next to me, but it wasn't enough. "Even if I found a dress today, alterations alone can take longer than the time we have left. We still need flowers. We haven't even decided on a menu! It's too much." My head felt like it was going to explode from the constantly growing to-do list it had been housing over the last several months coupled with the news about my dad.

"We can get Sarah on the phone right—"

I waved him away. It wasn't worth his energy to try to talk me out of it. "I take full responsibility. If I'd been more realistic about my capabilities, we wouldn't be in this position. But little Kim Long, as Hannah likes to call me, took a bigger bite than she could swallow. I made *Pastel Is the New Black* into a smashing success, but was it good enough for me? No. Silly me had to prove to everyone that Hannah Marshak didn't hold the monopoly on published authors from Liberty High School. But the joke's on me because *A Blogger's Life* is vapid and boring and my new novel is…" I fought to come up with the words to describe *Love on Stone Street*, but nothing came to me, unsurprising considering my writer's block.

Nicholas cocked his head to the side. "What's up with your book?"

"I'm finished."

His face lighting up, Nicholas said, "That's amazing! I knew you could do it. You can do anything you put your mind to." He placed a finger under my chin. "Including finding the perfect wedding dress in three months."

I shook my head. "You misunderstood me. The book isn't finished, but my writing career is and so is our November wedding. I'm sorry, Nicholas. I can't do it."

Nicholas studied my face for a moment like he was waiting for me to change my mind or at least explain myself better. He must have given up because without a word, he stood up and walked out of the living room toward the entrance of our apartment.

To his back, I asked, "Where are you going?"

Without turning around, he said, "Out for a walk. I need to think."

As my eyes filled with tears, I wondered if my writing career and wedding weren't the only things that were finished. I returned to the refrigerator and removed the bottle of Tito's Vodka from the back. A liquor-induced stupor was very tempting, but I knew my problems would still be there when my buzz faded, along with a nasty hungover. And, besides, I already had enough issues and couldn't afford to add "alcoholic" to the list. Instead, I grabbed a bag of Lay's Classic Potato Chips and a bottle of water and went back to the bedroom. I no longer had to worry about fitting into a wedding dress.

I was still in bed with a now-empty bag of chips when I heard Nicholas come home hours later. I was reading a great romantic comedy about two complete opposites vying for the same job and falling in love in the process. The novel was the perfect escape from my own cataclysm of an existence, and unless the author did something over the top, like throw in a serial killer or a pro-choice vigilante, it would be getting five pink champagne flutes from *Pastel Is the New Black*.

"Hi, baby," I said when Nicholas entered the room. The words came out so quietly, I wasn't even sure I said them out loud. I put my e-reader on the night stand.

"Hey," Nicholas murmured in an equally hushed tone while getting undressed.

"Where were you?" I'd assumed he went out for drinks with George or another friend to blow off some steam, but he didn't seem (or smell) like he'd been drinking.

"Nowhere." He slipped under the sheet and reached over to turn off the lamp on his nightstand. "I wish you'd talk to me, Kim. We can get through this."

I choked back a sob. I wanted so badly to believe him, but the weight of it all was crashing down on me. "I don't see a way to make this better. I'm sorry."

"So am I." He sighed and flipped over with his back to me. "Goodnight."

I was overcome with an urge to wrap my body around his, but I didn't give in. Instead, I reached over, turned off the light on my side of the bed, and curled into the fetal position. With our backs facing each other, we were a textbook image of a couple with negative body language.

Chapter 21

The next day, I went straight to Ground Support after work. Only this time, it wasn't to work on my novel; it was to draft an email to Felicia telling her I needed to opt out of my publishing contract.

Dear Felicia,

I'm so very sorry, but I'm not going to be able to produce the second book of my contract by the deadline. As you know from reading it, Love on Stone Street *is nowhere near publishable quality. I'm afraid I just don't have the* jen ne sais quoi *to write an engaging*

I stopped typing before completing the sentence—*Jen ne sais quoi?* I sounded like Hannah. Only she'd never find herself in this predicament. I let out a dejected sigh and deleted the last sentence of the email. I'd probably be penalized for breaching my publishing contract, but I had no idea in what way. The publisher had only delivered a third of my advance for the second book. They'd pay me another third when I turned in the manuscript and the final third would be paid on the publication date. I assumed I'd have to return the five thousand dollars I'd already received, but could I be subject to additional damages for pain and suffering, or more likely, wasting their time? It wasn't an arrestible charge, was it? Nicholas would know, but he'd left for work before I even woke up. If I asked Rob, it would open up a line of questioning I wasn't prepared to answer. I could say I was asking for a friend, but was anyone ever really asking for a friend? I doubted it. I scanned the space of the crowded coffee shop. I wondered if any of the millennials, hipsters, generation Xers, or aging baby boomers in line or sitting at the neighboring tables were lawyers.

My chest was tight with guilt at taking the chicken's way out of telling Felicia. The honorable thing would be to call her on the phone or even set up an appointment to meet with her in person.

Communicating via email wasn't only cowardly; it was unprofessional and mean. Felicia had been the dream agent—kind, patient, and encouraging. And here I was gearing up to send her a Dear John letter to part ways. Would she be considered in breach of contract with Fifth Avenue Press by association? I bit my lip and deleted the entire email.

My phone rang—Bridget. I was tempted to ignore it. If I didn't talk to her, I wouldn't have to tell her the wedding was postponed. Although she might be relieved since she was afraid she'd look too fat in the pictures. But the world didn't revolve around me and my problems and if something happened to Bridget or the baby, I needed to know immediately. If Jonathan didn't rise to the occasion, I'd practically be a surrogate father. I answered the phone. "Hey, Bridge."

"Are you busy?"

I sat up straighter in my chair at the panicked pitch of her voice. "I'm at the coffee shop. What's wrong?"

"You're writing? I thought..." She cleared her throat. "I hope it's going well."

"Not exactly." My face flushed with warmth. I had no desire to get into it now. "Never mind about me. What's up?"

"Can you come over? Things aren't going well with Jonathan." She sniffled. "We need to have a rap session and I want you there as a witness in case things get ugly."

I frowned into the phone. "You think he's going to yell at you?"

"Or worse. Please, Kim. I'm scared."

Had I been so wrapped up in my own problems I didn't realize Bridget could be in danger? I'd known Jonathan for almost twenty years and there had never been a violent bone in his body. Then again, people could change, or maybe the news of Bridget's pregnancy had woken up a latent demonic tendency that had been there all along. My heart raced at the thought. "When do you need me?"

"Now?"

"On it." I logged off my computer, tossed my purse over my shoulder, and hoofed it onto the street and into a waiting cab. If Jonathan was going to cause physical harm to my best friend and her unborn child, he'd have to do it over my dead body.

Chapter 22

Fifteen minutes later, I arrived at Bridget's building. I waved to the doorman, Joseph, and proceeded to the elevator. Once inside, I sent Bridget a text letting her know I was on my way up. Since I'd lived with Bridget and Jonathan for a week the previous year during my break from Nicholas and had spent so much time there over the years, the doormen rarely bothered to inform Bridget I was there. I wanted to give her a chance to warn me if I needed to arm myself before entering. As the elevator doors opened on her floor, she texted me back. "The door is unlocked."

I took a deep breath and stepped into the apartment. My eyes immediately latched onto Bridget, where she sat on her purple couch. At the sight of Caroline sitting next to her, my muscles relaxed marginally. If she wasn't such a whiz in business, Caroline would have made a stellar psychologist and could probably tame a lion. She was a welcome addition to our line of defense.

When I reached the couch, Caroline stood up and gave me a hug. During our embrace, I whispered, "I'm so glad to see you."

We separated and I turned to Bridget, who was still seated. "Did I miss anything?"

Bridget shook her head and bounced her knee. "We were waiting for you to start."

"Where is he?" I whispered.

"I'm right behind you," Jonathan said.

I whipped my head around and faced him. It was hard to reconcile that the man standing before me with a can of PBR in his hand was the same boy I loved in high school. As his hazel eyes did a sweep of my face, he looked sad and I wondered if he knew what I was thinking. I frowned, torn between a desire to hug the insanity out of him and an urge to kick him in the nuts.

He took a gulp of beer and motioned to the couch. "You should sit down."

Taken aback by his cocky attitude, I put my hands on my hips and turned to Bridget with a questioning gaze. "Who's running this show anyway?"

Jutting her chin toward the computer in front of Caroline, Bridget said, "You still there, Pia?"

"My Pia?" Why would my associate reviewer be involved in a heated discussion about Jonathan and Bridget?" A chill ran through my body. "What's going on?"

Bridget chewed on her lip. "I lied to you before."

My mouth fell open.

"I didn't call you over to discuss..." She darted a look toward Jonathan. "We're all here for you. This is an intervention."

My breath hitched. "A what?"

"We're worried about you," Caroline said. She pointed at the couch. "Come sit."

I backed up a step. "You guys are crazy. I'm going home."

Caroline stood up and approached me. "Please, Kim. Hear us out." She reached out her hand to mine.

My eyes watered, but I took her hand and allowed her to lead me to the couch. I couldn't make eye contact with any of them. I was too hurt. And I was angry. I paid twenty dollars to get here as fast as possible because I feared what Jonathan might do to his lover and unborn baby. Had I known it was a fabrication, I would have taken the subway and paid $2.75. Better yet, I wouldn't have come at all.

Caroline placed a hand on my thigh. "We know you're worried about your father."

I twiddled a strand of hair around my finger, pulling until it hurt. Without looking at her, I said, "Who told you that?"

"Nicholas," Bridget said. She drew me into a hug. "Your dad will be fine. I'm sure of it."

My lips trembled. "What if he's not?"

"Don't go there yet. You'll make yourself sick," Caroline said. "Nicholas also said you don't want to write anymore. Is it because of your writer's block? I'm sure it happens to all authors."

"I hope this isn't about what happened at Stony Brook. Even my mom said the lackluster response to *A Blogger's Life* had nothing to do with your books and everything to do with the snooty attendees," Bridget said.

"You've worked so hard to get where you are. You can't give up when you're so close to becoming the next Sophie Kinsella," Pia said.

I kneeled in front of the computer and gave Pia a timid smile. "I'm afraid I'm more cut out for reading than writing."

"And what's this about calling off the wedding?" Bridget asked, her eyes wide.

Jonathan stood before me. "What's wrong with you, Long? Nicholas is total husband material."

Bridget giggled and we shared a smile. Apparently, Jonathan's bro-crush on Nicholas was capable of amusing me even in the throes of an intervention. "I still want to marry him. It's the wedding I can't handle. Not in three months, at least."

Bridget and Jonathan's buzzer rang from the lobby.

"I'll get it," Jonathan said.

Bridget and Caroline exchanged a look. "Once we're all here, we'll get started," Bridget said.

"Who else is coming? Nicholas?" I suspected he'd spent the prior afternoon talking about me to my friends and hoping I'd be more open to discussion with them than I was with him. I was certain there was nothing they could say to change my mind, but I was trapped.

"It's not Nicholas," Bridget said.

The doorbell rang and Jonathan went to let in whoever it was.

Something pungent curdled in my core like spoiled milk. "Please don't tell me it's Natalie and Tiffany." I had a feeling Tiffany would actually encourage me to call it quits with Nicholas—return the ring, move out of our apartment, the works—so she could have him to herself. She was the last person I wanted to see.

Or so I thought until Hannah Marshak strutted into the living room and stood before me with her hands on her slender hips. Before I knew what was happening, she leaned down and kissed me on both cheeks. I inhaled her orchid-scented perfume as she wagged a forest green-painted finger at me. "For someone so little, you sure know how to make big trouble, don't you, Kimmie?" She was wearing black shorts that flattered her long tan legs, a red top, and Tory Burch black classic ankle-strap sandals. Her raven hair was held back in a smooth long ponytail and with just a touch of makeup on her large hazel eyes, she looked prettier than I'd ever seen her. At least writing professionally was good for someone's appearance. I could swear the dark spots under my own eyes had become more prominent in the last six months.

My jaw dropped. "What are you doing here?" I turned to Bridget and whispered, "What is she doing here?"

Hannah rolled her eyes. "I can hear you."

"I called her," Bridget said.

I continued to gape at Bridget, silently willing her to explain herself.

She shrugged. "I'm afraid she's the only one who can talk sense into you on the writing front."

"Me and your ginger-haired sister from another mother can finally agree on something." Hannah smirked at Bridget and acknowledged Jonathan with a jut of her chin. Then she noticed Caroline, who was still sitting on the couch, seemingly entranced by the production playing out in front of her. Extending a hand, she said, "I'm Hannah Marshak, although you might recognize me from the picture on the back of my books. I write the Paris Couture series."

Caroline introduced herself and stood up. "Your reputation precedes you."

Hannah flipped her ponytail. "Thanks." She looked up at Caroline and blinked. "You're tall."

Caroline scrunched up her face. "I'm five foot eight."

Hannah turned to me with a prominent wrinkle in her forehead. "I didn't know you had any tall friends."

Jonathan groaned. "Let's move on, shall we?"

"Fine." Hannah waved her hand. "Strawberry Shortcake called me yesterday, told me about your voice going on strike, and I've come to save the day—again."

I frowned at her. Again?

Hannah sighed dramatically. "Must I remind you of all the times I swooped in and saved your ass? Does 'The Shitter' ring any bells? Or how about when I singlehandedly got your book off the slush pile by personally handing it to Felicia? And let's not forget, you never would have dated Jonathan back in high school if I hadn't played matchmaker." She gave Bridget a once-over. "And if Kim hadn't dated him then, you probably wouldn't be with him now and pregnant." Her eyes bugged out. "You're pregnant!" She wiggled her nose. "Either that or you're in desperate need of a better core workout. I know some ace trainers if you want a referral."

Her atrocious bedside manner aside, there was more than a morsel of truth in what Hannah said, at least the part about giving me the goods on Daneen and making the intro to Felicia. Still, I didn't see a point in baring my soul to her. Even the girl who managed to out the brightest student in our sophomore class as a kleptomaniac couldn't help me now. She'd probably laugh and tell me I was "cute" for trying to be an author, but I should go back to writing my little blog and give *A-line in the Sand* a five-pink-champagne-flutes review while I was at it.

"I don't have all day, Long," Hannah said while examining her nail beds.

"Tell her," Caroline urged.

When I met Bridget's eyes, she gave the slightest nod of encouragement. In a split second, I saw a montage of all the times the two of us had gone head to head with Hannah when we were kids. For Bridget to call upon the mean girl now meant she was desperate to help me. Considering the embarrassment I already felt over Hannah being witness to my "intervention," I didn't have much more to lose.

I told her everything, from the multiple reviews citing *A Blogger's Life* as cavity-inducing in its sweetness, to my unsuccessful attempts to avoid the same in *Love on Stone Street*, to the death of my writing mojo even after a visit to a bookstore, and finally to the two hours on a spin bike that resulted in an overabundance of ideas and a paralyzing fear they all sucked. I even admitted to the lackluster response to my participation at the Stony Brook Book Fair. I left out the part about the publisher cutting my print orders in half. Even in my vulnerable state, I wasn't comfortable sharing less than mind-blowing sales numbers with Hannah. When I was finished, I channeled my inner tall girl and forced myself to take whatever ridicule Hannah threw my way.

"You want to quit writing all because some troll called your book 'vapid and boring'?" She shook her head back and forth. "I'm disappointed in you."

I knew this was a mistake. I'd confided in her and all she took from it was "vapid and boring." "Were you even listening to me?"

"I was, and I have flawless auditory skills, but I still call bullshit." She gawked at me. "I've known you a very long time and I can't remember ever seeing you without either a book or a pen and notebook attached to your miniature body. I used to tease you about preferring a made-up world to your real one."

I pouted. "I remember."

"So do I," Bridget and Jonathan said in unison.

Hannah glared from one to the other before turning back to me. "And now you're going to give it all up because of a few bad reviews? As a book blogger, you're a hypocrite, as a writer, you're a traitor to your craft, and as your mentor, I'm at a loss."

My body shook. "But..." I stood up to defend myself. "Wait. My mentor?"

She took a step closer to me. "I might enjoy teasing you about your height, but you're acting seriously small right now. You're a grown woman, Kim. Stop acting like a child."

"Hey, leave her alone," Pia said.

Hannah made a sour face. "Where is that noise coming from?" She motioned toward Caroline, Bridget, and Jonathan. "I need a few minutes alone with your friend. Can you guys take it somewhere else and bring the girl in the computer with you?"

Jonathan opened his mouth to object, but Bridget nudged him in the side. "As long as Kim says it's okay." She looked at me. "Will you be all right alone with Hannah?"

"Do I have a choice?" My bones already ached like I'd been through a beating.

Hannah rolled her eyes. "Haven't you ever done an intervention before? Kim has no say in the matter. But if you're worried I'm going to throw her in my purse and make a quick getaway, rest easy. Small doses are all I can handle."

"The feeling is mutual," I muttered.

Caroline picked up Pia and followed Bridget and Jonathan into the bedroom. I heard Pia say, "I'll remember your snotty comments next time I review one of your books."

When they were gone, Hannah turned to me. "Alone at last."

Sitting next to Hannah on Bridget's suede couch, my palms were sweating, my knees were weak, and my chest was tight. I never cared about being popular, so being on the outside of her exclusive clique in school didn't even register to me. Writing, however, was my life and this knowledge in Hannah's hands was dangerous. She could hit me where it hurt and we both knew it, but I was trapped.

"I'm going to tell you something I don't admit to many people."

I was staring down at my wobbling knees, but applied my brave face and looked up.

Her expression was grave, like she was about to tell me my grandmother passed away. "There are actually a few people who don't like my writing."

I knew this already, having stalked her reviews on Amazon and Goodreads, and waited for her to continue.

"Nineteen agents passed on *Cut on the Bias* before Felicia signed me."

My eyes bugged out.

She nodded. "Hard to believe, right?"

I gave her a closed-lip smile. "Totally." My rejection count was about the same, but I'd assumed representation came easier to Hannah.

"Here's the clincher." Her cheeks reddened. "I was also rejected by Fifth Avenue Press."

I blanched. "What?"

"You heard me. Too many romantic comedies on their list. The same reason Three Monkeys passed on you." She shrugged. "Ironic, right?"

My mouth opened, but words wouldn't form.

She swiped her palm against the back of her ponytail. "I spoke at a high school in Long Island last month. Since I was the most popular girl in my high school, I was positive the students would drool over me like they did at Liberty High. Guess what?"

"What?" I leaned forward.

"The kids wanted to know if any of my characters were vampires or saving the universe from imminent destruction. When I said 'no,' the questions dried up. I was out of there twenty minutes early. It was a bad match—just like you and the MFA wannabes from Stony Brook."

"Thank you for telling me—"

Hannah raised her hand. "I'm not done yet. Last week, I received an email from a reader telling me as an American, I had no business writing about Paris. I was desperate to tell her I was an American who lived in Paris my junior year of college and for a year following graduation and was therefore the ideal person to write my story."

I whispered, "Did you?" Engaging with critical readers was a well-known no-no in the industry and could destroy her career.

Hannah shook her head softly. "Fred wouldn't let me. You remember Fred Gordon, right?"

Fred was a nerdy but loveable brainiac from our high school. In one of our many futile attempts to take Hannah down a notch, Bridget and I had led Hannah to believe Fred was secretly the heir to the throne of Denmark by planting the juicy gossip in a fake diary. We'd hoped she'd make a fool of herself, but the plan backfired when Hannah not only became genuine friends with Fred, but came out looking like Mother Teresa for befriending someone of much lower social status. My cheeks flushed in shame at the memory of my deception even as my heart warmed at what a good friend Fred was to her. I couldn't hold back my grin. "Smart guy."

"The smartest," she said, her cheeks dimpling. "So, yes, that bitch of a reader didn't think I was the appropriate author to write the Paris Couture series, but did I change my setting to Paris, Illinois because of it?" Answering her own question, she said, "Of course not." She cocked her head at me. "I teased you relentlessly about your writing in high school and I'm positive it never even crossed your mind to toss your journal in the garbage can because of it. I was way more influential than an anonymous reviewer on Amazon, so why would you stand up to me yet give them so much power?" Hannah stared me down, but all I could do was shrug helplessly.

She let out a loud breath. "The point I'm trying to make is being a published author isn't always glamourous. As artists, we often have to face rejection, floundering sales, unsuccessful events, diminishing buzz, constructive criticism from your editor, and hurtful reviews. Negative feedback stings and probably always will, even after ten books under your belt. But if you're a real writer, which I thought you were, you dust yourself off and keep penning those stories. Of course, you should work on your craft and keep trying to improve your skills, but you also follow your gut and don't bend to the whim of every single reader out there. It's a fruitless exercise." She paused for a beat and studied me. "Am I making any sense?"

I wiped away tears I didn't realize I was shedding. "Yes."

She groaned. "Stop blubbering. Just remember, you're the writer and they're not. You'll never be able to please them all, but if you can appeal to enough of them to build a loyal and growing fan base, it's pretty wonderful." She glanced at her Tiffany East West watch. "Is my job done here? I've got things to do." She stood up.

"Thank you, Hannah." I lifted myself to a standing position and resisted the urge to pull her into an embrace. For one, she'd probably push me away and for another, hugging Hannah was way too weird.

"Don't mention it." She stared me down. "I mean it. Everything I said today stays in the vault. Or else."

I flinched. "Got it."

"You can come back now," Hannah called out.

A moment later, we were joined by the remaining members of my intervention team. They eyed us with nervous expressions.

"Mission accomplished," Hannah said.

Bridget raised an eyebrow. "You're not going to quit writing?"

"Definitely not." Somehow, I knew the words would flow again and I felt a rush of adrenaline at the thought of going back to Ground Support, this time to write. Thank goodness I hadn't sent my Dear John email to Felicia.

Bridget's face broke out in a huge grin and she threw herself into my arms. I squeezed her hard to express my thanks for her calling on Hannah despite our past and her misgivings as to whether the mean girl had really changed her stripes. It must have taken a will of steel, but my BFFAEUDDUP put aside her pride for me.

"When Topanga and Angela hug, it's my cue to leave," Hannah said.

Bridget removed herself from my embrace. "Thank you, Hannah."

"Don't mention it," she said with a wink in my direction before heading to the front door.

"Does this mean the wedding is back on too?" Pia asked. "I was excited to finally meet you in person."

Hannah stopped walking and turned around. "You called off your wedding?"

I nodded meekly.

The setting sun coming through the window reflected on Hannah's face, making her teeth glow when she smiled. "Strawberry Shortcake is unmarried and knocked up and Little Kim is a runaway bride. Too bad you two weren't remotely as interesting in high school. We could have been friends."

Chapter 23

I was desperate to make them understand why a November wedding couldn't happen. "Even if someone could promise my dad's memory loss isn't a result of anything serious, we're not even close to ready. I don't even have a dress yet." I dipped my chin to my chest in guilt over my lie to the girls. "I shouldn't have pretended otherwise, but saying it out loud only stressed me out more."

"My fault," Bridget said with a full lower lip.

"I accept full responsibility. I should have been more realistic. Planning a wedding around the release of my first novel was too much."

Hannah smirked. "If you ask me, your future husband should have let you bask in the glory of your debut rather than hijack it by proposing."

In defense of my man, I leapt off the couch, nearly knocking over the can of beer I was holding. It was the only alcoholic beverage currently stocked in Jonathan and Bridget's apartment and I was desperate. "It's not Nicholas's fault!" I could never think of getting a proposal and a book deal in the same night as anything other than magical. "But maybe we should have set a date further in the future," I conceded in a softer voice.

"You had no way of knowing how you would handle the transition from book blogger to published author," Caroline said.

I grunted. "You mean badly?" I took a sip of beer and snarled. Pabst Blue Ribbon tasted nothing like rose prosecco.

Smiling kindly, Caroline said, "I mean humanly."

"Two of the four times you went dress shopping, I distracted you from your mission." Bridget's quivering chin suggested she was on the verge of tears.

I darted a glance at Hannah to gauge her reaction to more blubbering, but she was silent. Since I couldn't deny Bridget's statement, I simply blew her a kiss to let her know it was a forgivable offense.

"What if I were to tell you I found a way to solve your dress problem. Would it change things?"

The intercom must have rang again without my hearing it because somehow Nicholas was standing in the living room. He looked delicious in an olive crew-neck t-shirt, tan shorts, and khaki leather boat shoes. Before I could answer his question, Hannah approached him. "It's the groom himself. Remember me?" She batted her long eyelashes.

Nicholas gave her an amused smile. "Bridget told me you agreed to talk some sense into Kim. How can I thank you?"

Hannah's gaze took a slow expedition from Nicholas's feet up to his face and she smiled slyly. "I can think of a few things, but Kimmie here would probably object."

I stood by Nicholas's side. "Yes, she would." I looked up at him, hoping to share a moment, but he wouldn't meet my eyes.

Hannah laughed. "I'm teasing. Another man already has my heart anyway." She motioned toward Nicholas. "Let's hear your brilliant idea for suiting Kim up for the big day."

Finally, Nicholas looked at me. "It turns out not everyone thought *A Blogger's Life* was vapid and boring. Does the name India ring a bell?"

Hannah gasped. "Don't even tell me Bibhu Mohapatra agreed to design Kim's dress." Her eyes opened wide. "Michelle Obama wore his designs."

Nicholas cackled. "Okay, I won't tell you that."

I knew who he meant. "India was the name of my bridal consultant at Kleinfeld." I couldn't forget the stunning and poised woman who tried to suppress my overzealous entourage.

"While you were getting your head shrunk by your besties here, I took a road trip to the store. India graciously agreed to speak with me in between clients. I told her your predicament and it turns out she remembered you fondly despite how the day ended. When I told her you were a published author and the name of your book, she was like a kid at the gates of Disney World." Nicholas turned to the others. "No exaggeration. The woman actually squealed."

My heart leapt. "She did?"

Nicholas nodded. "Yes, and she agreed to come in on her day off tomorrow for a do-over. Or in her words, a second chance to say yes to the dress. All she wants in exchange is a signed copy of *A Blogger's Life* and a selfie with the author." He scratched his jaw. "What do you say?"

"Say yes to the dress shopping or I'm going to jump through the computer and hit you," Pia said.

Nicholas put a finger up to my parted lips. "I know what you're thinking, but your father would be crushed if you postponed the wedding on his account."

I gave a reluctant nod, but I wasn't convinced. "What about flowers?"

"Who cares about flowers?" Jonathan said as if we were discussing something optional, like a chocolate fountain or a ring bearer.

"A lot of people," I said.

"I'm pretty sure three months is enough time to order bouquets for the bridal party, but Jonathan's right about flowers not being the be-all and end-all to a wedding reception. Instead of having flowers at every table, you can do something else, like candles," Caroline suggested.

"If you don't like the candle idea, I bet Natalie can come up with something off the beaten path," Nicholas said.

All eyes landed on me to make a decision. Even though it was closer to two and a half months than three, excitement built up in my belly against my better judgment. Then I remembered something else. "I'm blown away by India's generous offer to show me dresses on her day off, but I'm sure the store is way too backed up to fit my alterations into their schedule. As it's been pointed out to me repeatedly, my measurements aren't exactly off the rack."

I took the silence to mean no one disagreed with my statement and I feared all of Nicholas's efforts were for nothing.

Hannah's voice broke through the quiet. "Go get your dress."

My head whipped in her direction. "Do you truly think I can fit into a dress without major alterations? Aren't my boobs too big, my waist too small, and my legs too short?"

Hannah took a deep breath in and let it out slowly. "Yes, yes, and yes, but I repeat my earlier command. Go shopping for the dress and don't worry if Kleinfeld can't accommodate you for alterations. I've got you covered."

I froze in place.

Raising her chin in the air, she said, "You can't trust just anyone with a designer wedding gown, but I know people." She cocked one of her perfectly groomed eyebrows. "Can you please just trust me for once?"

I looked at Nicholas for guidance. He shrugged so I turned to Bridget, who gave me a thumbs-up sign. If Bridget, of all people, believed in Hannah, I figured I should too.

I grinned as my pulse raced in anticipation. The answer was a resounding and astounding "yes."

Chapter 24

A little while later, after I assured everyone the intervention was a success and thanked them for devoting their evening to curing my emotional ailments, Nicholas and I were in an Uber on our way back downtown. There was so much I wanted to say to him, but since we were sharing the car with several other commuters, I was forced to hold back temporarily. In the meantime, I squeezed his hand to let him know without words how much I cherished him and appreciated what he'd done for me by tracking down India. He squeezed back, but kept his stare on the windshield in front of us.

We arrived at our apartment building and walked through the lobby in silence. Once inside the elevator, I snuggled closer to Nicholas.

He stiffened at my side. "We need to talk, Kimmie," while looking straight ahead at the floor-display panel.

My heart jumped into my throat. "Okay," I said meekly.

The doors opened and he motioned for me to exit first. I led the way to our apartment with shaky legs and a queasy ache in my gut. It might have been the first time Nicholas ever pulled the "we need to talk" card. I'd done it the year before when I followed him to Florida. On the positive side, he wouldn't have gone through the trouble of scheduling a private meeting with India to shop for gowns if he planned to call off the wedding. But a gazillion other "what ifs" floated around my brain. What if the Soho Grand double booked the night of our wedding? Or my father's tests came back while I was at Bridget's, and Nicholas was going to break the news of his early onset dementia diagnosis? My breathing grew labored and the first thing I did upon entering the apartment was break out the Tito's.

I poured enough vodka to fill a quarter of the glass and topped it off with cranberry juice. "Do you want something to drink?" I asked

Nicholas, who was already on the couch.

Nicholas turned to face me, his arm resting on the top of the couch. "I'm good. Come sit."

I joined him on the sofa and took a gulp of my drink, cringing at the taste. "What do you want to talk about?" I placed the glass on the coffee table and braced myself.

Nicholas rubbed his jaw and appeared to contemplate his next words.

I hadn't noticed how exhausted he looked until now. He was already stressed over the impending appointment of an executive general counsel, and his fiancée going off the deep end only added to his bloodshot eyes. I ran my hand over his cheek, letting the coarseness of his facial hair scratch against my fingertips. "I'm so sorry, baby."

He extracted my hand from his face. "Do you even know what you're sorry for?"

I frowned. "For everything. For impulsively calling off the wedding and forcing you to pull together a support team to talk me out of my madness. For making you beg the most famous bridal shop in the city for a do-over." When Nicholas didn't respond, I took another sip of my drink. "Shall I go on?"

He winced. "You called off our wedding without even consulting me. Do you have any idea how that made me feel?"

I gulped. "It was all too much. The wedding, the writing, my dad. I was suffocating."

"And instead of coming to me for support, you made a solo decision to quit both—the wedding and the writing. We're supposed to be partners, Kim, but you didn't even think to lean on me. Why?"

I inhaled sharply. "I tried, Nicholas."

He crinkled his brow. "When?"

"Several times over the last few months, I told you how overwhelmed I was." I shook my head. "Maybe I didn't use those words exactly, but you knew I was stressed about not having a dress and the wedding plans in general. I told you about my bad reviews and Melina and Felicia's negative feedback over *Love on Stone Street*. Your solution was always to focus on the bright side." Letting out a heavy sigh, I said, "I tried, but I hit my threshold. I was so blinded by stress, I could no longer see any light." I patted his thigh. "I swear I didn't intentionally shut you out." It was true, but a twinge of guilt rocked my core anyway.

Nicholas's eyebrows drew together. "I thought I was giving you what you needed—reassurance, support, confidence." He scraped a hand though his hair. "I didn't mean to downplay your anxiety or minimize what you were going through."

I smiled gently. "Of course you didn't. I know my happiness is always your goal. I concede to not pushing back or outright asking you for advice. I kept assuming everything would work out on its own and why should I bother you with it? You already have so much on your plate."

Nicholas brushed a hair out of my face. "It's in the fiancé manual that we're supposed to be here for each other, no matter what else we have going on." He gave me a lopsided grin. "I'm surprised you haven't gotten to it yet considering how much you read."

I chuckled. "It hasn't reached the top of my TBR yet."

"How about I promise not to systematically attach a positive spin to all your genuine concerns if you vow to call me on it if I do," Nicholas said. "Because I want nothing more than to spend the rest of my life with you, but I can't have you bottle things up inside and then shut me out without warning."

I grinned and extended my hand. "You've got yourself a deal."

Nicholas kissed my engagement ring. "Can we seal it with something better than a handshake?"

Leaning forward, I said, "Like a pinky swear?"

"Something like that." Nicholas stood and pulled me up with him. "Come. I'll show you."

Later, after closing our transaction in an entirely agreeable and pleasurable manner, we lay on our backs in bed in sated silence. I consciously brushed aside my concerns about my father for the moment in favor of contemplating what I looked most forward to in the following day: getting back to *Love on Stone Street* and perfecting a draft both Melina and I would love or returning to Kleinfeld for my special shopping session. It was too bad I had to make it through a full day of work first. The pesky legal secretary gig stole all my fun. "What time can India meet with me?"

"Six o'clock. Does that work?"

"Of course. I don't even know if you mean a.m. or p.m. because, either way, I'll be there."

Nicholas chuckled. "I'm pretty sure it's p.m."

I wiped my brow. "Good. An appointment at sunrise would impede my beauty rest and I'm pooped. It's been a long day."

Nicholas turned on his side to face me. "You excited to go shopping tomorrow?"

"Sure am," I said, scooching closer to him.

He traced his finger along my arm. "Who do you want to bring with you this time?"

I'd been so overwhelmed, I hadn't even thought about who would join me in my next and, please God, final attempt to buy a gown. It was too late to invite my mom or Erin. And while I was positive Bridget and Caroline would cancel any existing plans to be there if I wanted them with me, the truth was I didn't. There was only one person whose eyes I wanted to see filled with happy tears at the sight of me in The Dress. He was lying right next to me. "You," I said.

Nicholas's beautiful brown eyes opened wide. "For real? Isn't it bad luck?"

"I seem to recall you saying screw the 'it's bad luck to see the bride in her dress' bullshit. I second your emotion." I shrugged. "Seriously, you're the only one I want there. Besides, how I look is a reflection on you. You don't want your friends, family, and work colleagues talking smack about your bride's unflattering dress and so I'm positive you'll tell me the truth."

"What if I purposely pick a dress that hides your sexy shape so no other man wants you?" Nicholas challenged with a raise of an eyebrow.

I did a sweeping motion up the length of my body. "It would have to be some dress to hide the sexy shape of all this action."

Nicholas laughed. "True, Kimmie. So very true."

"Does that mean you'll come? You might have to leave work a bit early." I held my breath.

"Even a Beatles reunion complete with Paul, George, Ringo, and John wouldn't keep me away."

"Consider me flattered. And exhausted." I kissed him on the cheek. "Goodnight, Nicholas."

The following day, I called my mom first thing. "Have you heard from the doctors yet?"

"Not yet, honey. It's only been a few days. I promise to let you know when we hear something."

"Can you put him on?" As David walked past on his way into Rob's office, I took the phone off speaker and whispered, "Have you filled him in or are you keeping it hush-hush for now?"

"Your father knows everything. He's a grown man, Kim, not a child."

I clicked the top of my retractable pen over and over again. "I know. I'm just scared."

My mom sighed. "I knew we shouldn't tell you. We haven't mentioned anything to your sister, so please keep it to yourself for now. Anyway, here he is."

When my father got on the line, I said, "Hi, Daddy. How are you feeling?" I hadn't called him "Daddy" since my age was in the single digits, but I was in a sentimental mood.

"No complaints, Tiny Kim. Honestly, I forgot a dentist appointment and my third cousin's name. My dentist is a sadist and my third cousin stole my girlfriend freshmen year in high school. I'm better off forgetting them." He laughed. "Seriously, don't worry so much about me. You've got a wedding to plan, right?"

"I do." I thought about my do-over with India later.

"Then get to it."

"I'll call you tomorrow."

"You don't need to call me every day."

"I want to."

"I appreciate your concern, but I'm the dad and you're the child. I'm supposed to worry about you. Not the other way around."

"Telling a daughter not to worry about her parents is like telling water not to get wet."

He chuckled. "Did you pen that yourself?"

I allowed a small smile. "I tinkered with it—made it my own."

"Goodbye, Kim. Talk you soon."

"Tomorrow."

"Soon," he repeated, hanging up before I could get the last word.

Chapter 25

"Do you like it?" Nicholas asked with a wrinkle of his nose.

I stood in front of the 3D mirror and gazed at my reflection. Mere moments earlier, I'd sworn this gown—a lace fit and flare Vera Wang in blush—was The Dress. How could it not be? Vera. Wang. In blush! "I thought I did."

Nicholas finished off his glass of champagne in one swig. "Then I love it too." He smiled, but it was the kind of smile you gave your very sweet colleague when he asked if you liked the bracelet he bought you for the Christmas exchange and you didn't. At all.

I stepped off the platform and stood before him. "But you don't." I wanted Nicholas's eyes to pop out in lust before misting with tears. Wrinkling his nose was not on the same level. "What's wrong with it?" I twirled to the best of my ability given the long train.

Nicholas sighed. "It's the color. I know you love pink, but isn't it overkill? Do you really need to match the cake? Can't you stick to a pink garter or something?"

Standing before the mirror again, I admired the intricate lace details of the fitted bodice. "How about if the dress was white? Would you like it then?" I was positive Vera Wang made the dress in ivory and crème as well.

Nicholas pulled a face. "Sorry." He frowned. "Do you wish you didn't let me tag along?"

"Not at all." This was true. I'd rather Nicholas voice his disapproval of the dress before we shelled out thousands of my parents' retirement dollars than be disappointed when he saw me walk down the aisle. I turned to India. "Next."

She smiled. "We'll get there. You've only seen two others so far."

If India was any nicer, we'd be inviting her to the wedding along with the plus-one of her choice before this day was over. I'd gushed over her willingness to work on her day off and she'd enthused about *A Blogger's Life*. We even took a selfie of us holding the book in front of the Kleinfeld sign for my Instagram and Facebook Author pages.

"We'll be back soon."

Nicholas beamed as a clerk refilled his champagne flute. "I've got nothing but time."

I followed India back to the dressing room, leaving Nicholas with his bubbles. I hoped the store had enough bottles in the back to keep him happy until we could agree on a dress.

"Can they make it without that stuff on the bottom?" Nicholas said, pointing at the layered skirt.

"Stuff?" I didn't think Pnina Tornai would appreciate her beautiful layered skirt referred to as stuff.

"It reminds me of duck feathers."

"So it's a no?"

"It's a no from me. The top is great though."

"This is more like it," Nicholas said, running a finger along one of the thin beaded straps of the Madison James gown I was wearing.

My heart jumped into my throat. This could be it. "Yeah?" The gown made me feel old-Hollywood glamorous, but I'd had my doubts as to whether Nicholas would like the slim sheath. It was reminiscent of scalloped shells.

He scrutinized me from my head down to the chapel-length train. "Not crazy about the lace though. Do they make it in plain silk?"

Nicholas whistled. "Wow. The back is just…" His eyes dilated. "Sexy."

"Isn't it sublime?" I admired the beaded detail of the open back.

"Stunning," Nicholas agreed.

I flashed India a broad smile and she crossed her slim fingers. Nicholas loved the dress. Finally.

Shaking his head, Nicholas said, "But why did the designer have to ruin it with those funny-looking shoulders?"

I was no stranger to experiencing an adrenaline high from a shopping spree only to crash later, but not even hours walking the floors at Bloomingdale's had prepared me for this. Getting in and out of heavy wedding dresses was laborious, not to mention sweaty. It also worked up an appetite as witnessed by the loud and embarrassing growl my stomach had just made. India had pinned dresses to my form in the double digits at this point, but none of them had made my heart flip with certainty. And Nicholas's critiquing skills could rival Simon Cowell, Gordon Ramsay, and Zac Posen's combined. Either there was too much going on or not enough, or he hated the neckline, the beading, the lace—you name it. His distaste had no limits. Any fears of finding the perfect dress early on and missing out on the whole shopping experience had been assuaged. Now, I just felt guilty for making India give up a day off when I was probably going to leave the store sans dress yet again.

While she kneeled on the floor to pin the next dress to my form, I paid no attention. I was thinking about what I wanted to eat for dinner and whether Nicholas would be up for stopping at Luke's for lobster rolls. And then she stood up and pushed me toward the mirror. "I think we have a winner."

My mouth dropped open and my eyes filled with tears. This was it. This was The Dress. I put a hand to my mouth and gasped. "India."

Standing behind me, India met my eyes through the mirror before wiping away a tear of her own. "I know. Shall we show it to Nicholas?"

I nodded, still unable to look away from my reflection. I hoped Nicholas would see what I saw because I didn't think there was a dress in the history of dresses that would make me feel more like a beautiful bride. The Martina Liana silk gown I was wearing had a body-hugging sweetheart bodice with blocks of asymmetrical pleats and ruching at the neckline and bust. The fit-and-flare skirt featured box pleat accents just above the knee. The gown closed in the back with a zipper under a strand of gorgeous silk-covered buttons that graced the mid-back of the dress down through the chapel train. It was perfect. I was positive my original entourage would approve as well. It wasn't a ball gown style, but even Erin would agree I looked like a princess. Nicholas's mom would love the strapless style and even my mom would say this one showed off my "girls" in a tasteful and classy way.

My legs shook as I followed India to the main room where Nicholas was sitting on the couch typing on his phone. Part of me dreaded the moment he looked up because if he found something wrong with this dress, I might have to return the ring.

I opened my mouth to get his attention at the same moment he lifted his head and saw us standing there. He met my gaze, started to smile, blinked, and then did a double take. He stood up and dropped his phone on the floor. He bent to pick it up and missed, fumbling it one more time before finally clasping it in his hands and placing it on the side table with his empty glass of champagne. I watched the scene with bated breath. At last he spoke. "Thank God you let me see the dress before the wedding day."

My heart stopped. With only half my voice, I whispered, "Why?" What was he going to hate about this one?

He shook his head in wonder. "Because what you just witnessed now—the groom falling all over himself—would be ridiculously embarrassing in front of a hundred guests."

I bit my lip. "Meaning?"

Nicholas smiled gently. "Let's put it this way. As far as I'm concerned you were meant to wear two things: your birthday suit and this dress." He faced India. "Please tell me you agree." His face turned pink. "At least about this being the perfect dress."

India nodded. "I do."

Nicholas turned to me and held my hand in his. "And you?"

"Yes!"

Looking at me expectantly, India said, "Kim, are you saying yes to the dress?"

I grinned. "I am saying yes to the dress."

The three of us clapped like over-excited tweens for a few seconds until India frowned.

"I hate to be a buzz kill, but the dress does need significant alterations." She pointed to the long train. "Besides shortening, it needs to be taken in at the sides and the top. Unfortunately, we can't fit you into our schedule in time. And this is not the kind of project I'd recommend entrusting to your neighborhood tailor."

I looked at Nicholas in a panic.

Rubbing my bare shoulder, Nicholas said, "Call Hannah. She promised she'd take care of it."

I nodded, while trying to brush aside the stubborn nervous knots in my belly. Hannah had insisted I trust her. I was halfway there, but erasing more than a decade of her mean-girl antics from my memory wasn't an easy feat despite the handful of nice-girl acts she'd performed during the past two years.

While Nicholas and India discussed payment and the best way to get the gown home, I called Hannah. Even though I hated being beholden to her for anything, if she came through as promised and found a way to deal with the tailoring of my wedding dress, it would be a huge monkey—make that ape—off my back.

The phone went straight to her voicemail. "Hi Hannah. It's Kim. Thanks again for coming over yesterday. You really helped me see the light." I swallowed hard. "I found the perfect wedding dress, but it needs major alterations which, like you said, shouldn't be entrusted to just any old tailor. I'm hoping you're still willing to help me." I rolled my eyes at how pathetic I sounded. "I'd like to take you up on it if the offer still, um, stands. Please call me back when you can. Thanks!"

I hung up and fought the urge to throw up. What if she was playing a cruel joke on me? Get little Kim Short to shell out thousands of dollars on an ill-fitting dress that falls down on her walk down the aisle. What if she paid someone to videotape it at the ceremony and play it on YouTube? What if she lied about the whole thing and never called me back?

Either I said it out loud or Nicholas was a mind-reader because he looked upon me with amusement. "Don't be silly, Kimmie. Of course, she'll call you back."

Chapter 26

Thirty-six hours later, Hannah hadn't called me back yet. In hindsight, her generic voicemail surprised me. I'd assumed her greeting would say something about being a bestselling author with a stellar fashion sense. Afraid I might have left a message with the wrong number, I sent her a follow-up text and asked if she'd received my voicemail. I told her I bought a wedding dress and wanted to take her up on her offer for help. Now I was afraid if I called the wrong number and left a voice message on a stranger's phone, I might have also sent the text to the same person.

Instead of returning my phone to my bag, I scrolled the list of recent calls and pressed send. "Hi, Mom."

"Still no news, Kim."

I pressed my lips together. "How do you know I'm calling about Dad?" I was, in fact, checking up on him, but it wasn't like I'd never spoken to my folks two days in a row before.

"I'm sorry. What's up?"

I wracked my brain for a noteworthy tidbit unrelated to my father to share. "I bought a wedding dress!" The moment the words left my mouth, I wished I could take them back. My mom was under the impression this was old news. Before she could question me, I confessed. "This time, I'm telling you the truth."

My mom was silent for a beat. "As opposed to the times you lied?" She didn't sound angry, just confused.

I told her about my failed attempts to go shopping and how I'd been about to confide about what a mess I'd made of the wedding planning when she told me about my dad. She kept silent through my description of the intervention, but then she gasped. "You were going to quit writing and postpone the wedding? Kim! What were you thinking?"

I slunk down in my chair and hoped Patty, the secretary in the cubicle next to mine, wasn't eavesdropping. "I choked under the pressure."

"All this worrying is unhealthy. I'm sure Rob needs you, so I'll let you go, but try to relax. It's a good thing you have that glorious man of yours to talk you down. And who would have thought Hannah Marshak of all people would come to your rescue? Maybe the bad egg isn't so rotten after all."

"Yes, indeed," I said with a trace of doubt. We hung up and I got back to work, but I spent the remainder of the day checking my phone for texts from Hannah and practicing patience. Poor Rob asked me to complete the simple task of reserving a restaurant for an upcoming client dinner, and instead of a seven o'clock reservation for the following Tuesday night for six people, I made it for seven people at six o'clock on Thursday night. By the time I realized my mistake, the desired slot was taken. I was afraid if Hannah didn't call me back soon, Rob would hand me my walking papers.

I was desperate to work on *Love on Stone Street* after work, but wasn't confident in my ability to get in the writing zone. Nicholas was staying late at the office and so I invited myself over to Bridget and Jonathan's apartment instead. I showed Bridget the text I sent to Hannah and compared the number on my phone with the one she had called for the intervention. Bridget confirmed the digits were the same.

"I got the same voicemail. Only the phone rang a couple of times first. She called me back immediately and said she'd screened the call. She said she obviously didn't have my number in her contacts." Bridget smirked. "God forbid Hannah waste an opportunity for a dig."

"Did you say the phone didn't ring at all?" Jonathan asked.

"Yes, why?"

"Nothing." He bent down to straighten the pile of *Entrepreneur* and *Inc.* magazines on the coffee table.

My inner alarm bells rang, since Jonathan was way too comfortable with clutter to ever do such a thing. "What are you thinking?"

He stood up to bring our coffee mugs and Bridget's cup of green tea to the kitchen. "Forget I said anything."

Red-faced, Bridget stood up and removed the dishes from his hand. "Spill," she demanded, her hands on her hips.

I looked from a decidedly miffed Bridget to Jonathan and made a mental note to ask how things were going on the pregnancy front as soon as I dealt with my latest wedding-planning catastrophe.

Jonathan sighed. "Often, when a call goes directly to voicemail, it's because the owner purposely ignored it." Gazing at me, he added, "But Hannah has no reason to do that to you."

I cringed. "She's Hannah Marshak. She doesn't need a reason."

Bridget shook her head vigorously. "No. Hannah seemed very sincere when she said she'd take care of things for you. You said yourself she's not the same girl she was in high school. She wouldn't renege on her promise."

My breath hitched. "You think?"

She nodded, but then bit her lip. "Unless..."

I leaned forward. "Unless what?"

"What if she thought she could help you, realized she couldn't, and is now too embarrassed to face you?"

"What exactly was her plan?" Jonathan asked.

"I don't know," I cried as tears blinded my vision.

Bridget glared at Jonathan. "Look what you've made her do. She's crying."

"Me?" Jonathan's eyes bugged out as he pointed to Bridget. "You're the one who said Hannah can't help Kim after all."

"I didn't mean..." Bridget frowned at me. "Don't listen to us. I'm hormonal and he's...he's..."

"I'm what?" Jonathan demanded.

"Nothing," Bridget muttered.

I stood up. "It's getting late. I should go home."

Bridget engulfed me in a hug. "Don't go. We can order more food. I'm craving fried chicken."

I stiffened in her embrace. "No thanks." I'd had my fill of poultry for the night, having already inhaled a container of Kung Pao chicken, but I knew Bridget was only trying to make me feel better. Or else, she was genuinely still hungry. I reckoned it was a combination of both. I pulled away and forced a smile. "She'll call me later. I'm sure of it."

Bridget's cheeks dimpled. "Of course she will. But why don't you send her an email or Facebook message just in case?"

I'd been afraid reaching out again would be a desperate stalkerish move, but Bridget had provided the validation I secretly wanted. "Great idea. Can I do it from here?"

"Of course."

I returned to the couch and opened Facebook messenger on my phone. After sending a brief message to Hannah asking her to give me a call, I sent an identical note to her email. I gathered my things, said my goodbyes, and headed downtown in much more optimistic spirits. I was positive I'd covered all the bases and unless Hannah had taken up a new identity and fled the country, she'd get back to me soon.

Chapter 27

Hannah posted two pictures on Instagram that night, both from the Upper East Side. One reported the completion of the first draft of *A-line in the Sand* and the other was a photo of a gorgeous Stella McCartney Noma bag she'd received as a gift from someone she called "a generous friend." Her identity was intact, but she still hadn't returned my call, text, Facebook message, or email. I was in full-on panic mode. As promised, rather than keep my hysteria to myself, I confided my worries to Nicholas. We were partners, which meant my problems were his, especially since this one directly affected him.

From next to me on the couch, Nicholas pulled his computer onto his lap. "I'm sure Hannah will get back to you, but just in case, let's see if we can find a highly regarded dress tailor in the area. If they're all booked, I bet they'll suddenly have an opening if we throw money at them."

"It might take more cash than we can afford." I wanted to be more positive, but lots of people on the island of Manhattan had money.

"Aha!" Nicholas said, pointing at his computer screen. "There's a list on Yelp of the best places for dress alternations in the city. We'll start from the top and keep going until we find one."

"You don't think Hannah will come through?" My lips trembled. I thought I was over being made a fool by the queen bee of Liberty High, but she seemed so earnest at Bridget's apartment. She'd tricked us all. I slid down the couch in despair as I pictured her bragging to Plum and Marla, her high school besties, about how she'd ruined my wedding.

Nicholas returned his laptop to the table and placed a hand on my thigh. "I do think you'll hear from her, but if it will make you feel better to have a plan B, we should put one in place. Agreed?"

I pressed my lips together. "Yes."

"Good," he said with a smile before returning his attention to the list.

As I read over his shoulder, my eyes locked on the name Tiffany's Tailors and Cleaners. "Tiffany called you on the landline last week, by the way."

Nicholas stopped perusing the list and looked at me. "What did she want?"

"She claimed to be looking for Natalie and thought you might know where she was. I'm positive she was full of crap. But why else would she call you?"

Without missing a beat, Nicholas said, "Because we're having a secret love affair and trying to find a way to break it to you gently."

His tone was so serious, I would have believed him if I wasn't acutely aware of his unequaled poker face. I gave him a playful push. "Stop it. It was weird. I thought you were going to talk to Natalie about her."

He scrubbed a hand over his face. "I forgot with everything else going on. I will."

I narrowed my eyes. "I'll believe it when I see it."

Waggling his finger, he said, "I did try once, but she was on call. No one under the age of forty listens to voicemails so I didn't bother leaving one. I'll try again."

My stomach clenched. "What if Hannah didn't even listen to my message?" Even if she hadn't, it wouldn't explain why she hadn't replied to my email and text.

Nicholas exhaled. "Kim." The trace of annoyance in his voice was unmistakable. "Why is this all hinging on Hannah? Is this another excuse to postpone the wedding?"

My head swung back. "Of course not."

"Then stop obsessing over her. My gut says she'll come through, but if not, there are at least three tailors on this list with stellar reviews. No matter what happens, your dress will fit on November tenth."

I swallowed hard and faced my fiancé with a timid smile. I doubted I'd be so patient if the roles were reversed. "You're right." I couldn't let my history with Hannah get the best of me. If she didn't come through, it wasn't the end of the world.

Nicholas squeezed my hand. "Let's give Hannah until tomorrow night. Deal?"

"Deal." The hourglass was running out of sand and if a Plan B was necessary, I wanted to initiate it as soon as possible. Still, I was determined to practice mind over matter and not even think about it until the sun went down the following day.

The wait was torture. I refreshed my Facebook and email accounts every ten minutes to see if Hannah had returned my messages. I would have done it every five minutes, but I was too busy trying not to get fired. I also knew the chances of a new email popping up increased the longer I waited. I received countless newsletters from other authors, daily deals from my favorite shopping websites, and more than one fake email from PayPal telling me my account had been suspended and urging me to click on a suspicious link to have it reactivated. There was nothing from Hannah. I wanted her to come through for me, not only for the sake of my wedding dress, but so I could finally put our tumultuous past behind us once and for all.

When my phone pinged a little before four in the afternoon, I nearly fell off my seat. Unfortunately, Rob was hovered over my desk asking me a zillion questions. I was dying to request a minute to check my phone, but didn't dare. I had put the device away to avoid the temptation to stare at it all day. I could see the light from the notification from where the phone was resting at the top of my purse, but couldn't read what it said.

Shoving a Post-It note in my face, Rob said, "Is this an O or a zero?"

"How can you not know? This is your handwriting," I teased.

He gave me a sheepish grin. "I scribbled yet another password too quickly and now I can't read what I wrote. I was hoping you could decipher it. You know my script better than anyone."

I squinted at the paper. "It's a zero."

Rob beamed. "Thank you!"

I rolled my eyes. "Glad I could help." My phone pinged a reminder of my unread text. "Anything else I can help you with?" Please say no.

"I don't think so."

"Great." I kept my eyes on Rob as I reached for my purse.

"Actually, can you call the librarian and ask when McCarthy on Trademarks and Unfair Competition is next being updated? It seems like it's been a while."

I returned my hand to my lap. "Sure thing." I noted his request on my desk calendar.

He scratched his head. "There was something else I wanted to ask you and I can't remember what it is."

"It will come to you eventually and I'll be here waiting," I said with fake enthusiasm. Please let the text be from Hannah.

"I guess I have no choice," he said in a resigned voice before backing away from my cubicle.

I waited for him to turn his back before plucking the phone from my bag.

"I remembered!" Rob said.

"Ask away," I said dejectedly, while marveling at his ability to take two steps away from me and two steps back before I could even manage to flip over my phone to see who texted me.

"My wife wanted me to tell you she loved your wedding invitation."

It was the one spot of color in my otherwise dreary day and my belly flipped in delight. "I'm so glad."

Rob leaned forward. "The planning is going smoothly?"

"Like a baby's bottom," I lied. Normally, I enjoyed confiding in Rob. Once you got passed his workaholic exterior, he was a great listener, but I wanted to put on a brave front. Despite a rocky start, Nicholas and I were finally getting our acts together. As soon as Rob left me alone, I'd read Hannah's text and feel so much better.

"Excellent. I'm sure it's a well-oiled machine given how well you organize my life." He winked and, at long last, returned to his office.

I counted to five, in case Rob wasn't quite finished with me. Then I removed my phone from the purse and read the message. My shoulders slumped. It was from Erin.

"What color nail polish do you want us to wear to the wedding? I was thinking the makeup artist should use purple eyeshadow to match the bridesmaids' dresses and maybe we can all wear our hair in similar styles. Coordination is so important for pictures. You've scheduled professional hair and make-up appointments for the bridal party the morning of the wedding, right?"

I rested my head on my desk and wept silently. Of course I hadn't.

Since Nicholas and I agreed to wait a full twenty-four hours to call a tailor from the time we had our discussion the night before, it was still too early when I got home from work. Instead, I group texted my bridal party about whether they wanted to have their hair and makeup done professionally or if they preferred to do it themselves. The vote for professional hair was unanimous, but everyone except Erin wanted to do her own makeup. I assumed my hands would be too shaky to apply mascara without accidentally blinding myself, and preferred a third party to take on the task of making my skin glow and my eyes pop on my wedding day. Erin said since she was the matron of honor, it made sense only the two of us would opt in for a cosmetologist. I knew Bridget was dying to chime in that, as maid of honor, her role was equally as important as Erin's, so I texted her separately and we shared a laugh before I implored her to let Erin's text go without comment. On Natalie's recommendation, courtesy of *The Knot*, of course, I reserved a stylist to do everyone's hair the morning of the wedding, including the mother of the bride and, if she wanted, the mother of the groom, from the deluxe suite we'd reserved at the Soho Grand.

When Hannah hadn't called, texted, messaged, tweeted, emailed, faxed, or sent a carrier pigeon to get back to me by the time I scheduled a makeup consultation, I resigned myself to call one of the tailors Nicholas had flagged. But as I stared at the phone keys, I felt heat flush through my body and my muscles quivered in anger. How dare Hannah screw me over this way? If she'd changed her mind about connecting me to her "people," she should at least have the decency to own up to it. I couldn't move on without letting her know what I thought of her latest prank. I placed Nicholas's list of tailors on the coffee table and called Hannah instead.

I assumed, based on her recent track record of being out of pocket, the call would go into voicemail, but she picked up. "Bonjour, Kimmie," she answered as if she hadn't been ignoring me for days.

"Bonjour," I parroted sarcastically. "Since you're clearly too busy living your fabulous life to get back to me about alterations for my wedding dress, I wanted to let you know I don't need you anyway. I'll find someone else. Someone trustworthy and reliable, who will have the courtesy to keep her promises and return my calls. Not someone who will pretend to want to help me only to stab me in the back with her perfectly manicured fingernails!" I paused to take a breath, but I hadn't even given her half my mind yet. I was poised to confront her for being the same beyotch she was at the turn of the century when laughter filled the silence. My insides boiled and I ground my teeth. "You think this is funny?"

She chuckled again. "I can almost picture you, red-faced with your tiny hands in fists and anger bursting out of your miniature body at my perceived deception. You're too cute."

"Perceived deception?" I had wanted to shame face Hannah with my tirade. Her calling me "cute" was not the desired response, but it seemed she was incapable of taking me seriously.

"Yes, perceived," Hannah said calmly. "I was about to text you, but you beat me to it. I had called in a favor to my friend and was awaiting details as to when she could see you and your little dress. I'm far too busy to give you bits and pieces of the plan in dribs and drabs, you know. Isn't it more efficient to get all the information in one shot? I figured you would be accustomed to this way of communication, being in the publishing industry and all." In a lower voice, almost as if she was speaking to herself, she said, "Although I suppose I should have realized you were panicking when you sent me a Facebook message and an email on top of the voicemail and text—kind of extreme. I'm sorry, I guess. Everything is all set now, but if you don't need my help anymore—"

"Wait!" My heart slammed against my chest. Dang it, I needed her. "I mean, I could call someone else, but if you've already gone through the trouble..." I let my head fall back and released a breath. "You can help me?" I crossed my fingers for a solid answer in either direction.

Hannah sighed. "Your dramatics are exhausting, but yes, I can help you. I'm dear friends with Kelly Dempsey. Of course, you've heard of Kelly."

I hadn't, but I wasn't going to admit it freely. Maybe she was Patrick Dempsey's sister.

"I met Kelly on the set of *Project Runway* while researching *Cut on the Bias*. She's such a sweetheart and was robbed of first place, but don't even get me started. Her clothing line is streetwear, but she's a gifted designer and seamstress. Her hands could turn the most hideous dress into a gown worthy of Fashion Week. Anyhoo, I told her about your predicament and she said she'd love to help you out."

"She...she would?" My voice trembled. "She wants to help me? But why?"

"As a favor to me. She adores me. I promised to write her into my next book, but between us, I'm positive she'd have agreed to do it either way. You'll have to pay her, obviously, but she promised she'd give you the friends and family rate."

I teared up at this latest unexpected act of kindness courtesy of a person I'd thought of as unkind for most of my life. "Wow. Thank you, Hannah."

"See? I'm not as untrustworthy and unreliable as you thought. Although you were correct about my flawless manicure and fabulous life." She snickered.

I still wished she'd kept me in the loop from the beginning, but I was ashamed of my outburst. I dipped my chin to my chest. "I'm sorry about going off on you before."

"Don't sweat it, Kimmie. It was fun."

My lips pursed at her definition of fun, but it wasn't worth arguing. "What next?"

Hannah gave me the address for Kelly's workroom and told me to be there with the dress on Sunday morning at eleven. I thanked her again and, exhausted, fell asleep on the couch with my clothes on.

Hannah scrutinized me from my head to where my toes were hiding beneath the train of my dress. "I approve."

Bridget giggled and I gave her a warning glare through the side of my face. I couldn't risk laughing with the multitude of pins in such close proximity to my skin. "I'm glad you like it."

"I was afraid you'd go for a Cinderella style which, while stunning on some, would be entirely inappropriate on you. But you were always so gaga over princesses and pink back in the day." She made a gagging motion.

Bridget smirked. "Admit it, Hannah. You knew Kim's dress would be exquisite and flattering to her shape." Her tone was light and if I didn't know better, I'd think she was even starting to like Hannah a little.

Hannah harrumphed. "I confess to no such thing."

Kelly, who was kneeling at my feet, stood up straight and circled me. She tugged at the dress in a few places before maneuvering me closer to the three-way mirror. "Magnifique."

I withheld a chuckle. No wonder Kelly, who seemed to be close to our age, got along so well with Hannah.

"I'll need about three weeks to finish, which still leaves you about a month before the wedding in case you need last-minute adjustments. Does that work for you?" Kelly asked, tucking a strand of ebony hair tinged with purple behind her ear.

"It's perfect. Thank you so much."

Kelly smiled. "Anything for a friend of Hannah's. She's my favorite author." She pulled Hannah into a side hug.

Hannah beamed. "Kim here is an author too. Thanks to me."

I bit my tongue and avoided making eye contact with Bridget. Must not laugh.

Kelly helped me out of my dress and she and Hannah left me alone with Bridget while I changed back into my street clothes.

"I can't believe I'm going to say this," Bridget said.

She patted her belly while she spoke and my face drained of color. "You're not going into labor, are you? Isn't it way too soon?"

Bridget shuddered. "Don't even go there." She chewed her lip. "If you asked me back in 1998, I'd have bet my entire collection of Polly Pockets against this happening, but you, Kimberly Michelle Long, are friends with Hannah Marshak. Dare I say it, good friends. I think you need to invite her to your wedding." She winced as if saying the words caused her physical pain.

I was, surprisingly, not thrown by Bridget's statement. She was correct on both counts. It occurred to me Hannah hadn't screwed me over since high school. In fact, the opposite was true. Despite being a pain, Hannah was a better friend to me than I ever was to her and maybe it was time to let my guard down and keep it there without waiting to be proved wrong at every turn. Inviting Hannah to my nuptials was the right thing to do. "I agree. But the invitations already went out. Will she think it's rude at this point? Like she was on the B-list?"

Smirking, Bridget said, "As if Hannah would ever consider the notion of being anything less than A-list."

"True." I gestured toward where Hannah and Kelly were deep in conversation on the other side of the workroom. "Let's get this over with."

I tapped Hannah on the back and when she turned around said, "Can I speak with you for a second?"

"You may." She followed me to a corner of the room. "What's up?"

The concept of asking Hannah to attend the most important event of my life so far must have freaked out my heart because it was beating at an uncomfortably fast pace. I placed my hand against it and took a deep breath. "I want you to know I appreciate everything you've done for me this past week."

"Week? Year is more like it."

"Hannah." I pleaded with my eyes for her to show a semblance of humility in this moment.

She waved me away. "You're welcome. Was there something else?"

I swallowed hard. "I'd like to invite you to my wedding. With a guest, of course. I just need your address to send out the invitation. You don't have to come, but I...I'd be honored if you did." It felt like someone was holding a lit candle up to my face and I fanned myself for relief.

Hannah's cheeks radiated light. "I wouldn't miss it." She cleared her throat. "I mean, if only to mock Jonathan's dance moves, of course." She recited her address and I typed it into my phone. "I don't eat beef or chicken anymore. I assume there will be a fish or vegetable option?"

I nodded, even though I had no idea. Underneath Hannah's address, I jotted down a reminder to call Sarah about the menu. Slowly but surely, the wedding was coming together. Maybe I was one of those people who worked best under pressure.

Chapter 28

TWO MONTHS UNTIL "I DO"

I took a sip of my honey latte and skimmed the café. Almost all the wooden picnic tables at Ground Support were occupied. Most of the patrons had on headphones, which made me feel better about talking to my mom in a public place. I crossed my fingers she'd answer since my calls over the last few days had gone to voicemail.

"Hi, sweetheart."

Her voice was cheery, but my suspicious mind doubted it was genuine. "Any news about Dad? Why haven't you returned my calls? What did the doctor say? Does he have dementia?" I saw no reason to work up to the point of my call.

My mom chuckled. "You sound like you're doing an interview for your high-school paper. Breathe."

I took a gulp of air. "No one will tell me anything."

"Haven't you ever heard the phrase, 'no news is good news'? Please stop calling every day. You're doing more harm than good."

I swallowed down the thickness in my throat. "I am?"

She blew out a stream of air. "Your father and I, along with the doctors, are confident it's nothing serious. We're trying to go about our lives on that assumption, but your constant phone calls and frantic attitude aren't helping."

"I'm sorry." I sniffled.

"I don't mean to be harsh, sweetheart. We both love you, but please enjoy this special time in your life and leave the burden of your father's health to us for now. Can you do that? I promise when we know something, you'll know something."

It was time to be brave. I wiped my eyes and sat up straighter in my chair. "If you say so."

"Good." I could hear her smile through the phone. "And Kim?"

"Yes?"

"Don't call us, we'll call you. I love you." She ended the call.

It wasn't my intention to pile more stress onto my parents' plate, and so I'd do what she asked and trust her promise to keep me informed. In the meantime, it was time to get my writing back on track. I was over allowing a small minority of naysayers to stifle my voice, but even as I sat in front of the computer, my thoughts were jumbled and my fingers hesitated to type complete sentences. I knew it was a matter of taking the first step. Just like the hardest part of exercising was showing up at the gym, the most challenging part of writing was getting those first words on the page. What was I so frightened of?

A master of procrastination, I checked my Gmail account. Among three discount book newsletters was an email from Josslyn Romeijn. I took a nervous bite of my veggie sandwich and opened the note from the unfamiliar sender.

Dear Kim,

You might not remember me, but we met at the MFA event at Stony Brook University last month. I bought a copy of A Blogger's Life *after telling you I didn't like chick lit. Well, I just finished the book and had to reach out to you. I loved it! I'd been feeling really frustrated with my long-term boyfriend and unable to tell him how I felt. Reading about Laurel and Henry's troubles not only made me laugh (and cry at the end), but it reminded me of how important it is to communicate with your significant other. I talked things over with my guy and things have improved dramatically. Thanks to you! I left a five-star review on Amazon and wish I could give it ten stars. You're so talented and I'm so sorry I almost dismissed your book as being too frivolous. The joke is on me since it saved my relationship. I cannot wait to read your next one and hope it comes out soon.*

Forever grateful and a fan for life,
Josslyn

I gasped and dropped my sandwich onto my plate. My lips curled up in the direction of the older woman sitting across from me. She returned my grin as if she knew I'd received my first fan mail. My heart danced merrily in the knowledge a love story of my creation not only converted a naysayer of chick lit to a fan, but helped cure the ailments of a reader's real-world romantic relationship. If that didn't qualify as "relatable," I didn't know what did.

My heart beating fast, I clicked to my Amazon page and read her review. When I finished, I went to reply to her email and noticed another new message—this time from Christine Bannah. I covered my mouth in shock as I read what she wrote about wishing she'd reached out earlier to say how nice it was to meet me at the Brooklyn Book Fair and following up on her offer to read an ARC of *Love on Stone Street*. I blinked back more tears at her kindness. Imagine that—an author of her status reaching out to little old me. Perhaps I wasn't the scruffy little nobody I thought I was.

I switched back to Amazon on my computer and read the reviews of Christine's latest novel, the fourth in her series set in a small town. I typically enjoyed the first book in this type of series the most, becoming so attached to the original main character, I had trouble connecting to a new one. Surprisingly, her latest was my favorite. It was fresh with delicious conflict on every page. Yet she had several unfavorable reviews, including readers who said it was more annoying than funny, there was no chemistry between the hero and heroine, and most of the characters were unlikeable. I didn't agree with any of them and my opinion was equally as valid as anyone else's, more so perhaps, considering the weight my blog carried in terms of influencing readers. I shrugged. It was impossible to please everyone.

My head jutted back at my epiphany. It was so obvious, yet even after hearing it from Hannah, it hadn't quite sunk in until this very moment. It was as if the line separating Blogger Kim from Author Kim finally blended, allowing me to accept that a portion of the reader community wouldn't embrace my books and some might even hate them. It didn't matter. I'd keep writing because not doing so wasn't an option. And even if it was, it was a choice I'd never make voluntarily again. The days of me pretending I didn't ache to create stories were over. Even the people who loved me made it clear they wouldn't allow me to hide from my authentic self. I couldn't remove the cheesy grin from my face as my eyes swept the room again. Tingling with joy, I was tempted to thrust a fist into the sky and whoop for all the patrons of Ground Support to hear. Hallelujah, I'd seen the light at last.

I had no idea how long this clear thinking would last and in case it was fleeting, there was only one thing to do. Josslyn was waiting for my next novel and I planned to deliver. I opened up my manuscript and typed. I kept typing until my fingertips were numb and my kidneys ached from holding my bladder. When I finally put the proverbial pencil down, I knew I'd created something Felicia, Melina, and my readers would love. Most importantly, I loved it.

Chapter 29

A week later, Bridget nibbled on a curly fry she removed from the plate of assorted hors d'oeuvres we were sharing at Stone Creek Bar and Lounge a few blocks from my office. "Thanks for humoring me, guys."

I waved the onion ring I was holding. "You don't need to convince me to eat fattening food." Bridget had sent me a panicked text early in the morning saying her craving for fried bar food was out of control and begging me to go to dinner after work. I invited Nicholas since his team was meeting with the company's outside counsel—Rob—and he'd already be at my office. Bridget agreed to come downtown to meet us.

Bridget frowned before darting a guilty glance at the platter. "Am I the worst soon-to-be mommy in the world? I was desperate for a break from my doctor-imposed diet." She looked down at her paunch and rubbed it. "I promise I'll be good again tomorrow, baby."

"I read somewhere when a pregnant woman has cravings, it's her body's way of expressing what her unborn child needs." Nicholas removed a mozzarella stick from the plate with one hand and squeezed my knee under the table with the other.

"Mothers are definitely intuitive." Case in point, mine had called the day before to assure me there was nothing new to report, but results were expected soon. Her maternal instincts must have kicked in because, after going three days without calling her, I was tempted to book a flight to Florida.

"Somehow I doubt my baby needs fried cheese, but I'll go with it," Bridget said with a chuckle. "Back to raw nuts and lean protein tomorrow."

I pushed my plate away. "If I gain or lose even a couple pounds, all the work Kelly's doing on my dress will be for nothing. Unlike you, I can't blame it on my unborn child's nutritional requirements."

When Nicholas's phone rang, he grabbed it and stood up. "I need to take this. Excuse me a minute."

I watched Nicholas's retreating back for a moment before turning back to Bridget. "How are things going with Jonathan these days?" I'd been meaning to confront her for weeks, but between my dad's health issues, and my wedding/writing disasters, I hadn't had a chance. I also wanted to wait until we were alone, which hadn't happened in a while, what with half of Liberty High's graduating class of 2003 invited to my intervention.

"He's doing and saying all the right things," Bridget said without elaboration.

I leaned forward. "Meaning?"

She sighed. "He accompanies me to the doctor. He doesn't let me lift anything. He watches my diet." She shrugged. "He's being supportive."

This all sounded wonderful to me and exactly what I'd expect from Jonathan, but Bridget's lips quivered and her eyes took on a shiny about-to-cry appearance. Frowning, I said, "What aren't you telling me?"

"It's nothing. He's just..." She picked at the shell of an onion ring. "It's like he's going through the motions, but without any warmth. He doesn't seem at all enthused about becoming a daddy very soon."

I tried to remember how Jonathan had acted last time I'd come over, but I'd been too preoccupied by Hannah's unresponsiveness. "How so?"

"I asked if he wanted to find out the sex and he said it was up to me." She widened her green eyes at me. "What expecting father has no preference on whether or not to learn his unborn child's gender? You either want to know or you don't."

In a gentle tone, I said, "Maybe he's being selfless and putting your desire to know or not to know ahead of his own." It hit me we were discussing the sex of my very best friend's baby and my pulse raced. "Are you going to find out? Did you already take the test? What are you having?" I didn't require solid medical evidence to confirm what I already knew—they were having a girl—but I wouldn't turn it away.

Bridget's eyes twinkled as she shook her head at me. "I don't want to know, but if I change my mind, you'll be the first person I tell."

I cocked my head to the side. "After Jonathan."

"Whatever. It's not like he cares." She dipped a pig in a blanket into mustard and took a bite.

I tapped her on the hand. "Of course he does. Where is he tonight?"

"At home, I imagine. He assumed tonight was just girls and said he'd do his own thing."

I felt a surge of guilt for leaving him out, but it was fleeting since it wasn't intentional. I didn't know Nicholas would be joining us when I accepted Bridget's invitation either. "What other evidence do you have to support your claim he isn't excited about the baby?"

She swallowed. "He has no interest in baby shopping."

I rolled my eyes. "When has Jonathan ever liked shopping?"

Ignoring my question, Bridget popped the remains of her pig in a blanket into her mouth and closed her eyes. "Yum."

I followed her lead, relishing in the salty goodness. "So delish."

Bridget opened her eyes. "Please tell me you're having these at your wedding."

"We are if I have anything to say about it," I said as Nicholas returned to the table. "Honey, Sarah knows to include pigs in a blanket at our cocktail hour, right?"

"I imagine she does if you told her," Nicholas said, taking a sip of his beer.

"I haven't spoken to her at all. Did you tell her?"

Nicholas paused with his pilsner glass an inch from his lips. "I haven't talked to her either." He placed his beer on the table.

A chill ran up my spine. "You mean recently, right? You guys spoke when you booked her new company for the wedding."

Nicholas's face drained of color and his mouth went slack.

"Did I say something wrong?" The hair on my arms stood up straight.

"I thought you booked Sarah," he said in barely a whisper.

"What?" My stomach curdled and I thought I might be sick.

"You didn't?" He still spoke at a library-appropriate volume.

"No!" I yelped loudly enough to be heard at a rock concert. "She's your best friend's girlfriend, not mine. I assumed you did it." I stood up and circled the table. "This can't be happening," I mumbled.

"Don't freak out," Nicholas said, rising from the table. He placed his hands on my shoulders. "We'll figure this out." He said it calmly, but the panicked expression he shot Bridget belied the tone of his voice.

Bridget looked from me to Nicholas and back to me, her teeth biting down on her bottom lip. "I should let you guys deal with this." She stood halfway up and then froze in place "Unless you need me? Do you? Is there anything you—"

"No!" Nicholas fell back into his chair and covered his face with his hands. "I'm sorry, Bridget. Just go. Dinner's on us."

She met my eyes and held out her arms.

I walked into them and let her hug me. "You'll figure it out," she whispered in my ear. "Thanks for dinner." She tapped Nicholas on the arm and hoofed it to the exit.

Nicholas placed his phone to his ear.

"What are you doing?"

"Calling Sarah."

I joined him at the table, my legs bouncing uncontrollably beneath me. A million thoughts raced through my head. Was it truly possible we were less than two months from the wedding and didn't have a caterer? Maybe it was another nightmare, like the one I had where I walked down the aisle naked. Only my dreams were way more imaginative than this. Mine would involve something like the caterer switched our entrees with those of one of her vegan clients and there wasn't a pig in a blanket or even a piece of fish in sight. Or maybe all the guests suffered from food poisoning and simultaneously threw up into their plates. Simply forgetting to book the job was way too vanilla for my nightmares. No, this was really happening.

I saw Nicholas's lips move and shifted my seat to better hear his end of the conversation over the din of the tavern.

"I'm good. How are you?"

My eyes bugged out. He was so not good! "Put it on speaker," I whispered.

"Glad to hear it," he said into the phone before mouthing, "What?" to me.

"Speaker."

He complied. "So, you know Kimmie and I are getting married on November tenth?" He asked it like a question and then grimaced.

I mirrored his expression. This conversation sucked.

"Of course. George is excited to be the best man. I've already told him he's not allowed to race the entire month prior so he doesn't end up needing a boot to walk down the aisle or worse, a walker. He's not getting any younger." She chuckled, having no idea this was no laughing matter.

"Not sure I trust him," Nicholas said with a grin before scratching his head. "The thing is, we purposely opted out of using the Soho Grand's catering because we wanted to support Gotham City Catering, and well, we both thought the other spoke to you about it and it turns out neither of us did."

"Oh, wow." Her cheerful tone dropped at least two octaves.

"You can imagine our stress level right now." Nicholas squeezed my hand.

My palm was sweating and I couldn't look at him for fear of releasing the tears still holding strong behind my lids. "Is it t-too late?" I stuttered. "Can we still book you?" I removed my hand from Nicholas's grip and crossed my fingers. I squeezed my eyes shut in silent prayer and tried to remember to breathe.

Sarah sighed loudly into the phone. "I'd be so honored to cater your wedding, guys—truly—but we're already booked for the tenth, in Brooklyn. My partner, Jane, is heading it up since I'll be a guest at yours." She cursed to herself. "I wish I knew about this sooner because we'd have reserved the date for sure. I'm so sorry."

"Not your fault," Nicholas said before closing his own eyes and shaking his head.

"Can you call the venue to see if they can do the catering after all?" Sarah suggested.

Nicholas opened his eyes and looked at me. He raised his palms in the air and shrugged. "Sounds like a plan. Thanks, Sarah."

"Keep me posted, please. And good luck."

I chewed on my lips to stop them from quivering, but it was no use. Without a word, I vaulted out of my chair and, with all the restraint I could summon, speed walked to the exit of the restaurant before letting it rip. The second I got outside, my eyes and lips betrayed me and I bent over and cried.

"Kim." Nicholas patted my back a couple minutes later.

I ignored him, choosing to continue sobbing.

"Look at me."

Eventually, my eyes dried up and I stood up straight. I was exhausted. Shaking my head at him, I said, "I don't want to cancel the wedding."

Nicholas whipped his head back. "The exact opposite of what I thought you were going to say." He grinned. "A good surprise for a change."

Pulling on my hair, I said, "What are we going to do about food, Nicholas? Order pizza from Little Caesar's? Pizza, pizza!" I joked, but it was because the magnitude of this particular wedding disaster hadn't fully sunk in yet.

"I doubt it will come to that." He drew me into a hug. When we separated, he said, "Let's go home and call the Soho Grand. It's more than possible they'll be able to take on the catering. I'm sure they'd welcome an increased budget."

"I haven't returned any of April's calls. She probably hates me." I pressed my head into the crook of Nicholas's arm and resumed weeping.

Nicholas gently extracted me from his armpit, took my hand, and led me to a waiting cab. "It's impossible to hate you, Kimmie."

"Maybe we should have a Plan B in case the Soho Grand can't accommodate us. I saw a movie on The Hallmark Channel where they hired a bunch of local food trucks." I frowned. It wouldn't work because in the movie, the reception was held on a boat docked in an area already populated with food trucks—unlikely to be the case outside of the hotel on a Saturday night.

"First things first. Let's call April."

I spent the entirety of the cab ride attempting to bargain with God in exchange for the Soho Grand adding catering to our contract. I offered to have all our flowers arrive wilted until I remembered we decided to go with candles. By the time, we arrived at our apartment, I'd accepted the fact that either the Soho Grand would feed our wedding guests or they wouldn't.

Chapter 30

Nicholas offered to call April if I was too flustered, but I said I'd do it. I was her contact person and it was me who had ignored all her calls. If anyone should be on the receiving end of her possible resentment, it was me. We sat at our kitchen nook—Nicholas with a beer and me with a glass of ice water—and left a bag of Peanut M&M's within arm distance. No matter what happened, chocolate was in reach.

I found April's number under "recent calls" on my phone, pressed "call back," and put the phone on speaker.

"April Mills speaking."

I took a deep breath. "Hi April. This is Kim Long. I'm calling about the Strong/Long Wedding on November tenth." I twirled a strand of hair around my finger. "I'm so sorry I haven't returned your messages."

In an upbeat tone, April said, "Don't sweat it, Kim. Life gets crazy sometimes."

Ain't that the truth? I made eye contact with Nicholas, who gave me a wry grin.

April continued, "I wanted to touch base with you about the outside catering company. Is there anything they'll need from us? We'd be happy to communicate directly with them if you have a contact number."

"Thank you so much. To be honest, there's been a slight mishap with our caterer." I cringed at my use of "slight" to describe the present scenario.

"Oh, no. Is there anything we can do to help?"

"Actually, I was hoping it wasn't too late to add catering to our contract with you." I closed my eyes and crossed my fingers.

"I don't see why not. Give me a moment to pull up your file," April said, sounding nonplussed.

I looked up at Nicholas with wide eyes and he gave me a thumbs-up sign. My heart rate slowed to an almost-normal rate.

"Got it. I see here you've booked the premium bar menu but opted out of the food. Is that right?"

"Correct," I confirmed. Since Nicholas's biggest concerns were music and booze, we'd spared no expense on both. We'd hoped to budget the remaining aspects more carefully. In addition to being a friend, Sarah's company was a new one with competitive rates.

"Of course we can handle the catering as well, if you'd like."

"You can?" I sat up straight in my chair and gave Nicholas a high five.

"Certainly," April said. "I'll email you some of our packages right away. They include the various menu options and price lines. After you look it over, just call me back. We need to finalize your choices for the décor of the room—linens, china, table and chairs, etcetera—anyway."

"Wonderful!" I beamed at Nicholas.

"We'll just need to know within thirty days of the wedding if you want to move forward with the food which gives you…" April paused, presumably to check her calendar. "Two weeks to get back to me."

"We'll only need a few days to ponder our choices. Seventy-two hours tops," I said with certainty. We'd once again walked through fire without getting burned and there was no way I was going to play with matches again. This shit was getting done even if I had to take days off from work to do it. I gave April my email address and thanked her profusely for being so accommodating. I ended the call, vaulted from my chair, and did a victory dance. Nicholas laughed before joining me in the Whip and Nae Nae.

I fell back into my chair and chugged my water. "Whew. What a relief."

"I told you it would all work out," Nicholas said, reaching into the bag of M&M's.

I shook my head at him. "I still can't believe you never talked to Sarah."

"I can say the same about you." He shrugged. "Bygones."

"Bygones," I repeated with a smile. Any anger I felt toward Nicholas disappeared the moment April said the Soho Grand could accommodate us. I also acknowledged my role in the misunderstanding. If I'd been more organized and followed up with him sooner, the entire mess could have been avoided. Thank goodness this was the only wedding I'd ever have to plan, at least for myself. My marriage to Nicholas would be until death do us part.

"April said she'd email us the paperwork tonight. Let's fire up your computer so we can review it while we're still motivated," Nicholas said.

"Brilliant." I jogged to the bedroom, unplugged my charging laptop, and brought it to the kitchen. I busted another dance move before sitting back down.

A few minutes later, I was no longer in the mood to boogie. I glanced at Nicholas timidly. "What do you think?" The attachment to April's email, listing the available catering packages, was on the screen.

He blinked at the monitor. "It's somewhat more expensive than I'd expected."

I chewed on my lip. "Mmhm." My hopes sank. The prices were way outside the budget my parents had given us. Unless we canceled the band, photographer, and videographer or downgraded the alcohol from premium to beer and wine, we couldn't afford the menu options for the cocktail hour and dinner with most of our wish list items on it.

"I can ask my folks for more money. Making the bride's parents financially responsible for the wedding is an outdated tradition anyway," Nicholas suggested.

My stomach churned with discomfort. "Even though I'm sure they'd help us, I'd rather not. They're already paying for the rehearsal dinner and our honeymoon. It's plenty. My parents would probably shell out more, but with everything happening with my dad, I can't bring myself to ask."

Nicholas tapped his finger against his cheek in thought. "Do we really need a fancy red meat option? Chicken and pasta is fine, right?"

I frowned. "All of your groomsman are serious carnivores. Let them eat meat."

"Buffet?"

"Your dad hates buffets—too many germs." He'd even hemmed and hawed when the family chose to go to a tapas restaurant the year before. He didn't like to share.

"It seems like you're suggesting my family is more high maintenance than yours?" Nicholas cocked an eyebrow.

"I'm saying no such thing. Have you met Erin?"

The laugh we shared dissipated as quickly as it began.

"I have some good news that might render all these financial concerns moot."

My spirits lifted marginally. "What? I love good news."

Nicholas grinned. "I'm 99 percent sure I'm getting the promotion."

My mouth opened and my eyes went wide. "That's amazing, sweets!" I pulled him into an embrace. "Congrats!" Then I frowned. "Why is this the first I'm hearing of it?"

Nicholas pressed his lips together. "It's not official and I didn't want to get your hopes up in case it fell through."

I tsk-tsked him. "According to the fiancé manual, it would be my job to lift your spirits with my slammin' bedroom skills if you didn't get the job."

Scooting his chair closer to mine, Nicholas said, "Makes me almost wish they'd pick someone else."

"No worries. I'll use you to hone my talents either way." I plopped myself onto his lap.

He chuckled and wrapped his arms around my waist. "With the raise in income, we can pick up any catering costs outside of your parents' budget. Can you say filet mignon?"

I returned to my own chair. "Maybe." Since I didn't want Nicholas to think I doubted his chances of getting the promotion, I was hesitant to voice my concerns over spending money we didn't technically have yet.

Nicholas yawned. "It's obvious we're not going to make a decision tonight and I'm knackered. Why don't we sleep on it?"

I nodded, even though I had zero confidence in my ability to fall asleep with this unresolved.

Stroking my cheek, Nicholas said, "Focus on the positive, Kimmie. We have options. We just need to choose one."

As predicted, the sleep fairy wanted nothing to do with me. I lay in bed, wide awake, trying unsuccessfully to remain in the same position and keep my eyes closed for more than two seconds at a time.

Mr. Sandman couldn't get enough of my fiancé, of course. I glanced over at him sleeping soundly. He was on his side facing me with a hint of a smile on his lips. Maybe he was in the middle of a pleasant dream where our wedding guests were feasting on sushi, lobster mac and cheese, and bacon-wrapped scallops. From the way Sarah had gushed when her company launched, they had an array of creative mouth-watering dishes on offer. The Soho Grand did too, but we couldn't afford them. Had we known we'd be using the established hotel's services, we'd have budgeted differently, but we didn't and we hadn't.

How important was food anyway? The reception was a celebration of our love and pledge to be legally wed. It wasn't about the food. Once our guests had two of the top-shelf specialty martinis, they wouldn't care what they were eating anyway. We'd have the basics and call it a day. Although...

Nicholas's father was a big-shot surgeon and his parents were very wealthy. The additional expense would hardly change their lifestyle. However...

My mom already felt awful about not being very involved in the wedding planning. If she found out we skimped on the catering or went to the Strongs instead of asking her for help, she'd be devastated. And my stubborn father's pride would be wounded—assuming he even remembered me. My heart hurt at the possibility he had early-onset dementia. I couldn't go there.

Maybe Nicholas was right. If he had the promotion in the bag, the extra cost wouldn't be a hardship. But I hated the idea of him blowing a year's worth of his increased income on a single day. We were going to move to a bigger apartment if he got a raise so we could start a family in a year or two. I'd also wanted to discuss the possibility of downgrading my day job to three days a week if we could afford it. More time to write books would be a life changer and a huge investment in my career. I'd been planning to discuss it with Nicholas once his promotion was a done deal. If we spent the money on the wedding, I could kiss part-time work goodbye.

I flipped onto my side with a grunt. Nicholas was right—we had plenty of options. But I still had no friggin' clue what we should do.

The next morning, we both woke up as indecisive as ever. We decided to let things simmer a bit longer and discuss it over dinner later. After work, I entered our apartment, hung my key on the wall organizer by our front door, and dropped my purse on a kitchen stool. Since I assumed I'd beat Nicholas home, I was startled by the sound of him calling my name. I turned around to where he was sitting backward on the piano bench. Skipping the usual greetings, I said, "I've made a decision." It hadn't been easy, and I'd changed my mind four times since lunch. When I still hadn't faltered from the choice made at four by the time I left the office at five thirty, I knew it was the right one.

Nicholas stood up. "I have too."

We exchanged grins and I was certain we were on the same page.

"Let's go with the lower-budget option," I said at the same time he said, "We need to splurge on the premium menu. We only get married once."

My breath hitched and I backpedaled. "If it's really important to you," I said at the same time Nicholas said, "Unless you're truly okay with the basic items."

Clearly, neither of us were glued to our initial decision. I threw my hands up in the air. "I give up."

Nicholas took my hand and led me to the couch. "How about neither of the above? I bet another third-party caterer can give us the menu we want at a price we can afford."

I groaned. "How many hours do you think it will take to find this unicorn caterer? Do you have time? Because I sure as hell don't."

"Valid point." He puckered his lips and touched them with a finger. "How about we flip a coin?"

"Or put all the choices in a hat and pick the winner?"

"Rock, paper, scissors?"

I snickered. "Six of one. Half a dozen of the other. Let's flip a coin." How we came to suggesting games of chance to decide the food for our wedding was beyond my comprehension.

Nicholas removed a penny from his pocket. "Heads for cheaper, tails for more expensive." He tossed the coin a few inches in the air and caught it in the palm of his hand. "Heads."

Even as my shoulders relaxed in relief, the subtle downturn of Nicholas's lips tore up my insides. Against my better judgment, I said, "Best of three?"

He grinned and repeated the motion. "Tails. One for economy. One for big-ticket. Tie breaker on deck." Nicholas held the penny between his fingers, ready to decide the fate of our wedding. "You ready?"

"Yes," I lied. I took a deep breath and braced myself.

"Here we go." When his phone rang, he said, "Hold that thought," clearly happy for the built-in excuse to put off the third toss of the coin.

I hugged my legs against my chest and enjoyed a moment of peace.

"Hi, Sarah." He looked at me and mouthed, "Sarah" as if I hadn't heard him greet her a second earlier. "Yes. She's right here." He paused. "I will." He placed the phone on the coffee table and put it on speaker.

"Can you both hear me?" Sarah asked.

"Yes," we said in unison. My heart pounded furiously.

"Have you resolved your catering issues yet?"

Nicholas paced the floor surrounding the coffee table. "Not exactly. You caught us in the middle of a coin toss."

Sarah laughed. "I hope what I'm about to say will make your decision easy."

I locked eyes with my fiancé and swallowed hard. "Okay?"

"It turns out our gig in Brooklyn is only for thirty-five guests. How many people did you say you were having?"

"If everyone says yes, the count is one hundred and four, but we've already had several declines and are still awaiting the rest of the reply cards." I dug my teeth into my lower lip and prayed it was the right answer.

"To be safe, let's go with ninety," Nicholas said.

Sarah exhaled into the phone. "I was hoping you'd say that. I spoke to Jane and we agree we have enough staff to cater one small affair and one medium one in the same night. If you had closer to two hundred guests, it would be a different story. The other event is also earlier in the day so there isn't complete overlap."

I beamed at Nicholas, who held up a finger.

"This is amazing," he said. "But before we get too excited, can you remind us of your fees? The Soho Grand is taking care of the alcohol and the décor. All we need is food."

Sarah rattled off descriptions of the various items on offer and with each price she quoted, my spirits soared higher and higher. If we hired Gotham City Catering, we'd be able to invest in a close friend's entrepreneurial endeavor while feeding our guests the menu of our dreams—exactly as intended from the beginning. We set up a time to meet with Sarah and Jane to finalize the menu. When we ended the call, both Nicholas and I wore fat grins and rosy cheeks. We took some of our pent-up energy to the piano, where we played a duet of "Heart and Soul," the only song I knew how to play, on the piano.

Chapter 31

ONE MONTH UNTIL "I DO"

Dear Melina,

I hope you're having a great weekend!

I wanted to check in to see if you'd had a chance to read the latest version of Love on Stone Street *I sent you. I think I finally got it right, but I'm absolutely willing to keep revising if you think it needs more work.*

Thanks so much!

Kim

I proofread the email with labored breath as if I'd taken back-to-back spin classes— something I hoped I'd never have to do again. I was hesitant to nudge Melina after only three weeks, but terrified she'd have major comments on the manuscript. I hadn't heard from Felicia yet either. I'd lacked the time to send the latest version to her first, but had blind copied her on my email to Melina. After a very rough start, Nicholas and I finally got our acts together as far as the wedding planning was concerned, but with the countdown at only twenty-seven days, the last-minute details would need to take priority over my blogging and writing responsibilities. I'd have minimal time to focus on new edits until we returned from our honeymoon the week of Thanksgiving. I was afraid the revisions would be so intense, I wouldn't be able to meet the mid-December delivery date.

I felt Nicholas's breath on my neck as he hovered over me. "Don't you have brunch with Caroline and Bridget today?"

"I do." I skimmed the draft email for the third time.

"Are you planning to wear your pajamas? Shouldn't you get dressed?"

I glanced at the time on the bottom of my computer screen. "Shit." With one final read, I pressed send on the email and bolted out of my chair to get ready to meet my friends. I'd probably be a few minutes late, but they could keep each other company in the meantime.

After my shower, I went to the kitchen to ask Nicholas if he'd mind doing laundry while I was gone. We were down to our last clean towel. He had his back to me with his phone to his ear.

"I will. Thanks for everything, Tiff—" He turned around before completing his sentence, saw me, and ended the call. Scraping a hand through his hair, he said, "Good shower, Kimmie?"

I gave him a hard stare. "Nice try. Was that Tiffany?"

He nodded. "She wanted to know if you found a good makeup artist for the wedding because she has a few recommendations."

I narrowed my eyes at him. "Why would she call you and not me?"

"She said she tried your number, but you didn't pick up."

"Oh really?" I walked to where my phone was charging on the counter. "No missed calls from Tiffany. Shocking." My skin burned with irritation.

He raised his palms. "Don't shoot the messenger."

I put my hands on my hips, almost losing my towel in the process. "Weren't you going to tell her to lay off?"

"I thought she'd been behaving lately, but I promise I'll talk to her."

I smirked. "Promises, shmomises."

He lessened the space between us and pecked my nose. "You're adorable. Now finish getting ready before I pull off your towel and delay you even further."

As tempted as I was to call Nicholas's bluff, I did as I was told.

Twenty minutes later, wearing a rusty rose floral print high-low wrap dress and open-toe faux suede heels, I kissed Nicholas goodbye. The Uber he'd called for me was already outside. "Please do a load or two of laundry if you get a chance."

Nicholas winked. "Yes, Master."

*   *   *

Bridget texted as the car was approaching Park Avenue Autumn/Winter/Spring/Summer, a restaurant near my office in the Flatiron neighborhood that changed its menu each season. Caroline suggested it after it was spotlighted in *New York Magazine*. I replied with a quick "About to walk in" before thanking the driver and closing the door of the black sedan behind me.

When I entered the restaurant, I was immediately drawn to the enormous tree in the middle of the space. Lights hung from the orange-leaved branches. The décor successfully evoked the autumn season down to the glass vases adorning each table and filled to the brim with green and pale brown acorns, pinecones, and red, yellow, and orange leaves. Even the waiters were aptly dressed in red plaid shirts. As my mouth watered in anticipation of my next meal, I hoped the food lived up to the atmosphere.

I gave my name to the hostess and followed her toward the center of the crowded dining room. As I kept my eyes out for Caroline's blonde head or Bridget's striking red locks, I caught sight of a woman who bore a marked resemblance to my mom. To her side was a girl with espresso-colored spiral curls. She looked exactly like—Erin?

My heart caught in my throat and I stopped in my place. What was happening here? One by one, the faces of the closest women in my life saw me approach and clapped their hands together. It dawned on me this was my wedding shower. The pile of gifts set off to the side confirmed my suspicion. In all the madness of the last months, it had never occurred to me my bridal party would plan something behind my back.

My mom was the first to rise from her seat. "Happy bridal shower, baby." She approached me with open arms. "I've missed you so much," she cooed.

"Mom," I said before squeezing her hard and inhaling her familiar floral scent. My legs shook beneath me and tears of joy threatened to ruin my eye makeup. It felt like an out-of-body experience as I made my way around the large round table to hug all the female members of my bridal party and...Tiffany. We came to face to face and before I had a chance to politely ask what she was doing there, she pulled me into a tight embrace.

"Surprise!" She let me go and giggled. "We got you but good."

"You sure did." I smiled awkwardly.

"Come sit," Bridget said, patting the empty chair between her and my mom.

It was an idyllic afternoon with only my closest friends and family members—present and future. The discomfort I felt over Tiffany's inappropriate inclusion was diminished by the company and the delicious food, including roasted butternut soup, salmon buccatini, kale salad, and avocado eggs Benedict. Bridget and Caroline took credit for putting the event together and they pulled in Natalie to help with the planning, much to Erin's chagrin. To my little sister's defense, she only threw stony glares in Natalie's direction when she thought I wasn't looking. And she vocalized, loudly, how she would have obviously assumed a larger role if she was local.

When the waiters began clearing the dessert plates, I switched seats with Natalie so I could bond with Mrs. Strong. She was gushing over photos of my gown when Tiffany said, "Who invited the groom?" in a teasing tone.

I looked up as Nicholas approached the table, along with his father and brothers, George, Gerry, and my dad. Overcome with emotion, I vaulted off my chair and into my dad's arms. I hugged him with one arm and grabbed onto Nicholas with the other to alleviate the guilt I felt over acknowledging my father before my future husband. I was just so happy to see him alive and well.

"How are you, Dad?" It was a casual question with serious undertones.

"I'm wonderful, Tiny Kim. Couldn't be better." He winked one of his brown eyes at me.

I scrutinized him. He was dressed in a pair of olive-green Dockers and an off-white sweater and looked exactly the same as the last time I'd seen him. He appeared no thinner or heavier than before, and I was almost positive he was wearing the same outfit too. "As long as you're sure." I glanced over my shoulder at my mother for confirmation, but she was busy greeting the Strong brothers. I'd corner her later. She told me not to call. She never said anything about asking her face to face.

While Dr. Strong described in excruciating detail the walls of

Keen's Steakhouse, which were apparently decorated with old pipes belonging to iconic figures from the past including Babe Ruth, Abraham Lincoln, and Albert Einstein, I snuggled into Nicholas's arms. He ran his fingers through my hair while Warren continued to gush over Keen's.

"I wouldn't recommend it to my heart patients, but it was by far the best porterhouse I've ever had," he said, pumping out his broad chest.

I looked up at Nicholas. "You agree?"

"I had the bone-in ribeye, but it was mad delicious. Instead of doing the laundry as instructed by my dear fiancée, I stuffed my face with half a cow. I hope I can fit into my tux next month." He dropped his hands from my head and rubbed his belly.

"No worries. I'll help you burn off the calories later." A quick check confirmed no one was watching us and I pinched his butt for emphasis.

"I look forward to it." He kissed the top of my head. "Now I can tell you the real reason Tiffany's been calling me."

My belly flopped at the mention of her name. "Why?"

He did a sweep of the restaurant with his arms. "Apparently, Natalie delegated some of her bridemaid's duties to Tiffany. She kept me in the loop regarding the plans so I'd know where you had to go and when you needed to be there. The venue changed twice before you wound up here." Peering into my eyes, he said, "I hope you liked it."

"It was perfect, but..." Something didn't sit right.

Nicholas crinkled his brow. "What's wrong?"

"I just..." I felt incredibly lame soiling an amazing afternoon with this, but I couldn't help myself. "I still don't know why Tiffany is such a big part of our wedding day. I know she's Natalie's friend, but she's not mine. And it's not like you kept in touch with her after high school either, so why?"

"Clearly, I leave a lasting impression on my old flames and Tiffany wants to live vicariously through my current one." He laughed, but when I didn't join in, he clucked his tongue. "Okay, let's find out what her deal is." He held out his hand and when I took it, we walked over to where Natalie was sitting with her brothers, sisters-in-law, and Tiffany at the table the restaurant had set up for our late arrivals.

Nicholas politely interrupted the conversation they were having and asked Natalie if we could borrow her for a minute outside.

When we stood awkwardly at the edge of the sidewalk, I broke the silence by thanking her for throwing an unforgettable party. "I honestly had no idea."

"We appreciate everything you've done for us," Nicholas said with a nod at his sister.

A blush painted Natalie's olive skin. "I wanted to hold it at a hot new poke restaurant downtown but was outvoted. Apparently, Erin isn't a fan of raw fish," she snarled.

Disregarding the dig at my sister, Nicholas said, "We're truly thankful for all your help, but we're a bit concerned with the significant role Tiffany's been playing. She's one of my ex-girlfriends, which makes it awkward for both Kim and me. And she's not even coming to the wedding."

Natalie rounded her shoulders and stared us down. "I was invited to your wedding with a plus one. Correct?"

"Yes," I said.

She swiped her bangs off her forehead. "I'm bringing Tiffany."

It was true we'd invited everyone with a date, but Tiffany? I glanced at Nicholas for his reaction.

"Isn't there anyone else you want to ask? Like a guy you're dating?" Nicholas said.

Natalie raised a dark eyebrow. "Are you suggesting I have to date a guy? What if I'm dating a girl?"

My jaw dropped. "Are you saying...?"

She locked eyes with me. "Yes. I'm dating Tiffany."

"You're dating Tiffany? Like romantically?" Nicholas asked, his browns eyes protruding like bugs.

Natalie folded her arms across her chest. "Yes. And before you embarrass yourself by asking for clarification, we are sleeping together—as in, having sex." She took a step closer to me. "I know she's been a holy terror with stories of the good old days with Nicholas. I've begged her to lay off, but she lives to get a rise out of me. Making each other jealous is practically part of our foreplay." Her eyes glowed with adoration I couldn't believe I'd never noticed before.

As if sensing us talking about her, Tiffany walked out of the restaurant, radiant in a salmon colored open-shoulder sweater dress.

Nicholas jutted his head at her. "You're a lesbian?"

She pouted. "Bisexual, actually."

"I prefer the term pansexual," Natalie said, draping an arm around Tiffany's back.

Tiffany settled into Natalie's side. "What is this about?"

I wasn't sure if I could believe my ears, but I forced myself to take an active role in the conversation. "Natalie told us you guys were dating. We had no idea."

Tiffany's blue eyes rounded and she placed her hand over her heart. "You didn't?" With a laugh, she said "Why else would I be around so much? It would be rather inappropriate of me to help plan my first boyfriend's wedding unless I was dating his sister, don't you think?"

Silence filled the air while our brains translated Tiffany's statement.

I stood like a statue as it all sunk in. The only movement I made was to clamp my hand over my mouth to stop my body from doing what it instinctively desired—laugh my ass off. Nicholas and his sister having a sexual partner in common was all too much.

After a moment, Nicholas nodded. "Rather inappropriate," he agreed, meeting my eyes. "Right, Kimmie?"

My torso shook and I sucked in my stomach to keep my core steady. "Indeed." I grabbed onto Nicholas's elbow and faced the girls. "Can you please excuse us for a second? I need to..." My lips quivered against my will. "C'mon."

Holding hands, Nicholas and I jogged to the end of the block and turned the corner. When we were certain no one had followed us, we stopped, faced each other, and burst out laughing.

Once we composed ourselves, we went back inside the restaurant to say our goodbyes. With the arrival of the men, we'd become a rowdy crowd. We'd been finished eating for almost an hour, and I didn't want to linger too much longer, especially since the dinner service would be starting soon.

It was time to politely lead our guests to the exit, but first I was determined to ask my mom if the test results were finally in. The last time we spoke, she'd said they were expected "soon."

The group had relocated to the bar area and I secretly observed my dad talking to Warren. He was probably faking an interest in whatever medical anecdote Warren was sharing. My father had a drink in his hands—a glass half-filled with topaz-colored liquid on ice. Knowing him, I guessed it was Scotch on the rocks. Either the doctor didn't rule out alcohol—a positive sign—or my father was being rebellious. My stomach churned anxiously and I looked for my mom.

She was talking animatedly to Jeanine, and when I tapped her on the back, she turned to me with bright cheeks. "There's our girl. We were just saying what a beautiful bride you're going to make."

My heart filled with confidence at the compliment despite the biased source. "Thank you. I hope you're right. Can I speak to you alone for a second?" I glanced at Jeanine and gave her a closed-mouth smile. "I promise to bring her back."

Jeanine placed her hand on my arm. "Take your time. In fact, I'm going to find Nicholas. I don't think I've hugged my baby boy today."

She scurried over to where my future husband was deep in conversation with George. As if sensing me watching him, Nicholas caught my eye across the bar and winked.

I gave a little wave and turned back to my mom. "Did Dad's test results come in?"

She drew me into a hug. "It's all good. The tests ruled out dementia. I would have told you earlier, but the results came in just this week. I was afraid if I called you, I'd manage to ruin the surprise."

"Thank God." My back relaxed in relief for a moment until I remembered something. "But why is he having memory issues? Isn't he too young to blame this on the regular effects of aging?" My parents were still in their fifties.

"The memory loss was caused by the statins in his cholesterol medication. They lowered the dose, put him on a strict diet and, although they'll continue to monitor him, they're confident the symptoms will disappear. Apparently, this is a common side effect." She took my hands in hers. "You're officially out of excuses for not fully embracing this joyous time in your life. If you're fortunate, it only happens once." She gestured toward Nicholas, who was at the bar doing shots with his brothers while Jeanine cheered them on. "You're a lucky lady. Now enjoy yourself." She gave me a stern look. "Or I'm grounding you for a week and removing your reading privileges."

She'd get no argument from me and knew it. I gave her another hug and joined my husband and future brother-in-laws for a shot. Vodka with a side of gratitude went down very well.

Chapter 32

I liked Tiffany a lot more after learning she had the hots for my future sister-in-law and not my soon-to-be husband. Still, I didn't quite believe Tiffany's only motivation for flirting with Nicholas was to make Natalie jealous, and it wouldn't have surprised me if she hoped for an eventual three-way with the brother-and-sister pair. Since the thought brought bile to the back of my throat, I tried not to think about it on a full stomach. Between recommending the makeup artist I ended up choosing and suggesting the venue for our rehearsal dinner, Tiffany contributed almost as much to the wedding planning as anyone else in the party. I declined her and Natalie's offer to sit in on our meeting with Sarah and her partner, not because of Tiffany, but because I feared Natalie would scowl at all our food choices and suggest ones better served during a challenge on Survivor.

Since Sarah would be a guest at the wedding and not involved in the food preparation for the event, she wanted to introduce Nicholas and me to her partner, Jane. They'd become friends while students at the International Culinary Institute. We met the two of them to finalize the menu at the two-room office suite they leased in Queens while they saved up to buy their own commercial kitchen. Sarah had explained if the venue where an event was being held didn't have a big enough kitchen to accommodate them, they rented the space, depending on the size of the party. In our case, The Soho Grand would give them full access to their kitchen.

Sarah told us to make ourselves comfortable at the small conference table. After offering an array of beverages, she made introductions.

Jane, a girl about my age with wavy shoulder-length honey-blonde hair, beamed at me. "I'm in such a state over catering Kim

Long's wedding! My best friend and I devoured *A Blogger's Life.*
Marissa threatened to defriend me when I said she couldn't come
today. Would you mind signing copies of our books for us when we're
finished?" She motioned toward the two paperbacks resting on the
radiator.

I'd noticed the books the second I walked in and had been itching
to peek at the titles. To learn they were copies of my novel left me
breathless. "I'm so happy you guys enjoyed the book. Of course I'll sign
your copies." I debated asking if they posted reviews on Amazon and, if
not, would they?

The gold flecks in Jane's brown eyes twinkled. "Yay!"

"Shall we get down to business?" Sarah asked.

"Of course." I bit my cheek to wipe the goofy grin off my face as
Nicholas nudged me knowingly.

Over the course of the next hour, we drooled over descriptions
and photos of some of the more creative cocktail-hour options on offer,
including fried chicken bites in mini waffle cones, fried mac & cheese
lollipops, tomato-soup shooters topped with a wedge of grilled cheese,
push-up ceviche, and Nicholas's favorite, oysters. We also chose pigs in
a blanket to avoid my pregnant best friend having a hormonal fit.
Sarah and Jane offered suggestions to make sure everyone from the
meat-eating father of the groom to the fish-loving ex-nemesis of the
bride wouldn't go hungry. For the main course, there would be a choice
between filet mignon, Chilean seabass, and vegetarian pasta. The
evening left me with a solid appreciation for Nicholas's best friend
George, without whom we might not have known about his girlfriend,
Sarah, and her new company. I was also grateful we were getting
married this year and not next because I had a feeling they'd raise their
prices very soon—as they should. A more established caterer would
probably charge at least $300 a person for what we were getting for
less than half the cost.

"I'm so glad you chose the pasta dish. The asparagus, snap pea,
and avocado pasta is one of my favorite recipes and has been a massive
hit at every affair where it's been featured," Sarah said proudly.

"We catered my ex-colleague Andrew's wedding earlier this year.
Fara, the bride, loved the dish so much, they had to drag her away from
her plate for the first dance. She asked one of the servers to keep it

warm." Jane's face lit up at the memory.

"I might have to rethink my filet mignon pick," Nicholas said.

I nodded in agreement, even though I doubted it mattered which dish I chose. Every woman I ever spoke to said she didn't eat a thing at her own wedding. Maybe Sarah would agree to put aside one of everything for Nicholas and me to eat in bed the morning after.

"Speaking of first dances, what's your song?" Sarah asked. "Unless it's a secret, of course."

When Nicholas opened his mouth to respond, I cut him off. "It's a surprise."

Nicholas cocked his head at me with his forehead wrinkled.

I blinked at him. It was a surprise—to all of us.

At home after the meeting with Sarah and Jane, we decided to get serious about picking a song for our first dance. I made us both a cup of Nespresso for a jolt of caffeine, and we silenced our phones and kept the television off to ensure no distractions.

"My vote is 'In My Life.' You can't go wrong with The Beatles," Nicholas said, scrolling his iPod from his spot next to me on the couch. "What do you think?"

I brought my mug to my nose and inhaled the nutty aroma of the coffee. "We can't use the same song as David." I wouldn't want my colleague to think I copied him.

"David used 'In My Life'? I'm impressed."

"Sorry, hon, but you're not the only Beatles fan on the planet," I said with a snicker.

Smirking, Nicholas said, "How about 'P.S. I Love You'?" He extended his legs onto the coffee table and sipped his Nespresso.

"Not slow enough." I grimaced at the image of us dancing our first dance to a fast beat. "Listen, I know you love the Beatles, but I'm already walking down the aisle to 'All You Need is Love' and we're entering the reception for the first time as husband and wife to 'Love Me Do.' Maybe we should cater to our non-Beatles-loving fans." I knew this was not something Nicholas wanted to hear, but it had to be said.

Nicholas clamped a hand against his mouth and opened his eyes wide in mock horror. "Who are these Beatles-hater guests of whom you speak? I'd like to renege their invitations." He chuckled. "Have no fear, the band has been instructed to play a variety of music of all different genres—something for everyone. Besides, the first song is about the bride and groom, not the guests."

I frowned. "Then if you must know, this bride isn't feeling any of the Beatles songs either. The lyrics should define us."

With a sigh, Nicholas said, "Fair enough. What do you suggest?"

"How about 'Grow Old With Me'?"

Nicholas's face lit up. "John Lennon?"

"I was thinking the Mary Chapin Carpenter version." I sat up straight with cautious hope.

He pursed his lips. "No. What else?"

I sunk back against the couch and scrolled the list of songs I'd jotted down in my notes. "What do you think of John Legend's 'Stay with You'?" I held my breath.

Nicholas made a sour face.

This went on for the next forty-five minutes. With each song choice the other tossed aside, I got more depressed. What if our inability to agree on a single song suggested a deeply rooted incompatibility or at minimum, served as a warning to avoid long road trips?

"I have an idea." Nicholas removed his legs from the table and stood up.

I looked up at him. "Do tell," I said, my tone lackluster. I had little reason to think I'd like this new pitch any more than I had the one before it and the one before that.

Nicholas's eyes danced. "How about we have two songs? One I'll dedicate to you and the other you'll dedicate to me. It will be a surprise, but we can't choose any of the tunes we've already discussed tonight."

The edges of my lips threatened to curl up at this proposition, but I bit down on my smile due to lingering doubts. "It's not very traditional. Would our guests think it's weird?" I twisted a strand of hair around my finger.

"Kimmie." Nicholas bent down and stroked my cheek. "My sister is dating my first girlfriend, your best friend is pregnant with your first boyfriend's baby, and your dress was altered by the runner-up of Project Runway as a favor to your high-school nemesis, who's now invited to the wedding." He gave a slight shake of his head. "What about our wedding hasn't been weird?"

The grin I'd been suppressing could no longer be held back. "Two songs it is."

Chapter 33

With only three weeks until the wedding, it was time to focus on the centerpieces. Nicholas and I had agreed—me reluctantly, him adamantly—not to stress ourselves out so late in the game by racing against the clock to choose the perfect bouquets to place at each table. Candles were a lower-maintenance option. They were also cheaper than flowers, and we welcomed the opportunity to save a little money. Caroline had assured me the right candle display could be sophisticated, romantic, and wow a room just like flowers. Bridget had volunteered to take charge of the design, and with her artistic eye, I knew we were in good hands. She wanted to get an idea of my preferences before working her magic and so the two of us went to Caroline's place after work one day the week after my surprise bridal shower to look at Pinterest for inspiration.

Caroline's apartment on the Upper East Side had always been large by New York City standards, but after she married Felix, they purchased the vacant apartment next door, thereby converting the one-bedroom/one-bathroom home into a two bedroom/two-bathroom space. From Caroline's living room, which was about the size of the studio I rented before moving in with Nicholas, Caroline said, "What do you think?"

I nodded tentatively and pulled on a strand of hair. "It's pretty." Not for the first time in my life, I was thankful I'd never gone to law school. From the way Caroline narrowed her blue eyes as she studied my face, it was obvious I hadn't convinced her. I'd never be able to work a jury. I stared down at the gray marble top of her six-person dining room table.

"You don't like it." It wasn't a question as much as a statement.

"I do." I took another look at the picture on Caroline's computer screen, hoping for love at second sight, but it was no use. The heart wanted what the heart wanted and, in my case, what it couldn't have—flowers. I had no doubt in Bridget's abilities, and when she was finished, I was confident the sounds of oohs and ahs would echo the ballroom as our guests entered the reception. But I'd always envisioned celebrating my nuptials to the backdrop of flowers in all different shades of pink, like rose and fuchsia and watermelon and coral. Sometimes I visualized small splashes of yellow, blue, and even purple. If I closed my eyes, I could practically smell the fresh blooms. All the candle displays we'd seen so far today were easy on the eyes, but they were all muted colors like white or cream, and I couldn't smell them no matter how hard I tried. I took a deep breath and focused on the positive—the likelihood of a guest having an allergic reaction to my wedding decorations was reduced significantly by nixing the perennials.

Bridget placed a pitcher of virgin sangria on the table and poured me a glass. I took a sip, letting the sweet liquid swirl around the insides of my cheeks. It was delicious, but the grape-juice based cocktail lacked the kick afforded by the non-virgin variety. Then again, it was better to have my wits about me than get drunk and decide bubblegum-scented tumbler candles from Yankee Candle were the way to go. Even though they were pink.

"What are you guys looking at now?" Bridget awkwardly lifted herself onto a black leather-upholstered chair and scooched it as close to the table as her six-months-along pregnant belly would allow.

"What do you think, Bridge?" On the screen was a photograph of a long farmhouse table decorated with modern white frosted-glass square vases, each containing a votive candle.

"Very elegant." Bridget scrutinized the picture while sucking on a curly strand of her long hair. After a moment, she brushed away the hair and rubbed her belly. "Something like this would be perfect if you were having a winter wedding. For your big day in early November, I think we should pick something warmer like—"

"Flowers?" I mumbled. Bridget and Caroline exchanged a look that sent a stab of guilt through my gut. My besties had already gone above and beyond their maid of honor and bridesmaid duties. I knew they had other, more important and probably more enjoyable, activities they could be doing tonight, and yet they gave up their evening to help me—again. I was the most selfish friend on the island of Manhattan. An attitude adjustment was in order. Adopting an upbeat voice, I said, "Let's keep looking. I'm sure there's something we can work with."

Caroline beamed. "That's the spirit, Kim."

I planted on a smile and for the next ten minutes, I pointed out the parts of the various candle displays I liked the most and which I hated. I was telling the girls the current display on the screen—votive candles in pink-tinted mason jars—rated a seven and a half out of ten when my phone rang. It was Felicia. I remained frozen in place, as if my limbs were trapped by invisible chains. Rather than answer the call, I stared at the display as it rang once, then twice, until an unseen force jolted me into action. "I need to take this," I said to the girls. My shoeless feet scurried to the other side of the expansive living room, which was so big, it might as well have been in a different building. Even without shoes on, the bottoms of my black tights were clear of dust balls when I sunk my butt into a cushion on the coffee-colored suede couch.

"Hi, Felicia." I winced at my failure to disguise the nervous edge to my voice.

"How are you, Kim?" She sounded wistful, like she was about to deliver unwanted test results.

Anxious, terrified, and having difficulty breathing. "I'm good," I said in practically a whisper. I swallowed hard. "How are you?" To keep my legs from bouncing, I lifted them onto the couch and sat cross-legged.

"Doing well. Listen, Kim, I was wondering if you had time this week to get together. Maybe meet for coffee?"

My next breath lodged itself in my throat and I inhaled through my nose and out my lips to avoid hyperventilating. "S-sure," I stuttered. "Um, when did you have in mind?"

"Is tomorrow good? I know you have work, but can you meet me at the Le Pain Quotidien on Thirty-third and Park at six?"

"Sounds good. I'll see you then." We said our goodbyes and ended the call. I stood still for a beat, watching the phone bounce on top of my palm until I realized the movement was caused by my hand shaking.

I'd only met Felicia in person twice—the day she offered me representation and when we went over the offer from Fifth Avenue Press. For her to suggest another face-to-face appointment meant something big was going down. This could be a positive development. Maybe Reese Witherspoon had approached her about optioning the rights to *A Blogger's Life* or something of similar awesomeness. On the flip side, she could deliver the news Melina hated my revisions for *Love on Stone Street*, the publisher was dropping it from their list, and she was letting me go as her client. In other words, it could be a dream come true or the end of my author life as I knew it.

"Everything all right, Kim?"

I raised my head toward where Caroline and Bridget were still sitting at the kitchen table and took the slow walk over.

"Who was on the phone?" Caroline asked.

"Felicia. She wants to meet me for coffee." I shivered.

Caroline furrowed her brow. "You cold? I can turn down the AC."

I rubbed my arms. "I don't know why she wants to meet with me, and anxiety gives me the chills."

Bridget's eyes lit up. "I bet it's because they're making *A Blogger's Life* into a movie. I think Liam Hemsworth should play Henry."

"A girl can dream," I said, with a chuckle. I wasn't surprised both our minds went straight to a possible movie deal. Sometimes I was convinced we shared the same brain. "But what if she's going to drop me as her client because my editor doesn't want to work with me anymore?" I truly thought I'd nailed the revisions this last time, but maybe it was wishful thinking. Strike three, you're out.

"Why would she do that?" Caroline motioned to an empty chair. "Sit. Do you want something to drink? I have wine." She darted a guilty look at Bridget. "Sorry."

Bridget shooed her away. "By all means, liquor up. No reason everyone needs to drink fake sangria."

"Thanks, but I should go home." I'd walk. It would take me an hour to get there from the Upper East Side, but the fresh air would do me good. I looked over at my three-inch leather boots where I'd left them by Caroline's front door and I could almost hear my feet whine in protest. I'd take the subway.

Caroline's head whipped back. "Are you meeting her now?"

"Not until tomorrow, but I don't think I can focus on the wedding right now." I glanced at the table where Bridget had scribbled notes in a black and white old-school composition notebook. I could make out the words "candles" and "pink." My stomach clenched with shame. "I love you both so much for trying to help me. Please know how much I appreciate everything you've done." I stood on my toes and reached up to hug Caroline. She smelled like Love's Baby Soft—so safe. I was reluctant to let go, but I did.

I was afraid to make eye contact with Bridget. I was carrying twice my weight in nerves and was afraid it was contagious. I should be the only one to have a sleepless night.

"Kim?" she whispered, forcing me to face her head on. Her eyes welled up and, although I was sure much of it was hormonal, I also knew she truly felt my jitters, almost like we were twins.

"Think positive. Don't make assumptions," Caroline urged.

Caroline was right, but it was easier to prepare for the worst than expect the best.

"And don't worry about the centerpieces. We'll take care of everything," Bridget said.

I jerked my head back. "No way." Bridget was my maid of honor, not my wedding planner. I told her as much.

"I want to. Let me do this for you." She cocked her head toward Caroline. "Let us do this for you. We owe you for not subjecting us to a crazy bachelorette party in Atlantic City."

I'd told the girls my ideal bachelorette party consisted of a relaxing afternoon being pampered at a spa followed by a scrumptious dinner with my two favorite girls. I'd always preferred the intimate company of a few close friends to hanging out in large crowds. I also knew if my entire bridal party attempted to put something together, Erin and Natalie would never agree on a venue. Erin would scoff at a clubby-type place whereas Natalie might consider a hotel lounge, Erin's likely suggestion, stuffy. A small sigh escaped my lips. "No Palace Spa, please. I can do without a verbal spanking from a naked European lady," I said, referring to the bath house the three of us had narrowly escaped two years earlier.

"No skinny dipping with Brooklyn's finest. We promise," Caroline said with a chuckle.

Bridget made a face like she'd had a bite of something unpleasant. "I would never subject this belly to public scrutiny," she said, even while lovingly patting her stomach. "Does this mean you'll let us handle the centerpieces?"

I looked from Bridget to Caroline and back to Bridget again. "You sure?"

"Do you trust me to choose something fabulous?" Bridget asked.

"I trust you with everything, even my credit card." I smiled at them. "Both of you." I tried to summon my emotions from only a few minutes earlier, when having a flowerless wedding reception felt like the end of the world, and I couldn't. If anything, the call from Felicia gave me some perspective on where my priorities lay.

I bid my best friends a good night with full certainty they'd whip up something spectacular for my centerpieces. Everything else would be revealed the following day.

Chapter 34

When I got home, I dropped my keys in the holder and hung my denim jacket in the hallway closet. I'd managed to distract myself on the subway with the latest book in my queue—a chick lit novel told from the perspective of a single, lovelorn guy—but the second I stepped onto the street, it all came back to me. I had promised Nicholas I would confide in him rather than bottle up my feelings like some sort of martyr.

He was in the kitchen with his head in the refrigerator. "I have some news," I said to his back.

He turned around. "Let me guess, there's a nationwide shortage of candles and we're forced to either borrow from our retirement funds or go on the black market to purchase our wedding decorations."

I rolled my eyes. "Nothing quite so dire."

Nicholas swiped his brow in mock relief. "I can handle anything else."

I told him about Felicia's phone call and our meeting for the next day. When I was finished, Nicholas gestured to a chair and told me to sit while he poured us both a glass of wine. "Don't let your inner demons spook you."

I gave Nicholas a knowing look. "Have we met?"

Nicholas smirked.

I took a huge gulp of wine, hoping it would alleviate the ache in my chest at least temporarily.

"In other news, guess who got the promotion?" His lips curled upward, leaving no mystery to the answer.

My mouth dropped open and my eyes welled up with happy tears. "Nicholas! That's fabulous." I leaped off the chair and into his arms. "I'm so happy for you."

He squeezed me hard before letting go. "I found out today."

"You deserve it." I reached for the bottle of wine and refilled both our glasses. "This is cause for celebration." I raised my glass. "To the new executive general counsel of Gracefully Made Cosmetics."

Nicholas clinked his glass against mine. "It never would have happened if you hadn't come to my rescue the day of the presentation."

My knees still stung at the memory, but it was well worth the pain. "You were the genius behind it, not me."

"But you made it possible for me to present it." Nicholas's face shined with love.

Melting a little, I said, "We make a good team."

"The best." He kissed me softly on the lips.

I remembered something. "If you got the promotion, I was hoping we could afford to have me cut back on the day job by a day or two a week to focus on my writing. But I should probably confirm I still have an agent first." My career prospects stretched out before me in a continuous stream of nine-to-five days at a cubicle, behind a desk, taking orders from Rob. At least he was a decent guy, unlike Darin Clayton, the partner down the hall. He was forever blowing his top, usually in the direction of his assistant. I'd have to up my game at work. If Rob canned me, I might get stuck with someone like Darin next time around.

Breaking me out of my depressing glimpse into the future, Nicholas said, "Let's sit down after the wedding and talk about you cutting your hours. If Rob's okay with you working part time, I think you should."

"Shouldn't we wait to hear what Felicia has to say?" I hugged myself to stop from shaking.

Nicholas frowned. "If the worst happens, it will suck, but you'll come through it. There are other agents and other publishers. *A Blogger's Life* is doing well. I'm sure you'll bounce back and find an even better team eventually."

My heart swelled with love at Nicholas's faith in me, even if I didn't share it.

He kept talking. "Promise me you won't give up your dream no matter what happens tomorrow."

"I promise to try." It was the best I could do without full-on fibbing to my fiancé.

The following evening at eight minutes before six o'clock, I walked the one block from the subway to the entrance of Le Pain Quotidien. I consciously took breaths at regular intervals to trick my body into thinking I was calm and collected, but I wasn't fooling any inch of it. I was dark and stormy like the cocktail. I was also over tired, the result of a restless night's sleep. I spent most of it flipping from my left side to my right and moving my pillow from behind my head to between my knees to the tips of Nicholas's feet. He slept right through it, since there wasn't a ticklish bone in his body. I did manage an hour or two of repose, but it was riddled with bizarre dreams. In one, Erin was querying a memoir based on the remodel of her living room.

I usually liked when work was quiet so I could catch up on my reading, draft reviews for *Pastel Is the New Black*, or promote *A Blogger's Life*. With Rob on a business trip to Baltimore, I had plenty of time for all those activities, but I lacked the focus to do them well. I couldn't with good conscience read a book when my heart wasn't in it, as any resulting review would come from a bad place in my psyche. The one writing-related task I accomplished was imagining mine and Felicia's conversation. Most of the afternoon was spent writing and revising the dialogue in my mind. Modified versions played out in my head continuously. In one scenario, we brainstormed casting for the movie version of *A Blogger's Life*. In another version, I thanked her for everything and left in tears. I both dreaded the meeting and was anxious to get it over with. The "during" would be painful, but once my fate was sealed, I might be able to fall asleep again.

With one last deep exhalation, I opened the door of the restaurant. I recognized Felicia from her trademark all-one-length honey-colored hair at a table near the front. She looked up from whatever she was reading and waved me over. This was it.

Chapter 35

I forced my lips to curl up in my greeting. "Hi there." For positive thoughts, I sang, Pastel book covers and *Real Housewives* marathons, snuggles with Nicholas, and mint chocolate bonbons in my head to the tune of "My Favorite Things" from *The Sound of Music*.

Felicia stood up and drew me into a hug. My body stiffened, since I wasn't expecting it, but I managed to lift my arms and embrace her slender frame before it was too late.

I sat down, ordered a cappuccino, and we made awkward conversation for a few minutes. I lied when I told her my day was decent and she complained about the rush-hour traffic getting across town from the West Side.

After the waiter brought over my drink and refilled Felicia's coffee, the mood turned serious. I bit the inside of my cheek and tried to maintain eye contact. I waited for her to say something, but she didn't and the tension in the air was palpable. Was she waiting for me to go first? I had no idea where to start, but opened my mouth and listened as a voice that sounded like a shakier version of my own said, "So, about *Love on Stone Street*." I was lost for what to say next and hoped Felicia would take over so I wouldn't have to.

Felicia nodded. "Yes. Great job on your revisions. I loved it."

"I know. I tried so hard but…" I blinked. "Wait? What?"

"The fire angle is really great. I could totally see this book on the small screen someday." Her eyes, the shade of acorns, danced.

"It is? You can? Does that mean you're not letting me go?" I swallowed hard.

Felicia furrowed her brow. "Letting you go where?"

"I, um…" I tucked a hair behind my ear. "Never mind," I mumbled with a grimace.

Felicia leaned forward. "Did you think I asked you here to terminate our contract?"

I touched my finger to my chin to make it stop quivering. "Either you were going to tell me Melina hated what I wrote again, they were terminating the contract for the second book, and you were dumping me, or that Amy Heckerling wanted to turn *A Blogger's Life* into the next *Clueless*. My money was on the former." I tapped my noggin. "There are no fifty shades of gray in my thought process—just Sylvia Plath or Sophie Kinsella."

Felicia regarded me with wide eyes. "Wow." She chuckled. "I'm both delighted and disappointed to tell you neither of those scenarios is accurate."

"They're not?" My muscles relaxed marginally, but my entire body shook with residual nerves. I shivered, wishing I'd brought a cardigan with me.

She smiled kindly. "As of yet, I'm not in discussions over film options. But our partnership is solid. I like working with you very much. You're talented. You welcome critical feedback and are open to revisions. You get things right pretty quickly." She cleared her throat. "Usually."

I fiddled with my napkin. "Why did you want to see me then?" My voice came out like a whisper.

Felicia pursed her lips. "Because many of my authors have struggled with their second book over the years. They fear they won't be able to do it again or the feedback from their first novel is a paralyzing distraction. I was afraid you were suffering from the sophomore slump as well."

I sat up straighter in my chair at Felicia's words. She was telling me I wasn't the only author who toiled through their second book and, in fact, it was common. What I thought might be a dreadful meeting was turning out to be exactly what I needed. The knots in my neck unraveled at the discovery.

"I'd wanted to reach out earlier, but I've been inundated the last few months. When Hannah mentioned you might need some coddling, I realized my agent-to-author skills have been deficient."

Grinning, I said, "Not at all" until what she'd said sunk in. "Hannah told you I needed coddling?" My voice shook again—this time in anger, not nerves. It was as if for every good deed Hannah performed, she was obligated to screw you over with the next. I took a sip of my cappuccino to avoid letting Felicia know what I thought of Hannah's disclosure of what I'd assumed was a private discussion between the two of us. She was the one who insisted it stay in the vault. Was this purposeful? Could Hannah truly think making me look emotionally weak in front of my agent was a positive thing?

Felicia made a pained expression as if reading my mind. "Please don't be embarrassed, Kim. It's perfectly acceptable to struggle. You don't have to pretend to have everything together all the time for my sake. In fact, it's much better for all of us if the lines of communication are open. We're partners and I need to know when you've hit a wall or if you think you might lose it so I can give you perspective and talk you off the ledge. I swear I don't think less of you if that's what you're concerned about."

"You don't?" I asked meekly.

"I've been a literary agent for almost twenty years. I've seen everything." She reached down and removed something from her large orange hobo bag. "I'm sure you'll hear from Melina soon, but in case you want a second set of eyes, I've marked up your manuscript. It could use a little fleshing out in parts and I've made some suggestions on how to increase tension before the fire, but otherwise I think it's wonderful." She handed it to me across the table.

I took it from her and placed it on top of my own purse. I was dying to read her notes this minute but checked myself. "Thank you so much for this."

"I'm old school and always work from a hard copy, but I'll send it by email too if you prefer digital."

"Thank you, Felicia," I said again while wondering if it was too late to invite her to the wedding. It was a struggle to remember our relationship was business-based because I worshipped the ground she walked on. I currently wished we could have a sleepover, talk about our favorite books, and play with each other's hair. I forced myself to focus when I realized Felicia had said something I was too busy daydreaming about our slumber party to hear.

Ten minutes later, she paid the bill, and we said our goodbyes. Though the walk to the restaurant from the subway felt like a journey down death row, I might as well have been walking on air when I headed back to the train to go home. Even if Melina didn't love my writing, Felicia did. Whatever happened, and with or without a movie deal, we were in this together.

Chapter 36

ONE WEEK UNTIL "I DO"

It was Saturday morning and I was on the phone with my father discussing last-minute travel arrangements for the wedding, now only a week away. I was still under the influence of gratitude for his wellbeing, but after confirming the change in his medication had done the trick with respect to his memory, my dad insisted we lay the topic to rest permanently. I was happy to oblige.

"Now enjoy your bachelorette party. Please be safe."

I could picture my dad cringing as he said this, his face flushed at the thought of his daughter dancing seductively on a bar somewhere. "Last I heard, massages were a relatively low-risk activity," I said to put him out of his misery. I glanced at my watch. Caroline was on her way downtown after picking up Bridget, and said she'd text when she was five minutes away. The three of us were heading out to the Ocean Place Resort and Spa in Long Branch, New Jersey for the night. We were scheduled for spa treatments later that afternoon and had dinner reservations at a restaurant in the hotel. The original plan was to stay local, but the resort was running an off-season special, and we thought the trip would be a nice escape from the city and a relaxing girls' weekend. I couldn't wait.

When my phone pinged with the arrival of Caroline's text, I told my father I loved him and was excited to see them on Thursday when they arrived from Florida. Then I ended the call, kissed Nicholas goodbye, and rode the elevator down to the lobby.

I walked out the door at the exact moment Caroline's black BMW pulled up. Bridget rolled down the window and offered to sit in the back since I was the guest of honor, but I motioned for her to stay where she was. She was pregnant and wouldn't be able to partake in any of the yummy cocktails before, during, and after dinner at the Seaview Restaurant located inside the resort. I also feared we'd be stuck in traffic and she'd pee in her pants. Despite all the reasons she could have insisted we stay in the city, where there were many hassle-free places to get a pre-natal massage, she put me first. The least I could do was let her sit in the front. I placed my overnight bag in the trunk, stepped into the backseat, and we were off.

Two and a half hours later, after checking into the hotel, we dropped our bags off in the deluxe room we were sharing and headed to the spa. I was eager to get lost in my warm stone massage and Bridget felt the same about her pregnancy massage. Caroline was getting the Ocean Place Fire and Ice facial. It sounded heavenly, but I was too afraid to mess with my face a week before my wedding. The last time I had a facial, before I could enjoy the post-treatment healthy glow, I had to wait out the three pimples that escaped when my pores were opened.

"I wonder if Nicholas left for his bachelor party yet," I said to the girls as we walked to the elevator on our floor. The guys were starting out with drinks at a closed-off rooftop bar before having dinner at a steakhouse and then "playing it by ear," which I assumed meant going to a strip club. I didn't ask. I didn't care—much.

"Jonathan better behave," Bridget said. Her worried expression betrayed the light tone of her voice.

"Of course he will." I hadn't seen evidence Jonathan was only going through the motions of pretending to be excited about his impending fatherhood. I'd witnessed no proof of the opposite either, but I wasn't at all concerned he'd misbehave at the bachelor party. I couldn't even picture him getting a lap dance.

Before Bridget could argue or request further reassurance, loud voices came through the thin walls of a hotel room. A woman's voice said, "Why do you care so much what treatment I get anyway? You're so bossy!"

Another voice said, "The Swedish massage is so boring. If you're going to spend money, at least choose something your partner can't easily do for free is all I'm saying. But do what you want."

"I will!"

The elevator door opened, preventing us from hearing what was said next. We stepped inside and Caroline rolled her eyes. "What a dumb thing to fight about."

"Seriously," Bridget agreed with a chuckle.

I laughed too, ignoring the uncomfortable knot in my belly.

A few minutes later, a member of the spa staff gave us a tour of the facilities and provided us with robes and slippers. The three of us commented on how much more attractive we looked in them compared to the bright pink and orange striped "uniforms" we were forced to wear at the Palace Spa.

We sat on comfy leather recliners in the mostly white oceanfront relaxation room and waited to be called for our treatments. Caroline closed her eyes, already a picture of requiescence, which I hoped Bridget wouldn't destroy with her loud chomping on a Granny Smith apple she'd plucked from the bowl of fresh fruit. I debated flipping through an issue of *Brides Magazine*. The cover promised two hundred and fifty fresh wedding ideas. With my nuptials only seven days away, it was probably a mistake to read about all the great things I wasn't doing. I decided Caroline had it right. I rested my head against the chair and closed my eyes.

From somewhere behind me, a girl said, "There they are." My eyes longed to stay closed, at least until my therapist came to pick me up for my massage, but the voice was familiar. Still, I remained unmoving on the assumption she wasn't referring to my party of three. It wasn't like we were the only people in the waiting room.

"She's going to be shocked when she sees me."

My heart skipped a beat and my eyes flickered open. "Erin?" I sat up and turned around. Next to the woman who'd handed me my robe a mere five minutes earlier stood my little sister, her curly milk-chocolate-colored hair a stark contrast to the crisp white of her robe.

"Enjoy, ladies," the woman said before excusing herself.

Erin smiled wide. "Surprise!"

"H-hi!" I exclaimed, darting a glance at Caroline, who was now sitting up and facing my sister. Bridget had frozen with her apple poised at the opening of her mouth. It was obvious Erin's appearance was as much news to them as it was to me. I stood up and gave my sister a hug. "I had no idea you'd be here." I wasn't sure how I felt about it either, which made me the worst sibling ever.

"I told Mom how guilty I felt not being part of your bachelorette party. I'm your only sister after all. When she told me what you had planned for this weekend, I decided to take the train and surprise you." She wrapped the tie of her robe tighter around her waist.

"You certainly succeeded. Are you staying overnight? Did you get a room?" The thought of four of us crowded into a single space was suffocating, but we'd make it work. I could sleep anywhere for one night. As long as Bridget got a bed.

Erin smiled slickly. "I did. And the best part? With two rooms, you don't have to squeeze three of you into one. You can stay with me!" she yelped, clearly under the assumption I'd be thrilled.

My eyes opened wide and my lips parted, but no sound came out. If I told my sister how excited I'd been to have an overnight with my two best friends, even if one of them was likely to fall asleep by ten o'clock, she'd be crushed. I was touched Erin made the effort to travel all the way from Boston, and it would be fun to bond with her. The four of us could all hang out together until right before we went to bed anyway. "Thank you, Erin. Sounds fantastic." I hugged her and, over her shoulder, winked at Bridget and Caroline with a silent, "It's all good."

The four of us agreed to meet at the heated soaking bath after our treatments and so, eighty minutes later, feeling more serene than a bride-to-be probably should, I changed into my bathing suit and headed over there.

When I arrived at my destination, looked into the tub, and saw the blonde and brunette duo leaning against the side with their eyes closed, I knew it had been too good to be true. They hadn't heard me coming and I bet if I was careful, I could back up before they realized I was—

"Oh my God, that was ah-mazing."

At the sound of Bridget's voice behind me, I jolted and lost my footing on the wet floor. I reached for Bridget's arm to keep me up, remembering just in time if I took her down with me, I could hurt the baby. I dropped my hand. In a single second, an hour's worth of thoughts ran through my head. I could not—would not—break or even sprain a bone a week before my wedding. I had an aisle to walk down. Even though no one would see the designer shoes I'd bought—inspired by my "naked" nightmare—under my dress, it was enough for me to know they were fabulous. None of the lawyers in my circle were personal injury attorneys, and we had too much going on to bring a lawsuit against the resort anyway. But as the linoleum floor loomed closer, I braced myself for the worst.

Just as I resigned myself to fall, a hand wrapped around my waist to steady me. "Easy there, bride," Caroline said with a chuckle.

I blew out a breath of relief. "You're my angel, Caroline." It was true, she had potentially saved me from broken, sprained, or bruised bones as well as potential litigation. Unfortunately, even she couldn't save me from my future sister-in-law and her girlfriend, who were apparently on the same wavelength as my sister in their decision to crash my bachelorette party. Both girls had opened their eyes by now and were waving us over.

Approaching the bath, I said, "Fancy seeing you guys here!" My voice suggested I was surprised even though I'd half-expected to see them since the fight we'd overheard in the hallway earlier.

Natalie lifted her arms out of the water and back down with a loud splash. "When Nicholas told us where you were going, we immediately called and reserved a room since I'm not on call until Monday."

Silently cursing Nicholas, I stepped into the bath and sunk to my knees, letting the hot water cover me up to my shoulders.

"I need pampering in a big way." Natalie dunked under the water and lifted her head back out. "Seriously, don't let shows like *Grey's Anatomy* fool you. Being an intern is the opposite of glamorous. I'm doing my rotation through colorectal surgery and spent all last week doing pre-op and post-op management for inflammatory bowel disease." She pulled a face.

Tiffany giggled. "TMI." She shook her head at me. "Sometimes the medical jargon is a turn-on. Other times, like now…" She wrinkled her nose. "Not so much."

Natalie kissed the top of Tiffany's wet head. "Wait until I get to the transplant rotation. Très sexy."

I observed the two of them in awe. Where were the public displays of affection when Natalie first brought Tiffany around? The energy I expended irritated by Tiffany's constant presence could have been better spent on other activities, like planning my wedding and finishing my book. Remembering both those tasks were now under control, I let myself enjoy the hot jets of water pounding against my back.

"We couldn't get treatments until tomorrow, but at least we're allowed to use the sauna and steam room the duration of our stay," Tiffany said.

"Let me guess, you booked the Swedish massage and Natalie chose something more unconventional," I said.

Tiffany's eyes opened wide. "Exactly. Natalie booked some lavender hydrating thing," she said with a smirk.

"It's called a Hydrating Lavender and Honey Body Wrap and it's the ultimate nourishing experience and something you can't get at any old spa," Natalie said assuredly.

I slid my body to the right to make room for Caroline next to me while Bridget sat on the edge with her feet in the water. I closed my eyes and held tightly to the serenity, even though my intimate girls' weekend was morphing into something entirely different than planned.

"We also changed your dinner reservation from three people to five," Natalie said.

"I guess I'll just order room service, then."

I opened my eyes—Erin. Crap.

"You're here too?" Natalie said, not even trying to hide her displeasure.

Joining us in the bath, Erin said, "No. I'm actually a hologram."

Natalie muttered, "If only."

Before this escalated into a full-on verbal sparring or, God forbid, something physical, I calmly said, "When we get back to the room, I'll call the restaurant. If they have a table big enough for five, they can easily fit one more."

"Depends on how big said person is," Natalie mumbled.

I whipped my head toward Natalie. "That was uncalled for." My sister and sister-in-law's personalities clashed like caffeine and sleep. I didn't expect them to become bosom buddies, but tossing out insults was unacceptable.

"Par for the course," Erin said, nonplussed, while Natalie pouted like a petulant child.

"How was the facial, Caroline?" Bridget asked.

"Divine. And the pregnancy massage?"

"Marvelous," Bridget said. "The perfect antidote to stressful city life."

I glanced over my shoulder at Bridget and mouthed, "Thank you." She winked.

My stomach in knots, I rested my head against the edge of the tub and tried to relax. Bridget and Caroline had come to the rescue with their well-meaning, albeit awkward, change of the subject—this time. Whether they'd be able to keep it up for the next eighteen or so hours, and if Tiffany would help or hinder the peace, was anyone's guess.

I moved my bags into Erin's room after we left the spa. Even though I'd miss gabbing with Bridget and Caroline while we did our hair and makeup, I couldn't argue how much more sense it made to share space with one girl instead of two in terms of getting ready for a night out.

It wasn't all bad. Sharing a bathroom with Erin while she curled her eyelashes on one side and I flat ironed my hair on the other reminded me of when we lived with our parents back in the day. Though I didn't appreciate Erin's accusation I'd invited Tiffany and Natalie for the weekend and purposely excluded her, I was fairly certain I'd convinced her I was just as taken aback by their appearance as I was by hers. She made me promise I was happier to see her than I was Natalie. The truth was, I was none too pleased either of them had crashed my weekend, but there was no sense hurting her feelings after the fact.

My voracious appetite and enthusiasm to dig into a delicious meal exceeded my anxiety as to how Erin and Natalie would get along at dinner. I was also comforted knowing alcohol would be in plenty. Drinking always made people more congenial—except when it made them contrary and violent. While the hostess led Erin and me to our table in the expansive Seaview Restaurant located inside the resort, I shuddered at the image of Erin diving over the table to strangle Natalie. I hoped it was more paranoia and less premonition.

The hostess stopped at a rectangular table for six where the other girls were already seated. Tiffany and Bridget sat on either side of

Natalie on one end of the table, but the chair across from her was open. Clearly out of her mind, Erin went to sit there, but as if competing in a high-stakes game of Musical Chairs, I stole the seat out from under her. I didn't want my earlier vision of Erin leaping across the table to become reality. Erin appeared not to notice I'd highjacked her first-choice chair and sat next to me on my right without a fuss.

"You both look so pretty," Bridget gushed.

"Yes, you look adorable, Kim," Natalie said.

"Thanks," I muttered before taking a huge gulp of water. Maybe if I concentrated hard enough, I could turn it into vodka.

Directing her attention to Bridget, who sat farthest away from her on the opposite end of the table, Erin said, "Thank you, Bridget. You're so cute, you put all other pregnant women to shame." She leaned forward, and looked over at Caroline, who sat on my other side. "I love your hair, Caroline. You look like a fashion model." Then she focused on Tiffany, who sat directly across from her. "Your gold dress is stunning." Turning to me, she said, "And, lastly, the guest of honor. I might be biased because you're my sister, but I predict you'll be the most beautiful bride ever. After me, of course." She chuckled. "Kidding." She regarded Natalie with a cold stare.

Caroline cleared her throat. "How about we start off with a cocktail and move on to prosecco?"

"Great idea," I said, practically giving myself whiplash in my frantic search of the restaurant for our waitress.

"This fried calamari is yummy," Tiffany said about twenty-five minutes later.

"Agreed. I try to watch my intake of fried foods for health reasons, but sometimes you just have to be bad," Erin said. She spooned more onto my plate. "Take the rest, Kim."

"If you insist," I said, happily ensconced in my early buzz. Nothing defamatory had been uttered by Natalie or Erin since the precarious start of the night. In fact, when Bridget, who drank seltzer and pineapple juice because she said it at least "looked like an alcoholic beverage," made the toast, everyone clinked glasses, including Natalie and Erin. I was finally able to relax and enjoy myself without waiting for the fragile glass to break.

"It's also really fattening," Natalie said. "But you can afford it,

Kim."

A piece of squid lodged in my throat and I made a conscious effort to swallow it down. It was possible it wasn't meant to be a jab at Erin. Maybe it was an innocent statement.

"Have you heard from Nicholas tonight?" Tiffany asked.

I glanced down at my phone in my purse—no new texts. "Nope. I don't expect to. Let him enjoy himself without the old ball and chain dragging him down." I smiled to myself as I pictured Nicholas's posse taking over a bar, doing shots, and being otherwise rowdy. And then the bitterness crept in. I bet Nathan and Jonathan weren't hurling passive-aggressive insults at each other while Nicholas tried to maintain the peace by subtly changing the subject. It wasn't fair. If Nicholas hadn't opened his pie hole and told Natalie where I was going this weekend, I'd be enjoying a quiet bachelorette party for three, as planned.

I removed my phone from my bag and sent him a text. *I hope you're having a great time. That would make one of us.* The regret inched its way into my gut immediately. It wasn't all Nicholas's fault. My mother was equally guilty for spilling the location of the party to Erin. Besides, this was my bachelorette party—hopefully the only one I'd ever have. I had to make the best of it, which included not holding a grudge against Nicholas and putting a downer on his night in the process. I sent him another text. *Ignore my earlier text. Love you! XO.* I fought the stubborn irritation lingering beneath my optimistic surface as I returned my attention to my companions.

"Wait until you see the centerpieces we designed, K," Bridget said.

"You haven't seen them yet?" Natalie asked, her brown eyes wide as saucers.

I shook my head. "I'll see them at the reception with everyone else."

"Do you at least have a general idea what they look like?" Erin asked.

"I gave Bridget and Caroline carte blanche to do what they wanted." After abandoning the girls in favor of fretting over Felicia's phone call, I wasn't about to complain about their selections. I figured it was safer not to see them at all until the deed was done. By then, I'd be too ecstatic about my new last name to cry about the lack of flowers at my wedding.

Erin's jaw dropped. "Wow. I'd never be able to relinquish control of something so important."

"We agree on one thing," Natalie said.

I jerked my head back. Was it possible I was witnessing a bonding moment between the Red and White Queens?

Natalie continued, "And I'm usually very chill and laid back."

Erin pressed her lips together. "Are you suggesting I'm uptight and rigid, Natalie?"

Natalie groaned. "It's not always about you, Erin."

Bridget clapped her hands together. "Dinner is here. Hooray."

Aside from the sounds of utensils clanging against dishes, we ate our dinners in silence. My salmon steak was perfectly prepared and lovely, but my taste buds experienced no joy. My spirits brightened when the waitress brought over a bottle of prosecco. I needed more booze to get through this night.

Caroline clinked her knife against her glass. "We have a surprise for you, Kim."

My heart raced. Had they secretly asked someone else to join us? Please God, not Hannah. I didn't think this night could get any worse, but Erin practically danced on the ceiling when I told her Hannah was invited to the wedding. I wouldn't put it past her to text Hannah a last-minute invite tonight. I faked a smile with cautious hope. "Have at me."

While the girls regarded me with goofy grins, Caroline reached under the table for the plastic bag resting at her feet. She removed a silver tiara and white sash with the words "Bride to Be" in hot pink. Placing the tiara on my head, she said, "It's not a real bachelorette party without props."

The girls broke into rambunctious applause. "Put on the sash, Kim," they demanded in harmony.

I did as told, my cheeks burning in embarrassment at the spectacle we were making. But the mortification quickly turned into excitement as it hit me I was getting married. This was my bachelorette party—my night—and they were all there to honor me. So what if Natalie and Erin didn't get along? They weren't the bride-to-be. I was, and I'd be damned if I let them ruin my last night out as a single chick.

Suddenly, I was in the mood to party. Had the circumstances been different and Bridget not with child, I'd have suggested going out. It was a college town, after all, and harmless flirting with young boys could be amusing. But all that really mattered was having fun with the girls I loved, even if they didn't all love each other.

When we entered the Seaview Lounge for after-dinner drinks, Natalie stopped in her tracks. "It's dead in here."

It was true; the place was virtually empty aside from a trio of middle-aged couples at a booth and two guys at the long bar. I pointed to the terrace. "Check out the ocean view, guys."

"Phenomenal," Caroline said. "Can we sit outside?"

"Let's find out." I walked over to the bartender to ask him.

Natalie tapped her finger against her chin. "Don't you want to go somewhere with more people, Kim? You're a bachelorette! You should be wearing a candy necklace and drinking from penis straws."

"I agree. This is lame," Tiffany said. "Who cares if we can see the ocean? I bet the view is more scenic where Nicholas is, if you know what I mean. Why should he have all the fun?"

Why indeed. I checked my phone for the first time since texting Nicholas earlier. He'd written me back—several times.

At 8:36, he wrote: *Why aren't you having fun, Kimmie?*

At 9:07: *Remind me to keep Neil away from gin at the wedding. He's plastered already.*

9:40: *Jonathan thinks they're having a girl!*

I tapped Bridget on the back. "Your man and I are on the same page."

"Regarding?"

I showed her the text.

She crinkled her brow. "It's just conjecture. I swear we didn't find out. But ask Nicholas how Jonathan sounded when he said it. Was he excited? Miserable? Indifferent?"

I did what she asked and returned the phone to my purse. "Can we sit on the terrace?" I asked the bartender, a young guy with a premature receding hairline but cute dimples.

He grinned, the crevices in his cheeks deepening. "Sure thing. And shots on the house because you're a bachelorette. What would you like?"

I considered the question. The wise answer was "nothing," but it was my bachelorette party and it was practically against the law to refuse free drinks from a bartender. "How about something pink?"

Nodding, he said, "You've got it. Make yourself comfortable outside and I'll bring them to you." He handed me a cocktail menu. "For after."

I took the menu and motioned for the girls to follow me outside. It was a perfect night in early November—comfortable enough to sit outside with a light jacket—and I hoped the weather would be as agreeable the following Saturday. The ceremony was being held outside on the terrace. I thought about where I'd be this time next week and my pulse raced in excitement. I'd be married and dancing the night away. I was super excited about the song I was dedicating to Nicholas and couldn't wait to find out what song he chose for me.

The bartender brought out a tray of shots—five Pink Starbursts and one virgin pink lemonade—and we tossed them back in unison. "What should we drink now?" I asked.

Natalie yawned from her chair. "It doesn't matter to me, but can we do it somewhere else? This place blows."

I glanced at the other girls. "Do you guys agree?"

Tiffany nodded, but her opinion mattered least.

"Sort of," Erin responded.

"I'm happy anywhere," Caroline said.

"It's your night," Bridget said.

I pondered for a moment. "I suppose we can find a bar off the premises. But we have to order at least one round of drinks here." Leaving without spending any money, especially after a free round of shots, was rude.

We made our drink choices and Erin and Caroline went inside to order them. When they returned, Natalie said, "Let's chug."

I took a sip of my mango martini and smacked my lips together. It was too delicious to ingest in one gulp. I was also pretty drunk already. If I had any chance of keeping up with Natalie and Tiffany, who were clearly more seasoned drinkers, I had to pace myself.

Reading my mind like only she could, Bridget gave me a slight smile. "Take your time," she whispered.

I moved my chair closer to hers. "Are you sure you're up for going out?"

She nodded. "I refuse to be a buzzkill at my BFFAEUDDUP's bachelorette party. If I get too tired, I'll cab it back to the hotel. No worries. If we can avoid somewhere too loud and clubby, I'd appreciate it though."

I lightly tapped my drink against her glass of water. "Done."

Erin looked up from her phone. "How about The Wine Loft? They have generous pours, according to Yelp, and a nice décor."

"And probably all women. B.O.R.I.N.G," Natalie said.

I thought this was a funny statement coming from a woman who was currently dating another woman, but kept my amusement to myself.

Gesturing to Tiffany, she said, "We were thinking Avenue Le Club."

"No clubs," I said with a reassuring glance at Bridget.

"Why don't we pay the tab and walk around Pier Village? There has to be a place we can agree on," Erin said, although it was obvious even she didn't believe her own statement.

"I'm fine with closing out our tab here, but I'm not making Bridget walk around aimlessly," I said.

"Thank you," Bridget whispered from next to me.

Caroline went to pay the tab. She insisted she'd get money from the girls later, but I was positive she was full of crap. I gave her a stern look, but didn't argue since she was one of the two people in attendance I wasn't five seconds away from punching in the face.

We gathered at the exit to the hotel, all of us reviewing Yelp from our individual phones.

"How about Jack's Goal Line Stand? They have an expansive beer list," Natalie said.

At the same time, Erin and I said, "I don't like beer." We shared a rare smile between sisters.

Tiffany sighed. "They have other drinks too." She flipped her long hair. "And plenty of co-eds to flirt with, Kim." She placed her hands on her hips. "C'mon. Nicholas is most definitely at a strip club. Surely you're entitled to flirt with some college boys. Or girls." She waggled her eyebrows. "The first time I kissed Natalie was at a college bar. Remember, Nat?"

Natalie's cheeks flushed.

"She's so bashful," Tiffany teased. "We were flirting with some young boys at Down the Hatch. They dared us to make out and Natalie, who had never kissed a girl, was drunk enough on tequila shots to do it. The rest is history." She winked. "I'm a great kisser. Ask Nicholas."

"Stop it." Natalie elbowed Tiffany before changing the subject. "We should hurry. Most places close at one and it's almost midnight already."

Before I could ponder how time flew so quickly when I was barely having any fun, my phone pinged—Nicholas. Assuming, he'd answered my earlier text about Jonathan, I said to Bridget, "Nicholas wrote back."

"What did he say?" Bridget asked.

There were a few of them:

10:06: *I miss your body. I wish you were waiting for me in bed. Neked.*

I giggled.

10:37: *Shots. So many shots. Rescue me?*

10:54: *I want Kimmie Long in my pants. Where are you, Kimmie Long?*

My heart swelled. *I wish I was with you, baby. More than you know.*

11:27: I viewed the text and froze.

"What is it?" Bridget said.

"It's a...picture." I handed her my device, my pulse racing.

Her eyes bugged out. "Oh, dear."

"What's so interesting over there?" Erin asked, reaching for my phone. She studied the picture with a furrowed brow. "What is that? A tree?" She handed it to Tiffany.

Tiffany glanced at the phone and yelped. "It's someone's hoohah!" She tossed my phone to Natalie. "Check it out."

Natalie's mouth fell open. "Where did you get this?"

I bit my lip. Why would Nicholas text me a picture of someone's...hoohah? Why was he close enough to one to take a picture in the first place?" It had to be a mistake. My stomach cramped and my dinner threatened to reject the digestion process.

Caroline scrutinized the text and shook her head. "I'm sure it's not what it looks like." She blushed. "Well, I'm sure it's exactly what it appears to be, but there's no way Nicholas took this picture and sent it to you." She continued to scroll. "There are more messages."

The six of us drew closer and read them together.

11:31: *Check out the magic carpet. Should I take a ride?*

11:46: *Just got lost in the trouble triangle. What about you? Having fun yet?*

Tiffany howled. "This is priceless."

Natalie put her hand against Tiffany's open mouth. "I agree with Caroline. My brother is as annoying as ants in your pants, but he's a stand-up guy. These texts didn't come from him."

Bridget said, "It must be a misunderstanding, K. Call him." The others vocalized their agreement.

I stepped to the side and took a deep breath. Nicholas loved me. He didn't want anyone but me. I knew this like I knew my own name, but I was scared. Aside from proving our disastrous organization skills while planning the wedding, things between us had been almost too perfect since our engagement. Maybe Nicholas got cold feet and was sabotaging our marriage before it even happened. There was only one way to find out. I pressed the call button.

The phone rang once, then twice, then a third time. My scalp hurt from pulling on my hair. Finally, someone picked up.

I heard music and muffled voices in the background. "Nicholas?" I said, breathless.

He didn't answer me—just a backdrop of more undiscernible noise. "Nicholas? Hello?" I removed the phone from my ear and stared at it. "Answer me, god dammit!" I expelled a loud groan and ended the call. I buried my face in my hands and when I looked up, the girls were observing me with unease. "He didn't say anything. It was just...static." My legs wobbled.

There was a moment of silence and then Natalie clucked her tongue. "I say you forget about this for now. His phone was probably stolen," she said.

"Or maybe one of his friends decided to play a trick on him." Tiffany pointed at Bridget. "Maybe it was your man, Birdie."

Bridget's cheeks burned the color of her hair and I thought blood might burst from her eyeballs.

Caroline squeezed Bridget's shoulder. "It wasn't Jonathan!" In a softer tone, she said, "But I agree it wasn't Nicholas."

"It wasn't Jonathan, but he'll know where Nicholas is. I'll call him." Her phone already to her ear, Bridget took a few steps to the side and turned her back on us. A drawn-out minute later, she returned. "He's on his way home already and has no idea where Nicholas is." She chewed on her lip. "Sorry, K."

"I say we forget about this and go out. Avenue Le Club is only a few minutes away. You can dance the stress away," Natalie said.

"She already said she doesn't want to go to a club," Erin said. "I think the wine place would be perfect."

"Perfect for a retirement party, maybe," Tiffany muttered.

"Stop it," I whispered. Please make it stop.

"What do you want to do, Kim?" Caroline asked.

"I want to talk to Nicholas," I said, blinking back the volcano of tears threatening to erupt from behind my eyes.

Tiffany tapped her gold strappy stilettos against the marble floor of the lobby. "Well, it doesn't seem like he's answering. The best revenge is to go out and have fun." She gestured to the exit.

"Yeah, Kim. Don't let this ruin your fun," Natalie said.

My pulse sped up and my body flushed with heat. These girls had no clue. On the outside, I'd been playing the role of sweet, agreeable Kim for months, pretending the tension and unsolicited advice didn't bother me because I didn't want to make waves, hurt anyone's feelings, or seem ungrateful for their help. All the while, I was exploding on the inside. I was positive Hannah Marshak would never have let this happen and from this moment on, neither would I.

I glared at Natalie, Tiffany, and Erin. "Fun? Would you describe this night as fun? Let me be the first to inform you no part of tonight has been fun. The three of you crashing my bachelorette party uninvited—not fun. Bearing witness to Natalie insulting my sister repeatedly—not fun. The constant need to reassure my sister I love her more than my sister-in-law—not fun. Listening to you argue about where we should go without even asking what I wanted—not fun."

The girls stared at me incredulously with their mouths open. Erin took a step back and Natalie's face was white.

I was reaching the point of no return, but I couldn't stop. "I purposely didn't invite you because I knew you'd act this way. I don't know why you hate each other so much, but it's not as much as I hate both of you right now. The fun part of this day ended the minute you all got here." My stomach lurched. I needed a bathroom—fast.

I ran to the ladies' room, into a stall, and immediately lost my entire dinner, two cocktails, a Pink Starburst shot, and two glasses of prosecco in one fell swoop. While washing my hands after, I checked out my reflection in the mirror. My hair, previously straightened with a flip at the end, was slick with sweat and stuck to my head. There was no color in my cheeks, unless you counted pukey green. I splashed water on my face and when I looked up, Bridget and Caroline's worried reflections joined mine in the mirror.

Bridget frowned at me. "Are you okay?"

Physically, my stomach was no longer in rebellion. Emotionally, I was drained. "I want to go to bed." I paused. "In your room." I couldn't deal with Erin right now.

"You got it." Caroline placed an arm around mine.

When we stepped out of the bathroom, I could see the other girls huddled outside the door through my side vision. I couldn't hear what they were whispering and I didn't care. I stared directly ahead as Bridget held my hand and led me to the elevator and up to the room. At some point while I was brushing my teeth, I heard Caroline come in with my overnight bag. I changed into my pajamas in silence, slipped under the covers, and passed out.

Chapter 37

My eyes opened and I was blinded by a ray of light coming in from the window. For a moment, I forgot where I was and then I breathed in the stale air of the hotel room. The instant appearance of knots in my belly awoke whatever senses had remained dormant and the events of the night before flooded my memory. Nicholas. Hoohah. Erin and Natalie. I swallowed back the thickness in my throat over the harsh words I'd uttered.

I removed my phone from the nightstand—no messages. It wasn't even 8:30—too early to call a guy the morning after his bachelor party. My fingers moved until I was staring at the picture Nicholas had sent me the night before. To hell with being considerate. I couldn't wait until a more "reasonable" hour to speak to him. I looked over to where Bridget was sleeping in the other double bed and Caroline on the pull-out couch. Not wanting to wake them, I slid my legs over the side of the bed and walked to the bathroom. I closed the door as quietly as possible behind me, sat on the edge of the bathtub, and called Nicholas. His phone went straight to voicemail. My lips quivered and tears choked the back of my throat. Where the hell was my fiancé?

"Kim?" Caroline called out. "Can I come in?"

I ended the call without leaving a message. Wiping my eyes, I said, "Yes."

She opened the door and, still dressed in her pajamas, gave me a timid smile. "Natalie sent me a text. They were hoping you'd want to join them at the breakfast buffet."

I hesitated. The mean things I said to Natalie and Erin the night before replayed in my head like an earworm. Though there was truth to most of what I said, I wished I'd had the self-control to keep my resentment to myself. I knew the girls, however misguided, meant well when they surprised me by showing up and I only needed to restrain myself for one more week. Instead, I'd alienated two-fifths of my bridal party.

"You're going to have to see them at some point. Might as well get it over with," she said.

I let out a strangled laugh. "Why do you have to be so darn logical all the time?"

Caroline shrugged. "It's what I do." She glanced at her watch. "Can I tell them we'll meet them downstairs at nine thirty?"

I nodded.

An hour later, I pasted on a smile to disguise my nerves as the three of us made our way across the restaurant to join the others. A symphony of opening words played in my head, but I had no idea what would come out of my mouth when I reached the table and came face to face with Natalie and Tiffany and...Erin? I froze in place. I knew I'd have to face my sister eventually, but didn't expect to see her at a meal organized by Natalie. But there she was, fully made up and dressed for an upscale ladies' lunch in black dress pants and a burgundy sweater to match her lipstick. I was wearing the same boyfriend jeans and white t-shirt I'd worn on the drive up, but at least I'd managed to shower and dab a layer of sheer gloss on my dehydrated lips.

"Good morning," I croaked. Avoiding eye contact, I pulled out a chair and sat down. While I stared at the white linen napkin on my lap, I summoned the guts to say something so I could manage a semblance of an appetite. I had no desire to ingest calories I was too distracted to enjoy for my second meal in a row. I also didn't like knowing Bridget and Caroline's money was going to waste. They'd paid for my share of the hotel room, and although I wasn't sure the Sunday breakfast was complimentary, I was certain none of the girls would take my money anyway.

I had to move fast before someone suggested heading to the buffet. "I'm sorry about going off on you guys last night." I looked at Erin and then Natalie. "I know your hearts were in the right place when you..." I searched the tablecloth for my next words.

"Crashed your bachelorette party?" Natalie cocked an eyebrow.

My cheeks warmed and I nodded. "I did put thought into what kind of bachelorette party I wanted, and I didn't take leaving you guys out lightly. It wasn't because I didn't want to spend time with you or think we wouldn't have fun." I bit my lip. "I'm lying. It was absolutely because I didn't want you guys here—together. Because I never have fun when you're together, thanks to the flying insults, jabs, passive-aggressive digs, et cetera. I couldn't choose one of you over the other..." My spidey sense honed in on Erin's inner thoughts and before she could vocalize them, I said, "I wasn't going to pick one sister, whether by blood or by imminent marriage, over the other, and so I chose neither of you." My heart ached at the word "imminent" since my future husband was currently MIA, having last communicated with me by texting a picture of another girl's whoopsie daisy. I paused for a beat while a server poured us coffee and said we could go to the buffet table whenever we were ready.

When she was gone, I jutted my chin at Natalie and Erin again. "I don't understand why you guys took such a dislike to each other. Maybe you'll tell me, maybe you won't. It doesn't really matter anymore." I stared them down like I meant business. "But I cannot and will not tolerate it in my presence for another second." My shoulders were heavy with tension despite the eighty-minute massage the day before and my eyes welled up. "I'll have you know planning this wedding coupled with writing my second book almost killed me and, as Bridget and Caroline are aware, I was this close to calling it off and dragging Nicholas to a justice of the peace. It's all good now, but I've already had enough stress to last me several rotations around the sun without playing referee between you guys. But I'm sorry I said I hate you. I don't." I took a sip of coffee to indicate my speech had come to an end and the floor was open.

Fiddling with her napkin, Erin said, "You had every right to be pissed at us for ruining what was supposed to be a great time. I'm sorry I've been so awful and needy. I've been your only baby sister for almost twenty-eight years and maybe I was subconsciously afraid Natalie would take my place." She dabbed her wet eyes with the napkin.

I studied her fondly. "Will it make you feel better if I promise never to boss Natalie around, make fun of her metal mouth, or insist she was adopted?"

Erin laughed. "Yes, please."

"Done," I said with a wink before turning to Natalie. "Do you have anything to say for yourself?"

Natalie grimaced and then let out a distressed sigh. Focusing on Erin, she said, "I'm sorry I've been so mean to you. I'm not sure why. Maybe it's because you get to sleep late seven days a week and I have to work eighteen-hour shifts at a hospital and maybe I assumed you were entitled and spoiled before I ever got a chance to know you. It's possible I was a teeny bit judgmental. Will you forgive me?"

With my fingers crossed, I watched Erin's face while she considered Natalie's apology. It wasn't the sincerest expression of regret I'd ever witnessed, but it was Natalie's best offer. I silently pleaded with her to accept it.

After what felt like eternity squared, Erin nodded. "I will. And I'm sorry too."

Natalie grinned at Erin before turning to me. "And I'm very sorry for my part in ruining your bachelorette party. From this moment forward, I promise to behave." She stood up and pointed at the buffet. "Now let's get some breakfast and enjoy what's left of this weekend." Her cheeks lit up. "We're going to be family in less than a week. Can you believe you're marrying my brother in six days?" She was halfway to the food table before I could respond.

As I trailed behind the others, I pictured Nicholas in his tuxedo, handsome as can be, approximately 144 hours from now, when I vowed to love him until death do us part. I had no doubt in my ability to keep my promise, and couldn't wait to say the words out loud in front of our family and friends. But as my thoughts once again traveled to the unexplained picture and texts on my phone, a small part of me was terrified I'd never have the chance.

During our meal, conversation inevitably turned to the text Nicholas had sent. Understandably, the girls were curious about the source of the photo and how I'd resolved things with Nicholas. Since he was currently unreachable, making resolution a temporary impossibility, I told the girls I didn't want to talk about it. Then I proceeded to shove scrambled eggs, bacon, and home fries into my mouth so I wouldn't be able to discuss it even if I wanted to without doing so with my mouth full and putting myself in danger of choking to death. On a positive note, everyone got along during the entire duration of the meal. In fact, Natalie and Erin agreed the French toast was divine and the English muffin on the eggs Benedict a bit underdone. Worse-case scenario, it was only a temporary truce, but it was still a vast improvement from the night before.

After breakfast, Natalie and Tiffany headed to the spa for their appointments and the rest of us checked out of the hotel. Erin joined us for the return trip to the city where she'd catch the train from Penn Station back to Boston.

When Caroline's car pulled up to my building first, I hugged Erin goodbye from our seats in the back. She confirmed she and Gerry would arrive for the wedding on Friday morning. When Caroline got out of the car to get my bag from the trunk, Bridget joined her.

"Thanks again for trying to plan a great weekend, guys. I'm sorry I lost my cool." Knots tangled in my belly. I was both excited to be home and regretful I hadn't taken more advantage of what the British chick lit authors referred to as a "hen night." My last hurrah as a single lady was a ginormous fail by all standards.

Bridget said, "The two of them deserved to be told off. Under the circumstances, you were an angel. If it were me, I'd have kicked their asses to Siberia."

I chuckled despite myself. "Natalie might have enjoyed that. She tried to convince us Siberia was an up-and-coming honeymoon destination, remember?"

Caroline regarded me with earnest. "The rehearsal dinner and wedding next week will put this debacle of a bachelorette party to shame. And years from now, you'll have a funny story to tell your children."

I nodded with fake certainty. "I hope you're right." First, I had to piece together the details of said story with Nicholas. I looked up at the window of our apartment, wondering if he was already home. Then I waved goodbye to the girls, grabbed my overnight bag, and went inside the building to find out.

The answer was no—he wasn't home. I tossed my overnight bag on the bed with a huff and fought the urge to call him. If it went straight to voicemail—again—I might do something hasty out of frustration, like throw my computer across the room, break an entire set of plates like I was reenacting a scene from *My Big Fat Greek Wedding*, or hack off a portion of my hair. The last one was unlikely, considering I was too vain to make any drastic changes to my appearance days before my wedding, but my patience was whittling to dust. Where in the name of Apollo was Nicholas?

I'd made a deal with myself to take off my author hat until after the honeymoon, aside from occasional posts on social media, but if anything could distract me from real life, it was immersing myself into a fake one. Right after I read my email. Some people couldn't leave their apartment without peeing one last time. I couldn't begin a writing session without first checking for new messages.

Thanks to my meeting with Felicia, I was less frantic about Melina's imminent comments, but when I saw her name on an unread note in my inbox, my chest tightened. I squeezed my eyes shut and said a silent prayer. Then, I opened my eyes and read the email.

> *Dear Kim,*
> *I'm writing about* Love on Stone Street. *I'm sorry it's taken so long to get back to you. You sent more pages than I was expecting, although I'm not complaining. I like where you're going with this—a lot. You had me scared for a while, but this latest round sparkles with the same charm as* A Blogger's Life. *I've attached an itemized Word document of my issues so far, but I think you're really onto something and I can't wait to read the rest—December 15th.*
> *Best,*
> *Melina*

Warmth radiated through my body and I bounced in my chair as I read through her comments. Her suggestions on how to increase the tension between the fighting families in *Love on Stone Street* before the fire that would ultimately lead to peace were much like Felicia's and both were brilliant. I got lost in edits until the sound of keys at the front door startled me out of my fictional universe. I'd managed to ignore the pit in my stomach while writing, but it deepened with a vengeance the moment Nicholas walked through the door in black jeans and an Eric Clapton t-shirt. The bottle of orange-flavored Gatorade he was holding clued me into his hungover state.

Greeting me with a wave and a sigh, he said, "What a weekend" before joining me on the couch and kissing my cheek.

"I bet," I said as my pulse raced. "Anything you want to tell me?" I cringed at how cold I sounded. I trusted Nicholas to know there was a rational explanation for the string of texts, but damned if I knew what it was, and I was terrified to find out.

Nicholas crinkled his forehead. "What do you mean?"

With shaky hands, I removed my phone from the coffee table and opened it to our text exchange. Handing him the device, I said, "You tell me."

Nicholas gave me a befuddled look and I observed his expression go from grudging to confusion to shock as he studied the photo. "What the?" He looked at me. "Who sent this to you?"

My mouth dropped open. "You did!"

Nicholas's eyes widened and he glanced at the picture again. Laughing, he handed the phone back to me. "I absolutely did not send you these texts."

"They came from your phone." I touched two fingers to my trembling lips.

Nicholas took my hand in his. "Kimmie. It would be one thing if you found a photo of another girl on my phone, but why would I send you a picture of another chick's 'trouble triangle' from mine? I haven't even seen one since before the first time we slept together almost three years ago."

I bit my lip. "I know. But...how?"

He blew air out of his cheeks. "Your guess is as good as mine. We left one bar a little after eleven and when we got to the next one, I realized I didn't have my phone. By then, I was too drunk to care." He reached into his back pocket and waved a phone in my face. "My new iPhone, courtesy of a trip to Apple Soho this morning."

I pushed my lips into a pout. "You didn't think of texting from someone else's phone to let me know at any point last night or today?"

Nicholas shook his head. "To be honest, no. It was late, I was drunk, and I assumed you were too. I figured I'd see you when you got home. I had no way of knowing someone sent you a pussy pic from my phone." He frowned. "Did you freak out?"

I cringed at the memory and lowered my gaze to the floor. "Sorta. And then I went off on our sisters before puking and passing out." I lifted my head.

Nicholas's mouth formed an O. "I need to hear this," he said before jutting his head back. "Wait. Why were our sisters there? I thought it was a party of three."

I clucked my tongue. "Someone told his sister where I was going and she took it upon herself to reserve a room with Tiffany and crash my private soiree."

"Oops." He shuddered. "Sorry."

"My mom made the same mistake with Erin for a dose of double trouble." I let out an exasperated sigh. "I'm over it."

Nicholas cocked an eyebrow. "Including the picture?"

My eyes met Nicholas's and froze there for a beat. He was telling the truth. I'd bet my writing career, the health of my father's brain, and my friendship with Bridget on it. Otherwise, I'd never agree to marry him and there was nothing I wanted more in the world than to be his wife. But I wanted some assurances first.

Positioning myself so I was sitting on his lap facing him, I said, "I promise to let it go if you vow to never—ever—send me a picture of another girl's private parts..." I raised my hand to Nicholas's opened mouth. "Whether knowingly or not...as long as we both shall live."

Nicholas gave me a devilish grin before slipping his hand under my t-shirt and expertly unhooking my bra. Nibbling on my ear, he said, "I do."

Chapter 38

ONE DAY UNTIL "I DO"

An article I'd read in one of my bridal magazines urged brides to consciously embrace the moment whenever possible. It was a lot easier to get lost in the planning and excitement of the events surrounding a wedding than it was to be a living, breathing part of them. I wanted to truly enjoy my rehearsal dinner; not look back on it after the fact with only a hazy memory of being there. So, after using the bathroom following the appetizer course, I paused to take it all in before returning to my seat.

Natalie had reserved the upstairs private room for the dinner. Members of the bridal party and guests from out of town sat at one long black table, which was lit by black and white Art Deco chandeliers. Giant black and white photos of Indian dancers decorated the bright white walls.

Everybody looked so relaxed, it was hard to believe how much we'd gone through to get to this moment. At one end of the table, Natalie and Tiffany giggled as if in their own little world while Nicholas's other relatives enjoyed a mini family reunion. My parents held court with my own kin on the other end. Someone must have said something funny because a boom of laughter erupted from the center of the table, where Nicholas was sitting next to my empty seat. We'd somehow managed to situate our closest friends around us without any complaints from even the most high-maintenance and sensitive members of our clans, i.e. Erin and Natalie.

Nicholas looked over at me, as if sensing me watching him. We locked eyes for a moment and he smiled.

I returned the gesture, my heart bursting with love, and joined my fiancé at the table.

When I sat down, Nicholas leaned into me and pressed his lips softly against mine. He whispered, "Hi, almost wife," into my mouth, leaving me fluttery from head to toe.

My tone as soft as his, I said, "Hi, almost husband."

"You look so damn sexy tonight, I could eat you up right now."

A warmth spread through me at the way his eyes looked into mine with unabashed desire. I had wavered over my wardrobe choice—a white sleeveless A-line mini dress with lace appliques and a very deep v-neck—fearing it was too risqué for my own rehearsal dinner. Given Nicholas's reaction, I was glad I hadn't chickened out, but the realization we'd be married the next time we were alone together left me wishing we could sneak away somewhere.

Nicholas pulled away from me and winked before focusing his attention on George and Sarah, who sat next to him on the other side.

I overheard Jonathan say to Bridget, "Maybe you should go easy on the shrimp curry. Do you remember what happened the last time you ate something spicy?"

From next to me on my other side, Bridget eyed the portion of the dish still uneaten on her plate with longing and dropped her fork. "You're right. I'll quit while I'm ahead. I don't want to have heartburn at my best friend's wedding."

Jonathan reached for her hand across the table. "You'll be able to eat almost anything you want in about two months." He frowned, "But you should still avoid fish high in mercury, caffeine, and alcohol while you're nursing. And probably dairy, chocolate, and citrus foods too." He glanced at me. "I read newborns have bad reactions to those foods."

My head swung back. Jonathan certainly kept up on the mommy dos and don'ts for a guy who, according to his baby mama, lacked enthusiasm for becoming a daddy. I'd be sure to say something to Bridget when we were alone later, but it seemed to me Jonathan was doing more than simply "going through the motions."

Later, when the dinner dishes were removed to make room for the dessert course, the fathers from both sides said a few words. My dad said he knew Nicholas was The One when we fought and my dad couldn't get me to smile from my eyes even after plying me with pink champagne and making him sit through "the sappy movie with the British guy all the girls love."

During Warren's toast, I stiffened at Nicholas's side. Thankfully, my fear he'd use the opportunity to disparage Nicholas's career choice even while wishing him success in marriage was unwarranted.

"In conclusion, I don't say it as often as I should, but I'm proud of you, son. Your mother and I did something right." Warren's green eyes twinkled as he raised his glass. "To Nicholas and Kim. A lifetime of happiness to you both."

When the clapping died down, Caroline clinked her knife against her glass of wine and stood up. "I was hoping to say a few words tonight since the toasts tomorrow are limited to the best man and maid of honor—"

Erin called out, "And matron of honor!"

"And matron, of course," Caroline said with a chuckle. "Kim and I met in a book club, but our shared love of reading is not what keeps us besties. Kim might be of tiny stature, but she has the heart of a giant, passion the size of the Great Barrier Reef, and the ability to love like nobody's business." She looked at me and smiled. "I speak the truth."

My eyes threatened to well up and I happily accepted the napkin Nicholas discreetly placed on my lap in case I needed it.

"I first noticed her capacity to love when she introduced me to Bridget, her BFFAEUDUP."

Keeping my stare straight ahead at Caroline, I took hold of Bridget's hand and squeezed it.

"It took months and a lot of prosecco, but they finally told me what the letters stood for. Unfortunately, if I told you guys, I'd have to kill you. Either that or they'd kill me." The table chuckled. "I'd never seen two women so well-matched. They got each other's jokes, had each other's backs, and seemed to communicate with a secret non-verbal language I didn't understand. It was like a platonic love affair for the ages and I admit I was envious at first." Caroline swallowed hard.

This time it was Bridget who squeezed my hand. I was in a battle of wills with my tears and holding the lead by a hair.

"Kim and Bridget were pretty much a party of two without any need for a third musketeer. But somehow, the two of them welcomed me into their fold—the Big Mac to their twin White Castle sliders." She raised her hand high and then low to emphasize the differences in our height. "And then a certain handsome and shaving-challenged attorney entered the picture." She nodded at my fiancé.

I glanced at Nicholas, who ran a hand along his scruffy jaw and winked at me. I rolled my eyes, even though his manly facial hair turned me on as much as ever.

"It was me who encouraged Kim to step it up a notch when Nicholas flirted with her at work. Clueless Kim thought he was simply being friendly by reading her blog, *Pastel Is the New Black*." Caroline snorted and wagged a finger at me. "Yes, Kim, because most guys take an interest in chick lit because they want to be friends with a girl."

Mine and Nicholas's faces turned matching shades of red.

"Nicholas brought out the best in Kim, encouraged her love of writing, and wouldn't let her live in fear of failure. He forced her out of her comfort zone. Now, she's a published author with a hotshot literary agent. Mostly because she's incredibly talented, but also because Nicholas believed in her when she didn't believe in herself."

In my fight not to cry, my tears had taken a substantial lead. I had soaked the napkin Nicholas had given me and was now wiping my eyes with the edge of the tablecloth. I'd be sure to bring a package of tissues to the wedding the next day.

"Like the end of a fairytale, here we are to witness the start of what I'm certain will be the happiest of marriages." Caroline looked at me and then at Bridget. "It's funny. Only a few years ago, we were three single gals in the city and now we've all found our other half." She paused to beam at Felix. "But I'm positive we'll always make room in our lives for each other. Right, Bridget?"

Bridget rose from her seat, her eyes a bright emerald green from the tears she'd shed. "I couldn't have said it better myself." Her lips parted as if to say more, but she gasped and placed her hand against her side. "Cramp," she said before falling back in her chair.

I sucked in a breath and faced my friend. "What happened?"

Jonathan stood up. "Are you all right, Bridget?" He glanced down the length of the long table and then at Bridget. She could have been a million miles away from the expression of terror on his white-washed face. A second later, he disappeared underneath the table and appeared by her side. He kneeled beside her and wiped a strand of hair from her face. "Talk to me."

"I'm fine. It was a cramp, but it passed." She smiled sheepishly down at Jonathan. "It was probably the curry. Like you said."

"You sure?" He didn't look convinced.

She nodded. "Positive."

He kissed her forehead. "I'm only looking out for you and our baby."

When he returned to his chair, this time by walking around the table, I stared her down, saying nothing and everything with a single look.

She shrugged before turning away and fiddling with her napkin.

I draped an arm around her and out of the side of my mouth said, "Do you still doubt Jonathan's devotion to you and future baby Middleton?"

She shook her head, trying to hide the blush in her cheeks with her long red mane.

I chuckled. "I told you so."

At the conclusion of the dinner, I hugged everyone goodbye with promises to get a good night's sleep. I assumed this was a white lie since "I slept so well the night before my wedding" was a sentence uttered by no bride-to-be ever.

Dr. Strong walked over to where I was standing with Caroline and Felix, trying unsuccessfully to express how touched I was by her toast. "I've ordered five cars for those of us heading to the hotel. We should rally the troops," he said.

I nodded my agreement and did a sweep of the room for Bridget, who would be bunking with me in the deluxe one-bedroom suite we'd reserved for the night and to get ready for the wedding the next day. She was talking to Nicholas—Nicholas! My heart slammed against my chest. Once we parted ways tonight, I wouldn't see him again until I walked toward him down the aisle. He was staying in our apartment, where the groomsmen would gather tomorrow for pre-wedding photos and most likely drinks. We needed a moment alone. I told Warren I'd be ready in a few minutes and joined my two favorite people in the world.

I placed my hand on Bridget's back. "We're heading out soon."

Glancing at me and Nicholas, she said, "Gotcha" and scurried away.

"Alone at last," Nicholas said.

I took a deep breath. "You ready to make me your wife?"

He flashed a cocky grin. "I was born ready, Kimmie."

I stood on my tippy toes and pecked his chin. "Do you promise to text me tomorrow?"

Wrapping his arms around me, he said, "Of course. You will know where I am at all times, even if I lose my phone and have to use someone else's."

"Cars are here." Warren's voice bellowed from the front of the room.

This was it. "I love you, Nicholas," I murmured in his ear.

He squeezed me tight. "I love you more, Kimmie."

"Sweet dreams, my sweets." I walked away, turning around once more when I reached the exit for one last look at my true love.

He blew me a kiss from across the room.

My throat threatened to close up, but I blinked back my tears and followed Erin, Gerry, and Bridget into the back of a waiting car. There would be no more tears tonight. Red and puffy eyes were a no-no on a girl's wedding day.

Chapter 39

TEN HOURS AND COUNTING UNTIL "I DO"

I opened my eyes and, expecting to see Nicholas beside me, blinked at the head of red curls splayed across the other pillow. Then I remembered why Bridget was in my bed. Today was my wedding day.

I pushed down on Bridget's back under the white comforter to wake her up. Even though we'd spent most of the night gabbing, I wanted a few more minutes alone with my very best friend of almost twenty years before my mom, Erin, and the rest of the bridal party joined us for hair and makeup. Bridget had tried to sleep on the pull-out couch in the adjoining room of the bridal suite, but I'd been afraid if we continued to shout at each other through the walls, one or both of us would wake up with a case of laryngitis. I also wasn't confident the roll-out cot could withstand Bridget's growing belly. The bed was big enough for the both of us without risk of accidental spooning.

I pushed her again—harder. Bouncing up and down on the bed, I said, "Wake up, Bridge. I'm getting married today!"

She stirred and flipped over to face me. "Morning."

I gasped. "Your lip!"

Touching her fingers to her mouth, she said, "What about it?"

"It's swollen. And your..." My eyes landed on the display of hives covering her exposed arm. "Holy shit."

Bridget sat up abruptly, tossed the blanket off her body, and clawed at her legs. "Oh my God, I'm so itchy."

My heart raced. "Stop it. Don't scratch. It looks like an allergic reaction. Do you feel sick?" I vaulted out of bed and paced the room. I had to do something. But what?

Bridget checked her reflection using the camera on her phone and promptly burst into tears. "This can't be h-happening. I c-can't r-ruin your w-wedding with my ugly f-face."

Only one of us was allowed to sob and it was me. But I was too busy holding back my own tears so I could calm her down. I could call Natalie, but her apartment in Murray Hill was too far away. I needed help now. My mom would know what to do. She always did, and she was right here in the hotel. I sat on the edge of the bed and took the phone off the receiver. "Don't cry, Bridget. It will be okay," I lied before asking the front desk to connect me to Peter Long's room. My legs bounced uncontrollably.

My father answered on the second ring.

"Dad! Can I talk to Mom?"

"Good morning to you too, Tiny Kim. How's the bride feeling?" The cheer in his voice made it clear the panicked tone in mine had gone completely unnoticed.

"I really need Mom." I bit down on my lip. Then I caught sight of Bridget's distended mouth again and quickly freed my lip.

A knock on the door sounded, followed by the hushed voices of my mother and Erin.

My dad said, "She's on her—"

"Gotta run." I lowered the phone, but had second thoughts at the last second. Raising it to my ear once more, I said, "Thanks, Dad. Love you," before placing it back in the cradle.

Within ten minutes, Jonathan was on his way and Bridget's obstetrician had traced the probable cause of her allergic reaction to the mangos in her dessert the night before. The doctor wasn't taking office hours, but advised Bridget to go to urgent care. He predicted they'd give her a safe antihistamine, which would most likely go into effect within ten minutes. They'd make her wait a little while before releasing her in case of a bad reaction to the shot, but the doctor saw no reason why the size of Bridget's lips wouldn't be back to normal and her skin hive-free in time for the wedding ceremony. Now she was weeping because she didn't want to abandon me on the most important day of my life.

"Remember the episode of *Sex and the City* when Samantha showed up at Carrie's book launch after her chemical peel looking like beef carpaccio?" I asked.

Bridget frowned, her giant lips taking up half the length of her chin.

I shuddered. "I'm sorry, Bridge. But this is worse." Drawing her into a hug, I said, "Better to miss the prep than the main event, right? And besides, chances are you'll be back before hair and makeup even get here." My skin tingled with excitement. "Listen to me—hair and makeup. I sound like an actress on a movie set."

"In that case, tell craft services to save me some lunch. With any luck, I'll be there before you finish your last single-girl cup of coffee."

As it happened, urgent care didn't open until nine and there was already a line out the door. Bridget was still in the waiting room hours later, when I was showered and getting my hair done. While Vicky, one of the two hair stylists I'd reserved, painstakingly blow dried my locks in small sections, I called her for an update.

"Jonathan insisted I wear ugly yellow dishwashing gloves so I can't scratch. I resemble the Strawberry Reef My Little Pony." Bridget sighed.

"My poor Bridg..." I clamped my mouth shut as my eyes stared into twenty-two-year- old Vicky's impressive cleavage and I inhaled her sweet-smelling perfume.

"Can you angle your head slightly down and to the right?" Vicky asked with a snap of her chewing gum.

"Sure." With some discomfort, I pressed the phone against my ear in my new position. "How many people are before you?" My tone suggested I wasn't all worried my maid of honor wouldn't be seen by the doctor until Nicholas and I had already exchanged rings. She couldn't possibly sense my fear that the longer she waited to get a shot, the more likely her mouth would grow so big, it would swallow her entire face until she couldn't see or breathe through her nose.

"Now lift your head an inch. Too much. There. Just like that. Don't move," Vicky said.

I wasn't blessed with enough coordination to play head Twister and hold a phone conversation at the same time. "Bridget, I need to go. You'll be fine. I know it." I tilted my eyes upward and whispered, "Please let her be okay." I swallowed hard. "I love you, Bridge."

"Love you too, K. I'll be there soon."

I wondered what Nicholas was doing. I pictured him in a tuxedo, surrounded by his groomsman and laughing good-naturedly at the jabs directed at his imminent loss of freedom and how it wasn't too late to change his mind. His smile would light up his face from the inside out, the way it always did when he was sincerely happy.

My phone rang—Nicholas. This was a phone call over which I'd risk spraining my neck. "You must have read my mind. I was picturing you getting ready."

"Was I wearing any clothes in this fantasy?"

"I didn't say anything about a fantasy." I snickered before catching Vicky's eyes in the mirror. She cocked an eyebrow and I saw my reflection turn pink.

"I wanted to check in and see how things were going. Is Bridget back yet?"

"Not yet." I instinctively reached for a strand of hair to twist around my finger before remembering Vicky currently held the exclusive license to my mane.

Nicholas exhaled. "Try not to fret, Kimmie. She'll be there soon. But if it's any consolation, all the guys made it here in one piece. We're currently sitting around doing nothing, but will uncork the bubbly in a little while. It will keep us entertained until it's time to put on our monkey suits." Chuckling, he added, "And if one of us gets an allergic reaction, I'm surrounded by medical professionals."

I groaned. "Duh. Why didn't I just send Bridget to your father's room? Or one of your brothers?" They were all staying in the hotel. It could have saved Bridget and Jonathan a trip to Urgent Care.

"Kim." Nicholas drew out my name and paused. "I was kidding. I don't think any of them keep a medical kit in their jacket pocket. Focus on this one fact: the chances of me leaving you stranded at the altar are negative infinity."

I smiled into the phone. "Love you."

"Love you more."

After that, the morning flew by in a whirlwind of constant activity. My bridal party (minus Bridget) catered to my every need—pouring me coffee, offering snacks with enough substance to get me to the wedding without fainting, but light enough to avoid bloat, and providing a steady stream of compliments on my hair and makeup. The attention reminded me of what Hannah Marshak probably felt like in high school. Only I knew my friends and family were lifting my confidence out of love, not just blowing smoke to avoid being jettisoned from the popular crowd.

Hannah. I was sure my teenage self would have nothing positive to say about inviting the Mean Girl to her wedding. I was almost as excited to see who she brought as her plus-one as I was to say "I do." Not really, but I knew if Bridget was here, we'd have fun guessing what her date looked like, did for a living, et cetera.

My stomach sank. Bridget was supposed to be in the rotation with Caroline, Erin, Natalie, and the mothers of the bride and groom for a professional blow out. Instead, she was in a waiting room reading *Better Homes and Gardens* and *US Weekly*, and that was only if she could turn the pages wearing rubber gloves. The doctor assured us she'd be okay, but I couldn't fully enjoy my last morning as a singleton without seeing for myself.

My mom stood in front of me, looking elegant in a gray A-line V-neck evening dress with ruffle beading sequins on the shoulders, and placed a hand to her heart. "You look so beautiful."

Widening my eyes, I said, "Yeah?" and examined my face in the mirror for the fiftieth time. Vicky had done my hair in a romantic side-swept low ponytail that fell in curls across one shoulder. Rowena, the cosmetologist Tiffany recommended, had followed up with a sweet and flirty sixties-inspired makeup application. I liked what I saw—me, only prettier—and was ecstatic for my mother's validation.

"Absolutely." A tear leaked from her eye.

"No crying or you'll ruin your makeup," I commanded.

"Fair enough," she said with a brisk nod. "Time to get you in your gown."

"But...but Bridget isn't here yet." I did a sweep of the suite. Nope, still not there. Once I got in my dress, the photographer would take pictures of the bridal party in all different poses. My heart broke at the thought of leafing through my album of Bridget-less photos.

Erin grinned. "Don't worry, Kim. I think between us, we can manage to button your dress without Bridget's help."

My sister looked adorable in her dark purple cap-sleeve swing dress, but she was missing the point. "Okay." I stood up reluctantly and walked unhurriedly to where my gown was hanging in the bedroom. Maybe if I got undressed in slow motion, Bridget would arrive by the time we were ready for pictures.

A little while later, five sets of watery eyes in various shades of brown and blue, none of them belonging to Bridget, stared at me. No one said a word.

"Well?" I held my breath.

Caroline spoke up first. "Stunning."

Natalie nodded. "My brother is one lucky dude."

The butterflies in my stomach did the two-step as I grinned at my two bridesmaids—Caroline in a purple folded cocktail dress and Natalie in a purple double wrap full shirt dress. "Thank you."

"You really look beautiful, Kim. And that dress." Erin's face lit up. "Thank goodness for Hannah, right?"

I choked back a laugh and turned to my future mother-in-law, who I was pleased accepted my invitation to get ready with the bridal party. "You look so pretty," I gulped. It was impossible not to see Nicholas in his mother's face, although Nicholas would never wear a silver sheath mother-of-the-groom dress—unless he had a well-hidden fetish for women's clothing.

Waving me away, Jeanine said, "Me? Anyone who even sees me with you in the same room should get his head examined." She stepped back and surveyed me from bottom to top. "Ravishing. Thank you so much for allowing me to be a part of this special moment." She turned to my mom, who I'd purposely saved for last. "What do you think of your daughter?"

My mom's faced glowed with love. "Kim ordered me not to cry, so I'll hold my tongue for now." She wiped her eye and whispered, "I love you."

A catch formed in my throat. "Me too."

The six of us shared a moment of silence. It was as if we were collectively too overwhelmed with emotion to speak.

"I'm here!" A door slammed against the wall with force, followed by loud footsteps barreling through the suite toward the bedroom. And then a miracle happened. Bridget entered the bedroom, red faced from exertion, but with normal-sized lips. "I'm here," she repeated with ragged breath. She took a deep inhale. "I just need to shower and…"

Her mouth dropped open. "Kim." She blinked at me. "You're so...so..." Her eyes filled with tears even as she smiled—like the sun shining during a rainstorm. "You're a bride."

Bridget showered and got dressed with the speed of a cheetah, managing to look like a pregnant supermodel by the time she joined the rest of us for pictures. And the best part was Kelly Dempsey had altered her beloved maid of honor dress to fit her expanding middle. Erin was right—thank goodness for Hannah.

Our cheeks sore from smiling, we took a much-needed pause from posing and began the countdown to the start of the ceremony. Nicholas and the guys would be driven by limo to the hotel. Once they were settled on the terrace, where the ceremony was being held, the bridal party would make our way upstairs to start the procession. My hands were shaking and the combination of excitement and nerves left me worried I'd lose the lightly buttered toast I'd ordered from room service and the raw almonds Bridget insisted I nibble on to keep my energy up. I sipped from the can of ginger ale Erin had brought me, having been where I was several years ago, but still able to recall the nausea.

I saw my phone light up before I heard it ring. It was Nicholas. I reached for the device, only for it to slip through my fingers and onto the train of my dress.

Caroline bent down and handed it to me with a smile. "Here you go, milady."

I took it, only for it to drop from my hand like it was made of satin. "Dammit."

She retrieved it again, this time, placing the device in my palm and curling my fingers around it to keep it secure. Only by then, it had stopped ringing. Her eyes kind, she said, "Just call him back. And don't forget to breathe."

I nodded, silently willing myself to get a grip. Without warning, excitement had turned to panic and my entire body felt like it was hooked up to an electrical current. I wasn't afraid to marry Nicholas. Doing it in front of a hundred people suddenly struck me as the worst idea since wearing short sleeves over long sleeves. All those people watching me as I walked toward Nicholas. What if I tripped? And did I really need my coworkers to hear the personal vows I'd written for Nicholas? Would our guests be overly critical because I'm a writer?

Would they even listen or would they'd be too busy counting the minutes to the cocktail hour? What if Hannah's date was some awful person from my past, like an episode of *This is Your Life*? Why hadn't either of us considered going directly to St. Lucia for an intimate ceremony on the beach?

"Stop it," Bridget said, interrupting my rumination.

"What?" I moved my finger off the call button and cocked my head at her.

Rolling her eyes, she said, "You've dreamed of a big wedding since before you even liked boys. It's just nerves."

I blinked at her. "How did you know?"

She smirked. "Really?"

Dumb question. I clasped her forearm. "I'm so glad you're here and not suffering from anaphylactic shock."

"You and me both," she said with a chuckle. "Now return your soon-to-be ex-fiancé's call so we can get on with the show and find out who Hannah invited to the wedding."

I did as I was told. "Sorry about before. Technical difficulties—twice. You calling to make sure I don't pull a runaway bride on you?"

"Not exactly." He paused. "We have a problem."

These were four words no bride wanted to hear less than a hour before her wedding, and my stomach dropped to my knees. Feeling eyes on me from all directions, I turned my back and and whispered, "What happened?" into the phone. I prayed it was something minor like they ran out of champagne or someone broke a glass.

"Did you know the President was in town?"

Scrunching my face, I said, "Um, no. Why should I care? Unless he wants an invite to the wedding." I laughed, hoping Nicholas would join in my mirth and relieve the tension.

He didn't. "What happens to the streets of New York City when POTUS comes to town?"

"Rallies, street closings, traffic." My own words sunk in. Crap on a cracker.

"The limo driver just called. His ETA is sometime between our first dance and the cutting of the cake. Neil ran down to the street—not a cab in sight."

I let my head fall back and closed my eyes, willing them to stay dry. Why did everything have to be a battle? Was this an omen? Or maybe it was a test. If we could jump over these hurdles and get to the finish line, we'd live happily ever after. If we couldn't, our marriage would be over before it started. Challenge accepted. "Walk."

"Did you say walk?"

"I did indeed. You're all able-bodied men. It's a beautiful day for a ten-minute stroll around the West Village. It's not like we've never walked to the Soho Grand from our apartment. The day you proposed ring a bell?" I tried not to think about how the traffic would affect our guests. From a glass-half-full perspective, an intimate ceremony might be possible after all.

I heard him say, "Everyone, lace up your shoes and reapply your deodorant. We're going for a walk." To me, he said, "You're a genius, Kimmie."

"Not as smart as you. You proposed to me, after all. Now go and be careful. I'm leaving my phone behind, so if you need to tell me you got lost in your own hood, were hit by a messenger bike, got pooped on by a bird, or were kidnapped by the President's motorcade, you'll have to wait until after the wedding." I took a deep breath in the realization this was the last time I'd hear his voice until he said his vows. "Make this happen, sweets. For me. For us. Please?"

I pictured his smile through the phone. "Easy like Sunday morning."

Chapter 40

I stared at Erin's advancing back, and as the opening notes of "All You Need is Love" rang in my ears, I held tighter to my dad's elbow. This was it.

"Ready, Tiny Kim?" he said.

All I could do was nod since my nerves had stolen my ability to speak. I just hoped it was temporary.

"Remember this. I might be giving you away, but I'll never let you fall."

I turned to look at my dad, who smiled at me through teary eyes. "Thanks, Daddy."

It was a short walk, probably less than one hundred steps. I didn't need a Fitbit tracker to tell me I'd endured more strenuous passages. But this was the most monumental walk of my life, and I was determined to focus on one thing and one thing only—getting to Nicholas on the other side. "Let's do this."

The moment I locked eyes with Nicholas, my nerves were replaced with an overwhelming sense of peace and certainty I was in the right place with the right man. Although I made a conscious effort to take note of the setting sun over the New York City sky and the Empire State and Chrysler Buildings in the distance, I didn't focus on any of the things I thought I would. There was no contemplation as to what my guests thought of my dress or how I'd worn my hair. I didn't peek through my side vision to see whether my coworkers sat on the teal folding chairs on the bride's side or the groom's. And I didn't give a single thought as to Hannah Marshak's date. All I saw was Nicholas, standing in front of a gorgeous circular floral arch. I could tell from the way he gazed at me like we were the only two people on the terrace—all he saw was me.

My father released me and lifted my veil. I gave him a hug and a kiss and watched as he shook Nicholas's hand and sat next to my mom in the front row. And then, I was staring into Nicholas's molten brown eyes. He took my hands in his. "Kimmie," he said.

The temperature outside was fairly mild for early November, but my skin tingled with goosebumps. "Nicholas." I felt movement from behind me as Erin arranged my dress and then Bridget took my bouquet of blush and ivory roses and hydrangeas. We released a giddy laugh and faced the non-denominational shaved-headed officiant, who spoke of marriage being a celebration of love, commitment, family, and of two people who are in it together and forever. And then it was time to exchange our vows.

Nicholas went first. "Kimmie, I remember when Rob told the squad he was bringing in a new assistant from his old firm. He described you as very organized, quick-witted, trustworthy, and loyal. He failed to mention you were also utterly charming and adorable, but those attributes were obvious to me from the get-go. Still, it took several months to work up the courage to strike up a non-work-related conversation, since contrary to your preconceived notion of me, I was not a player."

I shrugged sheepishly at my initial assumption.

"We've had our share of ups and downs over a relatively brief period, but what I learned from the tough times is how much happier I am with you than I am without you. What's funny becomes hilarious when I'm laughing with you. What's interesting becomes mind blowing when we experience it together. What's yummy is mouthwateringly delicious when we taste it together. And, yes, what's tiring is utterly exhausting when we muddle through it as a team. But we are a team, Kimmie—partners in everything. This does not mean I expect an invitation to your girls' nights or plan to start reading chick lit—unless you wrote it. It doesn't mean I expect you to share my encyclopedic knowledge of classic rock through the ages or that I'll endeavor to appreciate the nuances of the perfect romcom. It means when you're falling, I vow to be the one to lift you up. When you're feeling 'less than,' I vow to be the one to build you up until you're convinced, as I am, how special you are. When you get a bad review, I vow to feed you ice cream and distract you like only I can." He waggled his eyebrows as our guests chuckled. "I've never met anyone like you, Kimmie Long. You're four feet eleven inches of fire, bravery, passion, strength, and love, and I'm so honored you chose to share all of you with all of me. I will love you forever."

A tear dripped from my eye. "Showoff. I'm supposed to be the writer."

He winked. "It's not a competition."

The officiant scratched his silver goatee. "Your turn, Kimberly."

I took a deep breath and let it out slowly. "Nicholas, when I first met you, I thought you were out of my league. You were a successful, ambitious partner-track attorney. And you were gorgeous to boot. I assumed you dated pediatric surgeons, CEOs, and supermodels." My voice was shaking and I took a moment to gain my bearings. "During the cafeteria lunches we shared together and our first few dates, I learned you were so much more than perfect on paper. Yes, you were a hardworking and skilled lawyer who was beyond handsome, but you were also funny, kind, a really good listener, and a phenomenal kisser." I grinned at Nicholas, whose eyes were watering even as he smiled back. These words came straight from my heart and it felt brilliant to speak them out loud. "You saw so much goodness in who I already was, but also potential as to who I could be. You instinctively knew I had dreams beyond the comfortable life I was living and you gently coerced me to take more chances." I studied his face like it contained the meaning of life. "Seeing myself through your eyes made me realize you weren't too good for me after all. You were perfect for me and me for you. You never let me take the easy way out. While this habit of yours is frustrating at times, mostly when my comfort zone is to cower or give up, you're exactly what I need. My life has changed in so many wonderful ways because you've taught me that anything is possible." I swallowed hard. "I almost lost you twice, and it's not an experience I ever want to repeat. And so today, I vow to never forget why I fell in love with you or take our bond for granted. I vow to hug you with both my arms and my heart, and to always kiss you like I mean it. Through conflict and resolution, during periods of intense action and through the saggy middle, when the dialogue is stilted and the internal conflict in plenty, I vow to be your happily ever after and your one true love."

Nicholas squeezed my hand. "You win," he whispered.

I squeezed back. "It's a tie."

We began the exchange of rings and chuckled along with our guests when George pretended he lost mine. I laughed harder when Caroline removed a candy ring from her bouquet, claiming she came prepared on account of the series of wedding misadventures we'd suffered so far.

At last, it was time to be formally declared married. "By the authority vested in me by the State of New York, I now pronounce you husband and wife." The officiant beamed at Nicholas. "You may kiss the bride."

Right before Nicholas took me in his arms, he presented me with a smile filled with so much warmth and emanating so much joy, I thought we'd both explode from happiness. And then, I was kissing my husband—my husband—against a backdrop of applause and wolf whistles.

Chapter 41

The room grew quiet when the tall and lanky caramel-skinned emcee spoke into the microphone. "And now, ladies and gentlemen, we'd like to bring out our newlyweds, Mr. and Mrs. Strong, to dance their first dance as husband and wife." He cleared his throat. "As you know, it's customary for the couple to choose one song, but Nicholas and Kim wanted to do something different. Actually, rumor has it, the lovebirds couldn't agree on a tune and so they decided to have two first dances—one chosen by Nicholas and the other by Kim." He flashed his dimples. "But the joke's on them because they both chose the same song."

Our guests broke into laughter.

My jaw dropped and I looked at Nicholas in time to see him clamp a hand against his mouth. We'd spent a good portion of an hour naying each other's yays for our first dance, and yet with all the songs from which to choose, we separately picked the same one. I was convinced we were the most sublime of all the perfect couples in the world, and God had brought us together to show all the mediocre pairs how it was done.

"Let's hear it for Nicholas and Kim as they dance their only first dance together to 'Like I'm Gonna Lose You.'"

My chest was so full of love, I thought my dress might pop open to reveal my new lace bra and panty set. As the female vocalist's melodious voice rang in my ear, managing to sound exactly like Meghan Trainor, I stepped into Nicholas's arms and we danced like no one was watching.

Nicholas pulled me close. "We did it," he whispered.

"Are you referring to getting hitched or making it through the ceremony without any major debacles?" My eyes were closed as I moved to the rhythm, but I opened them when I felt Nicholas's warm breath on my face. I ran my hand along his smooth jaw. He'd shaved for the occasion.

"Both, I guess. But I was referring to the latter. If this wedding was a test from God, I think we passed."

I suppressed a laugh. "I thought the same thing when you told me about the street closures." Could we be any more meant to be? I remembered we weren't actually alone in the room and smiled at our guests as Nicholas continued to slowly twirl me around the dance floor.

"I'm conserving enough energy to consummate our sacred union later, but after that I'd like to sleep for a week."

I nodded up at him. "You can catch up on sleep on the beach in St. Lucia. I can already picture the two of us under an umbrella, sipping frozen drinks, and alternating naps with dips in the ocean." The view inside my head was divine.

The emcee asked the bridal party and their dates to join us, and my heart warmed as my dad led my mom to the dance floor.

I looked over Nicholas's shoulder and noticed Warren and Jeanine throwing curious glances at Tiffany and Natalie, who were swaying together. "Do your parents know Natalie and Tiffany's relationship isn't strictly platonic?"

Nicholas stopped dancing and turned around just as Tiffany pulled Natalie into a lip lock. He faced me again with a glint in his eyes. "They do now." We laughed together, but then Nicholas pressed his lips together.

"What's the matter?"

"Did you say St. Lucia before?"

I jutted my head back at the strange change of topic. "Yes."

"You mean St. Martin, right?"

"St. Lucia. Our flight isn't until later tomorrow, so we don't have to rush to check out." I leaned my head on his shoulder. Our first dance was almost over and I wanted to enjoy it.

"Um, Kim?"

I took a step back. "What is it?" The rapid beating of my heart told me something was very, very wrong.

Nicholas's face was devoid of color. "I don't think God is finished testing us."

I crinkled my brow. "Meaning?"

Nicholas grimaced. "You reserved us flights to St. Lucia, but we're booked for a six-night, seven-day stay at the Four Seasons in St. Martin."

My mouth dropped open. "You're punking me, right?" Bam, bam, bam went my heart.

Erin and Gerry glided over to us. "Enjoying yourselves?" Erin asked.

I nodded energetically. "Totally." Through my teeth, I whispered to Nicholas, "Please tell me this is a joke."

Nicholas planted on a robotic smile for his new sister-in-law and her husband. "Amazing time." He spun me around. "I wish I was, Kimmie."

Before I could stop them, my eyes filled with tears, probably ruining all of Rowena's handy work in the process. Nicholas put a hand on each of my shoulders. "We'll make a few phone calls and get this straightened out. I promise we'll have our dream honeymoon."

"I know. It's just so..." My body quaked and I shook my head emphatically.

Nicholas peered at me. "Are you laughing?"

I opened my mouth but couldn't form words.

"It's not funny." The corners of Nicholas's mouth twitched. "Not at all." He turned away from me and rocked back and forth, holding his stomach.

When the music stopped, we remained on the dance floor, lost in our own world.

"Everything all right, you two?" my mom asked, her eyebrows furrowed.

"Fine." I pressed my fist against my lips too late to suppress a snort. "It's all good. Right, Nicholas?" I nudged him from behind.

He turned around, red faced. "Couldn't be better, Mrs. Long."

She pulled him into a hug. "You can call me 'Mom' now."

Nicholas wiped at his damp eyes. "Mom, it is." His shoulders continued to shake.

"Oh, you sweet boy. I had no idea you were so sentimental." My mom turned to me. "Did you know?"

I nodded my answer while holding onto my sides. They ached from laughing so hard and I wouldn't be surprised if I pulled something. I might even be sore in St. Lucia. Or St. Martin. Or wherever we ended up. It didn't really matter as long as we were together.

Hannah, wearing a satin royal-blue backless knee-length cocktail dress with classic Christian Louboutin shoes, pursed her lips while surveying the room in undisguised surprise. She looked up at me from her seat at the table. "It's a very classy affair. Didn't you have your Sweet Sixteen in your parents' craft store?"

On any other day, my face would have contorted into a smirk, but not today. Nothing, not even Hannah Marshak—passive-aggressive frenemy extraordinaire—could push me off the happy plane I was flying. I did, however, wish Nicholas would tear himself away from Rob and Mrs. Rob on the other side of Hannah's table and join me. We were supposed to be partners "in everything" according to his vows. Shouldn't that include collectively greeting our most infamous guest? "Yes, Longing for Crafts was my first-choice venue, but the 'rents sold it five years ago."

"The decorations are gorgeous in a DIY sort of way," she said, pointing to the tall white candle and blush rose in a glass votive in the center of the table.

"Thank you." I smiled politely. Instead of being disappointed with the centerpieces, as I'd feared, I'd been delighted. Caroline and Bridget had created a warm romantic atmosphere for the reception. I doubted Martha Stewart could have done a better job.

Hannah's date rolled his blue eyes. "Everything is beautiful, Kim. Congratulations."

"Thank you, Fred. I'm so glad to see you, by the way." Hannah might never teach a course on the art of giving compliments, but she won some points for bringing Fred as her date. He'd matured from a short thick-glasses-wearing nerd into a very handsome, but still short, designer-glasses-wearing millionaire.

"Me too. I was sorry to miss the ten-year reunion, but Hannah wants to plan one for our fifteenth." His eyes sparkled.

"I'd recruit someone else to do the work, but under my supervision," Hannah said.

"Of course." Fred winked at me.

Hannah continued to circle the room, stopping to gaze upon Bridget and Jonathan in a conversation with Pia on the edge of the dance floor. "Strawberry Shortcake and Jonathan Middleton having a baby." She tut tutted. "My mind is still blown even though it's old news. I thought it would have been you and Jonathan."

"Well, I'm kind of taken now." I widened my eyes at Nicholas, who had finally looked my way, and waved him over.

"I know. It's just weird," Hannah said.

Nicholas joined us. "What's weird?"

Fred cut in as Hannah opened her mouth. "Hannah was saying how pleased she is her high-school pal, Kim, found true love." He turned to Hannah. "Right?"

Nicholas and I exchanged an awkward glance, while Hannah and Fred stared each other down.

Hannah frowned at Fred before turning to us and beaming. "Fred's correct. I'm so happy for you both. And I'll be sure to tell Kelly how beautiful you looked in your gown. The alterations are flawless." She turned back to Fred. "I called in a favor with Kelly Dempsey to do Kim and Bridget's alterations. Did I tell you?"

"Only three times," Fred said with a fond smile, before patting her on the knee.

Nicholas choked back a laugh and pointed between the two of them. "Are you two dating or just friends?"

"Just friends. Very old friends." Jutting his head toward the dance floor, Fred said, "Who's the pretty Asian girl dancing with Bridget?"

"Pia? She's my blogging partner." Pia was considering a double Masters in website design and had latched onto Bridget after my "intervention" as a mentor of sorts. Animated Pia looked like she was performing an African Tribal Dance compared to Bridget, who moved slowly to the beat while holding her belly.

"Is she here with someone?" Fred's cheeks reddened.

My eyes grew wide. I'd assumed Fred's metamorphosis from awkward teenager to rich and handsome adult included the ability to ask about a girl without blushing. Seeing a flash of teenage Fred in the successful adult version endeared me to him, but not enough to give him the answer he wanted. "She did bring a date. And she lives in

Michigan."

Fred shrugged. "Oh, well."

Hannah stood up. "I need to use the ladies' room." She grabbed her Dolce & Gabbanna beaded evening clutch and patted Fred on the shoulder of his dark blue suit. "I'll be back."

"I'll go with you, Hannah!"

The four of us turned to Erin, who had seemingly appeared out of nowhere.

Erin pouted her full lips. "I couldn't help but overhear you say you needed to use the bathroom."

Hannah gave Erin the Manhattan once-over. "You're the sister, right? Erica?"

"Erin," I corrected, while twisting my platinum wedding band around my finger. I was torn between pity for my baby sister—who looked crushed—and a desire to laugh. Apparently, marriage didn't make me a kinder older sibling.

Hannah lifted her gaze from Erin's silver strappy stilettos and nodded. "Fantastic shoes." She gestured toward the exit, said, "Let's go," and began walking.

On Hannah's heels, Erin gushed, "Thank you! I can't wait to read *A-line in the Sand.*"

Fred snickered. "Hannah and her fans—an American love story."

I chuckled. "We should make our rounds, but thank you so much for coming tonight. We hope you have a wonderful time." To Nicholas, I said, "Shall we?"

Nicholas shook Fred's hand before placing his palm on the small of my back and leading me to the next table. Into my ear, he whispered, "Looks like Writer Chick has it bad for Fred."

Stopping in my tracks, I said, "What did you say?"

"Hannah likes Fred. It's obvious." He gestured for me to keep walking.

I remained unmoving. "Sorry, dear husband, but Hannah and Fred? No way." I giggled and kissed him on the cheek. "Let's go," I said, grabbing his hand.

This time, Nicholas stood still. Cocking an eyebrow, he said, "You didn't notice the way Hannah pouted when Fred said they were just friends and then coincidentally excused herself to the bathroom when he asked about Pia?"

I frowned. "You're serious, aren't you?"

He shrugged. "Based on what I just witnessed, yes."

My mouth dropped open. I couldn't wait to tell Bridget.

Chapter 42

"Please join us on the dance floor for the last dance of Nicholas and Kim's wedding."

My shoulders dropped and a wave of sadness washed over me, even though I knew it was coming. The band had delivered a "three more songs" warning two songs ago. My feet were bloated and possibly blistered from dancing all night, my voice was hoarse from greeting all my guests, and my cheeks were sore from smiling. But my wedding—the day I'd dreamed about since I was a little girl and which planning had almost made me lose my mind—would be over in five minutes, never to repeat again, unless you counted video.

Nicholas and I had flitted around the ballroom from table to table, managing to say a few words to everyone, but only a select few would go home tonight being able to say they spent quality time with the bride and groom. I'd asked the band to dedicate "Nine to Five" to my coworkers and dragged everyone, including Rob, onto the dance floor. At least I'd created a special memory for the squad. And since it was the first time we'd met face to face, I couldn't end the night without a short tête-à-tête with Pia, so I dragged her to the bathroom when no one was watching.

With those exceptions, no one besides the bridal party and their plus-ones were given more than minimal attention, but everyone seemed to enjoy themselves. The dance floor was crowded at all times. Plates were empty save for crumbs when servers took them away. By all accounts, the event was success. I had the time of my life and as the band began crooning, "How Sweet It Is (To Be Loved By You)" for the grand finale, I almost wished we'd chosen "I Had The Time of My Life (And I Owe It All To You)" instead. Then Nicholas motioned for me to come hither to the dance floor and I knew it didn't matter anyway.

I needed to make this closing dance count—gather as much joy from these last three minutes as I possibly could. While Nicholas twirled his mother, I shimmied over to my own parents. I grabbed my mom's hand and spun her around and then my dad did the same to me. Erin joined us, and we sang about how sweet it was to be loved by each other. Then Gerry wrapped an arm around both of us and we swayed back and forth.

Knowing it would be over soon, I removed myself from the chain, stood off to the side and observed. I'd try to freeze frame the image of my favorite people—tipsy, smiling, dancing, happy—so later, when I closed my eyes, I could conjure up the memory.

Tiffany and Natalie were dancing in a small circle with Warren, who was laughing like life-saving surgery was far from his thoughts.

Fred twirled a glowing Hannah. When he let her go, they continued dancing with very little personal space between them. I suspected Nicholas was right about Hannah's less-than-platonic affection for Fred. I didn't think I'd ever be invested in Hannah's romantic life, as long as it didn't conflict with my own, but I sincerely hoped they'd wind up together. He was a positive influence, she genuinely cared about him, and reformed mean girls deserved true love as much as anyone else.

I turned away from my old classmates to spy on Caroline and Felix. Even though it was a semi-fast song, they danced forehead to forehead. It seemed their honeymoon phase was still going strong. I wished nothing more for my most sensible, logical, and practical friend than to always be this crazy in love.

And then there was Bridget— the other love of my life, my non-sexual soulmate, my sister from another mother. She was laughing at Jonathan, who'd crouched low to the dance floor to boogie with their unborn baby. My heart surged at the sight.

I felt someone watching me. I looked over and smiled at Nicholas, who'd also stopped dancing to observe—me. In that moment, we were alone in a crowded room. I saw no one but Nicholas as I swerved in between the dancing couples to get to him. "How sweet it is, Kimmie," he said, before dipping me into a kiss that made my foot pop up.

Best. Life. Ever.

Meredith Schorr

A born-and-bred New Yorker, Meredith Schorr discovered her passion for writing when she began to enjoy drafting work-related emails way more than she was probably supposed to. After trying her hand penning children's stories and blogging her personal experiences, Meredith found her calling writing chick lit and humorous women's fiction. She secures much inspiration from her day job as a hardworking trademark paralegal and her still-single (but looking) status. Meredith is a loyal New York Yankees fan, an avid runner, and an unashamed television addict. To learn more, visit her at www.meredithschorr.com.

Books by Meredith Schorr

JUST FRIENDS WITH BENEFITS
A STATE OF JANE
HOW DO YOU KNOW?
THE BOYFRIEND SWAP

The Blogger Girl Series

BLOGGER GIRL (#1)
NOVELISTA GIRL (#2)
BRIDAL GIRL (#3)

Henery Press Books

And finally, before you go...
Here are a few other books
you might enjoy:

BET YOUR BOTTOM DOLLAR

Karin Gillespie

The Bottom Dollar Series (#1)

(From the Henery Press Chick Lit Collection)

Welcome to the Bottom Dollar Emporium in Cayboo Creek, South Carolina, where everything from coconut mallow cookies to Clabber Girl Baking Powder costs a dollar but the coffee and gossip are free. For the Bottom Dollar gals, work time is sisterhood time.

When news gets out that a corporate dollar store is coming to town, the women are thrown into a tizzy, hoping to save their beloved store as well their friendships. Meanwhile the manager is canoodling with the town's wealthiest bachelor and their romance unearths some startling family secrets.

Pull up a wicker chair, set out a tall glass of Cheer Wine, and immerse yourself in the adventures of a group of women whom the *Atlanta Journal Constitution* calls, "... the kind of steel magnolias who would make Scarlett O'Hara envious."

Available at booksellers nationwide and online

Visit www.henerypress.com for details

JUST FRIENDS WITH BENEFITS
Meredith Schorr

(from the Henery Press Chick Lit Collection)

When a friend urges Stephanie Cohen not to put all her eggs in one bastard, the advice falls on deaf ears. Stephanie's college crush on Craig Hille has been awakened thirteen years later as if soaked in a can of Red Bull, and she is determined not to let the guy who got away once, get away twice.

Stephanie, a thirty-two-year-old paralegal from Washington, D.C., is a seventies and eighties television trivia buff who can recite the starting lineup of the New York Yankees and go beer for beer with the guys. And despite her failure to get married and pro-create prior to entering her thirties, she has so far managed to keep her overbearing mother from sticking her head in the oven.

Just Friends with Benefits is the humorous story of Stephanie's pursuit of love, her adventures in friendship, and her journey to discover what really matters.

Available at booksellers nationwide and online

Visit www.henerypress.com for details

Printed in the USA
CPSIA information can be obtained
at www.ICGtesting.com
LVHW012331231023
761893LV00003B/187